I0788139

songs
and
SWEETHEARTS
Untouchable

Songs and Sweethearts
Untouchable #10
Copyright © 2021 by Heather Long
Editing: Kira of Leavens Editing
Cover: Crimson Phoenix Designs

Songs and Sweethearts/Heather Long – 1st ed.
ISBN-13 - 978-1-956264-24-1

For Abby

Foreword

Dear Reader,

Welcome to book ten of the Untouchable series. Ten books. It hardly seems possible that we've had that many and yet, there are only two left after this one.

In all honesty, I don't even know where to begin with this note. The last book took us on such a wild ride through their first year of college. There were new challenges and conflicts. More, they had to wrestle with not only interpersonal drama but also changing expectations academically and in life.

Growing up is never easy. When you're a teen, you think you know everything. You know what you will never do and you make decisions about the things you will always do. Yet, adulthood doesn't come with an "easy" setting. If it did, well, I guess they wouldn't call it growing anymore.

Yet, here we are, picking up just a few days after the end of where the previous book, Defiance and Dedication, ended. Life isn't gentle and they used to say, life wasn't for the weak. What doesn't kill us, makes us stronger. Remember that.

It's not just about winning or losing. Sometimes, you have to lose to understand what you have. Sometimes, you have to fall so that you can stand back up again. Sometimes, you have to learn who your people are, who stands with you, and who will be there.

Without further ado, I'll cover that bit of housekeeping and then we'll dive in. See you on the flip side.

For those of you who have never read a reverse harem before, first let me thank you for picking this up and giving it a shot. Second, a reverse harem means the heroine will not make a choice in this book or any other between the guys in her life. It may take her a while to reach that conclusion, but it's the journey that drives it. There are many ways to frame this kind of relationship, currently reverse harem fits it very well.

Also, this is the tenth book in a series. If you haven't read the first nine, I encourage you to pause here and go grab them. While there may be no specific happy endings at the end of each of these books, there will be one to the whole series, that I promise you. Some of these books will have cliffhangers, largely due to the size of the story, but the happy ending has to be earned as part of the journey.

Again, thank you for reading and being on this journey with Frankie and the boys. I can't believe I can say this again, but you really haven't seen anything yet.

xoxo

Heather

Chapter One

IS THERE FREEDOM IN DEATH?

Frankie

The funeral took place just ten days after my birthday. I hadn't been to class since the incident. Finals were also fast approaching, but the school had notified me that I was passing all my classes and no exams would be required. Apparently, a death in the family qualified one for bereavement leave.

Odd, but it was hard to bring myself to care about it much. I'd seen my new psychologist twice over the last week and a half. But I found it difficult to discuss with her, because I found it difficult to even think about it. Rachel had all but moved into the brownstone with us.

Ian's and Coop's parents had flown up, along with Trina. Jake's mom and the girls arrived the day before. The brownstone was full to bursting and Archie arranged for a floor at one of the closest hotels to put them all up. There had been a discussion about that, and I was fairly certain I'd been

5

involved in it.

Hank arrived the day after my birthday, and he'd planted himself. Coop gave him his room at the brownstone. Kelly and the kids were coming for the funeral. I didn't quite get why they'd want to go to Maddy's funeral. She'd hurt so many of these people—and Kelly didn't even know her, but Hank had said she wanted to be there.

My grandparents had wanted some elaborate service at their family church. I declined. Maddy hadn't been remotely religious and I hadn't been raised that way. Graveside would be fine and I'd expected a small turnout, particularly taking her home to where she'd grown up.

Only that proved not to be the case. We had our own hotel suite, having come up the day before, along with a train of cars holding the rest of the guys' families. Kelly and the kids had been waiting at the hotel when we got there. I ended up carrying Chloe inside because she turned into a barnacle and wouldn't let go of me.

Not going to lie, I kind of loved the hug.

The graveside service was scheduled for mid-morning. I got up, showered, and got dressed almost mechanically. Black dress, black shoes, and my hair pulled back up and away in a tight braid. Jake had done it when my fingers wouldn't work. I didn't bother with cosmetics, but Rachel descended on me a half hour later with everything in tow. When she'd arrived, I had no idea.

Honestly, I didn't care how I looked. No amount of dark clothing and layers of cosmetics could change the shocked shell that had encompassed me since the sound of a gun cracked through the silence. It had been so loud it damn near deafened me. I waited for the pain to come, even as the warm spray hit my face.

The bullet hadn't hit me. It hit Maddy and I'd stared into her lifeless eyes, her expression still half-contorted by the raw fury she'd aimed at Archie and me. Maddy was dead.

Stranger still, Edward had killed Maddy. Her Eddie had stopped her from hurting his son. The agony on his face and in his eyes cut deeper than anything.

At least he could feel something for her loss.

I didn't. I didn't feel a damn thing. The guys moved around me, one always with me, they were there for hugs and for me to lean on. Jeremy and Hank bullied me to eat, while Rachel bullied everyone to leave me alone.

But no amount of self-reflection brought even an ounce of sadness at Maddy's loss to the surface. If anything, it seemed surreal. I'd actually gone to the coroner's to identify the body, though they'd all said someone else could do it. I'd needed to. I needed to see that she really was dead and that I hadn't imagined it.

Archie and Hank went with me, though they both tried to dissuade me from doing it once we got there. Honestly, I couldn't even seem to make the words work to let them know it was fine. Seeing her lifeless on the cold metal table didn't make it anymore real to me than it had when I'd seen her blood on the floor.

Or when I washed it off my face.

Or when the police asked me question after question.

What had she said? Could I remember the exact words? Had Edward given her a warning before he fired his gun? Did I know that he had a gun license? Around and around and around the questions came. The detectives seemed sympathetic, but they didn't let up. Dominic's arrival not only slowed them down, it cut them off.

I didn't know who had called him or what got him there, but he took a seat at the table, all business, and locked eyes with the officer interrogating me. There was now a wall between me and them and I could breathe. A little. They still had questions and I was willing to cooperate, but Dominic vetted every question. It seemed to go faster and easier with him there.

Eventually, they seemed satisfied and Coop was there when they wrapped. They hadn't let me and Archie sit, or talk, or even be questioned together. Ian had gone with Archie while Jake took care of phone calls. Coop had promised me Archie wasn't alone. Attorneys had shown up for him and for Edward, too.

I'd half-forgotten the whole nightmare had started out as my birthday, until we got home where there were balloons and surprises waiting. Jeremy ushered us in and made me tea that he insisted on bringing up after I showered. The guys stuck close, but as close as everyone was, it was still a million miles away.

Reconciling Maddy's actions and personality with the number of people who came to her service left me puzzled. Coop held my hand the whole time, even when I faded in and out of awareness of the funeral happening around me.

Whoever gave the minister his script hadn't filled it with platitudes. He discussed the effect of life and death, of choices, and consequences. If anything, it seemed more geared to those of us present than to the person going into the ground. Even though I'd seen her body, I still couldn't believe it. When it was over, people began to leave in ones and twos, or in families. The guys murmured plans between them. Rachel had an arm around my waist and hugged me to her side.

Dominic had come for the funeral as well. I wasn't sure who had invited him, but he offered me quiet condolences and a kiss on the cheek before he headed over to the cars. A whole train of them had come to the little cemetery. Rachel eventually gave me a hug and headed over toward the cars as well. Finally, it was just me, Hank, the guys and Edward. He'd been at the back for most of the service.

I'd known he was there, that there had been some objection from my grandparents, but it had quickly been silenced. Of everyone present, I thought he grieved the hardest. The sadness in his expression hit me like a punch to the chest. Silhouetted against the grave, he just seemed so damn alone.

Without thinking about it, I walked over to where he stood. "I'm sorry." The words were ash on my tongue, but at the same time, I meant it. I was sorry. For him.

He'd killed the love of his life and if I'd mocked it or scorned it before, I could not deny the pain in his eyes or the tears on his cheeks. After everything that happened, he chose his son. He chose Archie over my mother.

I would never fault that choice.

But I hated that he'd had to make it. I hated what she'd done to all of us.

"I'm sorry," I said, and the words came out rougher and harsher than I imagined. It was like I'd forgotten how to talk.

Pulling his gaze from the grave, he glanced at me. The raw emotion in his eyes hurt so much. "Thank you for letting me be here."

"I think you might be the only person who really misses her." I hated myself for saying it like that, but the beginnings of a wry smile twisted his lips.

"You might be right," he said with a deep sigh. "I wish...I wish I could tell you she was different when she was younger. That the choices we made changed her. I wish..."

Putting my hand on his arm, I stopped his next words. "I wish I could, too. But she was Maddy."

The wry smile turned wistful. "Yes, she was." He glanced at me, then just past me, and I didn't have to look to know Archie was right there. The guys would give me space and Hank was nearby, but Archie wouldn't leave me with Edward until he was certain.

Even then, he might not.

"I'm sorry, you deserved a lot better." That could have been directed at either of us, so I held out one hand to Edward, even as I reached back for Archie.

The older man gave my hand a long look before he accepted it, but Archie's fingers slid through mine immediately and he narrowed the distance between us until I could have leaned on him if I wanted.

"So did you," I told Edward. And I meant it. Archie loved me. He loved all of me. He even loved my need for the other guys. More, he accepted me for who I was and embraced the family we'd built. I couldn't fathom how Maddy couldn't see what she could have had with Edward or how he'd forgiven her so much and so often and yet she continued to twist and to use and to abuse.

"She's right," Archie said with a kiss to my temple. "You do deserve better. Maybe we can't be—you know—but maybe we can just be friends and go from there."

It was an olive branch, one Edward clearly didn't expect to be offered if the sudden way he squeezed my hand was any indication. "I'd like that," he said. "I know I don't—"

"That's the past," Archie told him firmly. "A past we can all put to rest now. We look forward. You saved Frankie."

"He saved you."

"I wish I could have spared you both. I'll never make up for the pain we caused either of you."

"You don't have to," I told him. "I don't know if any of us could. But Archie's right, I don't want to look back anymore." Not at my life with her. Not at the choices she made. "The only thing I'm glad for is that you guys came into our lives, 'cause it meant I got to know Archie."

As twisted as that might seem, I'd take it.

Edward stared at us both for a long moment then he tugged my hand and stepped forward, until he hugged us both. I wasn't the only one who froze under the sudden display of affection.

"Thank you for loving each other," he whispered in a voice so cracked with emotion it ripped through the numbness muffling the whole world, and pain burned in my eyes. "Thank you for showing me it can be done."

As swift and fierce as his embrace was, he released us and strode away without a word. Archie wrapped an arm around my middle and pulled me back against him. I swayed, half-dizzy. The picturesque little graveyard with its rich, verdant spring green color swam in front of me. Coop suddenly took Edward's place and he clasped my hand, then Jake and Ian were there, too. All four of them arrayed around me in a perfect circle.

We had a family. Ours.

I wasn't alone.

Still, I couldn't quite help looking at the grave as the workers came forward and the coffin lowered mechanically into the ground. The faint whirring of gears and pulleys a rather ignoble farewell to someone who had cast such a long shadow.

Despite the burning in my eyes, the tears wouldn't come.

I had no idea how long I stood there when Coop said, "We can skip the lunch. Everyone will understand."

"We can even just bring food up and you can get comfy," Jake offered. "No one is going to mind."

"No, they came all this way. I should at least thank them."

"Angel," Ian said and that pulled my attention away from the hole where her coffin vanished. "You don't owe anyone anything. They came here to support you. What do you need?"

I had what I needed.

"Food," I admitted. "I haven't been hungry. But I'm sure I need to eat." A fact Jeremy confirmed for me every day when he put something in front of me three or four times a day. Food had even come to our suite at the hotel this morning while we got ready, but I hadn't wanted any then. I might be able to choke some down now.

We turned away from the grave and headed to where the car waited for us, it shouldn't have surprised me, but it did when I found Hank and Edward talking. Jeremy stood at a discreet distance. I half-missed a step when Hank and Edward shook hands and Edward turned away to walk to his own car.

Alone.

"Fuck it," Archie whispered before he brushed a kiss to my cheek. "You good until we get to the hotel, babe?"

"Go," I told him. "He needs you."

Loosening his tie, Archie nodded and set off at a jog to catch up with him. I caught Jeremy's faint nod of approval as he moved around to open the door. Everyone else had hired cars, Jeremy insisted on driving us and wouldn't hear anything to the contrary.

Hank waited for us to get within earshot before he said, "Do you mind if I ride with you..."

I answered him with a hug. The world might be muffled again, but Hank had been here from the moment he heard, even though he had a life and a family, he'd still been right here with me.

"Thanks for being here...Dad," I whispered, and his arms tightened around me. He'd been here because we were family too.

"Always," he whispered back and I closed my eyes. Everyone waited for us, and I let myself glance back once more at the gravesite in the shadow of the trees. It really was a pretty little spot. Idyllic. Peaceful. Perfect.

All things Maddy had never been in life.

I was never coming back here again.

Chapter Two

I'VE SEEN LONELY TIMES AND FALLING RAIN

Frankie

The reception was also at the hotel, Archie or maybe Jeremy—hell it could have been Edward for all I'd paid attention to the details, had made arrangements to arrange for everything to take place there. Lunch would be served, the bar was open, and in lieu of pictures of the deceased, they'd put out wreaths of flowers in all different colors and types. Roses. Lilies. Carnations.

Chloe and Craig had been opening car doors as the limos and other vehicles arrived back at the hotel. Alec stood with his mother at the top step, until Craig opened our door. Hank slid out first and then held a hand out to me.

Coop gave my hand a squeeze and Jake let go of my other hand so I could accept Hank's offer. Ian had settled back into watchful mode. My awareness of the guys wasn't as dulled as everything else. Probably the only reason I caught the flash of a frown when I summoned a smile for my younger siblings.

As soon as I stood in the sunshine, Alec jogged down the steps. Chloe wrapped a hug around my waist and I dipped down so I could hug her properly. Then Craig gave me a hug, though his still held an element of shyness. It was dark haired and solemn-eyed Alec who surprised me by giving me a hard, swift hug.

"Mom said to tell you if you need a break or anything, just glance at me and I'll interrupt whoever is talking to you." The hurried whisper turned my plastered-on smile real.

"Thank you," I told him as I leaned back to meet his dark gaze. "I'll do that."

He nodded firmly. "I'm sorry you don't have a mom anymore. We decided you can share ours."

Heat flash-flamed against the back of my eyes.

"But Mom said to not tell her that today," Chloe snapped into the middle of our conversation. She wrapped an arm around my neck. "She's sad, remember?"

Alec huffed out a little sigh, then fixed Chloe with a look. "Craig is going to open more car doors than you."

She stomped her foot, stuck her tongue out at him, then took off as I rose to my feet. The guys were right there, no way they could have missed any of the interaction. Jake's faint snicker promised as much.

Wearing a bland look, Alec peered up at me and then at the guys. "More boyfriends."

"Yep," I said.

"Don't worry, little man," Coop told him with a clap on the shoulder. "I already passed on the warning to the rest of them. Jake and I will totally back you up."

"Huh," Alec said as he glanced from one to the other, then to my great amusement, he eyed Ian. "You're quiet."

"I have zero intention of ever hurting your sister again. So you can focus on those two. They'll happily beat each other up for you."

That earned him a middle finger from Coop—which also caused his mother to snap "Cooper" and he groaned—even as Jake laughed. It was absolutely ridiculous. And wonderful.

"I like them," Alec told me.

"Me too."

"We should go up," Hank said almost gently, as he put a hand to the small of my back. We'd slowed down arrivals by just standing there so I nodded, and with Hank on one side and Alec on the other, let them guide me up the steps to where Kelly waited. She wore a kind, patient smile. Hank greeted her with a quick, easy kiss. One she returned as she feathered her hand to his cheek before she glanced at me.

"I really want to give you a hug," she told me and before she'd even finished the statement, she cut Hank a look. "I said I wouldn't just grab her and hug her as hard as I think she needs or deserves, I didn't say I wouldn't tell her."

As reluctant as the chuckle was that escaped, it was still a chuckle. "I wouldn't say I'm wholly opposed to a hug."

Any other time this might seem weird, but talking to the woman who was ostensibly my stepmother on the steps to the hotel we were using to host everyone who'd come up for my mother's funeral and agreeing that I wasn't opposed to a hug from the former—well, it really just didn't register on the scale of weird in my life.

"Then brace yourself," she gave me the warmest of smiles with that warning and then descended one step, so she didn't quite tower over me, before she wrapped me up in a hug. These were the kinds of hugs that Sara, Alicia, and Carly gave. The kind of hugs that just wrapped you up tight and seemed to make a promise even as they hid you away.

"Oh, me too!" Chloe shouted somewhere behind me, and I barely had time to brace before an energetic young body clasped onto my hug with her mom. I loosened my hold on Kelly, a bit surprised I'd returned the hug with all the fierceness she'd offered it and then we glanced down to include Chloe too. "Group hugs are the best," she told me and I smiled.

"I agree." They really were.

More cars pulled up and I touched my finger to my right eye behind my sunglasses to ease away the tear before it messed with Rachel's cosmetics job. There were more car doors closing. Ian stood a couple of steps up, waiting for me. Jake and Coop were talking to Coop's mom and Trina. Jake broke away to jog down the steps when a car pulled up with his dad and Klara.

That surprised me even more than all the other families coming in. His dad had been in physical therapy after the wreck, there was still something wrong with his knee. He'd been scheduled for a surgery the last time we'd spoken to him and in the chaos, I'd kind of forgotten about it.

"Stop it," Hank said gently and I blinked before glancing at him. Kelly and the kids had gone on up when I'd gotten distracted, but he stood right next to me.

"Stop what?"

"That little downturn your mouth takes when you're thinking something bad about yourself," he commented. "My mother used to do that. Stop it."

I rolled my eyes. "I wasn't thinking something bad about myself. "

"Uh huh," Hank said. "Well, when you're ready to go inside…"

He trailed off because the car pulling up next held my grandparents. In all honesty, I'd had very little to say to either of them. Though less to her than to him. My grandfather just seemed—broken. My grandmother kept insisting she could explain, but honestly—I didn't care what her explanation was. Someday, maybe I would care? Right now? Nope.

Grandpa Ted emerged from the car with them. He'd taken charge of both through all of this, and I couldn't thank him enough. In a way, he didn't need my thanks or encouragement—they were old friends of his after all. At the same time, they blamed Edward for Maddy's death. The only person to blame for Maddy's death was Maddy.

The last thing I wanted right now was another argument. The lunch reception was more to make sure everyone who came got a chance to eat. "I'll be in in a sec," I told Hank. "I need a minute."

Turning away from the cars and him, I headed for the walkway that would take me around the hotel. I didn't even have to look to know Ian had fallen into step with me. They were all keeping one eye on me and when I reached out a hand, he tangled our fingers together easily.

No questions. No platitudes. No urgency. I just followed the walkway around the hotel toward the back, where they had a huge patio area and a closed off swimming pool. The hotel boasted two, an indoor heated one and an outdoor one that was far too cold to be open in April.

At the end of the walkway where it dead-ended into grass, I closed my eyes and tilted my head back. The building provided heavy shade, so the air was actually cooler here. Cool enough I shivered. Ian tugged off and draped his jacket over my shoulders and then wrapped his arms around me, and I leaned back into the hug.

"We can just go up," he reminded me quietly. "No one expects you to be a hostess."

I tried to smile, but it wouldn't come this time. "I need to see everyone who came. They came for me and that means something."

"I know, Angel." The hint of exasperation in his voice did what the soft reminder hadn't, it relaxed some of the tension coiling through my insides. I swore my skin pulled too tight everywhere.

"This is so weird."

"I know," he repeated, only this time he punctuated it with a kiss. "What do you need right now?"

"I wish I —"

His phone buzzed against me. The only reason I noticed really was it was in the inner pocket of his suit jacket. Tucking the purse under my arm I dipped my fingers into the pocket to pull out his phone.

The name on the front was Aaron Garson. He was the producer at Roll City Records. Instead of taking the call, however, Ian clicked the side to decline and sent the call straight to voicemail. "Let me turn this off. I thought I had it on Do Not Disturb."

"You can take his calls," I told him as I turned to face him. He'd had to let me go to take the phone and the look he gave me countenanced zero arguments. "Or you can wait and talk to him later."

"Precisely," he said in a firm tone. "They can wait. Today is for you. This whole weekend is for you. The rest of the month if you need it."

"Hell, Baby Girl," Jake said as he walked up behind Ian. "Take the rest of the year. We can run all the interference plays you need. One thing that we are both very good at." He lifted a fist that Ian bumped easily and I laughed.

"That's a football reference."

"Thank fuck you didn't say baseball like you did last time." Jake gave me a mock glare as he pressed a hand over his heart, but it was Ian who snorted.

"She knew what she was saying, she was just messing with you."

"Honestly, I thought it was about hockey after you had talked about learning to play," I admitted and that earned me a droll stare from each of them, only Jake's lips were twitching. "What? You can't tell me with all the slamming around they do on the ice that hockey doesn't have some interference in it."

They both turned their gazes skyward, though Jake was chuckling and Ian wrapped an arm around my shoulders and tucked me against him. "She has a point."

"She always has a point. The big question is will you watch me play if I play?" The last held just a hint of challenge.

"If it comes with hot cocoa and warm blankets, as well as someone to snuggle me, then yes."

"Done," Ian said and Jake grimaced.

"Wait—"

"Too late," Ian told him, the grin in his voice audible. "We'll keep her warm while you bust your ass on the ice."

"Just don't bust up your face please," I said, leaning up to brush a kiss to his jaw. He tilted his head and caught my lips in a barely there kiss, more pressure than anything. At the same time, he cradled my chin and let out a soft sigh.

"I'll do my best," he promised.

"Are we moving this all outside?" Coop asked. "Also, if there are free kisses and cuddles, Player Three should definitely be in this game."

Real laughter surfaced at the comment. Despite the light remark and easy grin on his face, Coop studied me with serious gray-green eyes. "We still doing this?"

'Yes," I said slowly. "I need to. Have Archie and his dad arrived?"

"Not yet," Coop said. "But I checked in with him. His dad's being reluctant because he doesn't want to set off your grandparents."

"Can I borrow your phone?" Mine was off and left in the room. I hadn't really thought I'd need one today. The guys had theirs and were always close by.

"Always." He passed it over and I pulled up the text message with Archie.

It barely said *read* before Archie responded.

I thought about it, then answered with the truth.

Passing the phone back to Coop, I took another breath. "I can do this."

"Hell yes, you can," Jake said. "Jeremy's got your back, so does Hank, and we're right here."

I smiled. "I love all of you."

The huddle pulled me right into the center with all three of them hugging me. We held there for the longest of minutes then Coop said, "If I fart right now, how long would my grounding last?"

"Dude," Jake scolded but I was already laughing. "She told you no bean burritos."

Ian gave him a playful shove, but I grinned. Coop winked at me and something aching and sore settled in my chest. I had told Archie the truth. I wasn't okay. I wasn't even sure what okay was supposed to look or sound like, but I'd get there.

Especially because I had my guys. I had my *family*. Despite his playful threat, Coop didn't fart or act like he would. As we got to the side entrance, I returned Ian's suit jacket to him and he pressed his finger to my lips.

"When you're ready to go, just give one of us the nod, Angel. The rest of us will take care of it from there, okay?"

"Okay."

But instead of opening the door, he held my gaze. "You're an amazing woman, Frankie Curtis. You're strong as hell and I believe in you and in that great big heart of yours. We're all going to trust you to know your limit, just trust us to go from there."

It was as much a request as it was a command, and I could obey that. I wanted to obey that.

"Yes, Sir, I promise," I said, holding up two fingers. "Scout's honor."

Jake corrected my finger positioning and Coop cracked up as I stared at my hand and then at Jake.

"That's 'Live Long and Prosper'."

"I know," he said. "Just testing."

I whacked him gently, but my smile was back when Coop pulled open the door and we headed inside.

Time to mourn, or at least—remember, I guess.

Chapter Three

EVERYTHING WRONG WITH...

Coop

No matter how many times we told her she didn't have to go in and greet all the 'mourners,' it seemed to have little effect. Frankie couldn't understand why so many people showed up to support her. These people weren't here for her mother—fuck that bitch and speaking ill of the dead—they were here for Frankie. They were here to show her that *she* was loved, and whether she came to the lunch or not, they wouldn't love her any less.

That was Frankie, though, chin up and charging forward, even if she had needed a moment to collect herself beforehand. I kind of didn't blame her. While we weren't *that* unruly a crowd, all of our families were here. I was surprised my father had shown up, but apparently, solidarity was the rule. Jake's dad and Klara had come over. They were sitting at a table with Jake's mom, and you couldn't pay me to sit in on that drama.

Hank and Kelly had brought their kids, though Hank had been a fixture at the brownstone since the "incident." I hated referring to Maddy proving how fucking insane she was when she tried to kill Archie and Frankie—again—as an "incident."

"Stop scowling," Rachel told me with a not-so-subtle jab to my sternum. I "oofed" out some air and she turned to face me with the fakest fucking smile ever, before handing me what had to be a glass of wine.

Nope, not even gonna ask.

"I wasn't scowling," I muttered. "Much."

"She's glancing at you every couple of minutes." Like I needed her to tell me that, but just as she said it, Frankie glanced over to where Rachel and I were standing. She was talking to Jake's sisters, who'd all surrounded her. Jake was right there, taking point. We would all be on hand to run all the interference she needed. I found a smile for Frankie and she nodded, some of the worry vanishing from her eyes.

"Thanks," I said from the corner of my mouth.

"Welcome," Rachel said, then hooked her arm through mine. "You can repay me by looking interested in what I have to say."

I quirked a brow and glanced at her. "Well, I'm usually interested, when you're not throwing elbows. But why am I specifically interested at the moment?"

"Do you need a specific reason?" She glared at me without losing her fake-as-shit smile. That was some master class talent there.

"Probably not, but now I'm intrigued."

She rolled her eyes and just when I thought she wasn't going to answer, she cut a look across the room to where one Dominic Walsh re-entered the ballroom they had set up for the luncheon. It was a serve yourself kind of thing, so no one really had assigned tables. He swept the room with one look and latched onto Rachel with a kind of laser focus.

One he transferred to me. The icy coolness in his eyes held all kinds of threats, so I slung my arm around Rachel's shoulders. "Got your back."

Mr. I-Like-To-Fucking-Flirt-With-Frankie could go suck a dick. Besides, if Rachel didn't want him around, we'd take care of it.

"Okay, I don't need a cuddle buddy," she retorted, but she didn't pull away as we moved to one of the high top tables. "Also, how is she? For real?"

"You know how she is," I commented, loosening my hold on her long enough to pull out a chair for Rachel. "Chin up, eyes forward, and determined to do everything *expected* of her and not remotely looking after herself." If I sounded pissed while I rattled that off, well, I was. Her cunt of a mother didn't deserve an ounce of the grief Frankie expressed for her. Worse, Frankie didn't deserve to suffer *more* because of that bitch.

"How are you handling it?" Rachel asked before tipping her glass up and sipping her wine. I barely gave my glass a sniff before I tossed the whole drink back in one swallow. Mom caught my eye from across the room as I lowered the glass, disapproval thinning her lips as she compressed them. I sent her what I hoped was an apologetic smile and set the empty glass down.

"I don't give a damn that the bitch is dead," I said in an undertone, careful not to let it carry. None of us were sorry to see her go. Except the one person she hurt the most. Just then, the doors to the room opened, letting Archie and his father in. Well, maybe the person she hurt the second most. "But I hate that Frankie has to deal with this."

"Yeah," Rachel said with a sigh. "I want to do something to fix it."

"You, me, and everyone else."

Frankie spotted Archie and his father and she murmured something to Jake's sisters before breaking away from them to cross the room. Bubba and Jake tracked her motion the same way I did. The minute she reached Archie and he wrapped his arms around her, I flicked my attention back to Rachel.

"I'm glad you're here," I told her. "I know you haven't liked being at the brownstone so much."

One corner of her mouth quirked upward. "I give you shit, but the sound proofing is much better than I thought it would be."

I chuckled. "Or we haven't been the horny devils you always cast us as."

Her snort said everything. One of the waiters came by and claimed my empty and then looked at me and I shook my head. Not that I didn't mind drinking, but I wanted my wits about me, and I didn't want to have to deal with my mother on the subject.

"Fuck," she muttered under her breath, and I shifted to stand a little closer to where she was seated as Walsh approached.

"Need something?" I asked him even though he clearly focused on Rachel and not me.

"Rachel," he said, ignoring me. "I'm not trying to be a pain in the ass."

"You're right," she responded. "You're succeeding. What part of 'no' are you failing to understand?"

I straightened and caught Jake's eye. He quirked his brows and when I flicked a look at Walsh, he nodded and said something to his sisters before heading to me. Tossing someone out of a wake, or post-funeral luncheon or whatever the hell we were calling this, might not be in the manners rulebook, but this guy clearly needed a message pounded home.

And honestly, I couldn't slug Maddy, but I could hit him.

Walsh sighed. "Do you want to have the conversation here? Or would you prefer somewhere more private?"

"I would prefer to not have the conversation at all," Rachel said. "I'm here for Frankie. That's why all of us are here. So get your brains out of your pants or just go away."

Jake clapped a hand on Walsh's shoulder. "Problem here?" The grip had to be tight because the lawyer tried to move but didn't succeed in dislodging Jake's hold on him.

"We're fine," Rachel said in a crisp tone. "The last thing Frankie wants is for a fight to start."

Fair enough.

She glanced at the lawyer. "If I promise to call you next week, will you stop?"

Hell no.

"He'll stop now," I said, pinning a look on him and if my expression matched Jake's, the guy would get the message *now*. "She said no. Doesn't matter what your question is or what you thought you wanted to hear. Leave her alone."

"Right," Jake said without letting Walsh respond. "Let's take a walk, shall we?" The fact he hauled him backwards didn't really give the attorney a chance to argue.

"Guys," Rachel said. "I can handle this."

"You don't have to," I told her and then gave her a kiss on the cheek. "We'll be right back." With that, I followed Jake and Dominic across the room to the exit. Bubba was already at the door, holding it open and waiting for the pair to step outside before he and I followed.

Outside and away from the hum of quiet conversation, Jake all but marched Dominic toward the parking lot. It was still considered early spring up here in the northeast. The air was chilly enough that being in a suit didn't bother any of us. That said, if we were going to actually fight, we needed to lose the jackets. I also had on a white shirt, so I really hoped this asshole wasn't a bleeder.

As soon as we were well and truly clear of the room, the attorney yanked himself away from Jake. Facing us, Walsh smoothed down his jacket. "Was that really necessary?"

Arms folded, Jake glared at him. "Yes, apparently you have trouble listening. Today isn't about you, so you and your objections can get in your car and leave."

The man sighed and then cut a look at me.

"Don't," I told him. "Rachel said 'no.' That's all I need to know. You want to pretend like you don't understand, fine. But she doesn't have to put up with you."

"Ever," Bubba tacked on. "Also, you're Frankie's *attorney* and this is a funeral for your client's *mother*. While we may not think much of the woman or her choices, you could at least respect Frankie enough to knock this shit off today. Especially when Rachel has been focused on being there for her."

"Facts," Jake finished. "So, get in your car and leave or I'll put you in it and you won't enjoy the trip."

Irritation flickered in the man's eyes, but he reached up to loosen his tie. "I'll go, but not because of your threats. Let's be clear on that."

"Whatever helps you sleep at night." Before the words even left Jake's lips, Dominic slugged him. He didn't telegraph the move. Fuck, none of us saw it coming, but Jake rocked back a step and then landed his own blow.

"Son of a bitch," I swore before wading in as Jake and Dominic delivered a series of blows to each other. I slammed into Dominic, trusting Jake not to hit my back as Bubba grabbed Jake, and then I drove Dominic all the way back to the wall. Pinning him there, I glared. "What the fuck was that?"

"Proving a point," the asshole stated even as blood dribbled from the corner of his mouth. "Remember, you chose violence first. I'm just responding in kind."

Was he for fucking real?

A door closed behind us. "Guys."

Frankie's voice hit me and I sighed. Goddammit. This was exactly what we'd been trying to avoid. I let go of the prick and dragged a handkerchief out of my inner pocket. Now I knew why Hank told all of us to carry at least two today. Though I'd thought it was supposed to be for Frankie.

With a droll smile, Walsh took the cloth and dabbed at his lip with a nod before he glanced past me. I shifted so I could keep Mr. Sucker Punch in my line of sight, and also check on Frankie. She stood there with Archie. For his part, Archie had his hands in his pockets and a dark look on his face, which he fixed on Dominic.

See, he got it.

But it was Frankie's expression that had me swallowing my next statement. That and the fact that Rachel stood right behind them. The ball-shriveling look she wore was one hundred percent focused on Walsh.

"Good luck, man," I told him with a slap to his shoulder. "You're toast." I walked away from him and glanced to where Jake straightened his own shirt. Like Walsh, his knuckles were bruised and a thin trail of blood leaked from his nose. He was already in the act of pressing a handkerchief to it.

"Can we not do this today?" Frankie asked and I exhaled, guilt twisting my guts into knots.

"My apologies, Frankie," Walsh said before any of us could respond. "Your boyfriends were merely acting on yours and Rachel's behalf."

She just lifted her brows. "Look, Dominic, thank you for coming and if Rachel doesn't mind if you're here, you're more than welcome to stay. But fighting? Or making her uncomfortable? Those are a no go for me."

"I'm fine," Rachel said quietly from behind her, but Archie rolled his eyes.

"If you were, they wouldn't have marched him out of here. So let's just cut the crap, shall we?"

"Rich Boy," Rachel said. "You want to talk about cutting crap, we can compare notes, but right now might not be the time." She started to move around Frankie, but to my surprise and *clearly* to Rachel's based on her expression, Frankie stopped her.

"No," Frankie said, looping her arm through Rachel's. "If you hate him then I hate him. If you want him gone, then I do. No one needs to cut the crap, but I'd really rather no one ended up going to the hospital today. I'm sick of them."

Fuck. Archie's expression transformed as he looked at her, and Bubba was already heading to join them. Yeah, *this* was what we didn't want to happen at all.

"My apologies. To both of you. I've been worried about Rachel and you. I know you have these guys to look after you, but I wanted to be here for Rachel while she was here for you. Clearly, that's not welcome, so I'll excuse myself. You shouldn't have to worry about this right now. Call me if you need anything."

Huh. That was decent of him.

"Both of you."

Okay, that took it a bit far and I glared at him. He just gave me a smirk.

"Rachel?" Frankie asked.

"Let me talk to him for a minute," she said. "You guys go back in or better, let them take you back up to the room. You look like shit on a stick."

"I love you, too," Frankie said with a faint laugh. "Come on guys…"

"You sure about this?" Jake asked and I didn't blame him. The whole damn reason we'd dragged the dick out here was because he wasn't listening to Rachel.

"I'll be fine, asshats, thank you for defending my honor or whatever. Now shoo, go hover over Frankie and make sure she eats something. She's looking pale."

Now that she mentioned it, Frankie did look a little pale still, I lingered by the door even after Bubba and Archie ushered Frankie back inside, with Jake following. I leaned back against the wall, hands in my pockets and I waited as Rachel and Dominic walked out into the parking lot.

You could learn a lot about a person watching their body language. Rachel's arms were folded tight, her spine rigidly straight and though she'd walked next to him and now faced him as they talked, she kept her distance. Dominic, however, stuffed a hand in his pocket while the fingers of his free hand kept twitching like he wanted to reach out to her. He leaned in, she didn't.

But he didn't move to invade her space and while they spoke, both of them kept the most neutral expressions in place. Like emotion had no part of their debate. Or maybe it was the opposite—there was far too much emotion between them. While I kept an eye on them, I did my best not to stare. That would be rude.

Eventually, Rachel turned and walked away from Dominic. Their expressions were unreadable. He lingered until she was almost to me and then he turned away and went to get in his car. I flicked a look back to Rachel who stared at me.

"And you're waiting, why?"

I shrugged. "Needed some air. Not everything is about you."

That earned me a reluctant smile. "Thank you."

"I'm sorry," I said with exaggerated shock, even putting a hand up to my chest. "What did you just say?"

"Not going to repeat myself," she countered and smacked her hand over mine. "Not everything needs to be discussed, Mr. Psych Major."

"You don't know what you're missing," I said before opening the door for her.

Her indelicate snort just made me grin again. Once we were back inside, I scanned the room for Frankie. Where was she? What the fuck?

"She asked for a moment," Archie informed me. He glanced past me toward Rachel, who was already being surrounded by mine and Jake's sisters. "Rachel okay?"

"Yep," I told him. "Walsh is gone. She doesn't have to worry about him for today."

Tomorrow? Well, not much we could do about that right now.

"You good?" I asked.

"Shockingly," Archie said slowly. "I'm fine. It was weird to talk to him in the car and we took a drive to air some things out. But—as bad as he's hurting, he's also trying to be there for me and for Frankie."

"That's weird." I winced. "I mean—"

"No." Archie shook his head. "Weird is the word for it. It is weird. I just need Frankie's grandparents to leave him alone."

"Has the district attorney said whether they're going to pursue charges or not?" That was the one thing still up in the air. He'd had a gun, but it wasn't registered in New York, though he had a carry permit from Texas. Clearly, he'd acted in defense of Archie and Frankie, but there was still a chance the DA would press the matter. They hadn't *so* far, but...

"No, but the attorneys don't think they will. No one else was hurt and he had a gun that day because he's been worried about Maddy for months. Worried what she would do. He always assumed she'd come after him directly..." Archie sighed.

"And he didn't say anything to you."

Archie shook his head. "I don't know what to do with this yet, so I'm going to just—worry about it later."

I nodded. Mom chose that moment to catch my eye and motion gently for me to join them. "I get that," I told Archie. "If he was anyone else, I'd say just—go with it. He's family. They're never going to be perfect." Look at my dad, then again... "But he's also the guy who protected you. That's got to count for something." Especially considering how much the man was hurting, and you'd have to be blind, deaf, and dumb not to see it.

"I know," Archie said. "Go on, your mom is gonna give herself whiplash if she keeps doing that nod."

With a chuckle, I left him to think while I made my way toward my parents. Hopefully, we could all get out of this unscathed. Well, no more hurt than we'd already been.

Chapter Four
WORDS BLEED

Frankie

"**L**et me get you a drink," Archie murmured after we went back inside. Rachel and Dominic were talking and Coop had been less than subtle in choosing to stay outside and wait. Honestly, I could kiss them all for looking out for her, even if I wished she and Dominic could figure out whatever was going on there. I needed to be more there for her and less—less the hot mess I'd become.

"Okay," I told him and gave his arm a squeeze. "I think I need a minute." The room was full of people I knew and cared about. Hank caught my eye and when he raised his brows in question, I shook my head. I was all right. For the most part. Coop's parents and Trina had taken to one of the tables and it looked like Carly and Coop's dad were deep in conversation. Trina was on her phone.

Jake's sisters had settled at a different table, talking amongst themselves, but their attention was laser-focused on where Alicia sat talking to Jake's dad and Klara. Not only was she talking, she laughed. Hope surged through me, not because Jake needed his parents back together, but because Alicia deserved some happiness. If this made her happy again? Then I was all for it. I loved that Jake and his dad had been mending bridges, and now Archie and Eddie were.

Speaking of Eddie, I did a quick scan of the room but didn't see him. Had he left? I also didn't see my grandparents. Dammit. They hadn't been outside, so that meant they may have left through the other doors and out into the hotel. Pivoting, I headed for the doors and pushed the crash bar to let myself out. I didn't have to go far to find them. Eddie stood in the hallway, his chin down, hands in his pockets as he spoke with my grandparents.

Correction, as my grandmother chastised him. Her voice didn't carry, but that was probably the only discreet thing about her current actions. Her eyes were glassy with unshed tears, her face flushed and her whole body seemed to vibrate with her anger. Next to her, my grandfather actually looked uncomfortable. It was Grandpa Ted who was trying to calm her down. He wasn't quite blocking Eddie from her, but he also wasn't letting her get any closer.

Anger spiked through me. The past few days had been absolute hell. I'd spent most of it trying to sort out how I felt. Even worse, trying to mourn a woman who had made good on a threat she'd made more than a decade before. She had tried to kill me. She tried to kill Archie.

Just…

I marched toward them, arriving just in time to hear Patience say, "I would think you could at least have the decency to let us mourn in peace without having to be face to face with her murderer—"

"He didn't murder her." I cut Patience off, and she jerked her tearful gaze to me.

"Frankie…"

"Shut it." I didn't have it in me to even pretend politeness right now.

I'd avoided them as best I could and done everything to try and respect their grief.

Shock rippled across Patience's face and Eugene glanced up from wherever he'd drifted during the conversation to focus on me. His rheumy eyes held surprise but not—disapproval. I didn't think he agreed with her, but he also couldn't stand up to her or to Maddy or to anyone really.

"Frankie—"

"I said shut it," I repeated. "Eddie is welcome here. Eddie is grieving. You could respect *his* grief too, but you choose not to. You could respect my needs as well, but that's not even in your wheelhouse."

"Darling, of course we do…"

I laughed. "Wow, you sounded just like her there."

Patience reeled back like I'd slapped her.

"She always turned it around so that she was the victim, so that everything she did was for the best and how could I think any other way about her." My chest squeezed and my eyes burned, but I didn't look away from Patience. "She was there with you on Long Island before the wreck with the Ferrari. You knew she was there. You *kept* her secret. Just like you walked away from me when I was a kid because she threatened to kill me if you tried to look away."

This time, my grandmother paled, even as embarrassment stained her cheeks. Unlike her, I wasn't keeping my voice down or being polite.

"You kept that fact from everyone, *including* me, after they pulled me out of that wreckage. She tried to kill Archie more than once and she didn't *care* if she killed me too."

Hand to her mouth, Patience flinched.

"So, spare me your morality play. This could be my funeral you were at, instead of hers, if Eddie hadn't come along when he did. It could be Archie's funeral. She was the would-be murderer, not him. It broke his heart, and if you're too damn blind to see that, then I can't do anything for you. I don't know if I can *ever* forgive you for supporting her and hiding her after everything she did. That doesn't mean you aren't my grandmother, and I will never talk to you again, but it does mean you don't get to dictate anything. Not about this. Not about anything. So, if you can't respect Eddie being here, then you can leave."

"She's right," my grandfather said before Patience could say another word, and she dragged her stricken gaze from me to Eugene. "Maddy bullied us both, but you kept trying to placate her. You covered up for her and funded her and then…then we lied to Frankie about all of it." He shook his head. "Maybe we didn't *help* her, but we didn't stop her either." The long sigh he let out sounded so weary.

That was why he'd been so sick and exhausted. Why he'd looked like his health had been taking a turn for the worse.

"I'm sorry, sweet girl," he told me and then he looked past me. "And I'm sorry you were caught in the middle of all of this."

"Why are you apologizing to him?" Patience demanded, the sheen of tears escaping her eyes. "He killed our baby."

"No, he didn't," Eugene replied in a firmer voice than I'd ever heard him use before. "She stopped being our baby a long time ago. We're going to go now and we're going to let Frankie have the time she needs." Then he looked at me. "Please don't be a stranger. Even if I would understand it."

"I'll do my best," I promised and when Patience pulled from him and took a step toward me, I just folded my arms and took a step back. Pain flickered across her expression, but I shook my head. "We're not there."

We might never be there again. They might never be able to forgive Eddie, and fine, it was what it was. But I couldn't forgive them either. Maybe Eugene and I might find detente. I didn't think he'd wanted any part of Maddy's plans, but he also hadn't said anything. Patience was still making excuses, and having been in their shoes and excused Maddy's behavior for years—I could imagine how it had to be for them.

Didn't change the fact that they'd risked Archie's life. They'd risked mine. If Jake, Ian, or Coop had been there, I had no doubts they could have been hurt, too.

"I think it's long past time you go," Hank said quietly, and I glanced to my right to find he'd moved to stand next to me.

"I agree," Archie said. "Grandpa…"

"I'll take care of it, Sprout. You look after our girl here." Ted gave my shoulder a gentle squeeze as he eased past me, and Archie came to stand at my left. Warm hands settled on my hips and I covered them with mine, threading my fingers through Coop's as he pulled me back to him. Jake and Ian moved into the space between me and my grandparents, like they would help them along as necessary.

"I had it," I said softly, gripping Coop's hands tighter when my fingers started to tremble. The shaking seemed to spread through me, but Coop just squeezed me gently and gave me both of his hands to hold.

"Damn right you did," Coop murmured next to my ear.

"We saw that, Babe," Archie told me, brushing his knuckles down my cheek. "Now, we're just gonna sort them out to their car with Grandpa. Okay?"

I nodded.

"We'll be right back." He glanced up and past me, and I knew he and Coop were sharing one of those wordless looks the guys had all been getting good at. I felt Coop nod.

"I got her." He rubbed his cheek carefully against my hair. "Don't I?"

I dug my nails into his hand, even though I didn't want to hurt his skin, he didn't complain and just returned the grip. "Yeah," I said when I could trust my jaw not to shake. Hank gave me a measuring look. I tried to give him a smile but I failed at it.

"You are one of the bravest people I've ever met." The words and sentiment startled me. "I'm very proud of you." Then he glanced past me like Archie had, though his focus was in a slightly different direction. "Tell you what, Standish. Why don't I buy you a drink?"

"Let me do the buying and I'd like that."

I closed my eyes. A part of me had actually forgotten that Edward was still standing there, despite the fact I'd moved out here to defend him.

"Frankie," he said quietly. "Thank you."

Sucking in a deep breath, I twisted to face him and Coop moved with me easily, not letting go of my death grip on him. "You're welcome—I may have a lot of complicated feelings where you're concerned, but I was there and they weren't. You don't deserve their vitriol."

"Well, you shouldn't have to defend me either."

"You're family," I said and it rolled right off my tongue and I gave a little shrug. "You're Archie's dad and you seem to be trying with him. So that makes you family." Complicated and messy didn't even cover it. "And you saved him." You chose him was on the tip of my tongue, but I couldn't bring myself to say it.

He nodded and his dark gaze dropped away from me, hiding the raw emotion. I swore he seemed to have aged a decade in the past several days. "Take care of yourself, young lady," he said when he lifted his chin, seemingly having gotten himself in check. "I mean it. Make sure my son looks after you."

"I'll look after him," I said but that just pulled a smile.

"Of that, I have no doubt."

And Archie always looked after me. Hank paused in front of me again. "Take a break from all the people, yeah?"

I summoned a smile for him. "I just need a minute."

"Take all the minutes. No one is going to mind, in fact, you might be safer from Kelly if she doesn't feel the need to pull you out of here herself." The last he delivered with a tease and a smile, which turned my own more genuine.

"I think she's great."

"Yeah," Hank said within a wink. "Me too." Then he pressed a kiss to my forehead. "I'll see you soon."

He and Eddie walked away—together—and not back toward the

ballroom but in the direction of the hotel's bar. Not a pairing I imagined being comfortable and yet they seemed at ease with each other.

The guys hadn't returned yet nor had Grandpa Ted, that left me and Coop alone in the hall. I tried to force my hands to relax, but I couldn't bring myself to let him go.

"I'm right here," he said quietly and I shuddered, leaning back into him and trusting him to keep me on my feet. I hated the shoes I was wearing. I hated the dress. I hated everything about this day.

"I want to get out of here," I said finally.

Air whooshed out of Coop. "Done. You want Rachel too? Or just us? Or alone?" The last he offered grudgingly but the guys would leave me alone if I asked for it. Probably not very alone, like they'd be right outside the door in case I needed them, but they would do it.

"Yeah, she can come. I just—I don't want any more expectations."

He gave me another squeeze. "I'll take care of it as soon as you're done with my hands." But he was already walking us carefully toward the lobby and the elevators. A giggle escaped at how silly we had to look, but Coop just hummed as we shuffle stepped our way across to the bank of elevators and he hit the button with his elbow. "Hey, look, it's Jake. You get to keep my hands after all."

"We're going up?" Jake asked.

"Yes," I said quietly. The relief in his expression reminded me that as hard as all of this was for me, but the guys had struggled as well and they had been worried "You can stay to see your parents and…"

"Trust me, they'll be fine without me." He had his phone out even as he loosened his tie. "Arch and Bubba were talking to Ted, but I didn't want you worrying about all of us."

"Text Rachel," Coop ordered as the elevator opened. "And probably Jeremy. Let him know we're going up to the suite for the night." The last was an executive decision but I was okay with it. More than okay. Coop leaned against the wall, and I leaned into him, as the elevator swept us upward.

Jake met my gaze as he finished typing in a text. "Hey, Baby Girl."

"Hey, Jake."

"Pajamas?"

"Hell yes."

He grinned. "I bet Jeremy can swing us some wine if he didn't already load us up."

I snorted. Jeremy was always looking after us. Didn't matter that we weren't twenty-one. He didn't judge or give us any side-eye. Well, I guess he never gave it to me. The guys earned his ire plenty of times. Especially the last time Ian and Jake were throwing a football at each other from one room across the stairwell to the other.

That memory had my lips curling upward. When we reached the top floor, Coop didn't do the shuffle walk, he just picked me right up. I let go of his hands so I could curl my arms around his neck and he slid his now freed arm under my legs.

Eyes closed, I tucked my head against his shoulder. It was just easier to let them make the decisions for a few minutes. "I got you," Coop murmured. Once we were in the huge suite, he carried me right back to the huge bedroom that came with it. Well, actually it came with two, but they'd all piled in here with me the night before, king bed or not. I'd ended up sleeping across all of them and no one complained.

Once in the room, he set me on my feet and then he bent down to help me out of my shoes. Jake was right behind us, shedding his suit jacket, before he was unzipping my dress. In about thirty seconds, I went from dressed, down to my panties, because even my bra had vanished. Then Coop was pulling one of my favorite t-shirts over my head. He cupped my face to kiss me lightly, before he ran his fingers through my hair like he could comb out the hair spray that left it stiff.

"I need to wash my face."

"Yep," he said and gave me another kiss. I think it was one of the first times in a long time they'd gotten me naked so efficiently, only to put me in another outfit. I sighed and when I wrapped my arms around him, Coop just hugged me tight. No rushing at all.

When I finally peeled myself away to go wash my face, he and Jake spoke in low tones. The door to the suite opened and then closed. "Don't everyone rush me at once, bitches, I know you were waiting for me to get here."

Rachel's voice made me smile. By the time I'd washed off my face and stepped out of the bathroom, Jake and Coop had both changed into shirts and sweats. Jake picked me up into a hug and I laughed as he carried me toward the sitting room.

"I can walk."

"Yeah, but Coop's been hogging you and I need some Frankie cuddle time."

"You're gonna make me throw up, aren't you?" Rachel sprawled on one of the armchairs, like us, she'd also changed into looser clothing. Though her pajama leggings were a lot classier and so was her button down top. I swore she looked almost too prim and proper. "What?" she glanced down at herself and then at me. "I bought them in the gift shop. Sue me, I sleep naked and didn't have any PJs with me."

"Damn, I did not need that visual," Jake muttered as he sat down and settled me in his lap. Coop draped my legs over his as he sat next to us. Rachel had brought more than the pajamas, there were two bottles of wine on the table.

"It wasn't for you," she retorted and for the first time in what felt like forever, a real laugh bubbled up from beneath the broken wreckage and debris of heartache that I couldn't bring myself to sort through yet.

The door opened again to Archie and Ian in.

"I come bearing pizza and chocolate," Archie announced and the smell of the pizza hit me, and my stomach gave a hint of a grumble. I actually couldn't remember when I'd last eaten. "Wine, some pizza, our woman and—"

"Rachel," Ian finished for him with a snort.

"Don't get all excited, boys, I'm here for Frankie."

"Aww," Archie said as he put the pizza on the table and went to sit on the arm of her chair. "Really? And see here I thought you've been harboring some fantasies about the rest of us."

"You mean throttling you?" she snarked.

"Oh, no," Archie said, smirk growing, and I groaned.

"Be nice."

They both paused to look at me and I gave them *both* a meaningful look.

With an exaggerated sigh, Archie said, "Fine, I was just going to say if she wanted to get dicked, I could recommend some better guys than Walsh. That guy's an ass."

"I think I'm giving up dick, the experiment is a bust. It's all vag, all the time, but thanks for the thought." Rachel's smile was too serene, but she shook her head at me and reached forward to flip open the pizza box. It was loaded with everything, including pineapple. The second box was a straight up meat lovers.

"Glasses," Ian announced as he carried them out from the little kitchenette that came with the suite. "There's also soda if anyone wants to skip the wine."

"Jere made sure to bring us some beer too," Archie said. He and Ian went to change, they didn't take long and when they came back, we all spread out and I sat on the floor in front of Jake so I could eat at the table. Rachel kept filling our wine glasses and the guys were giving her shit and she was dishing it right back.

This—this was better. I caught Ian watching me and I gave him a little smile, mouthing 'I'm okay,' and he nodded. No questions, just—just the guys and Rachel and this was what I needed. I was out of words. But I could soak up their warmth, their nearness—their stability.

OK TO NOT BE OK

Frankie

Three days after the funeral, we were back in the city and the guys had classes. I was supposed to be in them too, but I just couldn't seem to work together the energy to care. My academic advisor had confirmed what the bereavement emails offered. I could take all passing and it wouldn't affect my GPA. She suggested I should give it serious consideration and accept the offer. I'd think about it.

Hank had encouraged me to do the same before we parted the day after the funeral. He needed to get back to Boston and his life, and we had to be back here. As it was, I sat outside, not far from the building where Rachel would be leaving one of her photography classes. I was a horrible friend, I couldn't even remember which class it was. Just that we usually got coffee after these classes.

The last ninety minutes of sitting here hadn't gotten me any closer to answers or a decision about what to do. I could have stayed home at the brownstone. Jeremy probably would have fussed over me, and I could have curled up in bed and watched sad movies to try and make myself cry. So far, very little had worked. My eyes were still dry, and the world still felt like it was a foot back, or like there was this thick pane of glass between me and everyone else.

"Whatever is making you scowl like that, we need to find it and bury it," Rachel announced as she suddenly blocked out the sun I hadn't even realized was making me squint behind my sunglasses.

"Pretty sure we already did that," I told her as I stood, and Rachel's grin froze. "It's okay," I said, waving off the impending apology. "Really."

"Fuck my life," Rachel exhaled the words before raking a hand through her mass of messy hair. She was usually way more put together than this. "I'm sorry, I know I can be a thoughtless bitch…"

"Stop it," I said, hooking my arm through hers. "You're definitely not a thoughtless bitch. It was an offhand remark."

"But in hella poor taste," Rachel grumbled, bumping my shoulder with hers as we walked together toward the corner, where we could cross the street and head down to the coffee shop. "Fuck, I'm sorry, Frankie."

"You're forgiven," I told her easily enough. "And it worked, I'm not scowling anymore."

"Ugh." Tilting her head back, Rachel groaned. "Fine, but I reserve the right to try and make this up to you at some point in the future, even if you don't think I need to."

I rolled my eyes. "You're going to do whatever you want no matter what I say."

"This is true," she said, her smile restored. "I'm so glad you agree with me. It makes all of this much easier."

I snorted. "Right." At the crosswalk, we waited for the signal to change.

"Did you make it to class today?"

"Nope." I shrugged. "Jake came in with me. Dropped me off at the hall before he headed to his, and I stood there staring at the door for like ten minutes and then just went outside."

She didn't say anything and the light changed. Arms still hooked together, we crossed the street. It was a pretty day. Warm, breezy, and the sun shone down on us. Glare bounced off the windshields of cars and there were even fresh flowers in some of the large planters that marked the sidewalk.

Reds. Blues. Even purples. All very *spring* like.

"You know it's okay, right?" Rachel asked as we reached the coffee shop. I loosened my grip on her arm to reach for the door and opened it for her.

"That was what I was telling you." I glanced at her, but the sunglasses hid her eyes just like the pair I wore covered up my own.

"Nice." The corner of her mouth kicked up, but the expression was familiar. "That's not what I meant."

"I know," I said, following her inside and letting the coffee scent wash over me. The tables were all full, but they were almost always busy. Students came and went. Spots would open up, or we could take the coffees and walk back to Rachel's dorm or head uptown toward the park.

Lots of options now that the weather had turned.

Rachel gave me a look but didn't harass me as we stood in line. She did, however, glance over to the corner of the coffee shop a couple of times. The third time she did it, I followed her glance to see what had captured her attention. I half-expected to see Dominic sitting there at his usual table. Had it really become his usual table the last few months? He wasn't always here, but more often than not he was, and he always paid for our coffees before we got here.

Today—three people sat at that table. None of them Dominic.

"Maybe he's listening to you," I offered and Rachel gave a shrug.

"I just saw someone I thought I knew," she replied, her tone *way* too offhand to be real so, I did a scan of that side of the coffee shop. No one looked familiar to me, but then I didn't know everyone Rachel did.

"Still," I said. "If he's not here then maybe he's listening. That has to count for something, right?"

"Hmm." The noncommittal sound was as far as she went. Soon enough it was our turn and Rachel had her wallet out and paid before I could.

"I'll get it next time."

"Uh huh." The distracted look on her face wasn't one she affected. I'd seen it before. Back when she'd sit at Mason's, working on her poetry assignments or when she and—what was that girl's name? When she'd been dating her. What…fuck. She took her to the Halloween party and we'd all been having a great time. She was at Homecoming too.

Why couldn't I remember her name?

"Here," Rachel said, prompting me to take the coffee she held out and then she nodded to the door. "It's crowded in here. C'mon."

I followed her out, there were even more people crowding inside so we had to weave between them, and then we were outside. The air seemed fresher after the throng of people. Rachel turned a sharp right and we were heading away from the school and in the opposite direction from her dorm. Not saying anything, we just—walked. It wasn't until we'd gone three blocks and I'd drunk about a third of my coffee before I asked.

"Are we going anywhere in particular?"

"Yes," Rachel said and then stopped abruptly. "I mean, we don't have to."

I raised my brows. "Well, no, we never *have* to, but where are we going? Or where were we going?"

"Nowhere."

"Okay. Is nowhere still this way? Or do we have to turn at a cross street?"

Rachel glared at me. "You know, you're too adorable to kick right now."

I lifted my shoulders. "Should I work on that?"

"Yes." She exhaled. "I was heading toward the park, I need to take some shots—slice of life pics, and I figured you could use some air and..."

I waited patiently.

"And I can't believe he actually listened to me."

With a sharp shake of her head, she met my gaze.

"I didn't say that."

"Okay."

She frowned but didn't challenge me, and then we were walking again.

"You know," I said. "It'd be faster if we took a taxi or the subway."

"I know.""

I nodded. We were walking because Rachel needed to think. It was a nice enough day and I needed to think too. "I don't think we've ever done this all the way on foot before."

"Nope," Rachel said. "Well once, but that was when we had to do city shots and I made the hike with Angelica."

That was a new name. "Girlfriend?"

"Pffft," Rachel said. "She's in Life in Pictures class. We work together a lot, but she's so straight she makes rulers look curvy."

A rough chuckle escaped me. "That's a terrible description."

"It is what it is..."

"Skylar," I said abruptly, the name hitting me, and Rachel swung her head around to stare at me like I'd sprouted a second head.

"What?"

"I was thinking earlier about Homecoming and the Halloween party and the girl you were dating, and I couldn't remember her name. It was making me crazy."

"Why the hell are you thinking about *those* two nights?" The askance look on Rachel's face made me hesitate.

"I was just—thinking about you and worried about you. I know you said your experiment with..."

"No," Rachel said, dragging us to a stop and moving out of the path of other pedestrians. "Frankie—those nights were horrible for you. Why are you thinking about them right now?"

Well, I hadn't actually thought of it that way. I shrugged and glanced away from the intense worry now filling her expression. "I was thinking about you and Skylar—not the rest of that. And I couldn't remember her name."

"Why would you be thinking about me and Skylar?" Rachel turned the question over even as she asked it, like she couldn't believe she had to ask it. "I haven't thought about Skylar in—fuck I don't know how long."

"Cause you liked her and you were happy with her," I said and started walking again. The coffee had lost some of its flavor, but I downed it anyway. "You haven't been that happy lately."

She'd fallen into step with me. "Yeah, well, it has nothing to do with Skylar."

"No, it has to do with Dominic, a topic you don't want to discuss, even though you clearly have feelings for him and it's clearly upsetting you that he was around all the time." I shook my head. "Now you're upset that he isn't."

"I'm complicated."

The retort almost made me smile. "That's my line."

"I know, I'm borrowing it. Besties share shit."

"Yes," I agreed with her. "Then why aren't we talking about him?"

She didn't say anything and I let the silence go for another block.

"And we're still not discussing him, and that's okay." Honestly, it was. "I'm here if you need to talk, I need you to know that. You were there for me—you're always there for me."

"Frankie, your mother…"

"Is dead. She was out of my life for a lot longer than this and I don't—I don't know how to process that yet. I'm not even sure what I'm supposed to feel, much less how I do feel. So, I'm taking a page out of your book."

She slid her arm through mine. "You're worrying about my problems instead."

"Sure," I told her and sighed. "I just want you to be happy, Rach. You told me you were one hundred percent lesbian, vag all the way and you weren't into dick. Then you're experimenting with dick and not just one, a lot of different ones—some of these guys have hurt you."

"Eh," Rachel said. "Not really *that* bad. Besides—I wanted to broaden my horizons and see if I was missing anything."

I frowned. "And?"

She shrugged. "I don't know. Sometimes I enjoy it. Sometimes I don't. Not all dicks are equal, that much I can tell you. Girls kiss better. Some are better at cunnilingus, though not all guys are terrible at it. Some guys are two pump chumps and some stretch out your vag until you aren't sure you can ever walk again."

A sigh escaped her, and she directed us toward a trashcan along the walk and dropped her coffee cup in it. I dumped mine in too, since it was almost empty. When she tucked her head against my shoulder, I leaned my cheek against her hair.

"Are you alright?" I asked. "For real?"

"I don't know," Rachel admitted. That was a big thing for her to confess. "Sometimes I think I made a mistake being curious and other times—"

We were still walking, just slower, and the pedestrians around us just cut by and kept going. That was one of the other things about New York. Go slow or go fast, everyone else just kept moving. Like life, it kept going on.

"Other times," Rachel continued in a quieter voice. "I think I've lost my mind because I want too much and I know better."

That made me inexorably sad for her.

"What about you?" she asked, lifting her head and blowing out a long sigh like she was shifting some huge weight off her shoulders. "Are you alright?"

"Nope." That was the truth. "I don't think I've been alright in a while.

I just—I don't know how to put it into words yet."

"You know," she said. "It's okay to not be okay."

"So everyone keeps saying."

Well, not those words exactly, but the same sentiment. Sara had pulled me aside for a quiet word the morning after the funeral. She just wanted to check in on me, to let me know she was there if I needed to talk. That I could just call and she could chatter if that was what I needed. Carly offered me the same, and so did Alicia. Even Klara did and that surprised me, but I appreciated all of their efforts. It seemed to literally kill Kelly not to hug me, but when I was telling them goodbye, I'd given her a hug and she'd damn near squeezed the air out of me.

It had been a damn nice hug. Even little Chloe gave the fiercest of hugs. Alec had been pretty solemn, but he extracted a promise from me to text him, saying he'd check in with me every couple of days. He didn't want to hover. In some ways, he was so me. So mature for his age, but not because he had to be. Just because he was.

"I don't know how to be okay," I told Rachel. "I don't even know what I need to ask for it."

"That's okay, too."

We'd been walking forever. "Rachel…"

"Yeah?"

"Can we get a taxi now? Or an uber? Or I can call Jeremy?" My feet hurt. I was *not* wearing the right shoes for this.

"Yeah," she said, pulling out her phone. "I'll get us an uber. Want to go back to your place, put on pajamas and watch sappy shit on TV and be sad?"

Yeah. I kind of did.

"Jeremy will make us brownies, I bet."

"Sold!"

Twenty minutes later, we were back at the brownstone, curled up in my bed with the brownies that Jeremy had already made, and she picked

Steel Magnolias. We started there, followed it up with *Moulin Rouge* and then *What Dreams May Come*. When Coop found us, we were on *Titanic*.

He crawled right in and curled up on my other side and let me lean on him as Jack drowned. Spoiler, the boat sank. Still, even when he let out a soft, sad sigh and Rachel sniffled, covering it up like she wasn't crying for Rose, my tears still wouldn't come.

Maybe I was broken after all, even if it was okay to not be okay.

Chapter Six
KEEP BREATHING

Jake

When Frankie came down the stairs, pulling her hair into a ponytail to join us for our run, I didn't say a word. I didn't say anything when Coop eyed me blearily from over her shoulder and shook his head. She'd fallen asleep in his room the night before and we'd just left her there. I'd almost gone in to sleep with them but sometimes she just needed Coop. Just like she just needed Archie or Bubba, and every once in a while, me.

Putting a pin in that pity party that had no place in my head, I focused on Frankie again. The shadows under her eyes said she wasn't sleeping. Even when I did sleep with her, there was a restlessness to her and she'd snap awake from a nightmare with no memory of the dream. The way she grabbed onto one of us in those first few moments of waking, told me a lot of what I needed to know.

Fuck, I hated her mom. I kind of wanted to go piss on her grave. Bitch.

Rather than voice that, I grinned at her. "Baby Girl is going to join us today. All the inspiration I need."

Her snort and reluctant, if real, smile settled some of my concern and I dipped my head to meet her peppermint infused kiss easily, before she moved on to give Archie and Bubba their kisses. Coop just shook his head and I clapped a hand on his shoulder. A run might be what we all needed. Routines were good. At least that was Mom's advice when I talked to her a couple of days ago when she called to tell me she would be *joining* the girls when they made their summer excursion to Germany.

Dad had put in his papers to retire and Klara had eighteen months left on her tour. I really hoped this was a sign of good things for all three of them, but between the accident at the end of last summer and the funeral for Frankie's mom, there had been a dynamic shift between all three.

I couldn't say I would complain. Not this time. Not when I understood far more intimately how complicated relationships could get. Bubba murmured something to Frankie and she just shook her head.

"No, I need to get out of my head. As much as running sucks, it does tend to make me think about breathing and my side killing me and how sweaty I am."

Coop laughed. "I told you we could just stay in and have sex. I'd get you out of your head."

Fuck me. That sounded like a good plan and Archie's snort echoed my own. Yeah, but mentally? High-five bro, high-five.

"I know, but I kind of just wanted to be with everyone."

"Well," Archie drawled. "We could do that too. Wouldn't be the first time."

"Won't be the last," I tacked on and Archie grinned at me, though that smile vanished as Jeremy cleared his throat.

The flush on Frankie's neck suddenly crawled up to her ears and she buried her face against Bubba's chest. His resigned smile said it all. There was no getting around the part we were all having sex and Jeremy damn well knew it. However…

"As I see you are all about to partake of some…" Jeremy paused for a moment and I cut a glance at him. His stern look swept over everyone and included me. Shit, I hadn't been doing anything but standing here. "Exercise, I will hold off on breakfast for an hour or so. Then I thought we might discuss summer arrangements."

"Sounds good, Jere," Archie told him. "We're definitely gonna partake in some exercise. Group run. Let's go people…" He clapped his hands together. "Places to go and an ass to follow. Ow—sorry babe, I definitely meant *your* ass to follow."

I snorted because I didn't even have to look back to know Frankie flipped him off and then thumped him. As much as the two of us had disagreed recently, Archie and I were working on that. Though, I had to admit, the temptation to thump him had definitely diminished.

"Let's go," I said before Archie could cause any more embarrassment for our girl. He shot me a look, but there was no mistaking the humorous glint softening some of the worry in his eyes. Since he'd had as much trouble sleeping as she had that first week after everything went down—I had zero issues cutting him some slack.

He'd talked to us some, but not enough based on Coop's reactions. I had a sneaking suspicion he'd been talking to his father and grandfather about it and trying to make sure we were there for Frankie, along with him. Maybe I'd drag him to the gym for a few rounds in the boxing ring and let him get some of the agitation out.

We could definitely do that for each other. Bubba already had the door open. The five of us descending the steps had to be a sight. Some days, even when we ran together, we had ear buds and listened to our own music.

Sometimes, we shifted routes, like on leg days I didn't do the longer runs, but Bubba did regardless. Guy didn't hit the gym as often as he used to, and I should probably give him some shit. He was losing bulk. Then again, maybe he didn't need it as much anymore. Frankly I didn't either, but I also liked the workouts and the strength training.

I also hadn't been kidding about hockey. I was thinking about it and there were a couple of amateur leagues in the area. Not something I wanted to admit, but I'd missed sports this year. Missed the drilling and being on a team, forcing myself to push and work with others. That said, I also had missed a lot with Frankie this year because of my own dumb stubbornness.

Spring semester had been *way* better than fall, but that didn't change the fact I'd fucked up. We walked to warm up and let Frankie set the pace. It was only a couple of blocks over to the park. When she yawned for the third time, I took pity on her and dashed forward to lift her up. She squealed as I tossed her over my shoulder and jogged about fifty feet before Bubba intercepted and he lifted her and did the same.

Laughter wheezed out of her when Coop made a grab for her, but Archie beat him and carried her through one of the entrances to the park before he set her on her feet. "Y'all suck," she said, her face flushed pink, probably from a combination of entertainment and being upside down.

"I can," Archie teased her and moved in like he was gonna kiss her, but she gave him a playful shove and Coop managed to get in there and he picked her up and kissed her. A chuckle escaped me as Coop walked her backwards toward the brick wall and away from the path.

Bubba pressed two fingers to his lips and whistled.

"You're right," Coop grumbled as he lifted his head. "They suck."

"We're here to run," Bubba reminded him. "Not get in trouble for public indecency."

"Who's being indecent?" Coop demanded but Frankie answered for all of us, and his grunt when she squeezed him had me cackling all over again. "Okay. Fine, I'll take Frankie home and we'll be privately indecent."

"Nope," Archie said. "Frankie wants to run, so she gets to run. You need to think of something to make that thing go away. No one here needs to see it."

That pulled another giggle from Frankie, and I studied my baby girl. The laughter was there, but it didn't stay. The sparkle in her eyes, it had been absent for a while. Grief was an insidious thing. I swore it was like that bitch of a mother haunted her more now that she was gone than she'd ever managed in life.

And I had no idea how to fix this. Coop kept telling us we couldn't. We just had to be there for her. I wasn't the only one losing my mind a little. Thank fuck for Rachel—another sentence I didn't think I'd ever be committing to, internally or externally—but seriously, she had been a goddamn lifesaver with Frankie.

She had gradually begun to spend more time back at her dorm, but she was at the brownstone at least one night out of every three. None of us were arguing, because she and Frankie talked for hours, and other times they just watched every single chick flick known to man.

I swore my man card was in jeopardy with the sheer number of theatrical sob-fests we'd watched with them.

"Dude," Archie said, and I shook off the maudlin thoughts. Frankie was stretching, with Bubba supervising. "You okay?" He'd dropped his voice so it didn't carry and I rolled my head around. The cracks released some tension, but not enough.

Just… "I'm worried about her."

"Same," Archie answered, and he glanced over his shoulder at her even as he grabbed his foot to do some quad stretches. "But we're doing everything we can."

"Are we?" I wasn't so sure about that.

"What are you thinking?" Rather than argue, Archie looked interested. "I'm down with anything if it helps her."

"I don't know yet. We need to wrap up the academic year and talk about June." Our month. Archie nodded once. "But I think we should— fuck, I don't know. Take her somewhere she doesn't have to think about this anymore?" I was asking more than telling.

Releasing a sigh of his own, Archie gave a little shrug. "I've been thinking about that. A lot. Maybe taking her to Iceland or somewhere north where she can see the Northern Lights. Do something utterly unexpected and just keep her distracted with sex and play. At the same time…"

"Yeah," I agreed with the unspoken thought. "I don't know if that's what she needs right now either." It was hard to just—*wait* and see. Being there for her was what we could do. But until then, we what? Waited?

I'd never hated waiting more.

"Come on slackers," Coop called and I shook off the worried expression. Arch did much the same. We were all doing it. Tucking the feelings away and keeping our attitudes and expressions as upbeat as possible. "The sooner we get the torture over, the sooner we can go back to bed."

Right.

Or at least take a shower.

Maybe that was what we needed to do. Just—bombard her with happier memories and happier activities. Somehow, though, I didn't think so. I'd known Frankie for way too long. She was hurting right now and hurting somewhere we couldn't quite reach.

Fuck, I hated her mother.

By unspoken agreement, we set off at a jog, letting Frankie set the pace. It wasn't long though until she started pushing herself, going faster. We could keep up, but she was so focused, that even when the trail began to head uphill, she refused to slow or give in to the grind. If anything, she huffed harder, trying to keep up her speed.

Coop pushed to get ahead of her while Bubba stayed right at her side. He only surrendered the spot periodically to me or Arch. That was fine, we all had our parts to play. At the top of the hill though, Coop doubled over and wheezed.

"And I'm out," he said in between explosive gasps of breath. I slowed my pace, as did Archie, and we shared a look. Coop was giving Frankie a way out. Would she take it?

"It sucks," Frankie said, the panting making the words almost inaudible. "But I want to do that again. I want to do it enough that I don't feel like I'm dying pushing up that hill."

"You can," I said before anyone else could jump in with advice. "But you aren't doing it all in a day, Baby Girl."

Face flushed and damp with wisps of hair clinging to it, she gave me a look that made me just want to swallow the words to clear up the disappointment from her expression. "I know," she said, walking in circles and still panting hard as she tried to catch her breath. "I just—I want to feel something. I want to accomplish something. Everything is so…numb."

Bubba frowned. "Don't hurt yourself in the quest to feel something, please." The last word he tacked on and she paused in her circuit to look at him. "I mean it, Angel. We know this is hard. We want to do something—"

"Anything," Archie interjected. "Anything that will help you feel better. No matter how challenging that might be."

I winced. They had a point and she paused, head back to stare up at the sky, her chest rose and fell. The shallow, sharp breaths gradually deepened and Coop straightened. We were all watching her. All waiting. "I don't know what will work. I don't even know what I need to make it work."

Fair. "Well, the good thing is we don't have to know yet," I told her and when I held out my arm, she slid right up against me and I didn't care that we were both sweaty. I wrapped her up in my arms and hugged her. "You know that, right? We don't have to have the answers. We just have to get through each day. Then the next. And the next. Between us, we can do that."

I believed it fervently.

"I know we can," she agreed and then buried her face against my shirt. "I changed my mind. I don't want to run anymore."

"Oh, thank fuck," Coop declared. "I'll get us an Uber."

Her shoulders shook and, at first, I worried she'd started to cry but it was half-formed laughter that had her lips pulling up into a hint of a smile. "We can walk back, Coop. We're not that pathetic."

"Speak for yourself," he told her.

"You have to go to the edge of the park to get to the Uber anyway," Bubba pointed out.

"I hate you," Coop said.

"And by the time we're there, we might as well walk those last couple of blocks." Archie just grinned and Coop groaned. Drama queen.

"I hate you more."

"C'mon, Coop," Frankie gave my hand a squeeze before she walked over to grab his. "We'll race them back."

"Oh, that's it, I hate you most of all." He couldn't even get those words out without grinning like an idiot. As if we could hate her.

"Fine, how about whoever gets back first, gets to shower with me?"

Definitely motivated Coop, not that I kept track of his speed, I was too busy leaving them in the dust behind me. Bubba didn't even try to race, he stuck with her, and I was fine with that. I still beat Archie and Coop back to the house—Coop kept up way better than he pretended. We waited, sweaty and laughing on the steps, for her and Bubba to catch up.

"We gotta do something," Archie said.

"We are," Coop reminded us.

"Yeah, yeah." I waved him off. "There has to be more we can do than wait."

"Not yet," Coop said. "She'll ask when she's ready—when she figures it out herself. Until then, we just be the best us we can be. That's what she wants."

I frowned. "You sound very certain about that."

"I am certain about it." Coop shot me a measured look. "Her mother tried to kill Archie. Frankie's terrified of losing us. Of having *us* taken away from her."

Archie said nothing and I wanted to beat the shit out of myself.

"She's protecting us."

"Even from her," Archie finished for me, and I slumped back against the railing. Yeah, okay, we could keep breathing, but we needed to beat up her nightmares too, and that needed to start sooner rather than later.

Chapter Seven

MINDFUL DISTRACTION

Frankie

I stared at the closed door to the lecture hall and turned away. When I got back to the brownstone, I'd email the instructor and my advisor. Maybe taking them up on the offer for my classes was way past overdue. Still, I should be able to handle it. I pushed open the door to the stairwell and came to an abrupt halt.

Jake leaned against the wall, arms folded wearing a grim expression. Pulse rabbiting, I swallowed. "Did you forget something?" The ability to play this off like it was nothing fled the moment my voice cracked mid-sentence.

Instead of calling me on my crap, he just raised his eyebrows then held out his hand. "Give me your backpack, Baby Girl and let's walk."

A sigh escaped me. "Jake…"

"It's fine," he said, his eyes softening as he pushed away from the wall. "I mean, it's not fine that you thought you had to hide this from us—from me—but it's fine. We'll figure this out together, okay?"

I slid my arms out of the backpack that I'd barely opened the last few days, and Jake took the weight easily, hooking it over his shoulder. I blew out another breath and glanced down. Guilt chewed away at my insides, even as my stomach bottomed out. The warmth of his palm against my cheek had me looking up as he cupped my chin.

"I'm not mad," he told me. "I mean—I'm pissed about a lot of things, but I am not mad *at* you."

Closing my eyes for a moment, I leaned into his touch. "I'm sorry, I wasn't trying to lie to anyone."

"I know, Baby Girl. I don't have a single doubt, I promise." He hooked an arm around my shoulders and we walked down the stairs together. I leaned into his side as we made our way out of the stairwell. With Jake right there, even the heavier crowds and throngs of students parted. It was kind of funny, the guys never had trouble getting people to get out of their way.

Outside, the warm sunshine had me reaching for my sunglasses and Jake let me go only long enough to put on his, then slid his arm around me. I wrapped one arm around his waist and reached up to tangle my fingers with his hand on my shoulder.

Together, we followed the sidewalk toward one of the other coffee shops I liked near campus. This one wasn't super close and didn't have the foot traffic of the Pot Head where Rachel and I liked to go. The Perky Cafe on the other hand, was almost a joke in the bright, cheerful boho decor and the damn near chirpy bro-istas that worked there. They were never in a hurry, nothing ever fazed them, and they were always upbeat.

The fact a dispensary was around the corner wasn't lost on me. As it was, Jake pointed me at one of the tables on the patio. "I'll grab the coffee for us." Then he pressed a kiss to my lips before he headed inside. Sinking down to sit, I leaned back in the chair and let the sliver of sunshine cutting around the building warm my face.

There was traffic and people. When Jake opened the door to the coffee shop, sound washed out along with some piped in music. Yet when the door closed, the sound cut off and it was just me on a warm day in the middle of a city and it was almost—silent. No, not silent. Quiet. Slow.

The absence of loud noises added a peaceful quality to the spot. Jake didn't take long inside. When he exited, carrying two huge cups of coffee, a smile curved the corners of my lips. There was also a couple of brown bags gripped in one of his hands. He met my gaze with a smile of his own.

"I figured you could go for a couple of chocolate croissants." He set the bags down before handing me my coffee and I let out a little sigh.

"I really am predictable."

"No," Jake said as he dragged his chair out and around so that he was sitting next to me and half-facing me. "You're reliable. You're steady. You keep most of us grounded because you are practical as hell. So, when you're hurting and retreating—all we want to do, all *I* want to do is fix it for you."

Wrapping my hand around the coffee, I smiled for real this time. "You guys do take care of me. You do chase the bad stuff away…"

When he put his hand over mine on the coffee, I waited. The serious note in his eyes was hard to ignore, much less try to avoid. "Frankie—why are you hiding?" That question, that *demand*, from anyone else might have earned a sarcastic remark or a quip. Rachel had more or less asked me the same thing a few days earlier, and I didn't have an answer then.

"I don't know." That was the truth. "I want—I want to go back to my classes. I want to work on my degree. I want to sing with Ian and play with Coop and hang out with you and Archie while you build something that might blow up—"

Jake snorted but he didn't deny it.

"But even if I want to in here…" I tapped the side of my head. "My heart doesn't seem to see it or be able to feel it." The numbness was hard to describe because the word 'numbness' didn't exactly apply to it. I *felt* things but they were…

"Have you talked to your therapist?" Yep, only Jake waded through the weeds to get right to the heart of it.

"I've tried a couple of times. She's on vacation at the moment and my next appointment isn't for a couple of weeks."

"Can you call Erin? Or hell, we'll go get Coop and he can put on the psych hat and tuck away the boyfriend card…"

"Jake, I love you for trying to solve that, but Coop puts up with a lot from me now. I just don't know what to say to make this easier for anyone. I know I need to take the school up on their offer. The passing marks won't affect my GPA which is good, it won't help or hurt, I can still work on the info, and not have to stress about grades or exams."

"But?" He prompted as he gave my hand a squeeze before he let it go. I took a sip of coffee as I turned the question over in my head.

"But I really don't know." I raked a hand through my hair. I'd pulled it up into a messy bun and I tangled my fingers in the band holding it in place and loosened it so I could shake my hair out. "I want—" The words just stuck there as I looked up toward the sky, finger combing my hair. "I want my mother to have never been my mother."

Even saying that aloud didn't help. If anything, it made me feel worse.

"Baby Girl," he said in a voice so heavy with emotion it dragged over me. "If I could fix it…"

"I know you would," I promised him. "I *know* you all would. If I'm scared, I know you're going to tell me it will be all right. When I have nightmares, you're right there to hug me and chase away the demons in the dark. But Jake—I don't even know what this is. I hate her and I miss her and I don't know how I'm supposed to feel and then I just feel—nothing."

Somehow that seemed so much worse.

I rubbed my face then wrapped both hands around my mug. The chocolate croissants were still in their brown wrappers and I wasn't even sure I wanted one anymore. "Jake, I hate this."

"Baby Girl, I hate it for you." He leaned forward and his legs bracketed mine. "I would give everything I have to make this better. Would it help if you went to Hank's? Or if we went back to Texas?"

The intensity in his pale blue eyes held me riveted. Jake wasn't kidding. I had a feeling if I said I wanted to go anywhere right now, we'd go get a car and get on the road. They all would. I let go of the coffee and reached for his hands. When he gripped mine, I lifted my shoulders.

"That's the problem, Jake. I don't know what I need or what I want. Everyone—you, Coop, Archie, Ian—you're all right there to pick me up if I fall. You're looking after me. You make me eat." I made a face and the minute I mentioned it, he reached for one of the croissants and gave me a meaningful look.

"When you don't eat, we all worry."

I supposed. "I just don't know what this is or how to make it better. I want to scream. I want to throw things. I want to demand to know why she did the things she did." Even as my voice rose on each of those sentences, my eyes were bone dry and the back of my throat turned scratchy. "She was my mom, and once upon a time I actually liked her—like, I have good memories with her." Not a lot to be honest, and I had to struggle to think of them.

"One time, I remember we drove down to the lake? Or maybe up to a lake? We were on a speedboat. And I got to wakeboard. It was…awesome." But the guy we were with, her latest fling, he was a blur. What I remembered was eating the fish he'd caught, grilled over this portable stove he carried, and riding the wakeboard.

"Frankie, there is no right or wrong way to feel. I—I had issues with my dad for years because I firmly believed he chose Klara over us. Now I get that's not as simple as it sounds, but I was a kid and they didn't do as good a job explaining all of it as I'd have liked."

"And even if they had, Alicia is your mom." Jake loved his mom and Jake protected who he loved.

"Yeah," he said. "She is. Klara is great, I care about her, she is family, but in my head—she was on one side and my mom and us on the other."

He sighed and it was my turn to squeeze his hands.

"Frankie, if we ever have kids—"

I opened my mouth to say woah, but he pressed a finger to my lips.

"Not right now, probably not even in the next few years," he told me sternly. "I'm not ready and no one is going to push you into anything you aren't ready for—but I want to talk about this because it's important, okay?"

Who was I to deny that? "Having kids scares the hell out of me," I admitted. It wasn't that I hadn't thought about it. I had—usually in conjunction with I wasn't going to do my kids what my mother did to me. Still…

"Okay, when or if we have kids, we're all a part of this family. It's not just me, it's Arch and Bubba and Coop and you. We're a unit, the five of us. I know we can't all knock you up at once—" His grin turned positively devilish as my eyes widened. "Sorry," he told me in a voice that wasn't remotely regretful. "I'm just trying to picture what that would be like."

"I'm good, move on." I swatted him and he laughed. The rich sound of masculine amusement pulled a laugh out of me and some of the weight smothering me.

His smile grew and his eyes brightened. He really was a beautiful guy. The beard he'd been keeping had really grown on me and the curve of one of the dragon's wings edged the collar of his shirt. He'd also been letting his hair grow out some, so he had this kind of rumpled academic look. My hot nerd.

"Frankie?"

"Hmm?"

"What are you thinking about?" The timbre of his voice dipped, and it was my turn to a grin. A smile I felt all the way down to my bones.

"You—and how beautiful you are and how much I love your beard and your hair and—" I didn't get to finish the sentiment as he swooped in to kiss me. The massage of his lips to mine had me sighing into his mouth. He tasted of chocolate, coffee, and Jake. It didn't get better than that. He fisted my hair and tilted my head so he could change the angle of the kiss and then his tongue swept in to dance with mine.

The kiss seemed to go on forever and the sizzle of it crackled along my nerves. When he finally lifted his head, the only thing I could see was him. "I really do love you," I promised him. "You know that, right?"

"'Hell yes. I know it, Baby Girl. I know you love me. I love you too. You get why we're worried? Why I want to make sure you know we're here? It's like you're floating away from us or drifting out to some island, and there's a lake around you. I'm not letting this gulf widen. We're right here—if you need time, you get it, but I also don't want you to think you have to hide this from us." He groaned and ran a hand over his face. "Fuck, I'm currently thinking about you naked and sprawled on a bed so I can devour you from head to toe, and that's not conducive to being the emotional shelter I'm trying to offer."

The giggle that escaped was genuine. "Who says? If I've learned anything over the last couple of years, sex and orgasms chase away the tension and batter down the walls, and what we are when we're spent and wrapped around each other?"

"That's a good image," he admitted and pressed his forehead to mine. He wasn't wrong, it was a great image. In fact… "But Baby Girl, it's not just the sex. I want to be there for you."

"You are." I gripped his forearms and locked my gaze on his. "You're real and you're right here and you called me on my crap…"

"It's not crap," he chastised, and I shrugged.

"My point is—you help me every single day because you love me and you're here. You even blew off classes to ambush me because you knew something was going on and well…busted."

He nodded. "I just want that smile back for you. I want those shadows gone. If I could do anything in the world, it would be to take away the darkness she left here."

"Thank you." I wanted that too. "You know what I want?"

"Anything," he said and I smiled.

"You haven't heard what I want."

"Whatever it is, we'll do it."

"Dress up like chickens and scandalize people in the park with random facts about poultry and history?" Don't ask me where that came from, it just popped out.

"Slap my ass and call me Big Bird, Baby Girl. Whatever you want."

I wrapped my arms around him and laughed. Really laughed. A laugh that shuddered through me and I held onto him tight. "I'll slap your ass," I managed to push out through the laughter. "If you can get me home and naked in the next fifteen minutes, I'll let you do anything you want to my ass."

"Oh, fuck me," Jake swore and he gripped me tight. "Challenge accepted."

Goddamn, Jake was good.

We made it with three minutes to spare.

Chapter Eight
A HANDFUL…

Frankie

When I said Jake had me home and naked with minutes to spare, I wasn't kidding. I swore the wind whiffed past as he raced me up the stairs—into his room though, not mine—where he locked the door. If I tried to wrench my clothes off with the same speed he had, I had a feeling I would have tripped over my shoes still on my feet.

As it was, I landed on the bed with a bounce and Jake stood over me with a triumphant grin on his face. Granted, I was naked and he wasn't, but the dare hadn't been about him getting naked. A laugh worked its way out of me as I pushed up onto my elbows and studied him. After he double-checked the locked door with a great show and fanfare, he pointed his phone at me. At my raised eyebrows, he grinned.

"Do you mind if I give the guys something to be jealous about?"

I glanced down at myself. My navel piercing gleamed with the light hitting it from the window and that my nipples went taut from the cooler air in the room even if my skin was already feverish. "You know they get to see me like this too?" I teased and Jake let out a low, half-growl and then walked forward, phone pointed at my painted toenails.

"Yes," Jake agreed. "They do get to see you like this—but they aren't getting to see you right now…just this lovely tease." He made a show of moving the phone up my leg to my knee then to my hip. He angled it away from any sensitive parts even as he ran his fingers up my flesh teasingly behind it. "Roll over for me, Baby Girl?"

The combination of his fingers stroking light circles around my clit and the promise of sex in his voice had me rolling over with far less grace than normal. As it was, I half-trapped his hand by locking my thighs closed, before turning onto my stomach.

His chuckle was positively devilish. "You guys are going to hate knowing how wet she is." And then Jake kissed my shoulder and the stroke of his hand told me where the phone was going and then it was in front of me on the pillow and reflecting my face back at me.

I could see Jake just above me and the heat in my belly began to unspool when he tugged his shirt off and gave me an eyeful of his tattoo. It had healed so beautifully, and the color took my breath away every time. He cupped his palm over my ass and began to massage my butt.

"So what was our deal?" He murmured as he teased along the crack, adding just a bare amount of pressure to my anus. I clenched my thighs, but he tickled my clit as he worked his other hand free. "Tell the boys, Baby Girl."

I groaned because he was giving me just enough to feel him and to enjoy the contact but moving away before I could achieve anything remotely resembling friction. The heat of his palm rubbing my ass didn't prepare me for the sudden sting as he delivered a firm slap or the gasp that exploded out of me as he massaged in the heat.

"Tell them," he ordered and then pressed the sweetest kiss to my shoulder and another behind my ear. Each kiss laid against a tattoo that he traced with his tongue. Aching spread through my whole system, along with a flush of heat.

"If you could get me home and naked within fifteen minutes, you can do whatever you want to my ass or with it." The words came out on an elongated groan as he pressed two fingers into my pussy and stretched them even as he echoed the action with my ass. I didn't know which fingers to chase or how he'd managed to lube up his fingers.

"Good girl," he murmured with another kiss that ended with a scrape of his teeth over the shell of my ear. "Oh, look—Archie is calling."

Oh fuck.

"Answer the phone for me, Baby Girl." I could no sooner disobey that soft command than I could have stopped trying to chase his fingers. Even the texture of the comforter against my nipples added to the rough sensations storming through me.

I wiggled my arms forward and clicked the green phone. It took a minute and then the camera kicked on and Archie's face was right there. His pupils flared huge and his expression was all kinds of tense.

"Hey, babe," he said in a thick voice and I opened my mouth to greet him when Jake moved his fingers and filled my ass with one slick push and my eyes went closed as my mouth formed a soundless scream. The burn and stretch were perfect and added to the pulse of my clit in time with Jake's fingers slipping free to circle it again.

Too much and not enough. The sound that came out of me wasn't human. "That's it, Baby Girl," Jake said in a silky voice as he rocked his hips. The push and pull were slow, agonizingly delicious, and threatened to tear me apart.

"You're such an asshole," Archie muttered in a hot voice, and I forced my eyes open to find him staring at me, his face flushed and tense.

"I could have just recorded and sent you the video later," Jake commented and I swore, everything inside of me went taut. He'd been streaming that live to them. Then Jake drove into me again and a cry tore from my throat. I dug my fingers into the covers as he quickened his pace. "She's so fucking tight, so beautiful spread out for me and she's soaking my bed with a wet spot that I can't wait to sample."

A shudder redoubled.

"The way her cunt tastes right after she's come," Archie said with a sigh. "I fucking hate you."

"He doesn't hate us does he, Baby Girl?" Jake slid a hand around my throat and cupped it. His fingers helped to brace my chin as he lifted my head. "Look at him, Frankie. Tell Archie how it feels with my dick stretching your ass wide…"

"It's awesome," I whispered. "I can't feel anything but Jake…I want…" Forming words was hard. I cried out as the increased tempo not only added to the friction of my nipples rubbing against the covers and heating them, but Jake had locked two fingers around my clit. The thudding pulse was driving me insane.

"Dude, tell me you still have the new toy in your room?" Was Archie begging? I couldn't focus on it but I could hear the slap and slide of skin, and not just where Jake filled me.

"Archie….are you…you jerking yourself off?" The words barely made it out before he laughed, low and dark.

"Yeah, babe. I'd rather be there pumping into you, but you're so fucking beautiful right now and my dick is aching for you."

I licked my lips. "Let me see?"

He didn't need the question asked twice before the camera angle changed and I could see his dick in his palm, the tip red and angry with a drop of pre-cum already slicking it. When Jake switched his grip from my throat to my hair, I trusted him to keep my head up as I watched the screen. For a brief moment, Jake's thrusts eased off and I took advantage of the brief respite to whisper Archie's name like an oath. He was so close, I could tell from the jerking motions.

"Let me see you," I begged and he angled the camera up and I opened my mouth to encourage him when Jake shifted us upward and I forgot how to breathe. He filled me so full, the stretch had me gasping for air.

"Watch him," Jake ordered and then there was a bit of vibration right at my clit that began as a tickle then suddenly throttled upward. The fierce suction matched Jake's thrusts for intensity. I screamed. The pleasure was too much, far too much. Jake's laughter was wild as was Archie's swearing, and then I swore I split right down the middle.

The heat of Jake coming filled my ass but the pleasure exploding from my pussy and radiating outward made it impossible to just hang on. I sank into a blissful haze populated by twitching muscles and the heavy, thick heartbeat of Jake's pulse in my ear. At some point, he'd eased out of me and I was wrapped around him.

"I didn't imagine Archie was on the phone, did I?"

Jake chuckled and then his mouth was on mine. The kiss held so much pent-up emotion, I swore I wanted to sob under the caress of it. As it was, I dug my fingers into his shoulders and then sighed as he kissed away from my mouth to my jaw.

"Nope," he said, a pleased note in his voice. "I figure we'll be hearing from—"

The knock hit the door before he could even finish the sentence and Jake's deep chuckle delighted me on a primitive level.

"Right on time," he said, shifting me on the bed before rolling out of it. At the door, he didn't bother to pull on shorts or a towel as he opened the door wide.

Coop stared at Jake with a droll look, then past him to me. His smile was so big and wide, the room warmed under his attention. He didn't make a single step inside before Jake stopped him with a hand to his chest.

"You gotta pay the toll."

"The toll?" Coop demanded and I didn't mean to, but I burst out laughing. He sounded so offended and so put out. "C'mon, Frankie. I don't need to pay a toll. Player three can just jump in the game, right?"

"Wrong," Jake answered before I could. "First, the door was locked. Secondly, she gave me that ass to do with what I wanted and I'm not sure I want to share yet."

Rolling over on the bed, I kicked one leg up toward the ceiling as I watched them. I didn't think I could adore them more, but the haggling over getting Coop in the door was priceless. Jake flexed his ass cheeks. There was no way Coop could see it, but Jake was definitely flexing them. Biting down on my hand, I tried to smother my laughter, but it was like now that the giggles were getting out, they refused to be contained.

"Fine," Coop dragged out the word to make it clear it was not "fine" but he would definitely play. "What's the toll?"

"Oh, good question." He gave Coop a gentle shove and then closed the door and locked it before he could respond. Leaning back against it, he gave me a shit eating grin. "What's the toll, Baby Girl?"

I grinned. Playful, charming Jake was absolutely incorrigible. "Hmm…does he have to pay you or me?"

"Fair question." He tapped a finger against his lower lip and his quads flexed. The ripple of muscle over his arms and chest got my attention to his abdomen, but the flexing muscles pulled my gaze all the way down to his dick. It was already thickening up with interest and he'd cleaned up at some point.

Since my ass still felt stretched and my pulse beat a steady cadence in my pussy, I was more than ready for round two or three. Whatever Jake had in mind, I was down for. "He definitely needs to pay you, but I want to enjoy the benefits. How is your ass, Baby Girl?"

"Ready for anything you want to dish out."

His dick thickened and stretched. I licked my lips and made no pretense of checking him out. Opening the door again, Jake said, "C'mon in."

Snorting, Coop drifted inside and his hungry gaze pinned mine. Jake circled Coop and walked back to the bed, but Coop didn't take his gaze off me and I swore I soaked more of the sheets just thinking about what Coop wanted to do.

"Toll?" The thickness in his voice echoed the bulge developing rapidly in his shorts. The basketball shorts he'd been out in did *nothing* to hide that monster cock he kept tucked away for me. Sliding in behind me, Jake caught my chin and turned my head. I met his kiss tongue for tongue. He cupped my breasts and massaged them as he moved to line himself up his chest to my back.

"The toll," Jake said as he nudged he slicked his dick up with some lube before easing two fingers into me, "is to make Frankie come as many times as you can until I do."

Coop's brows shot skyward and I had to be honest, so did mine. Before I could ask though, Jake was pushing into me and I was stretching around his dick. The burn was over faster than before and I was so full.

But I could be fuller.

"Yes, you could," Coop agreed in a heavy voice as his eyelids dropped. Jake propped himself up against the bed, with my legs spread out braced open by his. I was pinned to him, impaled on his dick with my pussy, soaking wet and drenched with need, spread wide for Coop.

"But first the toll…then you can have her pussy for the rest of the day while I have her ass." I wanted to come and my hips arched, but I couldn't escape or move as Jake held me still. "You can handle it, can't you Baby Girl?"

Fuck.

Me.

"Oh," Coop said as he licked his lips. "We intend to."

There was no more room for thought or breath as he buried his face against my pussy. The pressure of his teeth and tongue delving in to devour me in the most sinfully carnal kiss shattered me. I was screaming in minutes. The first orgasm took me by surprise, and it took both of them to pin me still. Coop kept his shoulders braced against my thighs and Jake kept cupping and tweaking my nipples as Coop lapped up every drop of my desire.

Then they started over again.

And over.

The first tears I'd shed in weeks slid down my cheeks by the time I'd come for the fourth or fifth time. I'd lost count. The sensations were too much, and Jake exploded beneath me, his ragged breathing an echo of mine.

"Thank fuck," Coop swore as he lunged upward and then he was kissing me before he flattened me into Jake and filled me with a relentless thrust. The pressure went from mind boggling to mind blowing and I was spasming around Coop as he chased his own release, and the only time he let go of my lips was for Jake to kiss me.

When I surfaced again, I was sandwiched between them, all of us sweating and sticky. If it was possible to want more, I did. I barely took two swallows of the water Jake pressed against my lips before I crawled down to pull Coop's cock into my mouth.

We didn't leave the room for the rest of the day, but Jake made good use of my ass. I could barely walk the next day, but it was worth it. He and Coop camped out with me while I took care of closing out my classes.

One less thing to worry about.

At least until Archie and Ian made good on their promise to get Jake back for that video.

I couldn't wait.

No really, I couldn't wait. It made me ache just thinking about it.

Chapter Nine

NO FIRES HERE

Archie

"What about the island?" Bubba asked from the kitchen sink, where he was currently peeling and eating an orange. He'd already eaten one and was working on a second. We had roughly fifteen minutes, if we were lucky, before Jeremy returned from his morning walk to one of the corner stores to pick up something for dinner. I reminded him that we had to wipe up any evidence of us in the kitchen.

Since Frankie's birthday, Jeremy had been going out of his way to make sure her favorites were always on hand. Fortunately, Frankie loved food, so it wasn't hard to find things to make for her. *Unfortunately*, she hadn't been eating. If anything, her *lack* of appetite worried me more than anything else. I wasn't alone with that concern. Even her father called the night before and Bubba's mom had checked in an hour earlier while we'd been on campus.

"You ever think you'd be asking me about a private island for our summer getaway?" I couldn't resist tweaking him a little. In the past, we never talked about money. Some of that had been resentment and some of it had just been he didn't care. I could respect that. We talked more about money now, but it was more about logistics than anything else.

"No," Bubba assured me as he sectioned off a bit of orange and ate it. The quick suck of the juice off his fingers reminded me that I was hungry, but I wanted to wait for Frankie. Maybe I could talk her into going out tonight. I had "tickets" to surprise her with, but a lot depended on her mood. She'd been—distant wasn't the right word. "But then, I'd never stayed on a private island before last summer and that shit was excellent for her. For all of us."

"Agreed. That said, I put in a call, but the family might be using it, so I haven't heard anything yet. Which means, we may not find out until the last minute. Which—I mean we can plan by last minute." It wasn't ideal but we'd done it before.

I cut across the kitchen to the espresso machine and got it going, when an alarm went off on my phone that buzzed my watch. Jake and I had finished up the engine we'd been building for our spring project, and other than writing up the white paper on it, I was pretty much done with classes. Bubba had a couple of classes he was finishing up, but neither of us had actual tests. Coop was the only one with a heavy testing schedule, so we were all adapting the last couple of weeks to him.

I pulled the first two shots and added them to the cup as the sound of feet hit the stairs. "But if that's not doable, then we can spend the summer doing something else. We can stay up here or we can hit the road…"

Bubba glanced at the door as Coop appeared in it, hair askew and a wrinkle from a pillowcase on his cheek. "Dude, you can take a shower."

"Frankie's asleep. I didn't want to wake her up." He scrubbed a hand against his face. I added the steamed milk to the cup, along with another couple of shots and then the foam. When I handed him the cup, he stared at it with bloodshot eyes. "The next time I decide that I want to do eighteen credit hours and six of them include lab hours, hit me in the back of the head."

"Noted," Bubba said. "You have to be back on campus in an hour, right?"

"Yep." He yawned, then shotgunned the coffee. I was already making him another for the road.

"What time is the exam scheduled to get out?"

"It's two hours." It was barely four which meant the testing opened at five. I nodded and put the second cup into a disposable travel mug. The paper cups weren't ideal, but on the run they worked.

"Take a car home," I told him. "I can arrange for one to pick you up so it's there."

Coop stared at me for a moment, smothering another yawn before he took the disposable cup from me. "You know, normally I'd skip that but this time, it sounds like a plan."

"Good," Frankie's sleepy voice wrapped around all of us, even Bubba straightened from where he'd been cleaning up the orange scraps. "Sorry, I missed the alarm." She hugged Coop from behind and then glanced around him to me and Bubba. Her hair was a mess, tousled from sleep and she looked deliciously rumpled.

The idea of being the one who rumpled her even more sent a pulse straight to my cock, and the last thing I needed to be planning with right this second was my dick.

"Go back to bed," Coop told her and dropped a kiss on her head as he gave her a sideways hug. "Let me enjoy sleeping with you vicariously."

She pushed up on her tiptoes and gave him a kiss before squeezing past him to make a beeline to me and the coffee. That was my girl. She curled right up under my arm as I lifted it and leaned into me. Like Coop, I kissed her head but she was in full on adorable mode. She probably should be sleeping—if she was really sleeping.

There'd been a few nights I'd woken up to her not being in bed, or if she was, she was curled onto her side reading or playing on her phone. Her schedule was a little all over the place. "Where's Jeremy?"

"Out getting dinner," Bubba answered for me and when he held out a hand to her, she kissed my jaw and then let me get a real kiss before she went to Bubba. Making her coffee would go faster with two hands, but I'd rather have an arm around her.

"I'll be back," Coop called as he headed for the front door.

"Good luck," Frankie answered.

"I'll be back for you to kiss my wounded pride later." Coop responded and she snorted.

"His pride," she muttered. "He's gonna ace that test."

"Then you can help me celebrate." If I hadn't half-expected him to pop up around the corner like that, I might have jumped just like Frankie. As it was, she screamed, I laughed and Bubba chuckled even as he flicked a towel at Coop. Which probably saved his life, cause it got him moving before she could smack him.

"The man does like to live dangerously." I could admire that. "Your coffee, my beautiful lady." Don't ask me where the flowery bullshit came from, it just suited her right now and when she wrapped her hands around the cup, she trapped my hands there until I brushed a kiss to her lips. She settled back against Bubba.

"That's why we love him," Frankie said with a wink.

"That's why you love him," Bubba corrected.

Tipping her head back, she grinned up at Bubba. The smiles were coming back, slowly but surely, but they weren't quite touching her eyes yet. That, of everything, worried me most of all. "Why do you love him?"

"We're still trying to work that out," I answered, dry as a bone and she flashed that grin at me. Sure enough, the light in her green eyes was present but it was nowhere near the sparkle it should be. All at once, we were standing in that hallway and I found her mother pointing a gun at her. A gun she swung on me, and Frankie wouldn't move. She'd become a wall in front of me.

Bile burned the back of my throat and I turned away from them to clean up around the espresso maker. Bubba didn't usually want coffee this late and I could use a real drink. I also had no classes first thing in the morning, so I planned to indulge.

"When is Jake due back?"

"Later," Bubba said. "Let's take the coffee upstairs." Right, 'cause Jeremy was due back. I finished the clean-up and followed, but only after I got the whisky out of the cabinet. We didn't need a full wet bar here, though Jeremy could probably set one up. Beer and wine, we always kept in stock. The whisky? That had shown back up after Frankie's birthday.

A damn good reason to be there if there ever was one. Upstairs, Bubba and I settled Frankie on the sofa and she glanced between us. "What's up?"

"That transparent, are we?" Bubba teased her, but since I'd brought the bottle of whisky up with me, I figured that ship had already sailed.

"No," Frankie said. "But you both have been giving me a lot of space and then I find you in the kitchen planning…and you two don't hang out in the kitchen if you can help it." She pointed at me. "Especially since Jeremy forbade you from touching the stove."

"It was one adjustment," I muttered. "And I paid for the new stove, so I think I covered the oops."

Bubba laughed. Ass. But I lifted my glass to salute them and then took a drink.

"We were talking about summer," Bubba said. "June's gonna be here before we know it…"

"And June is for us." Don't ask me why the fact she said that last part like it was the automatic response, and a promise all rolled into one, eased some of the tension in my soul. I moved to sit on the coffee table, right in front of them both.

"It is," I said, agreeing. "But we have some flexibility."

Though she was tucked against Bubba, she shifted to rest her bare feet on the table between my legs. I curled an arm under them and lifted them to rest in my lap.

"What do we want to do?" The question was one we'd all been asking. None of us wanted her to worry, but we also didn't think we could take her wanting to get away for granted.

"That's kind of what we wanted to ask you, Angel," Bubba said and I nodded. "We've been debating where to go and whether to surprise you or…"

"…or find out if you had ideas. I mean you could want to go up to Boston for the summer." Personally, I was hoping not. I liked Hank. A lot. I was fucking grateful to the man for being a steady rock for her, but Hank, Kelly, and their kids demanded a lot of attention from Frankie and I wanted to be a little selfish.

Especially after… the image of her mother pointing that gun at her and me digging my fingers into her hips, but she was locked in place.

I tossed back the whisky and let it burn all the way down. She frowned at me and I found a smile as I rubbed her ankles. "So what do you say, Babe? Any ideas of how you want to spend the summer? Besides being debauched in every way we can figure out how to do it?"

Frankie's eyes widened and Jeremy cleared his throat in the same moment. The man needed a damn bell. And somehow, we needed to adjust that uncanny timing of his so it was someone else's cock he blocked.

"Nope," I said firmly. "Not apologizing for that one. We're all dressed and we're sitting in the living room. If I want to talk about debauching you, I'm gonna."

Bubba's lips twitched, but he glanced past me to where Jeremy had to be standing at the entryway to the room. "Good evening, Jeremy."

"Mr. Bubba. Miss Frankie. Mr. Archie."

Oh yeah, I was gonna get it. Oh well… "Good evening, Jere. Welcome back, and what delicious meal have you decided to prepare for Frankie tonight?"

"Actually," he began and I twisted to glance at him. The man wore a smug smile. "I was going to invite Miss Frankie downstairs to join me with tonight's meal preparation."

"Oh?" Frankie sat forward and tugged her feet out of my lap.

Oh, man, Jere, do we have to work on your timing.

"You mentioned wanting to learn how to make the Beef Wellington and that is Mr. Cooper's favorite."

Fuck. I saved my glare for him and smoothed it away when I glanced at Frankie. Her eyes had brightened, her whole expression had, and every objection I had vanished. "Why don't we all go down to help?"

"Cause we want to be able to eat the food," Bubba told me and Frankie cast me an apologetic smile.

I scowled, but Frankie cupped my cheek with a soft hand and kissed me. It was really hard to keep scowling when her soft lips brushed mine. "We can try another round of gourmet classes if you want…"

"Anywhere that isn't here," Jeremy said, and I had to laugh at that droll observation. Yes, I was forbidden from preparing anything *not coffee* in his kitchen.

"But I do want to make that for Coop and he's been so tired."

"No worries, Babe," I told her and tangled my fingers in her hair after I gave her another kiss. "Go ahead. I'll make Bubba play video games with me while we plot all the ways we can seduce you." Pressing my lips to her ear, I murmured, "Try not to think about how talented I am with my fingers when it's your sweet pussy I'm playing with."

A shiver raced over her and her face flushed. It was kind of nice that we could still do that to her.

"Promise?" She dared me and I grinned.

"Done."

Another kiss and then she was gone, chatting to Jeremy all the way down the stairs. Rising, I retrieved the bottle of whisky and poured myself another glass.

"You want to talk about it?" Bubba offered.

"Not really," I said and turned to face him. "I do want to figure out this summer though. With her. Or come up with ideas for her. But I need…"

"You need to help her." Like the sun needed to shine, yes I did. "We all do," Bubba agreed. "So we'll rope the guys into this weekend, all of us sit down and talk."

"Sounds good." I tossed the drink back, savoring the burn that steadied my nerves and made that image in my head waver. "If I could just turn back the clock a few minutes…"

"Same way we felt about Mitch," Bubba reminded me, and he wasn't wrong. "The difference is we're here. They're not. They're a blip on the road, we've got the long haul."

"Poetic," I said but he wasn't wrong.

"Maybe. But while we have a few minutes…" That got my attention. "The producers have been calling. I've put them off for the last few weeks…"

But it was a business and businesses needed answers.

Fuck.

"Want to tell me about the deal? Talk it through with me before you do with her?"

"Yeah," Bubba said slowly, "I would, because right now I just want to turn it all down."

"And what do you want me to do? Talk you into it or out of it?" Because it was always good to know what the end goal was.

"That's the million dollar question."

Chapter Ten

MOTHER'S DAY

Frankie

The day didn't register. Not really, until I heard Jake on the phone. He'd crawled out of bed when it rang and just before the door closed behind him, he murmured, "Happy Mother's Day—why are you up so early?" His soft laughter drifted back as he descended the stairs. I rolled over onto my stomach and stared across the empty room. Coop wasn't here, he had *one* more test and he'd had a study group that met at the library at the crack of ass.

I almost wished I'd gone with him. I'd volunteered. Just because I couldn't focus on my classes didn't mean I couldn't help him with his. I almost wished he'd taken me up on it, but he insisted I stay in bed and he'd kissed me before he'd left. Jake was there and he'd wrapped me right up in his sleep and it hadn't been hard to go back to sleep.

Wasn't sure what Archie and Ian were doing, but I wouldn't be surprised if they'd already gone out for a run. They tended to go a little later on Sunday mornings. Or maybe they were waiting on Jake. Sitting up, I ran my fingers through my hair and then reached for my phone where it sat plugged into a charger next to the bed.

A couple of messages from Rachel. One was a book recommendation that I just saved for later and the other was her move out date from the dorm was rapidly approaching. Since she wasn't taking summer classes, she was probably going to head home.

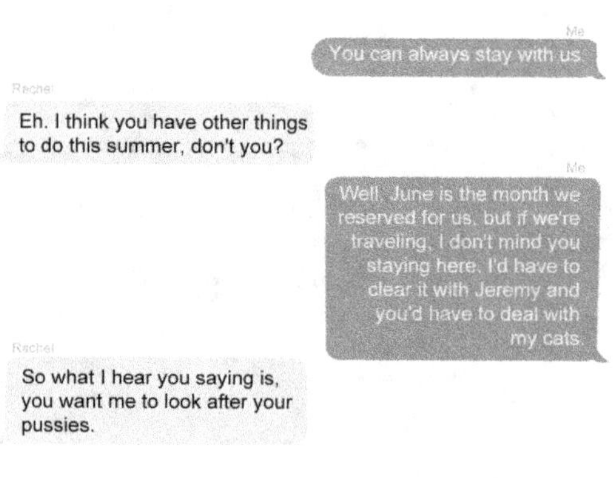

I rolled my eyes.

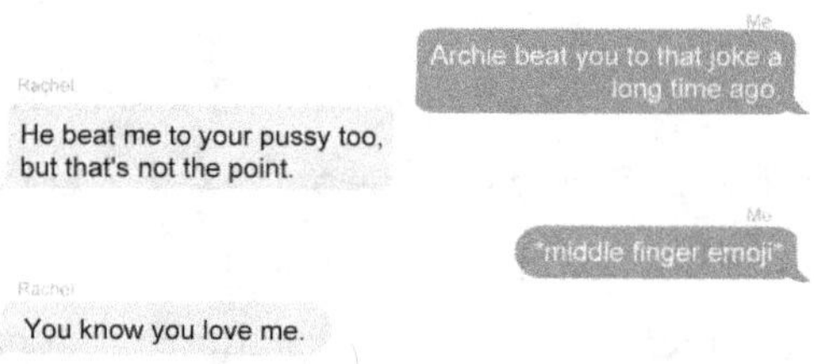

The guys wouldn't even blink. Granted, we hadn't actually nailed down our plans for the summer yet but then… the last five weeks had pretty much been one long train of suckage and they were trying to make it easier for me.

Maybe we needed to stop making it easier.

That was the most I was gonna get out of her and I could accept that. As it was, I hadn't actually meant to text her, instead I flipped to my other messages. They were all quiet. Well, not the one from Alec, but he was testing out dad jokes because he was determined to stump Hank.

To stump Dad.

I'd said it aloud a couple of times now, but I still wasn't all the way there in my head. Hank. Dad. I adored him regardless of his name, then again… he was amazing. How different my life would have been if Maddy had just made a different choice.

So. Many. Choices.

I switched from the messages over to the photo file and scrolled through it. It took a while, but I found her. The picture had to be from when I was fourteen? Maybe the first day of high school. She didn't like having her picture snapped if she wasn't ready for it. But I'd taken a picture of her while she stood in the middle of the kitchen, a mug of coffee in hand and a damn near blissful smile on her face.

It was a rare, rare moment of happiness and I'd just taken the picture. I'd also never told her I'd taken it because she probably would have made me delete it. Her hair wasn't perfect, she had zero cosmetics on, and she even had a bit of a wrinkle on her cheek from her pillow.

But the smile? It was not one I got to see often. I had no idea what we even said that morning, just that it had entertained her. I'd probably left right after, because Coop and I had to catch the bus. I stared at the picture for a long time, then closed out of my photos and dragged myself out of bed.

After a shower that lasted way too long, but I was kind of enjoying being under the spray, and getting dressed, I found Jeremy downstairs. He had the newspaper open and the television in the corner of the kitchen focused on one of the news channels.

"Good morning, Miss Frankie."

"Good morning, Jeremy." I waved him back to his seat. "You're already taking a break and I just want coffee."

Disapproval flashed across his expression, but he didn't voice it. "Mr. Ian and Mr. Archie had an early appointment today, so they've already left. Mr. Jake is on his way to the gym, said to let you know you should join him when you woke up if you wanted. And you know Mr. Coop…"

"He's at school. It's good. He's got studying going on, so that's cool. As for the gym?" I made a face as I filled a huge cup with coffee. It was just the straight, fresh-brewed stuff and it was very fresh if the scent was anything to go on. "I'll pass. I'm not sure what I want to do today yet…do you want me to start another pot of coffee?"

"Not yet," Jeremy said. "Unless you plan to give yourself a bad case of the jitters, which I do not recommend." The last he said over the top of his newspaper and I had to bite back a smile. The doorbell rang and he lowered the paper, but I waved him back into his chair.

"Stay there. Tiddles will be cross if you move—" I hadn't missed the fact that my boy was seated in Jeremy's lap, purring away. "And I'm already up."

I cut through the house, coffee in hand to the front door. We had a security panel now that included a screen to show us who was on the porch. Little changes like this had cropped up everywhere. Like, we'd *had* a security system before. What we had now was more in line with a fortress.

Then again, after Maddy? I couldn't really blame anyone.

The fact Dominic Walsh stood on my porch at—barely nine in the morning on a Sunday—already dressed in a suit and sporting a pair of sunglasses like he'd just stepped off the cover to GQ? *That* was weird. I hadn't spoken to him since the funeral, outside of a couple of contracts he'd sent over related to my trust fund. I'd read them, signed them, and messengered them back.

I pressed in the secure code, then unlocked the door before I opened it. He had turned away and seemed to be scanning the street, but faced me as the door swung inward. It was a beautiful day out there. The sun warmed my bare toes the moment it struck. "Good morning, Frankie."

"Good morning, Dominic. To what do I owe the honor this early?" I didn't ask, why didn't you call, because that seemed a tad rude, then again, you'd think he'd have wanted to call.

"If you're worried I thought I'd catch Rachel here, I promise you, that's not it."

I just raised my eyebrows and pushed the door wider. "Good. Cause she isn't here. Would you like to come in?"

"Thank you," he agreed, straightening his tie before he stepped inside. I waited until he was clear before I closed the door. "I have some files to go over with you, I've been holding off for the last few weeks, but some of them need answers and I thought it might be easier for you if I just briefed you on each offer—hit all the high points as it were—then I can leave the finals with you to read at your leisure."

That sounded about as much fun as a stick in the eye.

"Good morning, Mr. Walsh," Jeremy said as he joined us. "I was unaware you had an appointment today." The chastisement in Jeremy's voice spoke volumes.

"That's because I played it fast and loose to drop by." He flashed Jeremy a grin. "I promise to not take more than an hour of the lady's time."

"Hmm." Jeremy glanced at me and the question there was plain as day. Did I want him to get rid of Dominic? I had zero doubt that he could accomplish it.

"That's fine, we'll go up and sit out on the patio. It's a nice enough day." And it would be outside, so even the guys wouldn't be too ticked about having Dominic in their space. Particularly Jake. Oh—I should probably send Jake a warning, or not. If I did tell him *right* now, he'd be just as likely to show up and bodily toss Dominic out.

"Very good, Miss Frankie. Would you like me to bring your guest some coffee? Or breakfast?"

"Dominic?" I asked. "Coffee?"

"That would be great, but don't put yourself out for breakfast unless you're going to eat too."

"I'm fine right now, but maybe after we're done I'll eat." Honestly, hunger and I seemed to have parted ways. "Thank you, Jeremy."

"Absolutely, Miss Frankie. I'll let Mr. Jake know you won't be joining him."

Yeah. "Thank you." But I cut a quick look to Dominic then back and shook my head slightly. Jeremy nodded once. Hopefully that meant message received. I wasn't going to start keeping secrets, but if we could keep the blood spillage down, that would be great.

I took the lead and ascended the stairs with Dominic behind me. Thankfully, I had the big cup of coffee so I took a couple of healthy swallows on my way over to the deck doors. We had the garden downstairs, a semi-garden up here as well, but more an open deck with tables and chairs and then the roof. The house, for all that we were in the middle of a huge, bustling city, offered a number of quiet retreats.

"Shall I open the umbrella?" Dominic offered after I held the door open for him.

"Probably," I said. Then glanced down at my arms and legs. I was in cargo shorts and a tank top. The lack of tan was noticeable. But I didn't need to burn and I wasn't gonna go put on sunscreen right now.

He set his bag down on one of the chairs, then got the umbrella open. I should probably have grabbed my sunglasses but if it got too bright, I'd go back in.

When he held out a chair for me, I shook my head. "Don't suck up to me."

"Wouldn't dream of it," he promised and nudged my chair in as I sat down. "When it comes to ranking us in Rachel's estimation, I know where I land."

"And if we were ranking *you* two in my estimation?" I studied him as he pulled his sunglasses off and flipped them closed. He really did seem all put together, overdressed for a Sunday morning.

"I don't even appear on the scale with which you rate Rachel," he answered smoothly and the corners of his lips tipped upward. "That's as it should be." He opened his bag and pulled out three folders and his digital tablet, before he pulled out a chair and took a seat to the right of me but not across. "In the interests of not wearing out my welcome..." He motioned to the papers. "Shall we get started?"

Jeremy chose that moment to carry out a tray with a fresh pot of coffee and two mugs on it, even if I had my own and I hadn't even reached the halfway mark. There were some cinnamon toast sticks also on the platter and I quirked a brow at the man who made the best french toast on the planet.

"I know you said you might eat later, but I also know legal matters can be tedious and this will keep you fueled." Man didn't even miss a beat. Dominic waited for Jeremy to finish and go back inside before he began.

"First and foremost, your stocks in Standish..."

"I want those signed back over to Archie and his father," I said.

"I know," he commented, raising a hand in a gesture of asking for patience. "I attempted to make that happen and they both shot the idea down. I believe Archie's exact words were he'd give them right the hell back and Mr. Standish was a little more eloquent, but he insisted it was a family business and you're family."

The dry remark held a lot of judgment and I leaned back in the chair. Archie and I hadn't talked about this. I'd half-forgotten I'd even asked Dominic to do this in the days immediately following Maddy's death. I guess he'd been busy. "So if they don't take them, what do I have to do with them?"

They needed someone with more than a passing interest in what was going on to take over the stocks. Then again, what did I have to do? Read prospectus and vote periodically? I could do that. I just—I just wanted to undo some of the damage Maddy had done.

"Well, we have been diversifying your portfolio. I spoke to your attorney in Texas, he suggested we add it to the same management file we've been running for your stocks and bonds, see how it matures over the next couple of years and revisit when you're out of college. You may find that your position has changed or even the stock's interest has changed. We may also be able to persuade them to take the stocks back at that point. Though, I think you would be far better off keeping your assets separate in the event of any domestic changes."

Any domestic…

I shook my head. "Those stocks belong to Archie and his father. In the event of any domestic shifts, they will go back to Archie and his father. Am I clear?"

"Absolutely. Would you like me to draw up a power of attorney regarding that so that it's ironclad?" The very faintest of smirks touched his lips and I raised my brows.

"You might think being a smartass is funny, I don't." The flat tone in my voice erased his smile in an instant. "Death happens. Life happens. Domestic situations change. How I want to respect the people around me won't."

"You're right and I'm sorry." Dominic sighed and lowered his head. "I—I misspoke. I know things have been difficult since the incident with your mother and I wanted to try and make things a little lighter."

"Don't," I said. "I don't need to be handled." I had four wonderful men who did plenty of that, and Jeremy too. If Hank were closer, I had no doubt he'd be here handling me, or trying. I got it, I was a mess and they were all picking up the slack. "What I do need is for you to be straight with me. Don't waste my time. Don't joke and tease like we're friends."

"I'd like to be your friend," Dominic stated without an ounce of flirtation or even a hint of a smile. Then again, would I recognize flirtation if it bit me in the ass? Probably not. I reached for one of the cinnamon toast sticks so I could shut myself up. "As your attorney, I will always give you what I feel is the best advice and make you aware of all your options. While I was flippant about it, a power of attorney to be executed in the event that you can't do something? That will make sure your wishes are honored and it'll be far more difficult for them to say no."

I washed down the swallow of toast with coffee and sighed. "But not impossible?"

"Nothing is impossible. I mean that—the point is, if you want to make sure something happens, then we have to plan for all eventualities—short and long term."

"Like if we break up or if we get hurt or…" I didn't really want to travel down any of those roads. We hadn't talked about lifetimes or permanence, but we also hadn't ignored it either. We were building our lives *around each* other. Intertwined. Vital. Loved.

"Exactly. So, what I propose doing is we take Wittaker's advice, we add it to your portfolio and review it every quarter with your business manager." I had so many people working for me now it was kind of nauseating. "In the meanwhile, I'll draw up a few presumptive Powers of Attorney that allow you to dictate the disposition of your assets in a variety of events. You can review those and make any changes and we'll put it on file. They don't have to know. It's not a subject for debate. It's just making plans."

Making plans.

I kind of sucked at those of late.

Exhaling, I nodded. "That works for me and thank you. Also—Dominic, I can't really be your friend. Not until this thing with you and Rachel is resolved or solved." Or whatever. He studied me for a long moment, lips compressed. "She is my best friend. She will always come first. So you're my lawyer and I like you, but we can't be friends. Not yet."

"Fair." He closed that folder, then went to the next. "What I want to bring up now is the contracts from Roll City Records…"

Contracts?

I frowned.

"The negotiations have been pretty fierce, but we've gotten them down to pretty much everything your partner asked for and while I think the language could use some massaging, we conferenced this week and all of us feel this is probably the best case language to get you into a studio and recording this summer."

The offer.

The offer that had come when I'd gone to Hank's. I hadn't even thought about it in the last few weeks. Dominic pushed the file folder over to me, maybe taking my silence as thoughtfulness. "Now I want to give you the high level bullet points, make sure your concerns are all addressed and if you're comfortable with it, we'll conference with their attorneys and get this all executed."

"When this summer?" I asked, then cleared my throat when the words came out froggy. A swallow of coffee, followed by me draining the cup helped and I sat forward to scan the first page he'd opened the folder to.

"Mid-June, I think," Dominic said as he pulled out his phone. "They had a few dates. But I think they wanted you at their studios to do the first tracks, then maybe do a few appearances around the country to drum up interest. They have a whole formula they work to get this done. We'll still have the right of refusal on dates and locations, until we agree to them. At that point, they ask that we make every effort to meet those dates as they requested."

My head hurt. Mid-June? That was barely a month away. "When did the date negotiations begin?" The first couple of pages were standard stuff. The songs we would record, seventy-five percent had to be new material, we had leeway for covers. They would prefer we covered only songs from their label. There was information on photo shoots, album promotion, laying down the sounds and the tracks. We'd also need to work on finding a backup band or work out how we wanted to do live on stage performances.

Oh, I was gonna throw up.

"A little over six weeks ago, things stalled after the incident with your mother because your partner kept putting them off, but they've grown more insistent."

Ian was shielding me from this. Everything he could have wanted was right here and he was pushing it off to protect me.

No. Mid-June wasn't a great date, but Maddy wasn't going to cost anyone anything. Not me. And most certainly not Ian or anyone else.

"I understand that this may not be the ideal time."

"I don't think an ideal time exists, Dominic." I reached for the coffee pot and refilled my own cup. "Tell me about everything they want and what, if anything, we have room on."

Chapter Eleven

WITH A LITTLE HELP

Ian

Letting Archie talk me into a pickup game of basketball was probably one of the best and worst ideas we'd had in a while. Though, I had to respect burning off energy on the court as a far better choice than in the ring. If anything, after their previous disagreement, Jake and Archie were exhibiting a serious amount of caution in their interactions.

It was stressful at home. We were all worried about Frankie. Putting her first wasn't hard, but I was worried about Archie too. He'd been more guarded than usual and at the same time, there was a rawness to him when he was with her and an emotion I'd never seen in him before.

Fear.

We walked up the steps from the subway and he made a groaning sound that had me laughing. "Getting old there?"

He snorted. "You're up next—*old* man. You're about to turn the corner and no longer be a teenager."

I pulled the shirt away from my chest and flapped it a little to let the cooler air on the street help dry the sweat. I had no idea what it was with the subways, but they were not always cooler than the street. Since we were both hot and sweaty to begin with, it had just made me sweatier if possible. The sun was warm on my face, but the breeze helped as we headed home.

"Don't hate," I told Arch and gave him a gentle shove. "You can't help it if you're not the first in something."

He laughed, a real one this time and a genuine flash of a smile. "I'm technically third."

"Yep," I said and dug out the phone from my pocket. Frankie hadn't called us while we were playing, but I wanted to double check. Since Archie was doing the same damn thing, he just chuckled and shook his head again. "Besides, not too worried about birthdays this year. It just—doesn't seem as important. You know?"

"Yeah," he agreed with a slow nod. "Though don't tell her that. She loves birthdays for us."

I snorted. "She loves birthdays."

"True." Then his smile evaporated. "Because she likes to make other people feel special since she didn't get that at home."

"Not anymore," I reminded him and bumped his shoulder. "She has us now and we'll damn well spoil her every damn time and probably more."

He nodded, but his humor was gone before we even reached our street.

"Arch—"

"Don't say it," he told me with a shake of his head. "I know that I'm a fucking killjoy at the moment. But every single time I feel like I can take a breath—it's right there again and I keep thinking about how fucking close her deranged mother came to just…"

"But she didn't," I said firmly. "You have got to remember that no matter what *almost* happened, it *didn't* happen."

"Bubba, it's not that easy."

"Well, if it were easy, anyone would do it. We almost lost her because we were too damn blind to see what we were doing to her. Then I damn near lost her because I reacted too strongly in the other direction. We've had some near misses and the car accident—that was bad." Mitch bad. I could cave that son of a bitch's face in all over again. I'd at least had the pleasure of breaking his jaw and later his arm.

He'd gone to jail. And he'd died there, ironically enough. You'd think that would be the end of it, but I still had my moments. Moments where I'd snap awake after being "too late" to stop him. Walking in *after* he'd hurt her, to find him laughing about her and… I shook my head. Those were nightmares and I couldn't let them dictate our choices.

My choices.

"I know how it feels," I told him. "Maybe not exactly but I have ideas."

He stopped and looked at me. "Bubba…"

"I dream about what would have happened if I hadn't gotten to her with Mitch in time."

One sentence and Archie's whole expression transformed. "I wish that fucker wasn't dead."

I raised my brows. "Honestly, I'm glad he is. If it wouldn't have sent me to jail, I'd have happily killed him."

While I'd never imagined myself as someone capable of murder, I'd have made an exception for him. He was a special kind of asshole. The kind that should be fertilizer.

"Except I want him to suffer. The dead don't suffer." He pivoted on his heel and stalked off. Summing up his issue in a nutshell.

"Her still being alive wouldn't make Maddy suffer," I said, staring at his back as he stopped. "It would be Frankie suffering."

His shoulders slumped. "I hate that bitch."

"I feel you."

Sucking in a deep breath, Archie tipped his head back and stared at the sky. The sunglasses hid his eyes but I let him have the moment. "Are we doing the right things for her?”

“We can only do what she lets us do,” I reminded him. “Right now, she’s not ignoring her own needs. She pulled out of her classes—took the out the professors and her academic advisor offered her.”

He cut a look at me. “She *hated* that.”

“Yeah, she did, but she couldn’t focus. So, rather than forcing herself to do something she wasn’t ready to do, she took a step back. She’s letting us run interference and she is leaning on us. There’s not much more we can do.”

His face probably echoed mine. I wasn’t any happier with the idea. Fixing things was his kink. Not that he’d probably *ever* admit that out loud. Or maybe he would. Stranger things had happened. Just like I wanted to be her buffer, to keep her sheltered and safe, he wanted to erase all the bad and fix it so it never happened again.

“Fine, be the reasonable one.” He mock punched in my direction, the fist just barely glancing off my shoulder and then his reluctant smile turned up a notch. “Just—don’t tell her I’m freaking out about it? She doesn’t need to worry about me.”

“Maybe,” I said, then raised my hands when a glare replaced his smile. “I’m not going to go and tell her. Just like I’ve never told her about my nightmares. She knows I’ve had one or two, but she always just asks me if I *want* to talk about it.”

His frown deepened. “You lied to her?”

“Fuck no.” Probably came out sharper than intended but at least it relaxed his expression. “I don’t lie to her. But I don’t want to tell her either, so I tell her I don’t want to talk about it and when she asks if there’s anything she can do, I hug her and she hugs me back. Then I tell her that she’s doing it right then. None of that is a lie.”

“And if she asked you directly?”

“Then I’d tell her, but I still wouldn’t want to. I can’t ask her to trust me with her fears if I won’t give her mine.”

“Which is why you don’t push her to tell you.” He shoved his sunglasses up then ran a hand over his face. The longer we stood out here on the street, the more the sweat dried on me, but I didn't care.

"More or less, but I don't want her to ever feel like she *has* to tell me something she isn't ready to or isn't willing to talk about. All the same reasons we never ask her more than how it went with her therapist."

As much as I'd love to know all the details just so I could help, when she was ready, she would tell me or one of them.

"I kind of half thought she told you," Archie admitted. "Or Coop."

"Maybe," I said. "Maybe not."

"So don't hide it from her but I don't have to tell her."

"I didn't say that." I gripped his shoulder with a quick clap. "And I'll never tell you to keep something from her. She might be the right person to talk to, she might not be. The only person who can answer that is the two of you. The point is—don't lie. The minute we start lying, we start shutting her out and I can't do that again. I won't."

"You didn't lie to her before."

"No, but I wasn't honest then either. What I was worried about and what I was afraid of, I couldn't really voice to her, or to any of you. I was pissed at all of us and I was pissed at me. I took that out on her. So…for what it's worth, she would understand. Because I know she was afraid too."

"Yeah." He sighed. We stood there for a long moment. Finally, he tucked his sunglasses back down and gave me a nod. "Thanks."

"You're welcome."

"And for what it's worth—you don't have to keep that shit to yourself. If you need to talk, I may be an ass, but I know how to be a friend. You can talk to me too."

"I thought I was." I raised my brows and he smirked.

"You're an ass too."

"Sometimes." It was his answer and he gave me another mock punch but we were good and we finished the walk back to the brownstone without another word. We didn't need them.

"What. The. Fuck." Archie's sharp words fired out in a sharp whisper had me jerking my gaze up and down the street. "Why is that asshole here?"

The asshole in question, Dominic Walsh, descended the steps from the door with Frankie standing at the top of the steps watching him go. A car was pulling up to the front and he reached for the door of it and spotted us at the same time.

I doubted my expression was any friendlier than Archie's, but Walsh didn't wait for either of us. He just nodded and climbed into the car. It pulled away before we reached the steps.

"Hey," Frankie greeted us, and I tracked my gaze from the street to her. She looked particularly stunning with the sunlight gleaming off her golden hair. It was all pulled up into a messy bun, but there were tendrils escaping in haphazard curls. She wore a light, lace edged tank top and a pair of shorts. All gorgeous legs and slender arms, though her workouts with Jake had been putting some nice muscle on there.

"Hey Angel," I said as Archie still glared after Walsh.

"What the fuck did he want?" Yeah, the grouch routine was not going to go over well with her.

"To talk to me," she said, dropping one hand to her hip and her chin came up. Yep, she was not remotely interested in the caveman routine. "Don't even start with me, Archie." She didn't rush away as we climbed the stairs, in fact, she leaned up to brush a kiss to the corner of his downturned mouth before she pressed her lips to mine. "You two stink."

I grinned. "It's honest sweat."

"Well, that's something." But there was the barest hint of sparkle in her eyes. "Go shower and then come talk to me?"

"You could come shower with us," Archie said and then paused. I snorted as Frankie raised her brows. "Nope," he told her with a wave of his finger. "Don't. That came out wrong."

Her laughter was a miracle. Fuck, if it made her laugh like that, we could go take a shower in the big bathroom upstairs, it wasn't like there wasn't room in that shower for all fucking five of us. Archie stared at her a beat before he ducked down and scooped up a white cat who was trying to dart out the door.

"Saved by the pussy," he said with a wink and then kissed her before he carried Tory inside and left us on the steps. Frankie was still grinning when she glanced at me, and I held up my hands again.

"You want us to shower together, you have to come and watch."

"Tempting," she admitted, then backed up into the house. "But I really do want to talk."

Oh, that sounded bad.

I studied her as I followed her inside. She waited while I closed and locked the door and made sure the security system engaged before she walked up the stairs with me. Well, maybe she was gonna shower with me after all.

No complaints here.

Archie's door was closed, so I glanced at her and said, "Want me to grab clothes and use your bathroom?"

She grinned. "As long as you don't mind me being a voyeur. I have a feeling sex would derail our conversation and this is important."

"Okay, rules. I like rules." I hooked an arm around her waist and pulled her with me into my room where I closed the door and backed her right up to it.

"Ian," she warned.

"Shh, Angel, not sex, I promise." Then I dipped my head and kissed her. Not just a quick peck or a brush of lips, but a real kiss. One where her mouth opened, and a soft breath escaped. With an almost exasperated sigh, she opened her mouth to me fully and I swept my tongue in. She tasted like cinnamon, honey, sugar, and coffee.

A part of my brain registered that she'd eaten. That was good. Her lack of appetite worried me. Then she sucked on my tongue as she fisted my shirt and I braced my hands on the door on either side of her. All I did was kiss her. A slow, thorough plundering, until her breath came in sharper pants and she arched her whole body into mine.

It was with some regret that I finally broke the kiss and lifted my lashes so I could study her swollen lips and half-lidded eyes. The flash of her pink tongue as she licked her lips went straight to my cock, but I savored both her actions and my response.

"What was that for?" she finally managed to ask, and I brushed my knuckles down her cheek. It was the only touch I allowed myself because right now, Frankie was pure temptation. But she'd said no sex.

"That was to remind you that whatever we're in trouble for, you love us and I love you." Leaning in, I pressed my lips to her forehead and held there for a long moment. Her fingers loosened against my shirt.

"You don't fight fair."

"I'm not fighting," I promised as I straightened. "I just want you to know how I feel."

Her eyes brightened as she leaned back against the door, even as I backed off. I stripped off my shirt and took my time peeling out of my shorts, shoes, and socks. Not once did she look away and the flush to her cheeks had me puffing my chest out a little.

"I love you too," she whispered and I grinned for real.

"I will never get tired of hearing that."

With a groan, she banged her head against the door lightly. "Go take a shower."

"Yes…ma'am," I said, and I swore her eyes dilated when she opened them to stare at me. "Come and watch? I might need a little help when I deal with my dick."

Because right now, it was pulsing and hot. There was no way I wasn't jerking off in the shower if she wanted me to keep my hands to myself.

"Who are we torturing?" she asked as she pushed away from the door and followed. "You or me?"

"Both," I said. "Definitely both."

Chapter Twelve

FIGHTING OUR DREAMS

Frankie

Sitting on the bathroom counter while Ian showered proved impossible. He didn't say a word when I slid in behind him and wrapped my arms around his middle. Pressing my lips against his back between his shoulder blades, I closed my eyes as he stepped a little further under the water and it soaked over us both. The hot water couldn't quite compete with his hot skin.

Rubbing my cheek against his back, I grinned when he eased around and loosened my arms so I could lift them to wrap around his neck. His smile made my heart flutter as he ran soapy hands down my back to my ass and when he dipped his head, I rose up on my toes to meet his kiss.

The thick erection pressing against my stomach seemed even hotter than the rest of him. I swore he devoured me with the way his lips fused to mine, and then he picked me up, and I wrapped my legs around his hips even as he turned me under the spray fully. My hair flattened to my head, but I didn't care. The beat of the water just added to the sensations as he pressed me against the wall.

Sucking on his lower lip, I fisted his hair with one hand and slid another between us to wrap around his cock. The delicious groan he released as I began to stroke him sent another thrill through me. Need for them—all of them—burned so fiercely it threatened to consume me. Times like now, I just gave into the desire. I wanted him and he wanted me. That was all we really needed to know.

When he wrapped one damp hand around my throat, it was my turn to groan. The grip was light, but present. The caress of his thumb over my pulse point sent it racing.

"Let me see you," Ian ordered and I opened my eyes to meet his gaze. He pinned me there against the wall more fiercely with his eyes than he did any other part of his body. "Now let me have you."

I grinned slowly, as I arched my hips and he lifted to help me line him up. I teased his head along my slit, pulling a groan from myself at the ache unfolding within me. He tightened his hand a fraction.

"Now."

I swore I melted at that singular command, and then I was sliding down on him as he thrust into me. Head back against the tile, I panted as he seated his cock deeply and his own grunting groan tickled me. The gasping laugh I released smothered against his lips as he captured mine for another burning kiss.

Ferociousness marked his movements as he eased back and then drove into me again. The tempo went from slow to fevered on his first stroke. "Eyes on me," he said, and I laughed and groaned at the same time. It was damn hard to focus when all I wanted to do was feel. I stroked my nails over his scalp as he began to rock in swift, hard thrusts that sent pleasure spiraling through my system.

Every push bumped his pelvis against me. His breath came in hot little pants as we stared at each other. He squeezed my ass as he increased our rhythm and I squeezed my thighs against his hips, fighting against the slippery skin for purchase. The rub of his chest to my nipples just sent another pulse of excitement through me.

"You are so fucking beautiful," he whispered before he locked his mouth over mine. I swore my thoughts exploded like little fireworks when he worked a hand between us. I was already on the edge when he stroked my clit, and the world just cascaded into sensation. The first spasms of my orgasm earned a curse. "Fuck." The fight to clamp down on him as he kept retreating and pushing in again just heightened every single sensation.

It took serious effort to keep my eyes open, even if he hadn't continued the order. I wanted to see him. Even as I could feel him inside of me, I savored his expression as bliss stormed over me and his grin turned to a grimace and then our mouths fused as a hot rush escaped him and his pace stuttered. He cradled my head, keeping it from slamming into the tile, even as his body shuddered against mine.

The dizzying pleasure shivered over my skin and I swore the bands of tension, stretched so taut within me snapped as I sank down against him, boneless, and if Ian weren't leaning into me against the wall, I had a feeling we'd both fall. Not that I had any doubt whatsoever. The nibbling kisses roused me from the sensual languor and I tilted my head back to chuckle. We were still soaked and there was soap on Ian's cheek and I was pretty sure my hair was ratting since I never pulled it out of the bun.

Not that I cared.

"Hi," I said.

He grinned. "Hi. Better?"

"Always." I rubbed his shoulders. "Even if I said no sex."

"You did say that." He nodded almost agreeably. "Then you climbed in here and jumped me. What's a guy to do?"

"Rock my world?"

"Give me a few minutes and I'll do it again." He winked. Relaxed, playful Ian was a guilty pleasure of mine. Maybe because we had such a strained time in the beginning or maybe because he took control and looking after me so seriously, but I loved it when he let go. It was good for him. It let me feel like I was doing something right.

"Ahem." Archie's voice carried from beyond the door. "I'm waiting for my scolding like a good boy."

Okay. I lost it. Ian set me on my feet as I laughed. "Go away, Standish," Ian said. "We'll be out in a few."

His chuckle drifted back, and Ian smiled down at me as he raised his hands to my hair. With care, he freed it from the band and then began to stroke the tangles loose before he went to work washing it. Yeah, okay, I could just stand here forever as he worked his fingertips over my scalp.

"If I could purr," I told him in a low voice, "I'd probably be vibrating right now."

"Yeah?" Ian said as he moved me back under the spray and rinsed my hair. Then came the conditioner. One thing the guys had all gotten *really* good at, but Ian had seemingly mastered over the last year, was washing my hair. Boneless and putty could easily describe me as the tension from the last few days, and even some of my earlier irritation, just melted away.

"Oh yeah."

"Good." After he rinsed the conditioner out, he kissed a path along my jaw but when I half-expected him to capture my lips, he moved down my neck and then to my breasts. Desire kindled in the pit of my stomach…

"Ian."

"Let me take care of you, Angel," he murmured and then he captured one nipple in a hard pull against his teeth, and I swore my entire core went molten. When he dropped to his knees and lifted one of my legs over his shoulder, it was game over. The first brush of his tongue against my clit and I braced one hand in his hair and the other against the wall.

I was screaming before he finished with me and rose up to push into me again.

Longest shower ever.

Not that I was complaining.

At all.

By the time we made it down to the living room level and out to the deck, Archie was half-asleep in the sun with his head back and his feet up. There was a stack of sandwiches on the table under a clear cover so we could see them and cold drinks waiting in ice.

"I thought you guys were never coming down," he complained, and I bent to give him a kiss in lieu of an apology.

"We were distracted," Ian said without an ounce of remorse in his tone and I grinned. When Archie dropped his feet from the table and snaked his arms around my waist and tugged me onto his lap, I settled easily, cuddling into him.

"We were," I agreed and then nuzzled another kiss against Archie's freshly-shaven jaw. My hair was still damp, but I'd at least run a comb through it after we got dressed and before we drifted downstairs. It had been a while since I'd felt this "floaty."

Ian passed me over a cold can of soda before he popped one open for himself. He motioned to the sandwiches, but I shook my head. His mouth tightened, but relaxed almost immediately as though he ordered it to calm down.

"I did eat," I assured him. "Earlier, when Dominic and I were talking."

"Right. Dickhead was here," Archie grumbled and settled his chin on my shoulder. "What did he want?"

"He's my attorney."

"I know who he is, I just wanted to know why he dropped in. As far as I know, he didn't have an appointment. It's the weekend. You're taking some time to yourself and—"

I twisted a little and eyed him. His grumpy expression turned almost mutinous and I raised my brows.

"I don't like him." One sentence.

"I know you don't," I admitted. "I don't know whether I like him either."

That seemed to mollify him.

"That said, he is my attorney and he's been fantastic in that capacity. I don't have to like him for him to work for me." Something Archie had been stressing over the last few months, that business wasn't always about what we liked, even if we could do more about that.

"She's right," Ian said.

"You're a suck up." Archie was still grumbling, but there was absolutely no heat in the words. "Fine. Yes, you're right. Because I was right. Now put me out of my misery and tell me what he wanted, because the thought of him here flirting with you…"

I pressed a finger to his lips. "One, he didn't flirt with me. Two, even if he did, we know I apparently suck at picking up those cues. Three, he's on my shit list until he figures this crap out with Rachel and I told him as much. Four, he wants to be my friend, and I know *that*, because he said so. *That* said, I also know it has less to do with me and everything to do with Rachel. Until those two figure it out, then as the captain of Team Rachel, he and I cannot be friends."

Lips pursed, Archie stared at me. While the sunglasses hid his eyes, I could practically feel the weight of his stare. "Okay," he said finally, giving me a gentle squeeze. "Point taken. I'm sorry I'm being such a dick about it."

"You're forgiven," I said easily. "I know you think I'm a bit flighty sometimes…"

"Hey," he interrupted. "I've *never* said that or even *thought* it."

"Fine, I think I'm a bit flighty sometimes, and I agree I can miss the flirting. To be fair, I don't care if someone is flirting with me anymore." I gave him a pointed look. "I'm extremely taken." With that, I held up my hand where I'd slid the class ring back on. It had been a gift from Jake, but it also had their birthstones on it as well. Like the tattoo on my back, it was another sign that I was theirs and that was the only place I wanted to belong.

"We care," Ian said, pulling my attention. "But we also trust you."

"Yes," Archie said without hesitation. "Absolutely. I just don't trust that dick because he does flirt with you."

I rolled my eyes and he grinned.

"You love us, you love our possessive qualities too."

"This is true," I conceded and then settled back against him. "Even when I am not thrilled to hear you're putting your dreams on hold for me." The last I said to Ian as I locked gazes with him. Beneath me, Archie went still. Ian exhaled.

"Well, I'm definitely with Archie on the little shit stirrer now." Ian pointed to Archie with his drink before he leaned forward. "But I'm not surprised they reached out to him, since he was reviewing contracts with the entertainment lawyer."

"Exactly." I sighed. "Ian—I remember when we got the offer. You didn't have to keep shutting it down because of…"

"Because your mother tried to kill you," he said, his expression sober and his eyes grave. "She tried to kill both of you. Now she's dead. You had to see that."

Well, yes.

"The last thing you need to be worrying about right now was what is going on with the offer. We hadn't formally accepted, we didn't need to move forward on it."

"Maybe we didn't," I admitted, but that wasn't the point. "Ian, this is one of your dreams. Giving up dreams, even putting it on hold, doesn't come for free."

"Angel, the only cost I'm not willing to pay is you." The absolute sincerity in those words was hard to argue with, and I wouldn't dream of it. I got it.

"You want to protect me. I love you for it."

"The same way you want to protect us," Archie said. His hands tightened on me. "The same way you wouldn't step aside."

I covered his hand on my abdomen with one of my own. "I couldn't let her hurt you. Not any more."

"And we won't let this hurt you," Ian assured me. "Angel, this has been a challenging year, beginning to end."

No lies there.

"Do I want to dive into this with you? Yes. Would I enjoy the hell out of making this happen with you right there?" The expression on his face said it all. "But—this is important. Right now, we need to focus on what you need."

"We don't even know what I need." As much as I hated to admit it, the longer we sat here the more the numbness crept back in. "I don't know. I want to know. But I haven't even…I don't…I don't want to put dreams on hold anymore. I don't want Maddy to take anything else from me. From you. I want to chase this—if you still want it too."

"Yes, I want it. But I want you and our family more."

"Your family isn't going anywhere," Archie said before he kissed my bare shoulder. "I'd rather still have our June, but if we have to adjust, we adjust. If that means we go with you for those first few weeks, then that's what we do. I somehow doubt Coop or Jake will object."

Ian glanced past me to Archie. "We haven't even settled on the dates, and I don't know how much work this is going to be. Once we're committed, that can be a couple of weeks in a studio, maybe more, and we still have to make sure they sign off on the songs. This isn't going to be like the island."

"Then we tell them we can't start until July." I'd actually had time to think about this. "We can work on songs and lyrics while the five of us have our time. Then—we go to wherever. Maybe we can talk them into letting us do studio time here. Hell, I can afford to rent one for us if they don't want to put out the money."

"They can pay for it," Archie said. "They want you two under contract and to make Bound Hearts a thing, they can pay for it. We can also follow you if we have to."

Exasperation appeared in Ian's eyes as he shook his head. "What about Hank? The kids?"

"They aren't going anywhere." I loved them all. "I don't know whether I'm up to being smothered by them yet." It was—both intoxicating and suffocating at the same time. "What I do know is that I want us. I want this for you. I want to be a part of it." And not the reason we didn't get to do it.

"You know I fucking adore you, Frankie, right?" The declaration always gave me a little thrill. "I don't need you to strain or hurt yourself for me."

"And I don't need you to give up on a dream for me." Reaching across the table, I held out my free hand to him even as I laced my fingers with Archie's. Ian gripped my hand easily. "I love you all. This is our life. This is part of what all of us have been working toward."

He let out a long breath. "Then we have a family meeting when Jake and Coop are back here."

"After Coop's final," I suggested. He really had been buried lately. "No more stress for him until he's in the clear."

"Agreed," Archie and Ian echoed in the same breath.

I smiled and squeezed Ian's hand. He held my gaze for a long time, looking for something. Whatever it was, he nodded and relief sang through me. I had no idea how worried I'd been that he'd resist this, when it was something he'd poured so much of his heart and soul into. I needed this for him. Wanted it for him.

"In the meanwhile," Archie said as the air around us lightened. "Let's talk about June. Where can we go so that we can keep you naked and sated all month?"

I cracked up and even Ian started laughing.

"What?" Archie asked. "It's a reasonable question."

Chapter Thirteen
DANCING WITH OUR HANDS TIED

Frankie

"Are you sure about this?" Rachel asked as the guys shuffled furniture around. Coop had already volunteered his room.

"Yes," Archie said as he stopped in front of us. "She's sure. So are we. We're already making a space, Manning, so suck it up."

"Mr. Archie," Jeremy reprimanded from the first floor, and I had to bite back a smile as Archie rolled his eyes to stare at the ceiling a beat before he pasted on a smile.

"You're right, Jere, I should handle it with more grace and a little less attitude, but I guarantee you, Rachel would trust me far less if I were polite about it."

"That is very true," Rachel admitted, almost grudgingly. Then with a pained expression that so mirrored Archie's I had to bite the inside of my lip to keep from laughing, she said, "Jeremy, I should be the one to apologize.

131

I do have a habit of making life difficult for the boys and I don't want to put anyone out."

"I understand, Miss Rachel. However, Miss Frankie has invited you and as we have all established, you are more than welcome. You are not, in fact, putting anyone out as Mr. Cooper more often than not prefers to sleep in Miss Frankie's room. Could I interest you and Miss Frankie in some chocolate cake and coffee?"

"Excellent idea, Jere. Rachel, take our girl downstairs for cake and coffee while we he-men finish the heavy lifting up here." I didn't even see Rachel move but Archie let out an oof that descended into laughter.

"Yes, you he-men stay up here with your sweaty Ys and the double X's are going to hang out downstairs." She was already tugging me with her.

"Sounds great—and thanks for that." The droll comment had Rachel pausing on the steps.

"For what?"

Jeremy met my gaze and I lifted my shoulders in a kind of helpless shrug. To be honest, Rachel and Archie bickering was something we were all going to have to get used to, and it was generally nowhere near as heated as it used to be. He nodded before moving away from the foot of the stairs.

Archie smirked. "For showing me what I am not missing in having a sister."

"Ha!" Despite the scoff, however, she was grinning. "Better me than Frankie, right?"

He grimaced and I made a face. Her serene expression was damn near smug as she glanced between us.

"Too soon?"

"And on *that* note," I declared taking over, I gave Rachel a gentle nudge. "Thank you, Archie." I blew him a kiss and Coop popped up to mime grabbing it from the air.

"Ahaha! Mine!"

"Hey!" Archie turned and the moving turned into wrestling and Ian snorted as Jake darted around them to give me a real kiss.

"Go on Baby Girl, we'll get this all sorted and come down to join you. Don't eat all the cake."

"Like I would," I challenged.

He gave me a bland look.

"That happened *once, Jacob*. Once. I was also just starting my period."

He grinned, brushed his lips to mine and then sighed as something clattered and crashed behind him.

"Go, I got this."

Yeah, I didn't want to see what they broke, if anything. Rachel was already down at the bottom step waiting for me. She opened her mouth, but I gave her a sharp shake of my head. "Nope, you're done with objections. You finished those when you called me three days ago and said yes."

"Pfft. Says who?"

"Says me. And I have mentioned how glad I am that you took me up on the offer?"

"Yes," she admitted with a sigh as we walked through to the dining room where Jeremy had already set the table and put out a carafe of coffee and as promised, a dark chocolate fudge cake was waiting, with slices already cut. "Also, how do you not weigh five hundred pounds with him feeding you like this?"

I chuckled. "Genetics. Probably. I think I got a skinny butt to go with mildly insane and sandwiched up against pathologically devoted to studying."

That earned me a glare from Rachel *and* Jeremy. Though neither of them said a word. I didn't talk about Maddy. Not really, and I wasn't kidding. But, I let the subject flop around on the floor like a dying fish and stepped past it to the table.

Jeremy took a moment to pour the coffee and then glanced at us both. "Can I get you anything else?"

"No, thank you," I said softly with some apology too because Jeremy worried. "I think we're good and I can smell the pot roast for dinner."

Another of my favorites. I needed to make more of an effort to eat. In that vein, I served up a heaping slice of cake and picked up my fork. Jeremy gave another nod then excused himself.

"This is weird," Rachel admitted, picking up her fork and taking a corner of pure frosting off my slice of cake.

"Eating cake for lunch or having coffee? Or moving in with us?"

"I choose D, for all of the above," she said, then paused with a sinful look on her face as she licked the chocolate frosting off the fork. "This is amazing."

"He makes it himself."

"The cake?"

"Well, yes, the cake and the frosting. The man has a million recipes and he makes almost everything from scratch. He's got a gift. I think he went to culinary school somewhere between being a badass butler and surrogate father, but whatever he did before he worked for Archie's family, he keeps to himself." And it wasn't our business, so I tried not to pry. That said, I was deeply curious.

Humming, Rachel took another generous helping of the frosting and at my raised brows, she grinned. "What? I was just thinking I may ask him if he'll let me do a photo shoot with him while he cooks."

"Really?" Intrigued, I stared at her.

"I like people."

"No, you don't," I challenged that concept and finally took a bite of the cake. It was melt in your mouth perfect. The frosting was sinful without being overly sweet and the cake just came apart on my tongue. I washed it down with a swallow of coffee.

"Fine, I like faces and I like the stories you can find when you're not looking. Besides, it will help me flesh out my portfolio." She busied herself with another bite and between my one and her four, we'd begun to tear the slice of cake apart. "So, what's the plan, exactly? You guys were still debating it when I called."

We had. Twenty-four hours after Coop's last final, after he'd had sleep, food, and a generous helping of me—his words not mine—we had a family meeting about the contract, the recording time, and June.

"We're leaving on Friday," I told her. "It's a couple of days early, but the plan is to take a lazy drive down to Florida—we're renting a car, because we're coming back on the yacht and then we're going to cruise the Caribbean for a few days." It sounded kind of weird even as I said it. "Archie wanted to go to Iceland, but this isn't the best time of year for the Northern Lights, so we might do that for Christmas break."

I waited for Rachel to carve away more frosting from the back before I took my next bite.

"There's a lot of different places to go and I think the goal is to be 'aimless' and 'free.'" No schedules, no requirements, no places we absolutely had to be. The yacht would have a crew and we would take our time. "We'll let the moment decide for us, because Ian and I have to be in California at the end of June. KC and the girls are actually going to meet us there for a 'professional recording boot camp' in Los Angeles."

"Damn," Rachel said. "So you're not coming back here?"

"Maybe for a night or two. After talking to both Dominic and the entertainment lawyer, we negotiated a break for us at six weeks so we can take a week back here, then we'll likely spend the autumn doing a club tour. But, we have to be back here for Christmas. I already hate the idea I'm going to miss Archie and Coop's birthdays."

"You won't," Coop said as he came around the corner. "We're flying out to wherever you and Bubba are, remember?"

The warmth and confidence in his gaze bolstered me. It had been his idea. Because the tour was one of the things the producers were pushing for. When I emailed KC about it, she'd said it was pretty normal. That said, she and the girls invited themselves to join us for the 'boot camp' so she could also get a look at what we were dealing with.

"I know," I said with a sigh. "It just seems so far away."

"Well, not something to worry about right now." He tapped his finger against my nose and then swiped my hand holding the fork and its bite of chocolate cake, and I fed it to him.

"You guys are making me sick," Rachel commented.

"Too bad," Coop murmured before he gave me a chocolatey kiss that had me curling my toes. "Did you tell her yet?"

I shook my head. "Not yet, we hadn't got that far." I licked my lips because the cake tasted even better with Coop.

"Tell me now, before you make me lose my appetite," Rachel commanded, but the corners of her lips were twitching even as she peeled off more of the cake slice. Coop gave me another kiss before he walked into the kitchen and pulled out a can of Coke from the fridge.

"We don't know what your plans are for the fall semester, but with Ian and I gone. and Coop moving into my room and you moving into his— you're welcome to stay here for the whole year."

"What about when you guys get back after Christmas?" Rachel said with a frown.

"One of them always sleeps with me anyway," I said with a shrug. "Sometimes all of them. The point is, you don't have to worry about a new roommate or issues like that. Currently, we are planning through Christmas, but no one is going to kick you out if Ian and I are back here for spring semester. I already decided I'm not taking the fall off. I may only go to half-time with a couple of online classes, and work with Grandpa Ted while I'm on the road."

"He's going to mentor you, isn't he?" Rachel's smile grew warmer and far wider. "I knew it."

"Well, we were talking about it and one part of my degree includes some independent study. I've emailed my academic advisor about it. It's a little early for me to start work on it, but if I can get approval, then I won't have to worry about how many class hours I take and I can stay on track to graduate with the guys."

"What about Bubba?"

"His music degree makes their work ideal for his independent study. He needs to log performance hours," Coop answered for me as he came back out eating a sandwich. "He can also do some general studies classes online, and he'll have the best tutor on the planet already with him."

"Wow." Rachel considered me for a moment and then Coop. "You guys are okay with her being gone that whole time?"

"Okay with it? No," Coop said. "We don't have to be 'okay' with it. We support it. This is something she and Bubba want to do, and we want to be a part of the solution. Do we wish it could all happen while she was here? Duh. That said, not going to block either of them from pursuing this." He glanced over at me. "Just makes our reunions that much more special and phone sex—lots of phone sex."

I laughed cause Rachel groaned. Still, my humor was fleeting. Leaving to do this was equal parts terrifying and exhilarating. Exhilarating, because I wanted to be a part of Ian's dreams, and terrifying because I didn't want to leave the guys. We'd been in each other's back pockets the last couple of years, the idea of a week apart wasn't too bad, but months?

That was something else altogether.

"So, you want me to babysit your boys for you?"

"No, Manning," Archie answered. "She wants us to look after her best friend for her." I bit back another smile. "So just deal with it. If we can put up with you, you can put up with us." He swiped the last bite of cake off my plate and Coop swatted at him, then moved to put another slice to replace the one we'd just decimated.

"I'm going to weigh five hundred pounds," Rachel said as she drained her coffee, before taking a huge hunk of frosting for another bite.

"Well," Coop offered. "Archie and Jake run every day, I'm sure they'd love for you to join them." The perfectly angelic delivery almost made me choke.

"We have to make Coop come with us," Jake said without missing a beat, as he and Ian circled the corner. Jake had changed his shirt and his hair was damp. He'd probably showered before he came down. "You can help us get his lazy ass in gear."

"Hey!" Coop complained and Rachel let out a damn near evil chuckle. His eyes narrowed as he studied Rachel. "We're the BFFs, you have to be on my side."

"Says who?"

"Says Frankie," Coop replied firmly. "She's Captain of Team Rachel and in her absence, I'll be in charge. So you have to be on my side."

"I don't think that's how this works," she said with a skeptical cluck of her tongue. "If you're filling in as acting captain for my team, you have to be on my side, but I'm not required to be on yours."

They both looked at me and I picked up a forkful of cake. "I'm Switzerland, as long as you guys look after each other, and don't fight, I'll be happy." With that, I stuffed my mouth with cake to stay out of it.

"Huh." Coop frowned. "Fine. If I have to run though, you have to do movie nights with me. That's nonnegotiable."

"Wait…I went from just crashing here for a couple of months, to now I have to go running and do movie nights?"

"It's a fluid plan, Manning, get on board or get run over," Archie suggested as he dragged a chair out and poured himself coffee. "Besides, at least with us around, you won't have to worry about Walsh."

She rolled her eyes, but she didn't respond with a snarky comeback, which said more for how much she appreciated that sentiment than I think she realized. Still…

"Rach?"

She glanced at me.

"Thank you."

Her half-smile gave her away. "Fine, I'll stay and look after your boys. And I can deal with any pushy little bitches that get ideas, while I make sure they aren't pining themselves into a stupor over your absence."

"What pushy little bitches?" Jake asked. "Cause as far as I'm concerned, there's only one girl for us. We don't need to be reminded."

"Ahh, Jake, how quickly you've forgotten," Rachel said with a damn near aggrieved sigh, that just made me laugh. "Don't worry, sunshine, I'll make sure they keep their distance."

I caught Ian's amused gaze and he winked. Yeah, this was a crazy plan—but it just might work. We were all going to work on it together and if Rachel was 'looking' after the guys, they could look after her too. I hated the idea of abandoning her in the midst of all her relationship drama but Coop said he and Archie had it covered.

I decided, for all our sanity, to not ask what that meant.

At least not yet.

Coop and Rachel helped me decimate a second piece of cake, but some of the leaden weight in my chest had eased and by the time dinner was ready, Rachel and the boys were already arguing about the fall schedule.

This could work.

Chapter Fourteen
TROPICAL CONTACT HIGH

Frankie

"What about this one?" Coop asked as he held up a larimar beaded and shell necklace. There were chunky jewelry options but this one boasted a more slender design. I reached for it and it was almost soft against my fingers as I lifted it. "There's a bracelet too." He plucked another chain that was definitely shorter but just as elegant.

"Oh, I like these," I murmured as I ran the necklace over my fingers. They were cheerful yet sophisticated. They definitely said Caribbean beach vacation, but at the same time they wouldn't be obnoxious. The stone was a large part of that, the larimar mingled the blue and the white of the sky and the sea. "Are there earrings?"

Coop twisted to look as I cradled both the necklace and bracelet. We were in the market in Martinique. We'd reached the island the night before and had to wait for dawn to park in the port, or whatever it was boats did.

Ships. The yacht was a ship. If I kept calling it a boat, Archie's eyes might pop out of his head. Though—that could be fun too.

"Not exact," Coop said as he held the earrings he'd picked over to the chains. The color of the larimar was close, but not quite. The shells were great. It was just enough off that it would probably drive Rachel nuts. The shopkeeper glanced over at us. She had both a store just behind her and these huge carts filled with all kinds of jewelry.

"Excuse-moi," I called. "Avez-vous des boucles d'oreilles assorties à ce collier?" I held up the necklace and the woman smiled at me as she ambled over to where we stood. In the last hour since we'd arrived in the market area and began to wander, that was one thing I'd already fallen in love with. No one rushed. There was a kind of laissez-faire that I really liked.

"Ma sœur en fait. Je peux l'appeler si tu veux." Her accent was so different from what I was used to, but I loved the lyrical sound of her voice.

"Ta sœur fait du beau travail et je ne veux pas la déranger." I loved her sister's work, but I definitely didn't want to bother her.

"Est-ce la pierre ou les coquillages que vous voulez assortir?" Turning to the cart, she began to sort through it.

I stroked my finger over the larimar in the necklace. It was definitely the stone I wanted to match. Before I could answer her though, she pulled a pair out with a little sound of triumph and moved over to hold them against the necklace and bracelet I already had in my hand. They were perfect.

"C'est ce que je pensais. C'est ce que tu voulais, non?"

"C'est parfait! Merci. Je voudrais acheter les trois." Delight curved through me as the woman beamed at me and then she beckoned me into the shop. I pulled off my sunglasses as I followed her into the shade.

The tank top I was wearing was open in the back, with just a single string to keep it in place and the white shorts were cool. I'd stuck a hat on my head before we went out because despite all the tanning on the deck I'd been doing, including the topless and nude sunbathing when the crew was out of sight—something the guys kept a firm eye on—I didn't want to burn.

Fans circled lazily inside and the air on the island wasn't remotely hot. The constant breezes were wonderful. Even more, I just loved the atmosphere. She walked back to the register. On the wall behind her were pictures and she motioned to one before telling me about her sister. The woman was very pregnant in that picture.

Now I was *very* glad we hadn't had to bother her. I counted out the amount in euros and paid her.

"Hey," Coop said, sliding up behind me and then sliding a necklace on me before he did it up. I glanced down to see the single huge larimar hanging from the chain. It was exquisite. "I like this one for you—and look—it has a cuff and a ring." He held both out and I stared at them.

The shopkeeper watched us with a small smile. "Coop…"

"C'mon, let me drape you in beautiful—what is this again?"

"Larimar," I told him. "The gem of the Caribbean. Or so they say."

"Larimar. I want to drape you in larimar," he said then leaned in to murmur. "Then I want to see you wearing nothing but the larimar while I show you just what it does to me when you speak French."

He pressed a kiss to the butterfly tattoo behind my ear and I shivered. Dammit, even my nipples went peaked. The shopkeeper was still smiling at us and then she glanced down at my hands and the ring.

"Let's make sure this fits." He'd already wrapped the cuff around my upper arm and it was perfect. The silver, or maybe it was white gold, the metal was pale and it matched the necklace and the ring. They weren't a "set" but they definitely worked together. He slid his fingers down to my left hand and tried the ring on my index finger—too big. Then my middle finger—too small. I laughed when he stuck his tongue at me and then slid it on my ring finger.

Perfect fit.

A tiny little thrill skated through my system. "That seems right," he murmured. "You promised to marry me all the way back in Kindergarten, remember?"

How could I ever have forgotten? We'd been between the swings and the slide. "Oui, je me souviens, mon chéri. Je les aime. Mais pas autant que je t'aime." I pushed up on my tiptoes to kiss him and Coop's eyes flared. This close it was impossible to miss the way his eyes dilated, despite the sunglasses. The fact he was hard as a stone where he pressed against my hip was also telling.

"I heard the 'oui,'" he said and turned to the shopkeeper.

"I speak English," she told him and I swore Coop's ears went red and the shopkeeper's delight increased. "You chose well for your lady. Always take care of her and like the sea, she will look after you." While yes, I liked how her accent flavored her words in French, it seemed even more lyrical in English.

"Merci," he said and then cleared his throat as he reached for his wallet. She chuckled.

"He is a good boy," she told me as she rang him up. "I like boys who listen and value what they have in their lives."

"Oui, il est le meilleur. Mon ami et mon amour."

"Good." She counted out the change. "Then I shall pray for you both and your continued happiness."

"Merci," I murmured as Coop said it a little louder. She passed over my bag with the presents for Rachel. Interlacing my fingers with Coop's, I pushed my sunglasses back into place before we stepped outside.

"We're done shopping now, right?" The teasing tone just made me laugh. "Or do I have to suffer through more French?"

"Suffer?" I retorted.

He cleared his throat. "Yes, suffer. If you don't remember, I fucking love hearing you speak French."

Oh, I remembered. I twisted to walk sideways just so I could look up at him. "Je me souviens. J'aime que tu aimes quand je parle français."

He grunted, but his lips just kept twitching. "You said something about speaking French."

I laughed, for real this time. "You should have stayed in French with me. Then we could talk to each other in French all the time."

"If I'd stayed in French class with you, I'd have been passing out from all the blood heading south on a regular basis. I'm practically light headed now."

Shaking my head, I pulled at his arm as I headed for another shop. "I promise, I'll spend the whole night just speaking to you in French."

"You're killing me, Frankie," he grumbled, but came along without any real protest. "You're killing me."

"And you love it," Jake said as he wandered out of the store we'd been heading into. "We told you this was a French speaking island."

Coop muttered but let me go as I wandered into the shop filled with all kinds of snow globes. Granted, some of the port cities boasted these amazing tourist shops filled with all kinds of kitschy items, but some had hidden gems in them. The jewelry for example.

"Nice ring," Jake said in a dry tone.

"You snooze you lose, buddy," Coop retorted but I ignored them as I wandered through. We'd stopped at a few islands so far. Most of the time, we spent a day or two and then moved on. Though I was looking forward to swimming with Dolphins when we got to Grand Cayman, we'd had to delay that trip when a storm blowing through the region sent us out further into the Atlantic for a bit.

My stomach clenched at the one storm we'd already encountered while onboard. That had been freaky as fuck. I'd literally gone from lying down to standing up between one moment and the next, and I wasn't alone. On the upside, I didn't get seasick despite the storm-tossed waves—and now I had a firm understanding of what that meant—but I hadn't been able to sleep the rest of the night.

Archie had sat up with me as the guys had drifted to sleep. The captain had come down long enough to check in on us and to make sure we'd lashed down anything loose. All the little compartments everywhere made sense. The next day had dawn miraculously clear, blue, and stunning.

We'd had some cleanup to do in the galley, but the air was so much fresher and cooler than before the storm it wasn't funny. The water wasn't even rough anymore. The storms that blew through like that were both terrifying and impressive.

Still *that* storm told me I wanted nothing to do with a hurricane. Archie promised that the crew was well aware, and they were constantly checking the weather. It meant rerouting then we went a long way around, but we'd get to Grand Cayman eventually. We had all of June to sail and I loved the port stops almost as much as I loved just hanging out with the guys.

I had Rachel's gift, but I needed something for Jake's sisters and for Trina, Coop's sister, then for Chloe because she'd been all about guilting me when I told her we would be traveling for a bit, despite Hank and Kelly both scolding her. Chloe was a master at guilt.

So far, I'd sent her postcards from every port and even from some of the places along the way when we'd driven down to Florida in the first place. The snow globes reminded me of the beaches we'd seen. I wondered if they would like those or if it was too—simple.

As for Alec and Craig? Yeah, I wasn't even close to figuring out something for them. Maybe I should go back and get something for Kelly at the jewelry shop, but I didn't know her well enough. Then there was Jeremy…

"Baby Girl," Jake said as he slid up behind me. "You're about to rip that bottom lip open, you're chewing it so much. What's wrong?"

"You'll laugh at me."

"So?" he said with a shrug before he wrapped his arms around my waist and pulled me back against him. "You laugh at me. We laugh at Coop. It goes around."

"Hey!" Coop's protest came from somewhere else in the store, but I just grinned.

"True," I agreed then sighed. "Fine…" So I shared with him my dilemma and to my surprise, he didn't laugh.

"Buying for the girls is always a crapshoot," he told me. "You have to find equal value, even if you don't pick out the same thing for them. You also have to consider that what you send Blake, Becca might want, but if you send Becca the same thing, Blake won't like it as much. Louisa's pretty chill about all of it, but you still want to make sure she doesn't feel ignored."

"Well thanks for clearing that up for me."

He grinned. "You're welcome." Then he turned me around and tugged my sunglasses off so he could meet my gaze. "They will love whatever you pick out for them because it means you were thinking about them. Your little brothers and sister are exactly the same way. You want to get her that snow globe, don't you?"

I mean I did, but… "It's like showing her where I was when I wasn't going to visit her."

"Exactly," Jake said. "Believe it or not, that will be something she likes. It means even if you were far away, she was on your mind and you're sharing with her something you love."

This was true.

Lips twisting, I glanced back at the wall of globes. They were similar, but each one seemed a bit different. "I think Chloe will want something from the dolphins." Because *I* was legitimately excited about that.

"See," Jake said. "Now you got it." He dropped a kiss on my lips. "Don't overthink it, Baby Girl. You love those kids and every single one of them knows it. Not to be the mushy one—"

"—cause that's totally Coop's job," I finished for him. Coop's distant "hey!" made both of us grin.

"Exactly, but I can tell you from experience it's not the gift that matters. It's the fact you got them a gift."

"You're almost as wise as you are cute," I told him before giving him another kiss. He grinned, and it wasn't until I was a few feet away looking at another display before he responded.

"Wait, what do you mean 'almost?'"

Coop laughed his ass off and I just grinned. I did end up buying a pair of snow globes. One for Trina and one for Louisa. The one for Louisa had kids playing soccer on the beach. I thought she'd get a kick out of that. Her interest in soccer had been growing over the last couple of years and in the year since we'd moved to New York, she'd joined a team and they'd made it to playoffs in their division, but got knocked out in the first round.

Next year.

Trina would like it because it had a starfish shell on the beach in the globe, and I'd picked her up some decorative starfish shells at our last port. Something different.

I spent the next hour drifting from store to store with the guys. Archie and Ian were supposed to meet us for lunch, but they were running late. I wasn't too worried about it. There was no rush.

"This one," Jake said as he held the dress up to me and I looked at it. Well, dress was generous, it was more sarong than dress. I raised my eyebrows and glanced down at myself. "Don't even start on that question, Baby Girl. I love you in everything."

"He likes you out of it even more, and that dress has easy access," Coop offered and I rolled my eyes. I passed them my bags, with my hat tucked into one of them, and just took the sarong and went in to ask the shopkeeper if he had somewhere I could change. He showed me to a little room that basically had a half door for privacy. My head was visible and so were my legs.

The fact I could see Jake and Coop both *staring* at me wasn't weird at all. But I slipped out of the tank top and shorts, leaving me only in a pair of thin, lacy panties. There was a mirror to the side and I checked the sarong. The one I'd had on the island the year before had all these different ways you could tie it, and this seemed the same thing.

Unlike the island last year, we weren't somewhere private, so walking out topless was not an option. I finally worked it out so that it looped around my neck before crossing over and then falling in a simple shift to my knees where it curved. The fabric was very soft and the colors were a muted tie-dye pattern that went beautifully with the larimar stones in my jewelry.

I studied my appearance and turned from side to side before I scooped up my shorts and tank top and let myself out.

Archie's low wolf-whistle warmed my face. He and Ian must have shown up when I was getting changed. They both stared at me with something between hunger and admiration.

"Buy her your own presents," Jake said as he shoved between them. "This one is mine."

"She's already wearing mine," Archie drawled and my cheeks heated for real. Yes, the lace panties were from Archie. In fact, every scrap of panties and bras that had made it on the trip were new and from him. Most of them were red. The man did have his favorite colors.

Jake gave me a once over and I spread my arms and did a little twirl. "Do you like it?"

"Oh yeah," Ian offered from where he stood and Jake grinned.

"I love it. In fact…"

Coop showed up with two more in two different colors. "All three?"

"Yep," Jake said and they both turned toward the counter.

"Wait—" But neither was listening to me. Archie drifted up beside me and tangled his fingers with mine, then lifted my left hand and eyed the ring on it. "Coop got it for me," I told him and Ian, who had followed.

"It's beautiful," Ian said. "Matches the arm band and the necklace. I approve."

"Hmm," Archie said, trailing his fingers up my arm to my shoulder. Then he traced the infinity pattern of the tattoo. "I approve, but I'm feeling the urge to top it." Before I could protest, he clucked his tongue and wrapped his hand around my nape as he dragged me to him. "Wait, not it, you. Feeling the need to be on top of you."

He swallowed my laughter with his kiss. I had a feeling lunch was going to be brief at this rate, but I wasn't that hungry. Not that they listened to me. We found a place down by the water where we could eat and watch the waves. Listening to them razz each other as I sipped the cold Pina Colada and nibbled on the appetizers soothed some of the more bruised places in my soul.

To my delight, we didn't head right back to the yacht, though Archie sent Coop and Jake with the bags back there, we headed inland to a nice hotel and a nightclub for dancing. If I wasn't already in love with all four of them, I would have fallen for them all over again today.

Chapter Fifteen
SCREAMERZ

Frankie

One of the best parts of being on Martinique, we were legally able to buy alcohol and get into nightclubs. The hotel Archie chose was a really nice one, but he'd picked it more for the club *on* the property. When I saw the name, I gaped at him. "Archibald."

"Yes, Francesca?" His smirk turned positively devilish. Ian stood just a foot away, hands in his pockets and his own amusement right there. "Something you object to?"

I glanced at the neon sign that spelled out *Screamerz* then looked back at Archie. Mischief filled his dark eyes. Honestly, it was the first time in a *while* that I'd seen that much life and light dance into them. "Hmmph," I said, grasping my mock outrage with both hands. The boys wanted to play with me. Then let's play, dammit. "I don't know if I like what you're trying to say here."

Head cocked, I focused on the sign as if it really was the source of all offense. Then the doors opened to let a group of people out. They were laughing and still moving to the percussion beat of the music spilling out of the club. I pivoted to face them again.

"Where's the lie?" Archie asked, smirk still in place as he closed the gap between us.

With a heavy sigh and a roll of my eyes, I let him tug me close and I wrapped my arms around his neck. "Don't hear you complaining."

"And you never will, Angel." Ian grinned. "But this is all Archie, he wanted to take you dancing."

A shiver went through me and I locked my gaze on Archie's. "I like the idea of dancing."

"Me too," he murmured then dropping a kiss on my lips. "Tonight, we're just five tourists, getting lost in the music and the fun. We can drink all we like, I've arranged a suite for us upstairs. The guys are bringing back an overnight bag."

"No wonder they didn't complain about going back to the yacht." Suddenly the jewelry and the dressing up took on a whole new level. "Sneaky."

"Thank you." Archie winked. The roguish light dimmed as he sobered. "You don't have to, we thought—I thought this would be good for you and for me."

I cupped his face and kissed him fiercely. The press of his lips against mine sent liquid heat to pool in my system. He didn't move for the space of a second, then his arms banded around me as he claimed my mouth. The first stroke of his tongue left me hungry for more.

It was a strain to press closer and when his hands slid down to my ass and gripped it, I groaned. That was better. But I needed more—

Ian coughed.

Reality rushed back in as Archie lifted his head with an aggrieved sigh. "Cockblock."

"Exhibitionist," Ian retorted, and I swore my face scalded as I caught his indulgent smile. He wasn't the only one watching us though. A couple was on their way down the hall toward the club doors and they wore warm, if entertained, smiles.

Hiding my face against Archie's shoulder, it was impossible to miss the laughter shaking him. Laughter that delighted me. When I leaned back to meet his gaze, he cupped my cheek and my smile widened.

"I've missed that smile," he murmured.

"I've missed yours."

The light dimmed briefly then shone in his eyes once more. "We'll get through this, Babe, I promise."

"I know," I said slowly, and those two words unlocked some of the tension in my chest. I did know. I didn't know how or when, but we would. "I know we will. We're stubborn like that."

"Yes," Archie said with a slow nod. "We are. Now, I'm taking my girl dancing. You got a problem with that?"

"Not even a little." Any traces of embarrassment or worry evaporated. Nothing mattered but being here, in this moment, with them. Especially right now. "I love that my guys want to take me dancing."

"Did you hear that, Bubba?" Archie said, smug as fuck. "We're her guys."

"Was there ever any doubt?" Despite his dry tone, his expression warmed. "I mean, now."

"Yeah, I know what you mean. Don't sweat it. Let's go. I get the first dance and you get table duty," he said to Ian, and I frowned.

But Ian just shook his head. "No worries, Angel. I can guard the drinks and the table. Tonight is for these guys. Especially since I get you to myself for a while."

"Don't remind me," Archie growled, hugging me to him. "We're gonna have to factor some solo vacays in for me and the boys too."

Ian just laughed and I grinned. "Whatever you want." I meant it.

"Oh, Babe, you give me an inch and I'm going to run with it."

Like I didn't know that, but he didn't really give me time to respond as he gripped my hand and tugged me with him. Ian was already at the door and he dropped a kiss on my lips before he opened it. "Don't worry, Jake and Coop are going to join us."

"The dress. The jewelry. I'm on to you boys."

Archie snorted. "No you're not, but you will be."

The need to retaliate to his teasing slid away as the music rippled out to pull us inside. The percussion, the rhythm, even the guitars were all provocative. The music was both familiar and different at the same time. It tasted like the Caribbean, and maybe I'd watched too many movies, but if I'd walked in here blindfolded with no idea of where we were—I'd have said Caribbean something.

Ian gave my arm a light squeeze as he headed over to the tables. Although it was late afternoon—I really hadn't paid attention to how long we'd wandered the market—people filled the club. The music was like a caress, tugging, pulling, and guiding us out to the dance floor. To be honest, I didn't pretend to be the best dancer out there. I just loved moving to music.

This music was so great.

"It's zouk," Archie said against my ear as he slid an arm around me and began to roll his hips in time with the beat. I followed, letting him guide. I was definitely not nailing the steps, but I kept glancing at the others around us and soon we had it.

Belly to belly, we moved in sync and we didn't need to go far. It was a slow-quick-quick rhythm. We took longer steps on the first third and the fourth beats. Everything else had hips rolling and moving up and down together.

"It's what?"

"Zouk," he repeated as the music changed but I had zero interest in stopping. It was like a fever and I was having fun. "Folk music. Brazil has a form, but this one was developed here and in Guadalupe. It uses calypso, reggae, and a few other musical traditions."

The song picked up the pace and Archie's sharper steps had me laughing as we moved. I mean, I guess you could call it dirty dancing, but it was way more flirtatious than that and the only places we touched were breast to abdomen. The movement back and forth filled me with a kind of inescapable joy.

"That's a lot about a musical tradition."

"What? I research."

I studied him a beat as he drifted his hands to my hips. "And Jake loves history."

"And Jake, does in fact, love history as much as you do."

A group effort. He grinned and then we were moving. The faster beat had me lifting my arms as we danced. The couple next to us were amazing. The lady caught me watching them and I complimented her in French. Her body was like liquid grace ebbing and flowing with the music in a way I could only imagine.

She danced over to me and showed me a few steps. It was amazing. We never stopped moving. And when I had it down, she grinned and blew us a kiss as she danced back to her partner. I flashed Archie a grin. When hands landed on my hips from behind, the only thing that kept me calm and relaxed in the moment was Archie's expression. He lifted his chin as though saying hello and I tilted my head back to find Jake moving with me.

Someone had been practicing. "Been here a while," he said with a laugh, as I turned to dance with him. "But we wanted a turn to dance too."

By we, he waved to where Coop sat with Ian and drinks. The music slowed and so did my heart as I drifted into Jake. Wrapping my arms around his neck, I grinned as he matched me step for step.

"You tired yet?" The playful note reminded me of what had been missing the last few weeks. Or maybe not missing so much as I hadn't been able to feel it the way I would.

"No," I said. "Not even." I wasn't tired or hungry or thirsty. The music was in my blood and out here was right where I wanted to be. "Archie told me about the music and your research."

"A quick search is hardly research," Jake admitted, bending his head until his forehead rested against mine. "Archie was right though." His voice softened, admiration and respect joining the affection. A fresh wave of relief swam through me. The two of them fighting was not something I ever wanted to experience again.

Yeah, we would fight. Argue. Disagree. But not—not that kind of hostility that brought them to blows.

"Hey," Jake said, ducking his finger under my chin and I lifted my gaze to his. We'd moved to the edge of the dance floor. "What's wrong?"

"Nothing," I said and I meant it.

"Then why did you look so worried?" The tone and the expression were so Jake. Blunt like a mallet. No dancing around it.

"I didn't mean to—I was just thinking about you and Archie fighting and how much I hated it. Never want to do that again."

"Baby Girl, we're going to fight."

"I know you're gonna argue and be pissy. *I* get argumentative and pissy."

"Right," he agreed so swiftly that I raised my brows but he just grinned, not remotely repentant. "But we'll get over it. Loving you just gives us a reason to get over it faster. Besides, I like fighting with you."

"What?" Was he drunk already?

Jake's grin filled with mischief. "Fighting means we have to make-up—angry sex is fun. Angry sex that turns to make-up sex is even more fun."

I groaned and Jake laughed as he pulled me back to the dance floor. The place had a constant ebb and flow. Lots of people there, drinking, laughing, eating, and dancing. They came and went, but it was lively and I loved it.

"I think that should be a rule," Jake said as we moved so close I could feel his breath.

Sweat coated my skin and made the underside of my hair damp. My pulse was this living, throbbing beat that matched the cadence of the music. "What should be a rule?"

Breast to chest and resting his hands on my hips, Jake guided our movements so we were just this side of actually grinding and there was no mistaking the hardness of his erection. The moment I realized it was pressing against my stomach, my nipples peaked and a delicious heat unfolded in my system.

"Even when we're angry, we play, we fight, we fuck, we live." The intensity in his pale blue eyes held me captive for a moment. "Angry fucking can be fun—just like make up sex can be fun."

"And if angry sex turns into makeup sex?"

"So. Much. Better."

Laughter swelled out of me, and he swallowed the sound in a kiss that had my arms tightening around his neck and when he lifted his head, I sighed. The music changed, the tempo increasing and my body throbbed in time to it. But my stomach also chose that moment to make a desperate, if gurgling, sound of protest.

"Aha!" With that, he hooked an arm around me and we headed off the dance floor. I hadn't even realized how long I'd really been out there until we were *walking* and the muscles in my legs reminded me that athleticism was not my strongest area.

"I need to pee," I said just as we got to the table and I accepted the water from Coop. There were plenty of drinks there, though drunk definitely didn't seem to be the goal, and I was down with that. I finished the whole glass in three gulps then took the one from Archie. Holy crap, I was overheated and hungry and desperately thirsty.

After I finished the second glass, I glanced around and Ian nodded toward the hallway to our right. It was illuminated in a blue light, kind of like there were other colorful lit areas around the club. Now that I wasn't wholly focused on the music and my dance partner, I could appreciate the aesthetic. It was gorgeous. Ian stood and I shook my head.

"I can go, you guys can see the door from here." At my protest, Jake glanced down at me then down the hall, then at the guys. I got it and I adored them for their protectiveness. My track record with bathrooms *sucked*. First Mitch. Then my— Not even slamming the door on that thought could stop the whisper of *mom* from sliding out. "If it was out of your line of sight, I'd ask one of you to come along, but it's not." Maybe I should indulge them, but at the moment, I just had to pee.

"Go on," Coop said. "But you"ll forgive us if we don't see you back out in three minutes."

"Thank you." I blew him a kiss and hurried, not quite dancing to the door because holy fuck did I have to pee. The lighting in the bathroom wasn't at all dim or flooded in deep color like it was out in the club itself. It was lit warmly and brightly. There was a woman at the sink washing her hands who flashed me a smile and a nod, along with the sound of another woman peeing.

Bless the dress, because I managed to purge my bladder—oh thank fuck—and wash my hands in record time. I glanced at myself in the mirror and made a face. I was a bit sweatier than I realized, so I splashed some cold water on my cheeks. Thankfully, no cosmetics meant I didn't have to worry about runny eyeliner or mascara. I also didn't have to worry about blotting my face dry with a paper towel.

The cold water not only rinsed away the perspiration, it also cooled my flushed cheeks. After wetting a paper towel, I ran it over the back of my neck then met my gaze in the mirror. While I'd never list them on my favorite places, I wasn't afraid of public bathrooms before and I refused to start now.

With a firm nod, I dropped the towel into the trash and headed back out. We were having an amazing time and I was hungry. Four sets of eyes stared intently in my direction, and I smiled. I couldn't even fault the protectiveness. I hated letting them out of my sight too.

My stomach bottomed out. In less than two weeks, I would be doing exactly that. Leaving three of them behind. Nope, I scolded myself as I focused on getting back to the table. Don't—

Movement in my periphery and Jake's expression had me half-turning and I caught the hand about to slap my ass by the thumb and just twisted it. I kept moving and slammed the heel of my free hand right into the guy's nose. There were guys behind him laughing. They all looked about our age, and big. I didn't think I could take on all of them. Not that I would have to. The twisted thumb lock I used had my ass patter hitting his knees and swearing.

Letting him go, I backed off. Not remotely surprised when Jake surged past me and hauled the guy up by his shirt. I didn't even have to see his face to taste the rage in the air. Archie and Ian were both in front of me and Coop moved right up next to me. The audible crunch of Jake's fist connecting with the guy's jaw even with the music playing had me wincing. Waiters and a guy who had to be a bouncer were suddenly wading in to separate them. Ian got a hand on Jake's shoulder and hauled him back.

"Bitch," the guy said. Oh joy. American. "I was just being friendly."

You know what… "Fuck you," I said. "Slapping my ass is assault. Especially when I don't even fucking know you."

"Watch your mouth," Ian ordered the guy.

A manager interrupted. The ass slapper had a bloody nose and split lip. I had a feeling he'd have a fist-shaped bruise by morning. Archie was already talking to the manager and smoothing the situation over.

Well, smoothing it over for us. Mr. Grabby Hands and his friends got ejected. Apparently, the manager was the guy who'd been dancing with the girl who showed me how to dance earlier. When he asked me, in French, if I was all right and then glanced at my guys then the three who were being ejected, I assured him I was fine. My guys were just looking after me.

And fuck me, I might never go to the damn bathroom again.

Jake was still fuming when I reached out to take his bruised hand to get him moving, and we all returned to our table. The manager sent a fresh round of drinks over and they apologized for the behavior of the other guests—not like they were remotely to blame—and he wanted to comp our table, but Archie and I both insisted that wasn't necessary.

When he left us alone, I stared at the appetizers they'd delivered on the heels of the drinks. Accras de Moure—fried fish and super tasty. Conch stew, or was it called Lambis? I couldn't remember—it smelled divine and there were a few others I didn't recognize.

"I should have looked at the menu," I said even as I reached for the conch stew. Ian lifted the platter, even as Coop moved my drink so he could set it in front of me. "But right now, I think I could eat all of this."

"Eat all you want, we'll get you a menu if you want it. But it's in French so if you read it, you might send Coop off the deep end." Archie smirked but Coop just flipped him off as I took my first bite.

"Eat and talk French to me," Coop beckoned. "Make me your slave."

There was a deep moment of silence as the guys stared at Coop and I paused, spoon halfway to my mouth.

"I said what I said," Coop retorted. "Y'all can fuck off."

The laughter hit Jake first and then rolled around the table. I almost choked on my first bite cause I was grinning so hard. The little bubble of misery that had tried to invade earlier popped under the warmth at the table and I hooked my ankle around Coop's and then sighed as I took another bite.

My guys, good food, good music and… "I knocked the shit out of that guy."

"Yeah, you did," Jake said. "Nice hit."

"Loved it," Archie said. "I'm hard as a fucking rock and I can't tell you how sexy badass looks on you."

"You did beautiful, Angel."

"Tell me that in French," Coop dared me.

That just cracked us up all over again, but I did as Coop asked. It didn't translate exactly, but it definitely worked. "J'ai défoncé ce gars."

His groan made me laugh. "I'm yours. Take me now."

"Can I eat first?" Not that I didn't want to have him now, but holy fuck

I was starving.

"Yes," they all said in unison and Ian waved to a waiter. "Just getting you that menu."

Chapter Sixteen

MONKEY BUSINESS

Jake

Adrenaline still throbbed in my veins from that fucker trying to smack her ass as she walked past. Frankie hadn't even glanced at them, but I'd seen his head swing to look at her. He wasn't the first asshole to focus on her like that, and he probably wouldn't be the last. She was drop dead fucking gorgeous, inside and out. Jerks like him didn't even deserve to breathe her air, much less talk to her, and he was in motion to *touch* her?

I'd never have gotten there in time, even if I was already moving. Her reaction. Fuck me. *Her* reaction. It had been solid fucking gold. My baby girl caught his hand in a thumb lock and slammed the heel of her hand right into his face. He'd gone down like a little bitch. It gave me time to get there and get my hands on him.

The fight had ended too abruptly. No, we didn't need to end up in trouble with the law, that said, the guy could still walk, even if it looked like Frankie might have actually broken his nose. My girl. Fuck, she was awesome. As reluctant as I was to let that fight go, the sparkle in her eyes, the flush in her cheeks and the fact she dug into the appetizers the manager sent to our table were infinitely more valuable.

Man, if her punching some jackass brought our girl back to life, I'd go get us a whole lineup. Course, watching her read Coop the menu should not be this fucking entertaining. Archie hadn't stopped laughing since she began and even Ian appeared bemused. Going dancing had been a brilliant idea. I owed Arch for this.

We lingered in the club for another couple of hours. Bubba took her out for a spin on the floor. The style of dancing just encouraged intimacy—thank you Coop—but it was fucking fun. The whole point of June together was to have fun together, to not be dictated to by a schedule and after this year? We needed it.

"Man, stop glaring across the dance floor like you want to drag her away from Bubba." Archie tipped back the last of his beer and drained the bottle. It was only his second. Drunk was not the goal tonight.

"Actually, that sounds like a great idea," Coop said as he stood and headed for the dance floor. Chuckling, we tracked him as he slid over and right up against Frankie's back to dance, and instead of leaving, Bubba stayed and they danced with her between them.

"You know, I feel like we missed out on that opportunity," Archie mused.

"Nah, you had her to yourself and I had her to mine. Coop genuinely enjoys sharing her."

"So do you," Archie pointed out then added, "Fuck, even I do now."

I chuckled at the grim reality he seemed to make of the comment. "Yes, but she's going away with Bubba." The fact I could laugh about that at all was—it was good.

"That's gonna suck," he admitted and I shrugged.

"Yep, but we'll make it work."

"*You* were the one opposed to long distance relationships."

"I was." I paused as the waiter came by to clear some of the dishes and to see if we wanted anything else. Archie shook his head and asked for the check. After the waiter left us alone, I continued, "I still am. But this is important to them. I want it for them if they want it. You know?"

"Actually," Archie said with a bemused look on his face. "I do know, and I hated the idea when they first presented it. Loathed it, because that meant letting her go and then—then that shit went down with her mom."

It was the first time Archie had brought it up as more than a passing comment.

"Jake, she'd have *died* for me." He paused as the waiter delivered the check folder to pull out his wallet. Those six words held me captive as he handed off his credit card without even a glance at the check itself. After the waiter left, he met my gaze. "Supporting this dream and making it as easy for them as possible, is such a little thing. She's coming home. They both are. This is an adventure."

Shaking my head slowly, I bumped my bruised fist against his shoulder. "You're a fucking romantic, Standish."

"You just figuring that out, Benton?" He retaliated with a smirk. The waiter returned with the check and he signed the receipt and then stood. "No wonder you keep coming in second."

Jaw dropping, I stared at him. "You did not…" But he was already walking toward the dance floor, laughing at me, and fuck me if I wasn't laughing too. Still, he did have the right idea. There were way too many people in this club, but I followed him out to the floor and we joined the guys to dance with her. It wasn't exactly the form of everyone else out there dancing in their pairs. Then again, we weren't like these couples and that was more than okay with me. We only ever had to be us.

We were more than enough.

Coop

When it came time to leave the club, I just wanted to stay, but I also wanted to steal away with our girl and the night was far from over. Happiness shimmered over Frankie in a way that illustrated just how profound its absence had been the last few months. Archie's comment about her earlier badassery with the grabby jackass had just made me laugh. Then again, Frankie had been punching asshats on my behalf from the beginning.

She practically floated, still half-dancing with Arch as we left the club and headed for the elevator. The dress Jake had picked out was stunning on her, but the fact was, she'd make a burlap sack look good. And I may have slyly, or not so slyly, snapped a few pics at the market and then again when she was dancing.

The elevator let us out on our floor and it was quiet. While the hotel didn't boast a penthouse per se, Archie had rented something nearly as good. As soon as we left the elevator, Frankie gripped Bubba's arm and began to tug off her shoes.

"You okay?" I asked and she shot me a half-smile.

"My feet hurt. They were fine, then we sat down for a while before we started dancing again." She shot me an almost teasing grin. "Emmène-moi au lit."

Damn. It never failed. The velvety combination of her voice, that accent, and that language and what little control I'd regained over my dick fled. I stared at her a beat as the last two words sunk in. I actually knew what those words meant.

To bed.

Hell. Yes.

No sooner did she have her shoes dangling then I swept her right up. Archie burst out laughing. Jake scowled with no real menace, and Bubba just shook his head as I cradled her to me. "I know those words."

Arms looped lightly around my neck, Frankie laughed. The most carefree sound ever. A siren's call if I'd ever heard one. "Of course you do."

"Pretty sure I know all of them," Archie pointed out smugly.

I carried our girl and flipped him off at the same time. I could multitask like that. Still amused, Archie strode ahead to open the room. All four of us already had keys, cause Jake and I made a detour up here *before* we joined them at the club. Not only did we want to bring the bags in, but we also wanted to make sure everything was ready.

"Close your eyes, Angel," Bubba ordered and Frankie just buried her face into my neck. I didn't know which was hotter. The fact she obeyed him without even an ounce of teasing or *how* she obeyed him. Her breath tickled my throat and the ache that had been building in me all day, since I slid that ring on her finger, threatened to burst out.

But I couldn't chuck all our plans, even if I did plan to make some simple alterations to them. Possession was nine-tenths of the law and these fuckers had watched her tease and torment me with French all evening.

It had been epic.

Archie held the door for us. Jake and Bubba went first and then I carried her in. The room had been done up right. There were rose petals scattered *everywhere* and the room *smelled* like a rose garden. Though, to be fair Jake was right, rose petals on white carpet looked like blood stains, but we would skip mentioning that to Frankie.

Avoiding the little puddles of petals, Archie navigated to the doors to the bedroom and pushed them wide, as Jake went over to the doors to the balcony and pushed them open to let in the night breeze.

Bubba glanced at the three of us, before he nudged the lights down a little and then he disappeared into the bedroom while Archie folded his arms and leaned against the doorframe. Jake turned around and stared at me a beat before he chuckled and shook his head. Good, he got it. I wasn't letting her go.

When I locked gazes with Archie, he just rolled his eyes and nodded. Good men. Knew there was a reason I liked them.

"Ahem," Frankie said against my throat and I shivered at the delicious little vibration of those syllables. "Are you all done with eyeball charades?"

I blinked.

Equally startled expressions appeared on Jake's and Archie's face before Archie laughed. Like Frankie's earlier laughter, there was something just open and maybe a bit carefree about it. Not forced or contained. "Eyeball charades?"

"Yeah, when you guys have those silent, but intense, conversations about me without ever opening your mouths. It's really, really irritating sometimes."

I grimaced.

"But I kind of think it's sexy, too. Only—I might need to pee at some point and Coop could get tired of carrying me."

"Never gonna happen," I promised and then pressed a kiss to the top of her head. "And yes, eyeball charades is done and I won."

From the bedroom, Bubba's scoff carried and it was Jake who cracked up this time. "No comments from the peanut gallery," he called.

I snickered. "Shit, we're trying to be sexy and mysterious, not clowns." Dammit, I would not laugh. Then Frankie giggled and I cracked up as Archie started laughing all over again.

"Guys!" Bubba called. "Get it together."

"Fuck that," Jake said. "This is more fun. Open your eyes, Baby Girl."

He was right. A romantic evening had its time and place, which we may yet get back to, but I'd much rather just have fun. Listening to these two laugh for real? That was a damn gift I didn't mind receiving.

Frankie opened her eyes and the first thing she did was smile at me. The promise of the past, present, and future all rolled through me at the same time. The sparkle in her green eyes as she reached for me, and I gave in. Dipping my head, I pressed my lips to hers, giving her the hot, open-mouthed kiss I'd been thinking about since the dance floor.

Laughter rose up from my brother boyfriends. I flipped them off as Frankie's arms tightened around my neck, and then her mouth opened to me.

The first sweep of her tongue, and the rest of the room really didn't fucking matter. Just Frankie. Just right here. Just right now.

Archie

Frankie's soft moan went straight to my cock. It was already hard as a stone. I hadn't been kidding earlier about finding her defensive capability sexy as fuck. I'd meant it when I told Jake there wasn't a damn thing I wouldn't do for her. I'd already been in deep before, but the way she stood up for me and wouldn't retreat, no—there wasn't a damn thing I wouldn't do, give, borrow, beg, steal, or kill if it would make her happy.

"Bedroom, Coop," Jake said with a growl I felt in my soul. Coop didn't even pretend to be listening to us. Frankie's shoes fell from her fingers, and one moment she had her dress on, and the next it began to fall away. Then all I could see was the red lace panties she sported.

Holy.

Fuck.

Those were the new ones. All lace, no panels. Not even a little bit of peekaboo. The bra was the same, but there was no bra and no tan lines and yeah. "Bedroom," I echoed Jake and Coop dragged his head up to glare at me.

"Goddamn, guys, I'd let you kiss her."

"Right," Jake said. "You can keep kissing her *in the bedroom.*"

Eyes bright, cheeks flushed, and lips damp, Frankie glanced from Coop to us and then around the room. She wiggled a little and Coop grunted as he set her on her feet. What part of the sarong wrap dress hadn't already fallen away hit the floor, as she did a slow pivot to take in the room.

We'd scored one of the Royal Suites. We were on the highest floor. Everything in the room was lush and expensive, right down to the hot tub in the center of the sunken living room that looked right out the open patio doors where Jake stood. The water, like the floor, also boasted rose petals. I'd asked them for their honeymoon package. It seemed the easiest.

"Guys…" she exhaled the words. Her perfect pink nipples puckered and went tight as the breeze rushed in the open doors. One of her hands stayed on Coop as she turned, slowly giving us a view of almost every luscious inch of her—well no—every luscious inch. The lace had been a damn good call on my part. "This is beautiful."

When her gaze collided with mine, it was a sucker punch of heat, lust, need, and love all at once. "We just wanted to make tonight special," I told her. "And all about you."

"It has been amazing." It was like she didn't know where to look first but kept coming back to stare at us. "I love everything about this—and you—where's Ian?"

"In the bedroom," Bubba called, his tone dryer than the Sahara. "Where you should be, Angel."

Coop snickered, then Jake did. Frankie bit her lips and I chuckled. Jake was right. This was more fun. I held out my hand to her. "Come on, Babe. Come see what we have planned for you."

When she skipped over to me Coop mock-glared, but Jake cut her off just before her fingers brushed mine, scooping her up and then he gave me a wicked smile.

Ass.

But I laughed and moved out the way as he carried her into the bedroom. Her gasp of pleasure was all I needed to hear. The bed was easily as large as the one we had at home. A huge platform that took up the entire center of the room. The sconces offered a flickering light, giving us the illusion of candlelight while keeping it safe from fire.

Bubba sat in a chair at the end of the bed, his feet propped up on the bed itself and his bemused expression softened as Jake carried Frankie over to the bed. He flopped onto it with her and then she pushed up on her elbows to look around.

"You guys went to an awful lot of trouble to try and seduce me."

"Try and?" I snorted. "We do, there is no try."

"Okay Yoda," Coop said as he smacked a hand against my chest. "Save the proverbs for later." Asshole was naked as he walked up onto the bed, dick out and proud. Then again, he never had been shy.

Frankie grinned at him. "What are you guys doing?"

"They are giving me lessons," Bubba said finally, his amusement at all of our antics making me grin in spite of myself.

"Lessons?" Surprise filled Frankie's expression, but Jake fisted her hair and tugged, turning her to look at him.

"Lessons," he said. "Bubba has to take care of all of your needs for the next few months, with minimal support. So, we're doing him a favor."

Right. We were also torturing him.

Po-tay-to. Po-tah-to. It all worked out in the end.

She laughed as Jake kissed her and then groaned when he rolled her over. A minute later, he hit the comforter as Coop pulled her right out from under him, to sitting over Coop. Eyes still laughing and face deeply flushed, Frankie braced herself then looked at all of us before she looked down at Coop.

Yeah. Jake grumbled, but Coop took the cake.

"So—" Frankie said as she pulled out a clip from her hair and the rest of it spilled free. "Let me get this straight. We're in this romantic location so you guys can all have sex with me while poor Ian has to just watch."

"Nothing poor about me, Angel, have your wicked way with them. I'll take notes."

She wasn't alone in the laughter and then she ground her hips against Coop, and he let out a wild moan. Fuck. I didn't want to wait, but Coop won this round.

Surprise flickered over her face and then she shot a look at me. Understanding flashed in those eyes as we stared at each other. Her birthday. This hadn't happened. We'd had plans to repeat the birthday tradition just for her and then Maddy…

I nodded slowly and tears glimmered in her eyes and then a smile.

When she mouthed 'I love you," I pressed a hand over my heart. I loved her too.

Holy hell, did I love her.

"Okay," Jake grunted. "Stop the monkey business, because I'm horny as fuck and Frankie is everything I want to eat."

Crude, but effective. I could go him one better. "Peel off those panties for me, Babe. We need some pretty pink pussy and Coop's about to pass out from all the blood running to his giant cock. So, shut Jake up by sitting on his face and put Coop's cock in your mouth and give the man some relief."

Her pupils swelled at the command.

"Go on, I want to see your lips wrapped around his cock until you're gagging on it, and you have to make him come before Jake gets you off."

"Or what?" She and Coop asked at the same time, though hers was a lot breathier.

"Or you don't get to come tonight," Bubba said and it was my turn to stare at him. Holy shit. I hadn't really had a "punishment" in mind. Edging, however, was a wickedly cool one.

Raising a brow, I met Frankie's shocked—no not shocked, intrigued—and maybe more than a little turned on, look. The flush had spread down to her chest. Yeah. She was feeling it. I grinned.

"What's it gonna be, Babe?"

Chapter Seventeen

ON OUR SIDE

Frankie

The challenge in Archie's voice just added to the loops of tension coiling inside and out. I wanted them and what he was telling me to do wasn't a bad idea. Far from it. And I was a greedy bitch, I wanted all of them and I wanted them right now, but no matter how clever we'd been so far, that was a lot of dick. Another shiver went through me.

"Have I mentioned I love your dicks?" The words rolled right out of me. The thought crystalized and escaped my mouth. I wasn't drunk, at least not on alcohol, but I was feeling pretty fucking high on life at the moment. Life.

Our lives.

Lives we were going to live, dammit. Together. With each other. That was when it hit me a moment ago. All of this…the market, the dress, the jewelry—the rings on my fingers, never felt so warm or so right—the

177

dancing, the dinner, and now this romantic hotel room.

We never finished celebrating my birthday and we'd been in a holding pattern of sorts for the last couple of months, no more.

Coop made a sound below me and I rolled my hips against his very heavy erection. It was right there and if the panties weren't in the way, I could have just slid right down on him. Sometimes it felt so fucking good to just let him stretch me as far as he could. Other times, like now, I wanted to tease him and play.

"You may have mentioned it," Jake said and I glanced at him. His pale blue eyes practically glowed in the low lighting. I rose up off of Coop and he gave me a harsh frown.

I stood up on the bed, moving to stand between the two, rather than still straddling Coop's body, and I hooked my fingers into the sides of my panties, while I glanced at Archie. "Get that dick out, Standish. I want to see every gorgeous inch of it, down to the throbbing vein at the bottom, and the way it curves when you're really stiff."

He went absolutely still and I raised my brows in a challenge.

"Fuck me, talk like that again." He didn't waste time going for his pants and the bed bounced below me as Jake rolled off the bed, stripped and rolled back on so fast, I was left staring.

"Strip," Jake ordered. "I want to eat that pussy."

My nipples went hard and I ran my tongue over my lips as I glanced over at Archie. He had his dick out and proud, running his hand up and down the length of it. "I showed you mine, now show him yours."

Coop sat up and grabbed my panties, peeling them down for me as I laughed. This was—ridiculous and fun, need rippled through me and my core clenched. All four of them were laser-focused on me and I don't think I'd ever felt as beautiful as I did right now. Beautiful. Wanted.

"Baby Girl, don't make me come get you." The rumble of a growl in his voice made me move, it took almost no time to straddle his face and I frowned down at him. I didn't want to put all my weight on him but before I could adjust, he closed his hands on my ass and squeezed it, tugging me right down to spear me with his tongue.

Pleasure eddied up from the first stroke of his tongue and the need to clench had me grinding down with and against his hands.

"Don't forget the rules, Angel," Ian's voice, soft and authoritative, caressed my flesh like he was teasing his fingers over me. I tilted my head as I stretched over to press a kiss to Coop's abdomen, then I locked eyes with Ian as I wrapped my hand around Coop's girth. Jake was being slow, but thorough and his beard tickled, but each time I thought I would start laughing, he would change the stroke of his tongue causing me to tense up again.

It was fantastic.

Though the shadows hid some of Ian's expression, it didn't keep his slow nod and approving smile, as I began to lap at the tip of Coop's cock, slow then faster, swirling my tongue around it and pumping him gently with my hand. Unlike my pussy, I couldn't just deep throat Coop. I had to work up to the stretch, but I loved it.

A low, masculine groan pulled my attention to Archie and he'd pulled up another chair, but he had his hand around his dick, working it slowly and keeping it where I could see it. Sighing, I relaxed as I pushed down on Coop's dick until he pressed against my throat. Hollowing out my cheeks, I sucked deep and hard, tongue stroking him.

"*Fuck*" His strangled oath was amazing, and he fisted my hair as I pulled back. Then I relaxed more, only Jake found my clit at the exact moment Coop thrust. I'd gotten much better at my gag reflex, but I still choked and tears flooded my eyes. "Shit, sorry."

I rubbed his thigh to let him know I was alright. Jake squeezed my ass and then switched his rhythm again, like he wanted to give me time. God, I really hoped they had been kidding about that edging thing. Even as that thought crystalized, another shiver burst through my system and I rolled my hips. They could do whatever they wanted to me. I could take it.

I could take them. They were mine. This time when I swallowed down against Coop's thrust, he pushed into my throat and he began to swear again. Hard and harder I sucked. My jaw ached from the stretch and my pussy throbbed as the need in my belly stretched out tighter and tighter.

Did I even want to win? Coop's dick seemed to get even hotter and the salty hint of pre-cum flooded my mouth. Then he swore as he jerked and his body stiffened, the first jets of his release hit my throat and I swallowed hard. Pressed all the way against his abdomen, I couldn't risk breathing as he came. The crisp little curls of his pubic hairs tickled my nose. Coop swore again as he pushed up and deeper. There was zero way to breathe for a moment, but I kept rubbing his leg as I swallowed against the pressure, then he relaxed and his cock softened slightly.

The first deep breath was dizzying and then Jake locked on my clit with so much force an orgasm had me pulling up to scream. It was like a riot of tension. Too much. But even as I tried to ease off of him Jake pulled me tighter until I was seeing stars. Coop swept up, his expression blissed out and dazed as he smothered my cries with a kiss. He teased my tongue with his own, lapping at me like he was a dying man and I was his only chance to survive.

The second wave hit and I swore against his lips and tongue—in French. His answering groan had me clutching at him. Liquid heat spiraled through me and I swore I came over and over, I couldn't stop and I couldn't get free of it. Overload hit me and the next scream that came out of me involved darkness edging my vision, then everything whited out.

A moment later, floating and aching, I opened my eyes to Jake grinning down at me. Smug rolled off him. "That's one boys…"

Oh shit. They were keeping score and I laughed as he lifted my thigh and pushed into me. The first graze of his cock against my pussy had me spasming. The overload was still there and Jake didn't waste time, he pushed my leg up and my knee bent and pressed into me so deep it was hard to tell where he ended and I began.

"Love you, Baby Girl," he whispered almost soundlessly against my lips as he kissed me. I held on to him, digging my nails in as he set a fierce tempo, rocking us together. The grind and rub sent me spiraling and I clamped down around him. His expression was almost manic with joy and his beard fucking glistened. That barely registered as he gave a stuttered motion and then I lost the thread as I writhed. I couldn't get close enough and the spasms of pleasure as I came almost robbed me of feeling him as he did. The first hot jet of release hitting me though, and I was gone.

It was so fucking perfect, because Jake kept hitting that one spot as he rocked through his own orgasm. When he finally slowed and we collapsed together, I managed to cling to consciousness. Barely.

Over his shoulder, I caught Archie staring at me hungrily. Honestly, it didn't matter how shaky my arms and legs were or how much trembling held my system in its grasp, the heavy coil of desire began to stir in my belly again. Jake lifted his head and blocked my view. His expression was adoring and my heart thudded strongly in answer. Cradling his face, I brushed my lips against his. "Love you," I answered his earlier whisper and he smiled against my lips.

"Hmm…so much," he responded, and I grinned as he deepened the kiss for a beat. "But I have a feeling Archie's about to beat my ass if I don't move."

Archie snorted. "Trust me when I say it's not your ass I'm interested in."

I laughed as Jake rolled over and the breeze cooled some of the perspiration on my skin. I was hot, sticky, and when I sat up, cum trickled out onto my thighs and I really didn't care. Sex was messy as hell. Instead of being embarrassed or worried about it, I scooted toward the end of the bed. I made it to Archie before he could get out of the chair.

"You doing alright, Ian?" I asked as I braced my hands on the arms of Archie's chair.

"I'm fine, Angel. Are you enjoying yourself?"

"Very much." Tilting my head, I reached down to nudge Archie's hand off his dick. "Mine."

"Oh really?" he murmured.

"Yes," I confirmed, wrapping my hand around his dick and giving him a gentle, if firm, squeeze and he hissed out a breath. The silken skin of his dick was hot and the first pump seemed to make him swell even more, or maybe that was just wishful thinking. "Mine. And I plan on riding that dick until you come inside of me. I want to feel you, Standish. Hard and deep."

His grin was wild. "I fucking love when you talk dirty to me."

Easing forward on my knees, I bracketed his thighs and stroked him until I sank down on him. Archie was nothing, if not inventive. At the first brush of his cock against my pussy, he clamped his hands down on my hips and thrust upward. It didn't matter that I intended to ride him, he took over and began to pump into me hard and deep.

Fuck, he knew just how to rotate his hips to add just a bit of a twist. "You're cheating," I groaned and he snorted.

"All's fair in love, war, and fucking." Archie winked at me before he sucked one of my nipples against his teeth and I let go of the chair to hang onto him. There was something wild about every stroke of him pushing in against my overheated and sensitized flesh. At the same time, that wildness comforted me.

He chased our orgasms like a man on a mission and I clung to him, clamping down and squeezing at every opportunity. The relentless pace set off sparks in my system and I didn't try to fight it. Head back, I gripped his hair as the cries escaped me with his every push. Cries that became screams and laughter and maybe even a little bit of tears as he shoved me right past that edge.

This time, when I exploded and the world went white, I didn't worry about falling apart. Archie would catch me. He would fix it. They all would. Every missing part of me was right in this room. We fit together. All of us. When I opened my eyes next, my head was tucked against Archie's shoulder and he nuzzled a kiss against my hair.

"That's one for me," he murmured.

"Player Three is back in the game," Coop announced with a grin and even boneless, I could grin.

Player Three was *always* in this game.

Chapter Eighteen

MOURNING HAS BROKEN

Frankie

No idea what woke me, but Coop and Jake were both sound asleep on either side of me. It took a little effort to ease out from between them. Ian had ended up on the outside of the bed. The steady rise and fall of his chest told me that despite the growing light in the portholes, he was out. I yawned as I made my way to the bathroom. Waking before Jake and Ian took actual effort most days. Not Coop, between us we could sleep until noon if no one needed us.

After peeing, I washed my hands, then my face and brushed my teeth. Significantly more awake, I ran a comb through my hair but didn't worry about the wild waves and curls. The ocean air and sun had done wonders for my tan and it had also bleached out my hair more, but taming it with this kind of humidity was impossible.

Padding back into the cabin, I scanned around for Archie. He wasn't in the bed or sleeping in one of the hammocks that hung from the walls. Those things cracked me up. He and Jake liked them, but I preferred the bed. The swaying was weird enough, even if I had gotten used to it. The hammocks just made the rocking worse.

Smothering a yawn, I dug around for some clean clothes. A bikini top and shorts would have to do because we'd gone through most of our stuff. The guys didn't even budge, Coop had his face smushed into the pillow I'd been using. Grinning, I snuck a couple of pictures of him and Jake together— they almost looked like they were cuddling.

Mine.

Saving them into a private file on my phone, I snuck out of the room. The scent of coffee pulled me like a siren to the galley. The yacht's crew included a chef. He prepped most of the meals and made sure there was fresh coffee every morning. Ned was my favorite member of the crew. I filled a big tumbler with my coffee and then carried it with me up onto deck when I didn't find Archie below.

The sunrise was still showing off in spectacular fashion. The extraordinary colors were one of the main reasons I didn't object to being up this early. That, and the man leaning against the rail staring out at the water. On light feet, I moved over to join him. While the breeze was cool with the yacht moving at a good clip, the deck itself was warm and the rapidly rising sun would heat up the day.

Sliding up next to him, I bumped his hip and Archie turned, a smile already lighting his face as he wrapped an arm around me and tugged me close. His long-sleeved shirt wasn't buttoned and flapped a little, but I leaned into him easily. The brush of his lips against my forehead made me smile and I turned my face up and accepted the second, almost gentler, kiss he pressed to my lips.

"Good morning," he murmured.

"Morning." I took a sip of my coffee and then offered him a drink, considering he wasn't holding anything. The deep brown of his eyes softened as he closed his hand over mine and then lifted the tumbler to take a sip.

"Now I know you love me," he said in a voice still rough from sleep.

"You didn't know before?" I took a drink of my coffee and grinned because he didn't let it or me go.

"Oh, I knew it before, Babe. Trust me, I knew it before." The affection in his expression made my heart squeeze. "But you, letting me share your first coffee? That's like next level right there."

Chuckling, I rose up on my tip toes and kissed him again. This time a proper kiss, one where the flavors of coffee, minty clean, and Archie all mixed at once. He smiled against my lips, then thrust his tongue against mine, teasing and testing. The slow, deep exploration had my toes curling and sighing as I sucked on his tongue almost lazily. This was the best part of this trip. These moments, sweet, steamy, and most of all, safe.

"Better," he said as we broke from the kiss, and he took another sip of my coffee before offering it to me. "Much better."

Eyes half-closed, I rested my head against his shoulder and then looked out over the view. We'd be back in Florida soon, I supposed. "This afternoon?"

"Unfortunately." The reluctance in his voice seemed to mirror my own feelings on this. "Then we'll get you and Bubba on your way to California."

My stomach bottomed out. California. The other side of the country. Weirdly, the state I'd been born in but had zero recollection of. I'd grown up in Texas, far from Maddy's East Coast background and ties. I took a drink of the coffee to try and steady the sudden influx of nerves.

"Hey," he said, giving me a squeeze. "What's wrong?"

I shook my head. "I don't know. I mean I do, but it's not something wrong exactly."

"Okay, so tell me what it is. Maybe I can help."

I smiled up at him. "You always help." The day brightened around us and neither of us had sunglasses. The wind kept whipping my hair up and across my face, so I tucked one errant lock behind an ear. "You help just by being you."

"Well, now that we've established how fabulous I am—tell me what you were just thinking. Let me in, Babe. I promise, I won't judge."

"Even if it was a sex thing?" I don't even know what prompted me to say that, maybe I just needed a little levity.

"Not even if it's a sex thing. If you think I need pointers or improvement, I'll totally take that under advisement."

A laugh-snort burst out of me, and I clapped a hand over my mouth at the inelegant sound. The corners of his eyes crinkled as his grin grew wider.

"That tells me it's totally *not* a sex thing."

Rolling my eyes, I blew out a breath and my own smile faded. "I'm scared."

"Of what?"

"Of—going away. Of being so far away. Of screwing this up for Ian." I wasn't looking at him anymore, I stared out over the water. "That summer without you guys sucked. I hated it. I was miserable the whole time and this might be months longer than that." Worse… "What if I really can't do this thing? What if we get there and I sound terrible or they want something different or if…"

"Hey," Archie said softly and touched my jaw with gentle fingers to get me to look at him. "This is not that summer. Not even close. I promise you—none of us are going to start dating some other chicks cause you're in California with Bubba for months."

Shock rippled through me. "That never even occurred to me."

"Good." He was so damn firm, that I worried I'd insulted him.

"Archie…"

"Nope, Babe. That's not a problem, but when you're nervous—or scared—knowing some absolutes can help. So, the number one absolute is it doesn't matter if you're in California, New York, France, or Taiwan, we're together and no geography is going to change that."

Admittedly—that helped.

"Two—you can do this thing. I've heard you sing, I've *seen* you do it with Bubba, and I know you've got it in you. But if you don't *want* to, that's different. You need to tell us, tell Bubba, and let us figure everything out together."

"I want to," I admitted without hesitation. "I mean—I wanted it for Ian and then I wanted to just be a help and not a hindrance. But I do want it—for me, I mean, for us. I love singing with him and I love singing what he writes."

"Good." He nodded. "Three—I don't care what the label or the producers want. You stay true to you. Trust those instincts and that heart." He stroked his thumb along my jaw. "Trust Bubba. He won't let anyone do a damn thing that makes you uncomfortable, and I guarantee you, he's not going to let anyone put you in a spot you don't want to be in."

Love flooded my chest, chasing away the butterflies and the sinking feeling of unease. "You mean that."

"Yes, I do." Cupping my face in his hands, he straightened as he held my gaze. "Frankie, I trust you. I trust him. I trust you both to look after each other. If he wasn't going with you or you weren't going with him, this might be different. But this isn't an end, it's just another chapter. I can't *wait* to hear the stories you tell and the songs you record. You do know that I'm going to be your number one fan, right?"

I laughed. "Fans—that's so weird."

"Get used to it, Babe. You're the whole package. Killer body, gorgeous smile, fantastic voice, and a heart that never quits. Jake's gonna get a hell of a workout keeping the guys off you."

Right. I snorted. "And you're not going to let it bother you?"

His grin was slow, almost feral, but definitely devious. "Hell no. I'll just double your security at all events."

Laughter exploded out of me, because that really was the last thing I'd expected him to say. But it shouldn't have been. Not at all. Not when he was Archie. Of course he'd just hire security. "What am I going to do with you?"

"Keep me forever," he said, then looped his arms around my waist. "Deal?"

"Definitely."

"You feel better?" He studied me, still smiling.

"I do."

"Okay, good, then I can keep my ace in my back pocket."

"Your ace?" Now I was curious, and almost out of coffee.

"Now, I don't need to take it out of my pocket—so the ace in the hole is still mine." All I did was raise my eyebrows and Archie made a grunt of submission and mock sighed. "Well, if you're just going to beat it out of me…"

I snorted, but he just grinned.

"Do I need to remind you that I own a plane?"

I opened my mouth and then snapped it closed again. No, he didn't need to remind me.

"Actually, we own three planes, so even if mine is busy—pretty sure I can get out there as fast as you need to see me or…" He elongated that single syllable. "I can send it to get you the moment you need it, even if you just come home for twenty-four hours or four hours. We got this—*you've* got this."

"Now, I'm feeling a bit pathetic."

"Nah, Babe, don't. Did I make you feel better?"

"Yes."

"Then mission," he murmured, closing the distance before he kissed me lightly, "accomplished."

"One last concern?"

At my question, he glanced down at my cup and then tugged it from my fingers and pointed at the lounger. "Absolutely, let me get us more coffee."

I nuzzled a kiss to his jaw and then settled on the lounger to wait. He wasn't long. When he re-emerged he had my sunglasses with him, along with the coffee. I scooted forward at his approach as soon as he handed me my sunglasses and coffee, he climbed onto the lounger behind me.

Sunglasses on, I leaned back against him and cradled my coffee.

"There we go," he said, pressing a kiss to the top of my head. "Hit me, Babe. What can I fix for you now?"

"Weird question," I said slowly, turning the tumbler in my hand.

"It's about Edward."

"Yes."

"You can ask, Babe. Edward and I are in a semi-decent place at the moment. Ask me, I may know the answer. I might not. But if I had to ask him to get you the info, he'd tell me. He likes you better anyway." Despite the lightness of how he said that, I twisted to glare at him. "Easy, Babe, I promise. I was just kidding but sarcasm and Edward go hand in hand."

"Uh huh. I get that he was a dick to you for a long time, but he knows it too. Now. He chose you." It came out way more blunt than I'd intended. "He didn't kill Maddy for me. He killed her to protect you."

"To protect us," Archie corrected. "And I know that. I was there. Remember?"

I sighed. Archie didn't deserve me snapping at him. "Sorry, I'm not trying to be a bitch."

"You're not being a bitch at all. We just haven't talked about this."

I sighed and then twisted so I could sit sideways and see him. "I know we haven't. I don't even know what to say or where to begin. Everything about Maddy is this—knot of confusion and snarl of anxiety. There's relief. There's anger. There's hate. There's sadness. Most of the time—I feel nothing."

He caught one of the strands of my hair whipping out and pushed it back. I probably should have put it up in a pony tail. I was going to have so many damn knots. I knocked back more of the coffee, mostly for courage and to gather my thoughts.

"I hate this for you," he said quietly. "I hate it more than anything."

"I hate it for you, too," I admitted. "I hate that she blamed you for so much."

"Fuck her," he said with a shrug. "To hell with what she thought or did. She was right about one thing…"

I frowned.

"I would have gotten between the two of you for the rest of our lives. I would never have let her get near you again." His fierceness seemed to echo my own.

"And I refused to let her try and hurt you again."

"I know." This time he scowled. "It still gives me nightmares."

"Archie…"

"We'll get through this, you and me. You're allowed to feel how you feel. No one gets to tell you what is the right way or the wrong way to mourn. She might have been a bitch on wheels, but Edward is still grieving her too." He shook his head. "I want to ask him how he can and then it hits me—he loved her. Loved her more than I thought him capable of. He loved her like I love you."

Tears burned in my eyes.

"I'd never get over losing you. For all the epic shit he's pulled over the years, neglectful isn't downright evil."

No, Maddy cornered that market.

"Or malicious." He sighed. "So, we talk and I reach out now because… he saved you. He saved me." A faint smile touched his lips. "I still think he likes you better, but I won't fault him for that."

I snorted. "Archie…"

"I get it," he said without me finishing. "You're worried about the two of us. I promise—I'll keep talking to him. Weirdly, he's almost a likable jackass these days."

Extending my hand, I cupped his cheek and he took my hand and pressed a kiss to my palm.

"I'm okay, Frankie. As messed up as it sounds—this month helped a lot. Helped me paint over the cracks and the questions. I told you once, we're not them. We'll never be them. Believe me? Trust me?"

"Always." I wanted that. I wanted us to be more. "I love you Archibald Standish the Third."

He chuckled. "God that's a long fucking name and I love Grandpa Ted, but damn…I love you too, Francesca Curtis."

We both made a face. "No more full names," I suggested.

"Deal. Save that for when I'm in trouble and I have to talk you into bed and me out of trouble."

As amusing as the sentiment was, it was also the damn truth. "You're incorrigible."

"And you love me just the way I am."

Yes, yes I did. "So," I said, "Last day—how do you want to spend it?"

"Right here," he said. "With you."

Chapter Nineteen
CALIFORNICATION

Frankie

The flight from LaGuardia to LAX took almost six hours, but Ian and I had first class seats and watched a movie in and around his playing with lyrics. Our flight had left mid-morning, just fifteen hours after we'd made it back to New York. It had been a whirlwind in and out of the brownstone. Jeremy took over the laundry, even though I was helping. Ian and I repacked clean clothes, our guitars—yes I was taking mine—and the brand new laptops that Archie had waiting for us.

When I would have protested, he just smiled indulgently and waited for me to yell at him. Impossible man. So instead of arguing, I just kissed him soundly and asked him if he'd already copied over my backup drive. His delight and surprise rendered him speechless. Score a point for me, a fact I shouted out and had the rest of the guys laughing.

Jeremy tucked a couple of notes into my carry-on bag. Suggestions and contacts, he told me. If we ran into something we needed help on, he had friends out there, and I'd kissed his cheek. Then I made a huge fuss of my cats before we headed to the airport. Rachel was gone for the weekend and wouldn't make it back before we had to leave.

I texted her and we promised to talk soon and catch up. She also promised to look after the boys and Jeremy for me. I promised her hot girl pics from the California beaches. She conceded I was allowed to send her hot boy pics too, just in case I needed the excuse. God, I loved her.

Saying goodbye had been impossible, so I just refused. I hugged and kissed them before squaring my shoulders and heading through security. Glancing back once, I saw all three of them watching me as my phone buzzed three times in quick succession. They'd each messaged me a picture of me kissing one of them.

Laughter chased away some of the melancholy and Coop blew me a kiss before yelling out "Love you, Frankie!" My face went damn scarlet as half of security and the people in it seemed to stare at me for a second. Right.

I scampered away with Ian, who chuckled. Once on the flight, missing them tried to hit again, but I focused on sending them funny messages. Then Ian and I played with all the comfort features, besides the fact we were in these super comfortable seats. Since the west coast was a different time zone, our flight might take almost six hours, but we landed only three hours later on our watches.

Yeah, better not to focus on that. Staring out the window as we came in to land, it all hit me. "Ian," I said in a soft voice. "We're really doing this."

He stroked his thumb over the side of my hand. "Yes, we are. Feeling better?"

The earlier sadness had quieted. "I think it's gonna be weird for a while," I told him, but leaning my head against the seat and facing him, I smiled. "Thank you for looking after me."

"Like you have to thank me for that, Angel. I'm gonna miss them, too. I don't know how I'm going to get through a day without at least one argument with them."

His dry tone pulled a real smile from me and I chuckled. "I'm sure they're going to be harassing you."

"Oh, they are," he promised. "I am required to provide daily Frankie status reports."

"Well, I guess that seems fair since Rachel promised to keep me up to date on them."

"Exactly." He leaned in and brushed a kiss over my lips. "Thank you for doing this with me."

I pressed my lips to his and just held there as the plane touched down. "Here we go," I whispered.

All at once, my nerves were back but Ian's quiet steadiness helped. Well, that and the fact he grinned every single time our gazes met. He passed me my backpack and helped me into it, before grabbing his own out of the overhead. Next came our guitar cases. Then we were off the plane and headed through the airport for baggage claim.

"You know," I said. "Even if they lose our luggage, we can always busk for money…"

Ian snorted. LAX was like controlled chaos. So many people. Ian's hand was firm on mine and anytime it looked like someone would cut into me he just angled himself and his guitar case. It was like having my own private blocker.

The hike to get to the baggage carousel let me stretch my legs. We'd booked a suite at a hotel. The name was in my phone, I'd check it once we were ready to get a car. Renting a car at the ripe old age of twenty was apparently not that easy. Most of the places required us to be twenty-one. Whatever.

Ian left me in charge of his guitar case as he collected the luggage off the carousel. We had enough that I also snagged a trolley for us. I fired off texts to the guys that we'd landed and were going to be heading to the hotel soon. Jeremy had also arranged for a car service should we need it while in Los Angeles. More secure than rideshare and more convenient than taxis. Once Ian had our bags loaded, we headed out to find our ride.

The driver held up a sign that read RHYS/CURTIS and beneath it BOUND HEARTS. I chuckled. Ian glanced down at me. "I thought Jeremy arranged the car service."

"Pretty sure that's Jeremy too," I pointed out. "Archie isn't the only sly one in the house. I'd wager Jeremy is a great deal more sly than we give him credit for."

"No way am I taking that bet," Ian told me. "Nothing gets past that man."

Which fit for the guy who essentially raised Archie. He'd have to be clever as hell to keep up. The driver shook Ian's hand as we introduced ourselves and he nodded to the luggage. "I can take that for you if you like."

"We're good," Ian said. "Just lead the way."

The man gave us a nod and led us out to where the car was waiting. It was a nice limo, comfortable, but not huge. The fact I had any kind of room for comparison just made me laugh. The drive from LAX to the hotel easily took an hour or more, but our driver entertained us with great stories about the area.

The limo pulled smoothly into the loop in front of the hotel and our driver slid out of the car to circle around and opened my door. Ian waited for me to slide out before he followed. We'd taken our backpacks in with us and he lifted them out. Before he could hand me mine, a deep-blue hued menace crashed into me with a squeal, and I barely managed to keep us from toppling over.

"You're here!" KC's familiar voice made me laugh and then I returned her hug. Over her shoulder I caught sight of Aubrey and Yvette, the girls made faces, but as soon as KC quit squeezing all the air out of me, I got quick hugs from them too. "Hey Ian!" She said and blew him a kiss before she looked at me. "You are so here!!!"

The enthusiasm was contagious. Grinning and shaking my head, I said, "Yes, we're here, what are you doing here?"

"To see you two, your last email sounded freaked out."

"I am not freaked out, I'm fine."

"Freaked out, insecure, neurotic, and emotional?" KC countered, her eyes practically dancing with excitement. "We totally get it. Been there…"

"…done that," Yvette said and Aubrey added, "Trust us, we have all the t-shirts."

"And rehab bills." KC's smirk was adorable. "So, first things first, we're old hats at this business and I needed a break from the East Coast, so we're staying at my mom's place in Beverly Hills. They aren't there right now so it's even better." She glanced past me to the driver. "Car service or full time hire for the visit?"

"Car service," I answered and KC nodded. "Fantastic. I got this." Then she gave me another swift squeeze before she hurried over to our driver. I glanced at Ian in question.

"Don't try to resist," Aubrey suggested. "She needs this too." Yvette was already following KC and Ian gave a shrug.

"I don't mind, Angel. I just don't want us to intrude."

Me neither.

"You're not," Aubrey promised. "Her mom's place is huge. You'll have plenty of privacy too. We promise."

That wasn't actually what worried me, but I frowned as KC gave our driver information and he started reloading the bags. "Is she okay?"

"She will be." Well, if that wasn't the vaguest answer ever.

"Okay!" KC returned, a little breathless and flushed. "Paul is going to bring your luggage out to our place. You're riding with us. Our car is on the other side of the building." She was like a hurricane of nervous energy and vibrant affection. Ian handed me my backpack and I slid it on. He picked up our guitars. "This is going to be great. Do you guys want help with those?"

"I got it," Ian assured her.

"Great."

"Thank you, Paul," I said to the driver and he nodded before he climbed back in the car. He and the luggage were already leaving us before we'd gone inside the hotel to cross it to the other side. "We should probably cancel our reservations." And we'd need to let the guys know.

"Not a problem," KC said. "We can call them from the car. Are you tired? Hungry? Want us to stop somewhere and grab food? We really need to take you out to Mackie's."

"Later," Yvette said, her French accent lifting the word. "Let's not overwhelm them."

KC made a face then stopped abruptly to pivot and face me. I blinked at the intensity in her gaze. "I'm not overwhelming you guys, am I? I mean, I know this is a surprise—so like hey, surprise! But I thought it would be easier if you had a quiet place to retreat. Recording a first album is both exciting and nightmarish and we've been there and well—I mean—if you wanted to stay here?"

Ian and I exchanged one look and he just nodded before I glanced back at KC. "You're not overwhelming us, and this is a fantastic surprise. It really is." And I wasn't lying. I hadn't seen her in months. We emailed regularly and texted now and then, but the last three months had been…

"Good." Relief filled her eyes. "I felt so bad we couldn't make it to the funeral and I haven't stopped thinking about you. And I really want to do this for you."

It would have been impossible to say no after that. "You don't *have* to do anything. But I really appreciate that you want to."

"Same," Ian added. "Friends are always welcome."

"Wonderful!" KC clapped her hands. "Let's go."

I didn't miss the thankful looks Aubrey and Yvette threw my way. Whatever was going on with KC, I would try to do what I could to help. She may not want to talk about it in front of Ian, and that made sense.

It didn't take long to get us to their limo—it was easily a third bigger than our own. The driver wasn't that much older than us, at least I didn't think so, and his grin at the girls kind of made my skin crawl. Ian must have noticed the same thing because he blocked his view of me almost immediately. Once we were inside though, the privacy screen was up and Yvette passed drinks to all of us.

"Okay," KC said as she flopped back in the seat next to me. "Tell me everything about your schedule."

"Kait," Aubrey said with a sigh. "Maybe let them decompress."

Making a face, KC popped open her soda and shook her head. "You know how I am."

"Exactly," Yvette agreed. "So, we shall remind you that not everyone is prepared for your bouncing cyclonic energy. Especially when it's still early in the day." She'd slipped her sunglasses on and leaned back in the seat.

"It's after twelve," I pointed out. In fact, it was almost two.

"Exactly," Yvette continued with an airy wave. "Business can wait until five at least. Then we can have drinks and lubricate the discussion."

The girls all cracked up and I shook my head. This was their world, Ian and I were just the visitors. Still, the drive took over an hour and then some, to make it to Beverly Hills. Despite all the freeways, traffic made the journey a challenge and, I for one, was actually glad we didn't have to drive in it.

"Oh," KC said as we pulled up to what was easily the largest house I'd ever seen, and that was saying something. It was—*huge*. There was a colonnade along the front, the white columns soaring up and giving it an almost Greek temple-like feel in addition to the water feature fountain that was spraying in front. A pair of double doors were already opening as the car came to a stop. "Dix—he's our driver can take you anywhere you need to go, or you can arrange for your own service here."

A woman stepped out onto the porch and I shit you not, she was wearing a black dress with a white apron and sturdy shoes. Her steel gray hair was pulled back into a proper bun.

"That's Davina," KC said. "She's a doll."

A doll.

The severe expression on that woman's face didn't say doll to me. But the moment Dix opened the door to let us out, Davina's expression transformed to something far brighter. Relief nipped at me, as Ian and I let the girls get out first and then I glanced at him.

"Toto, I don't think we're in Kansas anymore."

He chuckled. "No, we're not—deep breaths. At least we like them."

That was very true.

We were definitely *not* in Kansas, Texas, or New York. California was a whole new adventure.

New chapter, that was what Archie called it. A new chapter for us and I followed the girls with a little more enthusiasm. I already had so much to tell the guys, it wasn't funny.

Chapter Twenty

YOU CAN'T MAKE OLD FRIENDS

Coop

Leaving Frankie at the airport was a hell of a lot tougher than I expected. I held it together as she and Bubba disappeared on the other side of security. Watching them leave was so strange. Parts of me wanted to shout "wait" then grab my shit and go with them. That wasn't the plan though.

So much of this hadn't been the plan. Long distance was not what we wanted. Right now though, it may be what she needed. Next to me, Arch and Jake wore damn near matching expressions.

"This is gonna suck," Jake said in a low voice.

"Yeah," I echoed, looking at Archie and he shook his head.

"But we're not gonna be little bitches about this." The announcement really didn't need to be said aloud, then again, maybe it did.

"Nope," I said with a great deal more conviction than I was feeling at the time. "This is going to be awesome for them."

"It better be," Jake said. "I don't mind going out there to crack heads if I have to."

I leaned around Archie to stare at him. "Man, you really do need to work on that anger management." I was only teasing him a little.

Instead of being offended though, Jake just cracked his knuckles. "Just big facts, brother, big facts."

"Agreed." Clapping us both on the shoulders, Archie said, "Okay, let's get the hell out of here before I go buy a ticket and join them."

Noted. We'd keep each other sane. And the first step to that was *not* buying tickets to follow them. "It's nice to know we could go after them though, right?"

"Yes," they said in damn near identical, if fervent, tones. Thank fuck these two idiots had gotten their shit together. The drive back to Manhattan was quiet, save for the music. Frankie texted our group chat to keep us in the loop from boarding, to the movie she and Bubba watched, to the meal they ate.

Back at the house, a kind of pall settled over everything. Archie and Jake headed off to their rooms and I headed up to Frankie's. In some ways, I was lucky. It hadn't even occurred to me when I offered Rachel my room that it would probably be better for her to have Bubba's since he would be gone as well. Then again, having her in my room gave me the excuse to soak up the comfort of being in Frankie's room where it smelled like her.

I crashed out there half-asleep when Frankie let us know about the change in plans from the hotel to staying with KC in Beverly Hills. It kind of made me laugh, if you'd told Frankie a few years ago that not only would she have met Torched, but become friends with them, she'd have flipped you off. Hell, she might yet flip me off and tell me to get the fuck out of here.

That said, I didn't hesitate to send her a message that read *Don't fangirl too hard.*

Sure enough, the middle finger emoji was her response.

As much as I missed her, I slept all right. A sound woke me in the middle of the night and I lifted my head to stare at Jake as he walked in and collapsed on the other side of the bed.

"Fuck off," was his only comment and he burrowed against the pillows. I grinned and went back to sleep and only woke when I caught Archie stealing a pillow from the bed.

A laugh escaped me, and he hit me with the pillow once before wandering back out. Man, we had it so damn bad. Rolling over on my side, I hugged her pillow to me. I'd made sure to keep her favorite in arm's reach. I might have to hide it later.

The next couple of days, I spent working out the applications and paperwork for my new volunteer gig at the college's mental health center, and another one for the local community center where I could work with children's playgroups. One of my professors actually spent time volunteering there as a psychologist for the kids, and offered it as a suggestion for a good learning experience.

Not only did I relish the work, I needed something to fill the hours to keep them from being empty. The background checks required for both would take about a week, but I was all right with that. I had plans for the rest of this week anyway. A savory scent greeted me when I got home. While I hadn't been hungry before I opened the door, my mouth watered and my stomach rumbled.

I inputted the security code before making my way through to the back of the house. The last thing I expected to see was Archie and Jake standing there, sweating in their workout clothes and both staring in the kitchen with the most bemused looks on their faces. Glancing past them, I blinked.

Not only was Rachel in the kitchen, she was working at the stove in bare feet and dressed in shorts with her hair pulled back into a ponytail. "I'm telling you, J," she said. "The tenderloin you made was amazing, but it can be better. This was actually my grandmother's recipe and there were actual fights over the table for who got the last piece."

"Indeed," Jeremy responded in the driest of tones. "There will be no battles in this household for who gets to try the dish." On the last, he glanced at us and I had to hide a smile because Archie actually looked torn between offense and shock still. "Boys."

Rachel shot us a look. "Hey guys."

"Hey," I said, easing around TweedleDee and TweedleShocked. "How's it going?" In the kitchen, I went to the fridge and cracked it open to get a drink. A huge pitcher of iced tea waited and I pulled it out.

"Not bad," she said, but neither Archie nor Jake had moved yet. "Did they forget who has custody of their shared brain cell?" With tongs, she expertly turned the bound meat over in the pan. The smell was even better here.

After pouring myself a glass, I said, "Probably flummoxed that you've already earned stove privileges. Jeremy doesn't just let anyone cook." That was putting it diplomatically.

"Miss Rachel is quite capable," Jeremy pointed out. "Though we have a disagreement on how tenderloin is to be prepared."

"Not a disagreement," Rachel countered. "Not at all. I just happen to have some expertise in this area."

I wasn't touching that with a ten-foot pole. "Tea?"

"Thanks," she said, and I got her a glass and poured her some.

Before I could ask if the guys wanted any, Jeremy fixed them both with a look. "The food does smell good, but it would smell better if a pair of someones would shower off the smell of grunge and teenage funk."

Hiding a grin, I returned the pitcher to the refrigerator. When I popped back out, Archie and Jake had taken off and I chuckled to myself. Leaning back against the counter, I watched as she mashed up garlic into butter, all the while keeping an eye on the meat in the big pan.

"How long until that is ready for sampling and are we going to be allowed to eat it?" Because if not, I needed to eat something now. Maybe Rachel hadn't been kidding about fights over the cut of meat with her family,

I wasn't. I might actually stab the guys if I didn't get a taste.

"About another forty minutes or so," Rachel said. "But I haven't made any sides with it."

I was about to say I didn't need sides, I could just sit down with one of the tenderloin roasts. Jeremy, on the other hand, cleared his throat so I kept that comment to myself. "Once you place it in the oven, I can take care of the side dishes. There's also a torte for dessert."

"You're going to break Frankie's heart if you made her favorite while she was gone," I scolded Jeremy in jest, and his expression made me want to take the words back immediately.

"Mr. Cooper, I would never," he informed me in a stern fashion. Right. He wouldn't.

"Sorry, Jeremy."

He nodded once, accepting the apology. Rachel maneuvered with a kind of smooth expertise as she plucked the browned tenderloins from the pan and set them in a huge roasting dish, before shutting the heat off under the pan. Then she spread the garlic and butter spread all over them. With care, she opened the oven and set the meat inside and then set the time before she went to get the pan.

"Miss Rachel," Jeremy said firmly and she scowled.

"I can clean one pan."

"Be that as it may, you will *not* in my kitchen."

The stare down was fascinating in the way they seemed to measure each other up. Who would back off first? My money was on Jeremy winning. Rachel was badass, but Jeremy was cultured, trained, and an experienced badass. Also, he won against Archie more often than not, and that just said he had everything he needed to handle her.

"Fine," she said with a sigh. She surrendered the pot and carried her iced tea out to the dining room as Jeremy swept into the kitchen. That was my cue to get out of Dodge. "Thank you for letting me do the prep work myself. I remembered how to do it, but it's more about measuring by eye than it is by any recipe."

"Understood, but I think I have the whole of it. We shall test your results and then I'll help you write down the specific measurements you used."

"Sounds like a plan to me."

Man, it was like being in the Twilight Zone. Still, cool, and Frankie would be happy that Rachel was happy. "I'm heading upstairs. I've got some work to do," I told them. "Give me a shout when dinner is ready?"

"Return downstairs in forty-five minutes," Jeremy instructed, "And there will be no need to shout."

"Yes, sir."

It wasn't until I was almost to Frankie's room that I realized Rachel was following me. "What's up?" The door was open and Tiddles and Tory were dead to the world in the middle of Frankie's bed, sprawled in the sun coming in the windows.

"Nothing, just thought I'd catch up," she said, not coming all the way in but instead hovering in the doorway. "I guess that was weird."

Setting my drink on the desk, I flipped open the laptop to turn it on. "What? You cooking with Jeremy?"

"Yeah, I got the impression Rich Boy and Dickhead didn't like it."

I shrugged. "Archie's banned from touching the stove and Jake can cook, but he'd rather let anyone else do it." Kind of like me, though I could come through in a pinch. "Frankie's the only other person we've seen Jeremy literally *not* complain about touching the kitchen appliances."

Arms folded, Rachel studied me. I pulled out the chair and then waved her into the room.

"I don't bite," I reminded her. "And I wasn't kidding about having work…but I can do it and talk at the same time." Besides, if she was following me, she may actually want to talk and I didn't want to shut her down.

"Does he let her do dishes?" Rachel asked, wandering in the room.

"Nope," I said. "Though she's been known to just do them anyway, while he scolds her. I think they both enjoy it, so make of that what you will."

"Don't tell Rich Boy, it's taken me three weeks to convince Jeremy I wouldn't blow up his stove. I couldn't figure out why he thought that was even possible. Now I get it."

I laughed. "He didn't blow it up—exactly." Still better to not discuss it. I typed in the name of the tattoo and piercing shop Jake and I had gone to.

"Well, hopefully he lets me do a little more after the tenderloin comes out delicious. It's weird, I didn't realize how much I missed cooking until now. The dorm room has a kitchenette but it's really not the same thing at all."

Wandering slowly around the room, she seemed to be looking everywhere but at me. I let her have her space and then clicked over to piercings. I needed to confirm my appointment and with it coming up, I really needed to settle on what I wanted. They said five to six weeks for healing, so the window of time was perfect.

"You guys have a good June in the Caribbean? I saw some of the pictures. Looked fun."

"It was great," I said. "Did Frankie tell you she punched some asshole in the nose who tried to get frisky with her?"

"She mentioned there was an incident." Rachel paused. "Did she really pop the guy?"

"Oh yeah," I said, pride fisting in my chest. "It was fucking fantastic. Didn't need any rescue at all, not that Jake didn't get a couple of hits in himself."

"Because of course he did," Rachel said with a laugh and shook her head. "I like it. Good for her."

The quiet extended as I clicked back and forth between two piercings. Rachel moved over to the window and finally sat down on the window seat.

"How is she?" Real concern colored her voice. "I mean really."

"She's alright," I said, lifting my gaze to meet hers. "Promise. She's still working through things, but she's getting there and she's eating again."

After the night she punched that guy, she'd shown more appetite. While she wasn't back up to her normal levels of devouring everything not nailed down, she did seem to be way more interested in food.

Exhaling a slow breath, Rachel nodded. "I've been worried."

"We all have been," I told her. "But she needs time and support. We're all doing that, and she'll be alright." I was a hell of a lot more comfortable with her being so far away now than I had been at the beginning of summer. "How about you? How are you doing?"

"Me?" She seemed surprised.

"Yes," I said, making a face. "You."

She shrugged. "I'm fine. Just—figuring shit out. I took a summer course just to have something to do. I'm glad I did and wished I hadn't at the same time."

"I get that." And I did.

"Glad you do." Pushing up from the window seat, she went back to pacing. The air practically crackled with everything she wasn't saying. I wrestled with whether to ask or to wait. Ultimately, Rachel wasn't one you pushed. She needed to reach out on her own. All I could do was be available, so I went back to studying the piercings.

"You're really going to do it?" she asked from just behind me.

"Yep," I said. "Don't tell Frankie, it's a surprise for her."

"Dude," Rachel said. "You have my word."

"Just trying to decide what I want," I admitted. There were different values to the different piercings. Some were more for my pleasure while others were more for Frankie. The ones I really wanted would be for Frankie. Then again, I also didn't want to add so much metal to my dick that it might fall off.

"Want some advice?" Rachel offered after a long moment, and I turned around in the chair to stare at her. On the one hand, this was Rachel, she probably had some idea of what she was talking about. On the other hand, this was my dick and I didn't generally discuss that with just anyone.

"You know what," I said after a minute. "Why the hell not? What do you think? I want something more for Frankie than me."

"Then you want that one," Rachel said pointing to the upper left-hand corner on the screen.

"Do I want to know how you know that?" Cause I was leaning heavily toward no.

"Nope," she said, confirming it for me. "But if you want company, I'll tag along and be moral support."

Snorting, I studied the piercing. "I might need more than moral support before they're done."

"Don't worry," she commented, squeezing my shoulder. "You can take it."

She was almost to the door when I said, "That sounded like a compliment, Manning."

"Ask me no questions," she called as she began to descend the stairs. "And I'll tell you no lies."

Scratching my jaw, I kept chuckling after she vanished and then studied the piercing again. Simple, but elegant, I guessed. I glanced down at my dick, even happier that I'd snuck Not So Little Coop into Frankie's suitcase. Mine was definitely *not* going to like me for a while.

"But it'll be worth it, buddy, trust me."

Nothing Says Love Like Metal

Coop

"**Y**ou good?" Rachel asked as I paced back and forth on the sidewalk outside the shop. It was hot as fuck out here, but I'd rather wait where I was boiling, than sit inside listening. Once I got in there and he got started, this was gonna be it.

"Yes." I nodded. Then paused to glance at her. "Also, no."

"Thanks for clearing that up." She leaned against the side of the building, arms folded, and wearing sunglasses that hid her eyes. "You don't *have* to do it."

"I know." And I did. I absolutely knew that. No one was making me. Especially not Frankie, who'd only expressed an interest. Not So Little Coop made her pretty fucking happy though. More than happy. She'd delighted in it. "Let's be honest, of the four of us, I'm the only one likely to go through with it."

"Eh, Rich Boy might if she persuaded him. Not sure about Bubba or Jake, but you're a fucking prince for wanting to do this for her. Just don't do it only for her."

That was odd advice. Good, but odd. I paced a few steps away, took in a few deep, lungfuls of air, before I faced her again. "Explain."

"Body piercing, any body modification or mortification as the case may be, should reflect the person doing it. You have to want it, and want it for more than someone else, so that the pain is worth it." She grimaced. "I might be saying this badly, but the thing is—if you only do it for her, then you might end up resenting her."

Never going to happen. "I understand what you're saying. Fact is, there's nothing I won't do for her. But I wouldn't do this if I didn't want to do it."

"You realize you're saying you want to do it for her."

"Yep."

"What about you?"

"If it makes her happy and she enjoys it, then yeah, I'm doing it for me. I like making her happy."

"All right then." Rachel nodded. "You ready?"

No. "Not yet." I resumed my pacing. She didn't offer a single critical word. When the door jingled, my time was up. I pulled my phone out of my pocket and fired off a message to Frankie. Yeah, I was nervous. This was my dick. But I wanted this for her. For me. For us.

Me
I love you. Was just thinking about you. Missing you. Did you find Not So Little Coop yet? You're not allowed to play with him unless I'm on the phone. Yes, I know, mean.

I signed it off with a kiss emoji. It would be a bit before she read it. But I could almost hear her laughter, see the way her lips would curve as she fought a smile, and how her eyes would roll at me for being so melodramatic.

It was enough.

Inside, Rachel hesitated at the door. "You sure you want me in here?"

"If you're squeamish," I told her. "It's fine."

"Not squeamish," Rachel protested though the hint of a wince said otherwise. "Just trying to respect your privacy."

Chuckling, I held out my hand. "I need you to hold my hand, not my dick." Weirdly, that was true. She gripped my hand lightly and nodded. Then we both listened as the piercer went over everything. What to expect. How to clean it. What to do in case of swelling—no I didn't laugh—or severe inflammation. Definitely not laughing at that.

Fortunately, I'd never been a shy guy so when it came to dropping my trousers and the guy offered me something to clean my dick, I went to work. Rachel said absolutely nothing, just waited until it was time and then offered me her hand again.

"Here we go," my guy said, and Rachel made a soft grunting sound.

I glanced at her. "What?"

"My respect for Frankie just went up to a whole new level. That's a lot of dick, right there."

I was still laughing when the first pierce went through the soft flesh.

Chapter Twenty-One

WE SING THE SONGS

Ian

KC and the girls dragging us out to KC's mom's place in Beverly Hills turned out to be a damn blessing for Frankie. It not only distracted her from missing the guys quite so much, but it also gave us a resource about what to expect when we headed in for our first studio session.

"Don't be surprised if you don't get shit recorded the first day," Aubrey offered. "You guys are gonna need to coordinate with whatever band they're setting up for you. There's sound blending. There's chemistry. Then there's picking the songs out and working on them. Studio time is expensive, but cutting a first album is a lot of work. You're also a duo and not a whole band, but even the three of us had to work with musicians and it takes some time to get the right harmonies."

Honestly, that was probably the best thing I could have heard, because our first day at the studio with Boone, the new producer in charge of our "album," and Lauren, the music engineer had not been great. Discussing our sound and finding out what they thought would work versus our plans was something else entirely.

Still, it had been an experience and the girls assured us later that was "normal" so our next visit to the studio was to start putting the band together and maybe to lay some tracks. Give the mix engineer something to work with. When KC offered to have her driver ferry us, Frankie had declined. As it turned out, Jeremy arranged for Paul to be available to us for the whole trip and she didn't want to take the paycheck away from him.

Lauren waited for us at the studio when Paul dropped us off. "Hey," she greeted us with a wide smile. "C'mon in, Boone's not here and that's a good thing. I actually want to get the two of you in the studio and comfortable. I'm pretty sure Tuesday was not fun." As it turned out, Lauren was from Texas and she and Frankie hit it off.

The fact she relaxed the minute she realized Boone wasn't here, told me I needed to deal with that situation. I'd tackle that as soon as he showed up or I'd call him. "I think it would help if you got a better feel for us," I said, carrying our guitars and following Lauren into the studio. "Before we pick out other musicians."

"Okay, actually…" Lauren paused and actually glanced at the studio booth then checked her phone. The deep black of her hair made the single blue streak in it stand out. "Let's talk about that."

I set the guitar cases down as Frankie folded her arms to study Lauren. "Why do I not like how you said that?"

"Because you probably want to keep your style as close to you as possible and not mix it up," Lauren offered with an easy smile. "And I get that. A lot of musicians want that. Here's the thing, we're not saying change who you are."

"But?" I supplied and Frankie flashed me a quick smile. No, I got it, she was in full defensive mode for me.

"But, being flexible lets us all experiment. You guys are amazing, no lie. I've heard your whole demo and it's great. The fact that you did all the work for it and laid down all the music yourself, I'm seriously impressed." The absolute sincerity in her voice went a long way to easing my own discomfort.

"Despite that, you still think we should experiment?" Frankie frowned.

"That's the whole point. You guys have fire and chemistry, it plays right through the vocal tracks. But you haven't established your style yet. You're Bound Hearts, but who is Bound Hearts? What kind of music do they make? What is their sound?"

"Our sound," Frankie said slowly.

"Yes, and no."

"Thanks for clearing that up." Frankie huffed a sigh, but Lauren's laugh pulled a hint of a smile from my angel. No matter how tough she was, Frankie was also in her heart and soul, a genuinely nice person.

"That's my point," Lauren said. "Right now, you're thinking about this as a you and Ian thing. But Bound Hearts is a collective effort. Who you choose to be and what sound works best for you, isn't going to reflect on who you are as people. Frankly, most people won't care about who you are, but what your sound is and how it makes them feel."

Frowning, Frankie glanced at me.

"Give us a sec?" I asked Lauren and she grinned.

"No problem, I've got the mics off in here, so no hot mics, you'll have your privacy and I'm going to get some coffee. Be back in—ten?"

Another mark in the pro column for Lauren. "Ten would be great."

"Awesome, you guys want anything? I'm just gonna run to the place down the street."

"Thank you," Frankie said as she gave our order then Lauren let herself out and closed the door behind her. I glanced at the recording booth again. All the lights were off and the mic lights were off. Frankie pivoted to face me. "Thoughts?"

I spread my hands as I turned Lauren's words over in my head. "We knew this might be an issue," I began. "When we went through the contract negotiations we did fight for the final approval on the sound."

"So if we have final approval, why not experiment?" The earlier skepticism was gone and all that remained was a genuine question. "Are you okay with that?"

"I don't want to close the door on possibilities." Moving over to her, I caught her hands in mine and pulled them up to my shoulders. She didn't hesitate to wrap her arms around my neck. More of the tension bled out of her. Yes, we needed to work on this. I didn't want her wound so tight that she lived in defensive mode. "I've found that being open to what can happen is far more rewarding."

Understanding flared in her green eyes. "Well, in that case, I think we should set some hard limits and some soft limits."

Chuckling, I dipped my head and kissed her. She tightened her arms and I lifted her up so I didn't have to twist my neck and she didn't have to strain hers. The softness of her lips beneath mine was everything, and the last of the tension in her seemed to loosen as she slid her fingers into my hair. "Hmmm," I murmured. "Limits are good things."

"Yes, they are," she said in a soft voice. Combing her fingers through my hair, she sighed. "I don't want them to mess this up for you."

"Nothing will mess this up for me, Angel. This—is not something I imagined happening, much less like this. So, we'll let them give us some suggestions and we'll experiment. We might not like everything…"

That had been our rule with our play. We experimented. Found what we liked. Discarded what we didn't. She gave a little shiver. Damn, I loved how she could follow my train of thought so easily. "As long as you're happy…"

"As long as *we're* happy." I couldn't stress that enough. "This is us. We both have to approve. If you really don't like something, I want you to say something."

Head back, she stared up at the ceiling for a moment and then nodded. "I promise, I'll say something."

"Good." I flicked a look at the clock on the wall and then kissed her again. We didn't have time for what I'd like to do to her, but I had a plan for our next studio day. I should have put it into play today, but we'd been up late the night before and Frankie even later, talking to KC. I'd wanted her to have as much sleep as possible. "You ready to do this?"

At her slow nod, I set her on her feet. She ran her hands over my chest and I squeezed her biceps. "Ian?"

"Hmm?"

"Go out with me tonight?"

The questions surprised me.

"We've been with the girls almost every night and I love them, but…"

"I get it, and yes," I told her, brushing my fingers down her cheek. "I would love to take you out tonight. Or lock us in. I'm open to negotiation."

Whatever she might have retorted with we didn't get to discuss because Lauren returned with our coffee. "Hey!"

I had to hide a laugh at her very natural exuberance. Especially when Frankie flashed her an equally warm smile. There was my girl. She was right. We definitely needed a night to ourselves.

"So," Lauren said after she handed me my coffee and then stepped back to stand with Frankie. "What do you two think?"

Frankie gestured to me and I nodded. "We discussed it. And as long as you don't mind that we will veto anything we aren't comfortable with, we're willing to do some experimenting."

"Yes," Lauren fist pumped. "You two are the best. Alright, let me get into the booth and get things set up. Let's get you both into headsets and then we'll get started."

"Don't we need to pick out the music?" Frankie asked and Lauren grinned.

"I already have a few tracks lined up—just samplers. But we'll lay some of the lyrics down in different styles after we do a couple of run throughs. Sound good?"

I wasn't sure how much I cared for being manipulated. I definitely didn't care for the fact she'd played Frankie. But one glance told me Frankie was a little more comfortable with it. So, I'd let it go. For now.

"Sounds good," I agreed and moved over to one of the stools. "But why don't you give us a list of what you picked out? Then we'll go from there."

The lights came on behind the window and Lauren inclined her head. She flipped a switch and her voice came over the speakers. "Why don't we kick it off with how you composed November Dreaming first? We'll use that as our baseline."

November Dreaming was a ballad and it was personal as hell. Part of the reason that KC insisted we use it on the demo was the emotion in it. It was a song I'd been writing for Frankie when Thanksgiving happened. I checked with her first because it might be too personal to play with.

"I'm okay with it if you are. I love that song." The admission sent a wave of warmth through my chest. "But I love you more."

"I love you, Angel." More every damn day.

Lauren let out a long sigh. "I love you both. But that emotion right there—that intensity. Bring that when you're singing. Let's lay that down first, then we'll play with it."

Right. Play with our feelings. Frankie picked up the headphones and put hers on before she took a sip of coffee and I followed suit.

This whole thing didn't feel real and at the same time, when the first notes began to filter through the headset—it was all too real. Frankie locked gazes with me and I focused on her. Forget the studio, the recording equipment and anyone else listening to us. It was just me and Frankie. That was what the song was about in the first place.

It was about a dream of making better choices and the reality of learning from the bad ones. It was about hearing each other and really listening. In the end, it was about trusting the other person to know their own heart and to trust her with mine, in the hopes that she'd trust me with hers again.

A dream that became so much better in reality.

Frankie sang the first couple of lines and then paused and the music stopped.

"Ian?" Lauren said as Frankie gave me a questioning look. "You good?"

Hell, I was way better than good. We were taking a dream and spinning it into a reality. "Sorry, let's start from the top. I'm ready now."

This time when the music started, I moved my head slowly in time with it and played the notes with my fingers. Frankie sang the first line and I joined her on the second. Three more lines together completed the intro, detailing our September right down to the invitation to Homecoming. The bridge was mine as was the next series of verses before we hit the chorus and she blended back into the song. The next bridge was Frankie's and the deep, soulful sound as she sang the words about letting me go to protect her heart hit a little deeper.

She'd made that choice because she'd gone through so much push and pull with Maddy, she couldn't bear to do that with me. I followed her lines with my own, each one underscoring the misunderstanding. Writing that had been like tearing open my own soul to examine it and I'd do it again and again if I had to—whatever it took to make things right between us.

The next bridge was for both of us. Missing each other. Fighting for our friendship. The near miss at the dance. The weeks that followed. The chorus brought us back to November Dreaming and she held that note near the end of the refrain that tugged at my heart. The next bit was mine.

How I wanted her back. Needed her back. I'd wait and fight for as long as it took and then Frankie came in with the next lyrics, the promise of chasing dreams, grasping them, and holding on—and we finished the song together with a simple pledge to keep November's dreams alive before the music trailed off and then one last repeat of the chorus before the outro, which was a single line.

"Trust me," I said, not singing anymore. "Trust me with your heart and I won't let you down. Ever."

Chapter Twenty-Two

PICK-UP GAME

Archie

I was already ten minutes late as I crossed the lobby on the way to the executive elevators. I'd texted them from the subway, but it didn't change the chafe that lateness rubbed off on me. Lunch with Edward and Grandpa Ted had been booked for a week. Normally, only Grandpa could have convinced me to make the trip across town to the corporate building and then only if he insisted. Instead, this had been my idea and it irked me to be late for it.

As it was, Edward's message in response had just said *Take your time*. I swiped my badge to access the elevator and checked my watch once more, before stepping and choosing the fortieth floor. While not the top floor, it was where the majority of the executive offices and the dining room were located. It was just after eleven, which meant it was eight on the West Coast.

I fired off a quick round of messages to the group chat for Bubba and

Frankie both, then one to just Frankie.

Morning, Babe. Lunch with Grandpa and Edward today. Miss you.

Her response dinged my phone before I reached my floor.

Miss you too. So tired.

She included a picture of herself, hair askew and eyes heavy-lidded with sleep. She was still in bed and fuck if that wasn't an image that made my cock leap.

Call you later?

I smiled at her and sent a thumbs up.

Go back to sleep, Babe. Love you.

Her response was a big fat heart that exploded and a lipstick kiss.

I missed her like I'd miss a limb. Maybe more. That little bit of contact was a cool brush of her fingers against my cheek and a phantom kiss, both of which helped to soothe the aggravation of being late. The doors opened to the dark green painted and wood paneled walls. Expensive artwork of various countrysides from around the world decorated the walls.

This office had been Grandpa's base of operations for years. Every touch here reflected him, though the vases in the corners and the expensive flowers brought in fresh regularly were all reminiscent of Nana. She didn't like his long hours or when he forgot to come home for dinner. So she'd been the inspiration for the dining room, with its comfortable appointments and high-end chef. Even after Grandpa retired to spend more time with her, the facility remained firmly in place.

Grandpa used to bring me up to the New York offices once every couple of months for a "business lunch," where we could be men together. Muriel had wanted nothing to do with Standish or its subsidiaries. A blessing, I supposed. Nana supported Grandpa's work and his company in her own fashion.

Frankie would have the office right next to mine. Only, she'd be more likely to use her office than I was, and I was more than okay with that. Hell, I was okay if she didn't want anything to do with it.

Pushing in the door to the dining room, I found Grandpa Ted and Edward already seated and in quiet discussion. They didn't look up immediately at my arrival, which gave me a chance to study them both. Grandpa had always been athletic, but he'd slowed considerably over the last few years, especially after Nana passed and Edward—he'd aged so much over the last few months. Maybe he'd stopped giving into vanity or maybe he had begun to gray after everything with Maddy. It wasn't like he was old.

Hell, he was barely into his forties. Still, there were tired lines around his eyes and deep grooves etched into his cheeks. The resemblance between Edward and Grandpa had never been so striking. Though, by far, Grandpa had always been the happier of the two.

"There he is," Grandpa Ted said as he glanced up from the table. "Don't hover in the door, Sprout. We held lunch for you." Despite the scolding note in his voice, his eyes twinkled and he nodded to the chair between them.

"Sorry about being late," I said as I crossed over to join them. A waiter hurried over with a menu and a fresh glass of water for me, along with a soda. My standard drink order—when I was eight. Not that I was complaining.

"Nothing to worry about," Edward said. "Is everything all right?" He gave me a studious look and I could almost hear the question he wasn't asking.

"It's great. Jake and I just got caught up on the new engine we're rebuilding and then he wanted to head out to the airport to talk to some of our flight crews on maintenance. I gave him access," I said, then paused to glance at the menu. I already knew what I wanted. "Cheeseburger, extra fries, and hot fudge sundae."

Grandpa Ted chuckled. "Make that two."

To my surprise, Edward shrugged and said, "Three." Then he handed our menus to the waiter as I stared at the pair of them. While I wasn't exactly hiding my surprise, it caught me further off guard when Edward grinned at me. "Not everything is filet mignon and french-styled creamy potatoes with little garnishes that no one else even wants to eat, but look pretty."

I snorted. I couldn't help it, but Grandpa laughed. "I don't get to eat a good burger that often anymore. Doctors keep changing my diet around so much it's ridiculous. Old coots want to take all the fun out of living."

"Dad," Edward said, leaning forward to pick up his coffee.

"Don't you start," Grandpa told him with a light jab of a finger in his direction. "I gave up cigars and liquor. They can take my beef when I'm dead. Now, we're not here about me. How's our girl doing?" He fixed his gaze on me.

"Frankie's great, Grandpa. She and Bubba are working on their first album and apparently, it's a little insanity generating, but she's doing all right. Did she talk to you about the mentorship?"

"She did," Grandpa answered. "I'm more than happy to take that on, I let the college know. She's still on the books from her internship. Eddie never had her taken off."

Maybe that should have startled me, but then again, Edward thought of Frankie like his daughter. Where that had once irked me because of the way he and Maddy *seemed* to be trying to hurt her, I actually kind of appreciated it now.

"Maybe I should have…" Edward began but I waved him off.

"It's fine. I get it. You were looking out for her." That was all it was. Since Maddy told him that lie, he'd wanted to do right by Frankie and even now, "I get it."

"Are you sure?" His shoulders sagged a fraction and the worry knitting his brows together in a frown gnawed at me. "I know you wanted me to fuck off where she was concerned."

"Edward—Eddie," I conceded. "It's fine. You didn't know what was truth or lie. You did what you thought was best. I'll always want what is best for her. So, keeping her on the books is fine. Just—respect her wishes when she expresses them and you won't have any trouble with me. She actually likes the company."

Edward and I stared at each for a long moment and then he nodded once. "Thank you."

"You're welcome." As stiff and unyielding as those words had once been, they came a little easier and more natural. "She has asked about you a couple of times. Wants to know that you're doing all right."

"That's very kind of her."

"She's an extremely kind person." Nothing like her mother at all, but we didn't have to say that and there was no reason to jab at that wound.

He let out a little sigh. "I appreciate that and let us know if she needs anything. We have offices out there and we can make any arrangements either of you need."

"I think I've got it covered, but I will definitely keep that in mind."

Our burgers came and the smell hit me, reminding me just how hungry I was. Jake and I had gone straight to the shop after the gym. Fortunately, we had a shower at the shop. I'd managed to grab a shower before changing to come uptown.

"So, what did you want to call this meeting for, Sprout? Or were you just checking up on the old men?" Grandpa asked when we were about halfway through the burgers.

"You're not catching me in that net, Grandpa. I start referring to you as old men and you'll both do something to prove me wrong."

Edward's quick laugh pulled a chuckle from me because it was so abrupt and filled with genuine humor. He grinned at me. "I forget sometimes just how much time you spent with Dad while you were growing up."

"I like to think he helped to make me the man I am," I said, the compliment flowing off me easily.

"Me too," Edward said, and it was a rare moment of real understanding between us. "I'm very glad you had him."

I nodded then took a bite of burger rather than let that much emotion crash over me.

"Enough of the sappy stuff. No women here to impress and we don't need to be shedding tears." Grandpa cleared his throat and then took a long drink of his water. But I didn't miss the way he dabbed at his eyes. Nor did Edward from the way he hid a smile and cut a look at me. It was—almost conspiratorial. Damn. I just grinned and took another bite.

After I finished that, I said, "I did actually want to talk to you guys about the old machinery shops out in Brooklyn. The ones we took over when we acquired the Timekeepers—the old horology company?"

Grandpa frowned briefly. "We merged the operation with Benedict and Miller after we acquired all their patents. Do we still have the machinery shops?"

"Last I checked," I told him. "I noticed they were still in our assets when we got the last fiscal reports. They haven't been in operation in more than a decade, but we still have the real estate and the buildings, as well as whatever equipment is still inside of them."

"What about them?" Edward asked. He'd wiped his fingers off and pulled his phone out from his inner pocket. "Do you have a plan?"

"Jake and I do," I said. "We want to keep working on engines, customizing them, building them out and making them more efficient. I love the Tesla I got for Frankie, but I can do more with that kind of engineering. Maybe even push the self-driven car features, but making the most efficient engine while still making it powerful—that's a goal. There's also some robotics work we've been tinkering with but…"

"You need more space for something like that," Grandpa said, his expression thoughtful. "You've always been tearing things apart looking to make them better."

"Thank you," I said, straightening. "Try telling Jeremy that. I'm banned from my own kitchen."

"What did you do?" Edward asked. "Blow up his stove—again?"

"Look, the first time, I was testing a theory and it didn't blow up. Exactly." I'd also only been eight. I should get some slack for that. "And this time, I was trying to get it to turn off when the meat reached a certain internal temperature—I didn't expect the result I got."

"I haven't seen any fire claims for the brownstone," Grandpa said, caution in his voice and glee in his eyes.

I sighed. "I didn't burn it down." Then again, I wouldn't mention that was because Jake had been right there with a fire extinguisher. "Anyway, we're fine. The stove is fine and I got him a much nicer one as an upgrade."

"And you're banned from touching it," Edward said, making no attempt to hide his amusement and I lifted my shoulders in a shrug.

"For the moment," I agreed, because it was true. Though freaking *Rachel* had somehow passed the golden standard. Though, it shouldn't surprise me, she won Frankie's trust and now she had Jeremy's. "Anyway," I said stressing those two syllables. "The machinery shops?"

"We still have them," Edward said as he glanced at his phones. "Properties are up to date on taxes, though we haven't done an inventory in a while nor any safety inspections. If you want to use them, then we'll get a couple of our engineers over there to take a look, and bring in the city inspector so we can get everything up to code. You'll also need security and equipment."

Grandpa nodded slowly. "I don't mind turning it over to you, Sprout, but Eddie's right. We'll make sure we get it all sorted out for you. Probably take four or five weeks, I would imagine. That enough time? If you need a bigger place sooner, we can always look at renting you a space in the meanwhile."

I'd thought about that. "Five weeks is great. That means we could move some of the ongoing test pieces out there once school is back in. I do have one other favor…"

"Name it," Edward said.

"Jake's talking about getting a pilot license so he can get a feel for the plane engines. Probably small personal plane first, but I get the impression he wouldn't mind a commercial license and training."

"That's not a problem. We'll just get him working with one of our pilot's for training and licensing. He'll have to pass certifications and I know you'll cover any insurance rider he needs to carry."

Without a doubt.

"You don't want to learn to fly, Sprout?" Grandpa said. "Or is this your way of buttering us up and easing us into the idea?"

I grinned. Sometimes, Grandpa knew me too well.

Edward exhaled. "Your mother will have a fit."

"What she doesn't know won't bother me in the slightest," I told him. "Besides, I'm almost twenty."

"Fair," he said. "Just—exercise more caution than when you were learning to drive a car, please." He grimaced the moment the words were out of his mouth. The car accident. It was written all over his face. I waved him off.

"It's fine and I will. Jake's more into that area than I am. I want to tear apart the codes and work more with the internal systems for monitoring, and how we can use it to apply to vehicles, then in turn apply it to aircraft. But one step at a time. Gotta build it before I can race it or fly it."

And I wanted to do both. But—again, one step at a time.

We spent most of the hour they'd scheduled for lunch and the following hour they hadn't, debating different ideas and discussing the things we could do with the machine shops, eventually. I had to talk them out of sending out engineers to oversee me and Jake. While I would talk to one of the company's safety engineers to make sure we had everything we needed, the shop was for us to experiment and to build. We wanted to do it our way.

After, Grandpa had to go because he did have some overseas calls he had to take before it got much later there, and Edward walked me to the elevator and then rode down with me. We were both silent, but it wasn't the thick silence, crackling with animosity and all the things we didn't say. He waited until we were outside to ask, "Do you have a car coming or are you taking the subway?"

"Subway," I said. "What's up?"

"Just wanted to talk for a minute and I'll walk you to the station if you don't mind."

I didn't, so I motioned for him to go ahead.

"How are you doing?" I asked him as I loosened the tie I'd put on for the lunch and tugged it off before stuffing it in my pocket. "I mean, really."

"I get by," he said. "Oddly, Hank Jackson has become a regular caller on my blotter. He checks in once a week. He'll be in the city in a couple of weeks for some—conference or other. We're going to have dinner."

"That's cool." Sounded like Frankie's dad was just like Frankie. He was keeping an eye on Edward. "You know—you don't have to be a stranger if you want to drop by the brownstone or you know, get a pickup game sometime." I frowned on the last. "Do you even know what a pickup game is?"

Edward actually glared at me. "I'm in my forties, Archie, not dead. Of course, I know what a pickup game is."

Smirking, I loosened the two buttons at my collar. "All right old man, the guys and I usually have a game on the weekends. Jake and I tend to do more one on one, though if you show up, I'll drag Coop and we can play two on two."

We were at the steps leading down to the subway and Edward pondered me for a minute. "You on my team?"

"Why not?" I said and then held out my hand. He grasped it for a brief, if firm, handshake. "Just make sure you know what you're doing."

He laughed. Really laughed and clapped my shoulder. "I won't let you down."

For the first time in my life—I believed him.

I Just Called to Say, I Want You

Frankie

"What are you wearing?" Jake asked in a playfully leering voice and I glanced at the upper corner of the screen where he watched me via the video chat.

Glancing down at my tank top and shorts, I looked at him again. "Theoretically or actually?"

His grin grew, the flash of teeth sending a shiver through me. "Let's go with actually, and if I need you to give me a different mental picture, we can switch gears."

"Uh huh. I thought we were going to talk about your new project with Archie."

"Yeah, that's fine, going great. We're working on some things, have some other things in the hopper. But the project with Archie has nothing on your breasts or your pussy, Baby Girl, and I'd much rather discuss those."

The pussy in question clenched at the suggestion and I glanced at the room behind me before looking back at the screen. "Jake…what if I wasn't alone?"

"What if you weren't?" The question made my eyes widen. "It's been a while, but I thought the element of being caught turned you on."

I squirmed a little in the chair. Granted, we were at KC's mom's place, and we had loads of privacy. In fact, the only reason Ian wasn't here was his guitar had snapped a string. Rather than drop it off, he'd taken it to be repaired and was waiting on it.

"It does," I admitted. "But when was the last time we made out somewhere someone could catch us?"

"The deck of the yacht comes to mind," he said and I swore the temperature in the room climbed. "So, go and make sure the door is closed—but don't lock it."

I touched my tongue to my teeth and pointed a finger at him. "You too."

"Already done," he said and when he leaned back, all I could see was the dragon covering half of his bare chest. The camera didn't allow me to see much more but I hurried over to the door and nudged it closed.

The household staff didn't come in the rooms when we were in them. Though I half-thought they had to have a camera somewhere stalking us to know when we were out.

Moving back to the desk, I picked up my laptop and carried it over to the bed.

"Look at you, Baby Girl, already thinking ahead."

"Uh huh." I sat down and maximized the screen. Jake sat back sprawled on his bed and he was gorgeously nude. In my absence, he'd made himself comfortable and had already begun to stroke his cock. The fact it was thick and erect made my insides clench up again.

"See something you like?" His voice dropped to an almost seductive tease.

"Oh yeah." I definitely did. It wasn't until he cleared his throat and reangled the camera so I couldn't see him anymore that I snapped out of my trance. I really had just been staring at his dick like some first time virgin. Oh boy.

"Can I see something that I'd like?"

I dragged the tank top off, but I had to stand up in order to shimmy out of my shorts.

"Oh, that's nice—hold right there," Jake ordered. "There's that lusciously bitable ass I enjoy fucking so damn much."

Every single muscle in my body clenched at that one. His soft laugh told me he knew that, too. My heart raced and I had to keep licking my lips.

"Turn around," he said. "Slowly."

When I faced the computer and the bed again, he gave me a low, appreciative whistle. "Your nipples are all flushed and pink. Are they aching for me to suck on them, or do they want me to pinch them?"

"You're really good at this," I said with a half-laugh.

"I've got lots of inspiration. Now answer the question." The little whiplash of command turned me on almost as much as it did that anyone could just walk in that door right now. But I kept my focus on Jake.

"They want to feel your teeth," I said. "The bite and the scrape. The hard pull." Man, it was definitely getting hotter in here. "What about you? Are you imagining that's my hand while you sit there and just stroke yourself?"

"Your hand," he said, his voice so low and deep it made me shiver. "Your mouth. Your pussy. Even your ass. Nothing compares to your touch, Baby Girl or your body. This is just a poor substitute. Up on the bed, I need to see that pussy. But I want you to play with those tits, pinch, squeeze, tug. Keep your eyes on me. I want you to feel me."

The tension going taut in my belly pulled so fiercely I thought I might orgasm just from the words. That wasn't possible, right? Archie's dirty talk had a way of inflaming me, but holy fuck this was different.

I cupped my breasts, massaging them, then pinching them.

"Harder," Jake ordered. "Make them sting."

I twisted as tightly as I could stand it and between the sharp pull and the bite, it sent liquid heat pouring through my body.

"That's my precious baby girl. Close your eyes and lay back, use your foot. Angle the camera down—there—right there. Oh, look at her. She's all pink, damp, and sweet. Positively swollen and begging for me to eat you out until you scream. Or maybe I'll work you over with my fingers first."

My hips lifted almost involuntarily.

"Fingers it is, touch yourself for me, Frankie. Tease that clit, it's so full, it's peeking out at me." Jake kept talking, every single word guiding my hand to tease, stroke, rub, and increasing the pressure. It was like having him there, a phantom of him and when his voice strained, I let out a little whimper.

"I need you," I admitted. Needed him there. Fuck, I wanted to feel him come.

"Come, Baby Girl. Come for me. Come all over those fingers and I'll come all over mine. Just imagine it's me and we're right there…"

That shouldn't have worked. It shouldn't have blown my mind like that, but I did, the first cascade hit me and I would have stopped. I always had when masturbating before. That first release enough. But Jake growled and I put my fingers back. It was too much and not enough. The calluses on my fingers weren't like his and my nails were just a bit too long, but I spread myself wide so he could see and when I came the second time, he let out a groan so blissful I had to twist and see.

He had spilled all over his hand just like he promised, and he wore this lazy, satisfied grin. My heart swelled at the sight of it. "I can't wait until you're back in my bed, Baby Girl."

I licked my lips. "Next time—I want to do that to you."

"I'm in."

I just had to practice so I didn't sound like a dork. There had to be books or research material on it, right?

Chapter Twenty-Three
WONDERLAND SUCKS

Frankie

It had been two weeks of day in and day out at the recording studio, remixing, working over vocals, switching up styles and then working with different musicians until Boone put together the group for us. If not for Lauren and Ian, I might have bailed on this during the first week. But somehow, Ian found a way to make it fun and Lauren proved to be a staunch ally in our corner. When Boone wanted us to take a harder edge to the music, something neither of us wanted, she went to bat and became the difficult one.

It was both sweet and amazing. I kind of hoped if we ever did this again, she would be the one in the sound booth. Even when I messed up or we had to do repeated takes to nail a particular set of lyrics, she was always patient. Bless Ian for reworking lyrics on the fly, sometimes what worked at one tempo just didn't at another. He never seemed to grow impatient. Despite our attempts at privacy, KC and the girls were such sweet hostesses.

Couple that with the late nights at the studio, and the only real alone time we seemed to get was when we were passing out.

Not that half-asleep sex with soft touches and lingering kisses wasn't great, but I had begun to miss Ian almost as much as I was the guys in New York. Today had originally been booked as a down day, but Boone called us right after we got back to KC's place the night before to find a party in full swing.

Instead of a day off, Boone wanted us to do a cover shoot, cause they were trying to work out the "vibe." So instead of resting, we were up at six-thirty and in a car and on the way to the photographer's studio, which turned out to be almost two hours away. Even with coffee in me and KC—who was still up from her party, waving us off—I slept curled up next to Ian in the back all the way there. We'd missed a few messages from the guys and I hated it.

I'd barely talked to them this week, doing a lot of hit or miss texts. Even Rachel had been the same, though she swore the guys were good, if busy. She was also worried about me. I couldn't even tell her I was fine. It would have been a lie.

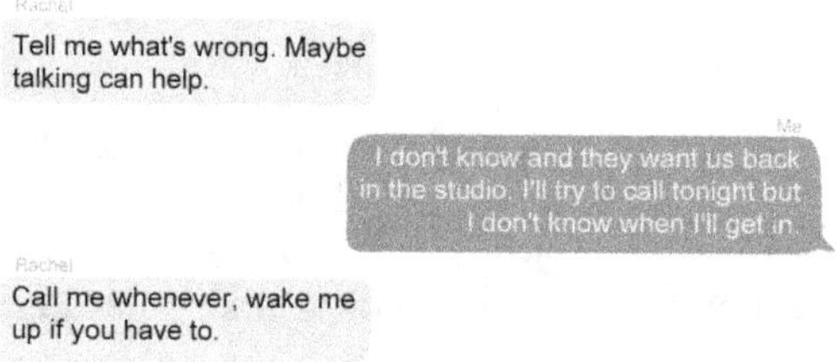

Yeah, I didn't call her whenever. I didn't want to wake her up. Boone wasn't at the studio when we got there, nor was Lauren. It made sense Lauren wouldn't be, she was the recording engineer. She had her own work to do. The photographer wasn't there either, but his assistant was. She hustled us inside then sent us to separate rooms for hair and makeup.

Sammie was the girl in charge of getting me ready and she gave me a once over, critical look. "When was the last time you had a facial? Eyebrows? I think we can polish some of this and thin them out." She didn't wait for me to answer, just talked a mile a minute. "I know it sounds like a lot but high-definition photography means every pore you own will be on display, so we're going to minimize that."

She paused to look at me again, her expression studious and her eyes thoughtful.

"Something wrong?"

"Nope, just—doing you up in my head so I know where to start. I think we go with outfits, they have a couple they want you in for the first shots. Come on. It's kind of like playing dress up on someone else's dime and that's not only fun, it's super fun." There was something wickedly familiar about her smile. She had a bit of a Rachel-vibe, fast and brash, but no meanness in it at all.

"I'll take your word for it on the super fun part," I said, but pushed out of the chair to follow her into the dressing room. Five minutes later, I stared at the three outfits she'd lined up and then back at her. "For real?"

The first one was basically a leather bra over a pair of bootie shorts that would leave half my ass hanging out. The only way that one could be bad was if it was a g-string. The second was a lacy top, off the shoulder, still left my midriff bare and a skirt with slits up both sides.

Marginally better.

Marginally

The last one was a pair of ripped jeans.

Just the ripped jeans.

"I almost hate to ask this, but where is the top?"

Sammie laughed. I might be rethinking my opinion of her. "Relax, I know it probably looks worse than it is."

Nope, not possible. Still, I locked my jaw together and stared at her.

Still grinning, Sammie pointed to one of the posters on the wall. It was a band I had a passing familiarity with. The girl on the album cover had on a pair of deep black stilettos, a mini skirt so short that if she bent even a hairsbreadth further, she'd be flashing her vagina at the world and no top, just bare skin. With one hand stretched up to the sky, her dark hair spilled down and she wore a teasing smile as she glanced back over her shoulder.

"Not making me feel any better."

"We painted her top on." She pulled out her phone and hit a few keys to open a folder then she held it up for me. Same chick from the front. Definitely wearing nothing but paint over her breasts. Granted, it was a really lovely paint job, but I could see her nipples and no amount of paint would make me feel like I was clothed. "I get it, it's overwhelming, but I'm thinking we start here. I have a good idea of how they are making up your partner. This would go well with his look and I think they wanted to do some motorcycle shots. Maybe silhouettes."

My stomach sank through the floor.

"Sweetheart, you have nothing to worry about. You're drop dead gorgeous at nine in the morning with zero makeup on and your hair up in a ponytail. Trust me, this will look so much better than you can imagine."

I chewed my lower lip. I wanted to call Rachel and bring her in on this, or maybe Coop. Though Coop had a whole new schedule and he'd been putting in a lot of hours lately. I needed to check in with Jake and Jeremy about Coop, cause he'd looked a bit ill.

Dammit. I didn't want to chicken out of this and at the same time, I really wanted to be anywhere but here. Deep breaths. I closed my eyes and tried to concentrate on calming my racing pulse down. "Are you sure?" I finally asked and looked at Sammie. "I know I sound like a whiner, but when we dove into all of this, going topless in a room full of strangers wasn't exactly on my bucket list or even on the list of oh, this might happen."

Real laughter escaped her. "Girl, you're not even close to whining. Trust me, I've worked with some real divas. You're fine. Come on, let's give it a shot, if you don't think you're drop dead gorgeous, we'll work with something else. You'll be wrong, but I'll allow it."

I snorted and relaxed—a little. "All right. You only live once." And even if I couldn't walk out there, I bet the guys would love it. Still, stripping down to my panties in front of Sammie was a little nerve wracking, she kept up a steady stream of easy chatter that relaxed my jangled nerves.

Paint first. Fuck that was cold. I swore my nipples pulled so taut they were gonna fall off. She didn't let me look at anything she did. "Not until we're done," she told me firmly. "Trust me when I say this is one time when you want the full effect, not just the partial."

At least she turned up the heat some because I was freezing. People also kept coming in and ducking out. Not a single one even glanced in my direction. Not that I didn't tense up every time someone came in. Somewhere else in the building music cranked up and Sammie grinned.

"Davish is here," she said. The paint was still drying and it was still cold as hell on my skin, but she'd moved on to my face. My hair would be last and it was all twisted up on top of my head as she shaded, contoured and added texture—whatever the hell that was—using more makeup than I even owned, much less wore.

All told, by the time she finished with my hair and took a step back, we'd been in here two hours. It didn't take me two hours to get ready for *anything*. Not prom. Not homecoming. Not a funeral.

Nothing.

"All right," Sammie said slowly as she curled her fingers in a beckoning gesture. I was already in the ripped jeans, we'd put those on between cosmetics and hair. They were the only thing I was sure I was comfortable with—except for the strategic rip just under my right ass cheek. I was pretty sure Jake's head would blow off his shoulders if he could see this outfit. Archie would want pictures though and so would Coop for that matter, so when Sammie held up her phone, I fought my initial negative response.

"One picture," she said. "Just give me a smile. You look like five million bucks and if I swung that way, I'd want to bang you. Totally."

I laughed. It was like a dam cracked inside of me when I let out the sharp sound and I would have clapped my hands over my mouth but she'd reminded me a dozen times already that smudge proof didn't mean I couldn't eat my own lipstick off and to stop biting my lip. She snapped a few pictures.

"Perfect."

My face ached as I blew out a breath.

"All right, look at my masterpiece. I dare you to tell me you don't look fantastic."

I pivoted on my heel and faced the mirror. At first, I just looked at the jeans. It was easier, especially since I was barefoot and the tears were familiar. Then I flicked my gaze upward and froze. The woman staring back at me from the mirror wasn't me.

Not even close.

The paint she'd drawn on my chest feathered like an angel's wings only in reverse. If not for how tight they were, I wouldn't even be able to see my nipples. The color of the feathers was a silvery gray and it gleamed and glittered against my tan skin. My navel piercing also stood out, shimmering in the light. She'd had me take off my other jewelry, but she'd added some kind of glitter to my cosmetics and my face was all kinds of shimmery from the frosted silver she'd down to my eyes and the deep red of my lips to the way my hair had been blown almost all out.

But it wasn't me. The woman staring back at me for the longest moment was Maddy, all done up in her perfect poise and frosted looks. She'd always looked so together and I'd always been a wreck.

"You don't like it…" Sammie said but the rest of her words kind of faded out as I kept staring at Maddy. We'd always looked so much alike, people joked we could be sisters. But I'd never captured that kind of effortless ethereal she had possessed when I was younger.

Tears burned in my eyes and my heart was racing too fast. A hand on my shoulder was like ice and I shook it off as I shook my head.

All at once I was standing in front of her as she pointed the gun at me—at Archie. "I tried," she told me in that empty voice. It was like she was disappointed and at the same time, not so much. If she had to kill us both. She'd do it.

Empty.

So goddamn empty.

The world around me just crumpled and wavered. I fought to lift my head and all I could see was Maddy. Only this time Ian was behind me. She didn't care who it was though. She would never care.

Just like she never really cared about me.

So why the hell did it hurt so much…

Brother Boyfriend Broadcast

Ian
She's asleep. Not restful, but asleep.

Archie
What the hell happened?

Ian
Far as I can tell, they did her makeup and hair and when she looked in the mirror she saw Maddy

Jake
...

Coop
...

Ian
Yeah, my thoughts exactly. I think it was the straw that just cracked through the rest of it. I already told the label we might be a few days and I sent a message to KC and the girls. I did not tell any of them where we were

Archie
Solid plan. I'm gonna have the security guys just keep a closer eye for a few days while you look after her. When she's awake...

Coop
Yeah, I want to talk to her. Fuck, I want to be there.

Jake
Me too.

Ian
Soon as she's awake, we'll all talk to her. If she wants a plane back to New York, we'll be on a plane.

257

Jake
Agreed

Coop
Get something to eat. Look after yourself.

Archie
Take care of our girl.

Ian
I will. Talk to you soon.

Chapter Twenty-Four

BROKEN WINGS

Frankie

I'd cried so damn much, my eyes had almost swollen shut. It was like once the tears started, I just couldn't get them to stop. I tried, I kept trying. Nothing worked. Ian had pulled a shirt over my head and then told them we were going. I think. Maybe that was what he said. It seemed a lot angrier than that. Or maybe that was me.

At some point, he bundled me into a car and then we were moving. I barely paid any attention to the journey. Nor to where we went. I wished I could just hate her and be done with it. Why did I mourn for a woman who never loved me? Why would I even begin to miss her? The first spray of water hit me and I slid down the wall, registering we were in a shower. Ian sat down next to me. His clothes soaking through.

I pulled my knees to my chest and hugged them, he didn't push me to do anything else as we sat under the water. It was like it could cry for me and the tears burning tracks down my cheeks didn't hurt as much. When he eased my head onto his shoulder, I closed my eyes and just held onto him.

Eventually, I couldn't breathe through my nose and my throat had gone scratchy and harsh. My eyes hurt like hell and the water had gone chilly then back to warm. Not once did he leave me, stroking his fingers through my soaking hair.

"I'm sorry," I managed to croak.

"Shh," he murmured and then pressed a kiss to my damp temple. "You have nothing to be sorry about, Angel. I'm right here and I'm not going anywhere."

That was what he'd been saying for the last little while and the words finally sank into my bones. I gave a shudder and sniffled. "I messed up."

"No," he assured me. "You didn't."

"But the album…"

"Fuck the album," Ian said and I tried to blink against the soreness in my eyes and focus my watery gaze on him. "I mean it. Fuck the album. I told you before we ever started this—it's an us thing. You're hurting, they can wait. If they want to sue us, let them. I bet you that yours and Archie's attorneys will eat them for lunch."

That shouldn't make me laugh. Even the harsh chuckle that escaped hurt my chest. "Poor Sammie."

"Who the hell is Sammie?"

"The makeup artist—I ruined all of her pretty work." I glanced down at the streaks of glitter and paint rippling over my torso. It had begun to give up the fight against the constant stream.

"She'll be fine." The firmness in his voice pulled my gaze back to him. His hair was plastered to his head. The hint of eyeliner beneath his eyes just made his blue eyes pop even more. Twin sapphire suns staring back at me. "She was the one who came to get me when you started crying and stopped talking."

Oh God. Humiliation crawled through me and when I would have looked away, Ian tugged my hair gently, keeping my attention on him.

"Stop it."

"I—"

"No." That single syllable held absolutely no room for argument. "Just—stop it. You've been running away from dealing with this for months and we've all let you because you needed the time. You couldn't figure out your feelings."

I hadn't been able to.

"I trusted you with you, Angel. But now I need you to trust me with you."

"Of course, I trust you."

"Good." He pressed his lips against my temple and just held them there. Seconds ticked away and I closed my eyes. Clenching his shirt, I flexed my fingers.

"Ian, I don't know how to do this. She tried to hurt Archie. She did hurt me—over and over."

"I know, Angel," he murmured. "But this is about who she was, who she should have been. You're mourning the loss of the mother she should have been to you."

The knife gouging into me twisted. "I look just like her."

"No you don't."

"I saw her in the mirror—"

"I don't care what you saw, Angel. You don't look like her to me or to anyone else who knows you. Do you resemble each other? Yes. But you know who else you look like?"

I couldn't swallow around the lump in my throat.

"You look like Hank. I see it in your expressions and your smile. I see it in your actions and in that great big heart. Everything else is smoke and mirrors."

I wanted to believe him. I really did. But the tears just started flowing again. He didn't even try to make me stop. Eventually, he did get me to my feet and we washed off the paint and the cosmetics. He helped me with my hair and we shut off the water. My fingers were prunes and I dreaded their poor water bill. Gradually the numbness crept in, trying to deaden all the broken pieces of my soul digging into me.

He toweled my hair while I sat on the toilet. I didn't have to do anything. Eventually, he walked me back into the bedroom and got me under the covers. When he wrapped his arms around me, I fell into darkness. When I jerked away, I actually screamed, and then warm arms were around me and turning me around. It was dark in the room, but Ian was there. Head against his chest, I focused on the steady thump of his heart and the soft words as he coaxed me back to sleep.

At some point, I swore I heard Archie but when I turned over, he wasn't there. Jake's and Coop's voices came and went. But I didn't want to try and fight against the dark cloud squeezing all the air out of me, so I just went back to sleep.

The next time I woke, Ian was saying, "She's finally letting it out, but just stay available cause she's going to want to talk to you guys."

I peeled open my eyes. They stung and felt heavy with crud, almost like they'd sealed while I was asleep. The movement got Ian's attention and he smiled down at me. He was sitting up, but he was still right next to me.

"Hey Angel, Arch is on the phone."

He didn't wait to see if I wanted the phone and just handed it to me.

"Hey," I said, then coughed. I sounded rough and my throat was like I'd been swallowing glass. A headache began to pound behind my eyes and my nose was so stuffed up, I couldn't breathe. This was horrible.

"Hey, Babe," Archie said in a soothing voice. "I'm going video now."

"I look terrible."

"I bet I look worse," he retorted.

"Impossible." It was a weak reflection of the conversation Coop and I usually had but the phone buzzed. With reluctance, I pulled the phone from my face to find Archie staring at me and he wasn't alone, Coop and Jake were with him. Tears filled my eyes all over again.

"No," Coop said. "She definitely wins this one. You look worse, Frankie. But I bet Jake could fix that if you wanted. Blackeye? Bloody nose?"

Laughter whimpered out of me, but it was still laughter. "No fighting."

"Damn," Jake muttered. "I was looking forward to the freebie."

Archie just snorted, but all of their gazes were so concerned. Coop still looked a little pale to me, but fuck my eyes hurt and it was hard to focus. I pulled the phone back some and it was Jake who frowned.

"Baby Girl," he said with so much love in his voice, I wanted to cry all over again. "We can be out there in a few hours."

"No," I said, sniffling as I tried to sit up. Ian took the phone for me and held it.

"Man, I've missed those breasts," Archie said with a sigh. "Though— wanna tell me why they're gray?"

A watery laugh escaped as I glanced down. The light from the window slanted into the room offering enough illumination to see the remnants of the body paint. "Album cover shoot. They wanted me in jeans and topless with wings spray painted over my chest."

Coop whistled. Archie looked intrigued, but Jake leaned toward the screen. "Bubba?"

"It looked fucking amazing, bitch at me later," Ian ordered and then he slid an arm around my shoulders and moved to tuck me against him so we could both look at the screen.

Jake didn't look remotely pleased and for some reason, that just made me feel better. Archie, however, drummed his fingers.

"The makeup artist took pictures," I said, then rubbed at my nose. I was such a hot mess. "If you want to see."

"Sammie is a girl, don't give yourself a stroke, Jake." Ian's easy tone pulled another smile from me.

"I miss you guys," I said, not even trying to do the brave thing.

"Then we're coming," Coop said.

"No," I whispered, then sniffled. "Ugh, I sound horrible and my throat hurts. I don't want everyone dropping everything for this. I wrecked the shoot. I don't want to wreck any other plans."

Archie let out a faint growling sound and I blinked. "Babe, I love you, but if you need us, we're on a fucking plane. Stop worrying about anything being messed up. *You* come first."

"And I love you for that so much," I said. "I do. Right now, I don't know what I need. Seeing you guys is everything though."

Coop eased down onto his elbows. I couldn't really tell where they were in the house. "Okay, then get up, wash your face, brush your teeth, let Bubba ply you with coffee while you try to eat something. And in an hour, tell us what you need."

Both Jake and Archie looked like they were going to argue, but Coop held all of my attention. "I love you and I'm always going to need you."

That earned me three nods and smiles, concerned smiles, but still smiles. "We love you too," Coop said. "So fucking much."

Another swallow and the lump in my throat didn't get any smaller, nor did the jagged broken feeling go away.

"Give us until tonight, guys," Ian said. "It's after twelve here. By the time you got a flight, it might be tomorrow morning before you got here anyway."

"Point of order," Archie said. "Private plane. That said, we'll do it your way. It's four here now. If I don't hear from you guys by eight, we're going to be there by tomorrow morning."

That wasn't a request. I touched my fingers to the screen tracing the line of his face. "Thank you."

"For what?"

"For being you."

The guys didn't linger on the phone though they clearly wanted to, and I was loathe to hang up, as well. Ian waited until they were off the phone though before he cupped my cheek. "I'm going to go make coffee, you can get in the shower or go soak in the hot tub.”

Hot tub.

That was when it hit me. The bedroom we were in… I glanced around. It wasn't the one at KC's.

“Where are we?”

“Archie's dad's place in Malibu.”

Oh.

“I called them yesterday once I got you in the car, Archie said to come here and Edward texted me the codes to get in. He also sent his housekeeper around to stock up for us.”

“I didn't even know he had a place here.”

“Well, now you do, and I wanted you to have some privacy. KC's a great girl, but she's got to learn some boundaries and right now—you don't need to deal with that.”

I licked at my chapped lips. “There's a hot tub?”

“Yep,” he said and slid out of the bed. Before I could follow him, he scooped me up.

“Ian!”

“Hush.” He punctuated the order with a kiss. “My way, remember?”

Right. I did and all at once more of the tension just bled out of me, and I curled up to his shoulder as he carried me into the bathroom. I must have really been out of it to completely miss not only was the bathroom totally different in layout, it had a whole other color. Sure enough, in addition to the huge shower we'd been sitting in, there was a hot tub right in the middle of the bathroom.

Setting me down on the tile, I gave a start that it wasn't freezing cold under my ass.

“Heater under the floors in here,” he told me with a smile. In a couple of minutes, he had the tub filling with water and the jets churning. He added a little something from one of the canisters, I couldn't tell what it was, but the water shifted colors—oh wait, maybe that was the lights under it. “Slide in," he told me. "Don't go to sleep. I'll be back in five minutes."

"Thank you," I whispered and he brushed his fingers against my cheek.

"You never have to thank me for looking after you." He waited until I was in the water before he left. The heat was like being enveloped in a hug and it illustrated just how sore every muscle I had was. Leaning my head back, I relaxed as the jet at my back pounded against the tension there and the rest of me half-floated. My nose began to clear a little, and the rich scent of roses filled the air.

Oh, that was nice.

I didn't know whether it had been five minutes or not, but I blinked my eyes open to find Ian sliding into the water with me. "I told you not to go to sleep," he teased.

"I'm apparently a bad girl," I said, then yawned as I reached for the coffee. "Maybe you should spank me."

"Oh," he said in a voice that held a promise in it. "I intend to."

Another flood of relief went through me.

"You should have told me," he said in a gentle voice.

"I told you I wasn't sure how I was feeling."

"No," he said, in that same even tone. "You should have told me you needed to cry." At my frown, he continued, "You told me yesterday in one of your crying jags, that you didn't know why you were doing this when you hadn't been able to all this time."

It was the barest hint of a scold that made me blush. Or maybe it was the heat from the water. Cradling the tumbler of coffee in my palms, I took a long drink. Man, it helped with how cracked and painful my voice was. "I didn't know I needed to." That admission cost me nothing. "I still can't even figure out why I'm so—lost feeling. By the end, I hated her. I hated what she tried to do to Archie. What she did to me. What she could have done to all of you—and my God, Edward and her parents. She was poison."

"She was still your mother," Ian reminded me and I made a face.

"I know she was."

"Then cut yourself a break," he continued, stretching his legs in the water. "You're allowed to feel whatever you're feeling. You owe no one an apology or an excuse. If you're hurting, you're hurting."

A long sigh escaped me. "Ian...I shouldn't feel anything for her but relief that she's gone."

"If you were her," he said in the same gentle tone. "That would probably be how you feel. But you're not her, Frankie. Stop telling yourself you have to be."

Surprise flickered through me at that. I wanted to argue that point. I really did, but... I couldn't. Was that what I'd been doing? Wrestling all of it away so I could ignore her the way she had me? Yes, I hated her. I hated her so much for everything she'd done.

I kept turning those words around in and around. I definitely hated her. But... "I loved her," I whispered. "I loved her and all I wanted was for her to love me, too."

This time when the tears slid down my cheeks, I didn't try to stop them. When Ian pulled me into his lap and put the coffee to the side, I held onto him. The heated water couldn't quite warm the chill from my soul, but Ian cradled me close and buffered me against it. "I know you did, Angel. That's one of the things we all love about you. That huge heart of yours."

At least with them, my heart was safe. Big or not.

Chapter Twenty-Five

BINDING WOUNDS

Frankie

By late afternoon, we'd called the guys back and I had a good chat with them. I would be okay. I was pretty sure, even if my nose was red and my face blotchy. Instead of getting off the phone, we moved their video call to the television in the living room of the Malibu place—right, more on that later—and I heckled them as Ian played video games with the guys. They tried to get me to play, but I wasn't up for beating on them.

Instead, I found some paper and a pen, writing down all my feelings. One of the drawbacks to California was my therapists were in New York and Texas. Apparently, there were legal snafus that didn't really let them treat people across state lines and I didn't have anyone here. So, writing out my feelings seemed to be a way to go. The guys played for a couple of hours and we signed off when our pizza arrived.

I promised them all I would call the next day. The fact all three of them sent me text messages made me smile. It wasn't until I was checking the list that I realized I had another text message. This one from Sammie. When had I given her my phone number? Grimacing a little, I flicked the message open.

Hopefully, I hadn't freaked her out to the point she was like never going to want to work with us again, but all I found was a link and a message.

Oh man, now I felt even worse. That was such a nice thing to do. Really, genuinely nice. And I wasn't sure about the photo, but I forwarded the link to the group chat with the guys, along with her message. I wasn't ready to look at it yet, but they could.

That comment made me burst out laughing.

"You look amazing," Ian said from the doorway, boxes of pizza in his hand along with a bottle of wine. "Absolutely gorgeous."

His phone was sitting on the coffee table and I sniffle-laughed "You say that just because you love me."

"I do love you, but I'm saying that because you're beautiful." He set the wine and pizza boxes on the table before he moved over to the sofa. With a gentle nudge, he eased me down onto my back and then walked up my length with his hands on the sofa until he hovered over me. Ian blotted everything out. "I talked to Boone and Lauren earlier," he murmured, kissing one corner of my mouth, then the other. "Everything is on hold for the next five days."

"But the schedule—" I didn't even get to finish the thought before he claimed my mouth with his. He tasted like chocolate chip cookies and coffee. The warmth radiating off of him spread over me as he made himself comfortable in the cradle of my thighs. Despite the rampant ping-ponging of my thoughts off each other, bit by bit, I relaxed as he teased my lips apart and then kissed me slowly, deeply, tongue stroking mine until I had my arms wrapped around his neck.

"Hmm," he murmured, breaking the kiss to press a line of kisses to my jaw. A shiver went through me. I'd only put on a t-shirt after the bath, between his kisses and snuggling, it had ridden up and the weight of him pressing against my naked thighs had me arching my hips. "As I was saying…" He nipped at my pulse point before drawing a circle around it with this tongue. "I spoke to them. Everything is on hold. KC and the girls know we'll be back in a few days. We'll stay here…" he reached my tattoo and kissed it so tenderly I wanted to cry. When he moved to my earlobe, I let out a little cry, the hard suck sent a bolt of pure sensation straight to my pussy.

Between us, my phone vibrated, but I ignored it in favor of getting my hands under his shirt. The heat rolling off him was even more profound on bare flesh. Ian moved back to my mouth, the connection sizzling through me as he kissed me until I forgot I had to sniffle, to breathe, and I was gasping when he let me have air again.

His blue eyes had gone deep and dark. "Just you and me," he said, running a hand down my side to my thigh and lifting it higher. My nipples ached under the fabric and when he lifted away from me, I slid my hands against his basketball shorts and dragged them down until his cock could spring free.

Yeah, I hadn't thought he'd put on anything beneath them. His weight came down again and his dick was right against my pussy and every time I raised my hips it ground me against him. If I hadn't been clenching against the emptiness in me before, I would be now.

"Ian," I whispered.

"Hmm?"

"Five days?"

"Five days." He confirmed.

The aching need in me unfurled. "That's a lot of sex we can have."

"Oh, among other things." Then he claimed my mouth again and we reached for his dick at the same time. Sometimes we liked to play. We really loved it. And other times, like now, I just needed him. Needed to feel him, and no sooner did we line him up then he pushed into me with a ferociousness that had me gasping.

Almost too much, but I needed more and when I moaned, he pulled back and then drove into me again. Our teeth clashed along with our lips and tongues. It was like we were fighting to devour each other. He reached out with one arm and shoved the coffee table away and then he rolled off onto the floor, taking me with him.

Ian took almost all of the force, but the action sent him deeper against me and I snapped my head back as another moan ripped out of my already sore throat, and I didn't care. He shoved my shirt upward—well his shirt really—and I went to raise my hands, but he got them bound behind me, tangled in the shirt. It pushed my chest out and arched my spine.

Gripping the shirt to keep my wrists locked together, he began to piston his hips upward into me, even as he pushed me forward and then he captured one nipple against his mouth. The sting of his teeth sent a whole new sensation to collide with the others and I shouted in surprise. It only seemed to spur him on, as he sucked the nipple until I swore every ounce of my blood pounded toward it, slingshotting between my pussy and my breast, then he released it. Only, then he blew against the pebbled flesh and the overload threatened to crash my synapses.

He moved to the other nipple and repeated the process. The sting of pain, the suction of too much pressure and then the release. Heat flushed against my chest and I rocked my hips in time to his thrusts, rotating my hips to a rhythm I swore he was humming and I recognized. It was all sensation and feeling.

He freed my arms, only to roll us over again and he rose up, lashing my wrists together over my head. "Keep them there," he ordered in a voice thick with heat and then he dragged one of my legs up and rested my ankle at his shoulder and then the other. The stretch burned and gave him access to push deeper.

Sweat slicked my skin as I began to mutter, "Fuck," over and over again.

"Fuck what?" Ian asked in a voice that would not be denied, and I clenched down against his cock, desperate to keep him inside of me and at the same time so hungry for the pounding he was setting me up for.

"Fuck me," I managed in a raw voice, my throat strangling the sound.

He went still, his dick no deeper than the tip as he pressed forward, half folding me, and the burn from my legs only amplified the pulse pounding away in my core. It was like a half-echo of what his cock felt like and it wasn't enough.

"Fuck me, what?" The command snapped my gaze up to him and every other worry just slid away. The only thing here was me and Ian and this moment.

"Fuck me, Sir. Please."

"Such a perfect girl for me." Then his mouth collided with mine and he pistoned into me so hard and deep I was crying against his mouth as the first orgasm struck, but Ian didn't relent, he thrust me from one to the next, and I was thrashing but I couldn't escape from the way he bound me with his shirt and his body. The first hot rush of release burst through my system like a white hot flare and I floated away on a scream.

When I drifted back, Ian was cleaning me up with a damp washcloth. My legs were spaghetti and my arms were just as rubbery. I lifted my lashes as I stared up at him, his concentration absolute as he wiped away the mess. With a second cloth, he ran it over my nipples and I shuddered. Oh fuck, they felt bruised in the most delicious way.

"How are you feeling, Angel?"

"Better," I admitted. "Greedy."

"Greedy" He lifted his gaze. "You want more?"

"Yes please," I said, this time not even bothering with hiding the cracks in my voice. "Please, Sir, may I have some more."

The corners of his lips curved upward, and I went from being on my back to over his lap and his hand landed with a stinging slap against my right ass cheek. I laughed and screamed in the same moment.

"That's for being a smart ass," he said, a smile wreathing his voice. He rubbed out the heat, spreading it around before he delivered another sharp, stinging strike. "That's for not telling me you needed to cry." More heat, more massaging and then he laid down the spanking motions in swift succession, so fast I couldn't catch my breath. "This is for blaming yourself and not letting yourself have a break."

When he was finished, my ass was on fire and there were tears on my cheeks, but I was still laughing through my sobs.

"How we doing?" he asked, massaging the flaming skin and I tilted my head to look up at him. The adoration and concern in his eyes so evident they might as well be branded onto my skin the way he was on my soul.

"I love you," I whispered.

"You want more?"

I nodded.

"It could be a long night, Angel." The warning I understood, but I didn't think I could describe to Ian what I was feeling right now, but I would try.

"I need this," I said. "Just—I need you. I need you to take over. To take it all. Take me."

He studied me for so long I thought he was going to say no, but he finally nodded. "I've got you," he whispered so much like he had while I'm sobbing. "I'm right here. I've got you."

A fresh wave of relief hit, and I shuddered when he eased me off his lap.

"On your knees, Angel, hands behind your back." I obeyed, shutting off everything except Ian and me and this moment, and when he tipped my chin up with his fingers, my heart soared at the love in his eyes. "Open that beautiful mouth—and keep it open, I want to fuck your throat."

I swore my core clenched again, but I relaxed my jaw as he instructed and thrilled to the first push of his cock past my lips. Hot, thick and tasting of us both, I took it all. The next few hours drifted by, we would take breaks and he would cuddle and feed me. Then he would tie me down or up, once he spread me out on the island in the kitchen and ate off me like I was his platter.

He put me back together, bit by bit, until all the scrapes and bleeds were bound up and my body pulsed with the feeling of him. Then we started all over again.

The next morning, I woke up sore and aching. Friction was a hell of a thing, but the bruises on my heart were easier and when Ian carried me into a bath, I just let him control everything. Just for a little longer. I needed this and it was okay to need this.

Things We Could Be

Coop

Istretched out on the bed and crossed my legs at the ankles. That lasted about three minutes and I shifted again. My dick and I were getting along again, though he might never forgive me for the hardware upgrade. The phone against my ear rang twice before Frankie answered.

"Hey." While I hated anything that made her cry, I had to admit the huskiness in her voice was sexy as fuck. "Ian said you were going to call."

"Man, he's getting really good at playing your social secretary. Good training."

I gave it a beat and her soft huff of laughter eased some of the tension in my shoulders. Honestly, I'd been worried about her since the first call from Bubba that she'd burst into tears. We'd all known they were coming, we just hadn't known *when*.

Selfishly, I wish she had when we'd been on the yacht, when all of us would have been there for her. At the same time, I was damn glad she'd had the break. She'd *needed* it.

"I'm not training him," Frankie protested, but there was a smile in her voice.

"You say no, I say get him tiger. How are you, Beautiful?"

"Hanging in," she said, sniffling. "I feel kind of stupid and overwrought, but managing. Ian's been taking really good care of me."

"Good. He loves to be there for you when you need him." He just didn't love it when life pushed her so hard she needed us that way. That, however, was not why I called. "I love to be there when you need me too."

"You always are. Even when you're not here, you're here."

"Yeah? How's that?"

"I can hear you—in my head. I hear what you would say or joke. I'll hear Archie and his snark, as well as his sweet."

"What does Jake do, threaten everyone around you?" I couldn't resist. Her laugh was worth it.

"Pretty much. He also reminds me that I can take care of myself and kick ass. So, yeah, you guys are always with me." She sniffled and then there was a whoosh.

"You laying down on the bed?"

"Well, yeah—a bed."

"Good. Can I make you feel better?"

"I don't know," she said, there was just a spark of her in that comment. "Can you?"

A grin spread across my face. "Oh, I bet I can."

"Hmm…"

"Ouch, you're wounding me."

"Ha, you just want me to go get Not So Little Coop."

My dick gave a half-hearted twitch. Yeah buddy, me too. Me too. "And if I do?"

"Well, I don't actually know if he's here."

Oh fuck, that was right, they were at the Malibu house.

"Then you better go see if there's a really big cucumber in the kitchen. We're gonna need it big."

Laughter rolled out of her and I grinned. The things we could do for each other. The things I wanted to do for her. There might still be tears in her laughter, but she was laughing.

Chapter Twenty-Six

WINGMEN

Jake

I checked my watch as Coop descended the stairs. He moved slow, but he was moving better than he had in the last few days. "You good?"

"Yeah," Coop said with a grimace, sounding anything but good. Then again, if someone rammed metal through my dick, I'd probably sound like a little bitch crying or making someone else bleed. Coop was going to get zero shit from me right now. Man was a goddamn saint. "Just a little tender. I was gonna try the jeans. Definitely not ready for them."

It was my turn to wince. "Shit, I didn't even think about that."

He chuckled. "I'm good." Instead of jeans, he'd opted for slacks and a button down with the sleeves rolled up. "Come on, we don't want to be late. I know she was gonna finish up that session at the studio then head over to The Crayon Club."

"Why the fuck is it called that?" I'd actually *yet* to hear the why behind this and Coop just shrugged.

"Cause love's a rainbow? I don't fucking know. But it's one of the few nightclubs that caters to the college crowd *and* doesn't card you to get in the door."

They'd card for drinks but not to pay the cover and get inside. Didn't matter, we weren't drinking. "Oh, wait," I said digging a hand in my pocket and pulling out the pair of silver rings we'd picked up. "Put it on."

Coop snorted and jammed the ring onto his finger, before he called. "Jeremy, we're on our way out. We'll be back later with Rachel."

"If she doesn't get lucky," I added under my breath. That was the whole point of us going. She wanted to get out of her rut, and apparently we were making her stir crazy with our so-called pining. After Frankie's meltdown last week, we'd all been on edge. Bubba had it in hand though, and she'd been sounding better each day we talked to her.

When Rachel dropped the bomb that we were going out with her, my natural inclination had been to tell her to go get fucked. Coop and she had hit it off the last few weeks and she'd actually been a hell of a support for him after he got pierced. Not that I minded helping a guy out, but there was only so much of checking his dick for him I could do. Holding his hand while they pierced it? Yeah, I was down with Rachel taking that hit for all of us.

The car I'd ordered was waiting for us. We could have done the subway, but the stairs might add to the chafe for Coop. Besides, we'd never gone to this place. "You talk to her today?" I asked once the car was on the move.

"For a little while," Coop said. "She's talking more. I think she's in a better place with everything now."

"Good." I hated it when our girl was sad. I'd beat the shit out of anyone who looked at her sideways, and had, on plenty of occasions. But when it was her own heart inflicting the damage on her? I hate feeling fucking helpless to do anything. Bubba and Coop were way better at this. Though, when she told me about writing in her journal, I'd actually thought that was a damn good idea. Even if she hadn't kept a real diary since she was like twelve or something.

"Call her tonight when we get back," Coop suggested. "She's going to want all the details on Rach's night anyway."

I laughed, then rubbed my hands together. "Hopefully, tonight pays off for her. She's almost as mopey as she accuses us of being."

"We *are* mopey," Coop said. "But we have a reason and so does she."

"Okay, don't get your panties in a twist. Tonight is about kicking that dick to the curb and letting her find something better to bury her face in."

Coop rolled his eyes at me.

"Dude, I'm being fucking supportive here."

Then he laughed.

Whatever. I was a great fucking wingman. "Just you wait and see."

"I can't wait."

I ignored his dry tone. Coop didn't have to be the life of the party, he just had to back me up. Granted, I had zero interest in picking up chicks, but I did know how to do it. Just had to figure out what Rachel was interested in that wasn't blonde, green-eyed, and tattooed on my back as well as my heart.

It took twenty-five minutes, with traffic, to get to where The Crayon Club was located. While summer was waning, the evenings were still light enough to mean we got a good look at the area. It wasn't all that bad. Little shops, restaurants, and a couple of art galleries. I mentally made a note of those. They would work for a roaming date one night.

The car let us out about a quarter of way down the block. Music from inside the club was audible out here. A strong techno beat. Not my favorite, but certainly not the worst. Thankfully, there was no line to get in and I paid the guy for our covers, then described Rachel since I was paying hers too.

Once inside, Coop and I took a beat to study the place. The place had three levels and all three had dance floors. This floor also boasted a couple of cages with dancers in them. They were dressed in the skimpiest bikinis and hosed down in glitter. They gyrated their hips and worked the bars like they were fucking them.

Damn.

Coop tapped me and held up his phone. The text from Rachel said second floor and she was on her way. It only took a minute to locate the stairs. I didn't rush them, I figured if I took my time it would be easier on him. The interesting part was the second floor had a whole different vibe, the straight up rock music was far more familiar and funnily enough, turned down. No dancers in cages, but more dancers on the dance floor.

"Go get a table," I told Coop as I headed for the bar. The place was maybe half-full. Lot of girls dancing with girls and a few guys with guys. There were some threesomes out there too and male-female pairings. I got why Rachel liked the place, even if I thought the name was dumb.

The bartender was a pixie-like blonde with super short hair and a lip piercing. "What can I get you?"

"Two cokes," I told her, holding up two fingers. "And three water bottles. They do any snacks up here?"

"Just standard appetizers and bar food. If you wanna eat you gotta go down the block to JJ's." She gave me a smirk as she used the drink wand to fill two glasses for us then passed over the water bottles. "Bar food's not bad here though. If you're hungry."

"Nachos?"

"You got it. That's thirty-eight bucks."

Fuck me, shit was expensive, but I peeled off two twenties and a five and handed those over. "Keep the change."

"Thanks sweetie." She winked. "I'll get your nachos over to you in a few."

I nodded but she was already on to the next patron. Coop had grabbed a table not far from the dance floor with a damn good vantage of the stairs. Not a bad place to check out everyone coming and going. He'd also acquired a friend. A guy with dyed black and white hair leaning against the table, a flirtatious smile on his face.

Lips twitching, I schooled my features and narrowed my eyes as I reached the table and set the drinks down. "Hey Babe," I said, voice bland. "Did you make a friend?"

"Sure did," Coop said, grinning at me. "Gib, this is Jake. Jake, this is Gib."

The guy grinned at me, the eyebrow piercing flashed under the lights as he held out his hand. I gripped it in a quick shake. "Nice to see you Gib, too bad you need to go now. Coop's taken and he knows better than to flirt."

"Aww, all the good ones are." Gib grinned at me. "You're more my type anyway. I like 'em tall, dark, and with an edge." The playful flirtatiousness amused me, but I just waved my ring wearing finger at him. "I was just telling Coop here, there's a group of us over at the back table if you want to join us. It's ladies' night tonight, so the girls tend to get a little territorial over the dance floor." He waved to a table in the corner with four or five guys at it. A couple of them blatantly checked out Coop, but the rest ignored us. Coop didn't even glance at them.

"Thanks man," I said. "We're just flying backup for a friend. But if it gets too hot out here, we know where to look for backup."

"Sounds good." With that, Gib left us to our drinks.

"Thanks babe," Coop said, grinning like the little shithead he was. "Don't know what I'd do without you."

I just snorted. "Lucky for you, I like you."

"I know," he said, rubbing his ring. "You show me every day."

Staring at him, I shook my head. "You think you're funny."

"Nah, I know I am. There's a difference."

"Dick." But I had to laugh, cause I did like the asshole most days. "I ordered us some nachos."

"Sounds good. Rach is about a block away and in a mood." He showed me the phone and the series of increasingly creative invectives.

"Why she being pissy at us?"

"I'm going to guess Walsh made an appearance at her shoot."

Fucking asshole. "Maybe we should have picked her up." I owed the dick for the sucker punch. I took a long drink of the coke and Coop shook his head.

"She can handle him, she just has to decide what she wants to do with him."

"Hopefully get rid of him, right? That's why we're here?"

"We're here because Rachel's our friend and she wanted to get out of the house for the night and to get us to stop pining."

Good luck with that. Then again, being here kind of reminded me of being in Martinique and taking Frankie dancing. It was like a kidney punch when it hit me how much I missed her. I'd never wanted long-distance. That was why we'd agreed to the same college. If Bubba wasn't out there with her, this would be a fuckload harder though.

"Stop glaring at the dance floor," Coop advised. "You're making some people nervous."

I blinked and then glanced at the couple who'd been dancing closer to us. They'd moved. Fuck. Shaking it off, I twisted to watch the stairs and caught Rachel ascending them. Despite her attitude in the texts she'd sent Coop, she looked a lot happier when she saw us.

Aww, we made Cactus Queen happy. Why did I think I was gonna end up getting nailed by the prickles in the ass if we fucked this up? I waved her toward one of the seats and the water bottles. "You want something else?"

"No, water is great," she said and this close I caught the hint of sweat on her brow and the fresh scent of perfume. Normally, she didn't wear it around us, or I hadn't noticed it. Maybe it was to cover up the sweat. She set her bag down on the seat next to her. "Thanks. We ran late on the shoot and then the light was being pain in the ass." She twisted the top off the lid and did a quick scan of the bar itself.

"You get everything you needed?" I had no idea what that was, but she'd been doing shoots like this for the last week. Her mood had a fifty-fifty chance of being shit if she hadn't gotten what she wanted.

"I did, I think. I'll know tomorrow when I start compiling everything and cleaning up the shots. I'm too tired to even think about it tonight."

"Well, that's why we're here," Coop reminded her. "Time off for you. No more work."

She laughed. "There is no rest for the wicked. Classes start week after next."

Yeah. They did. And Frankie was on the west coast nursing a bruised and wounded heart, courtesy of her bitch mother. If she wasn't already dead, I'd be tempted to kill her. I just might drive up to Connecticut and piss on her grave. It wasn't that long of a trip.

"Stop scowling," Rachel advised. "Your face will stick like that."

I snorted and shot her a bland look, but before I could comment, the blonde pixie bartender came over to deliver our nachos. She gave Rachel a much warmer grin than she'd given me and I raised my drink for a sip when she said, "It's been a while since you were in. Can I get you anything? I have some of your favorites back at the bar."

"I'm good," Rachel said in a tone so chilly it actually cooled the room down. "Thanks."

"Don't be a stranger." She ran her fingers down Rachel's arm and I raised my brows at Coop. He gave me a quick head shake, so I bit my fucking tongue even if that was the last thing I wanted to do. The pixie sauntered off and Rachel didn't even watch her go to catch the swaying hips and little show she put on.

"Don't ask," Rachel said, before she reached for one of the nachos.

"I wasn't," I told her. "But it would help if you could give me some idea of what you're looking for? Small? Tall? Stacked? Flat? Ass? Curves? Blonde? Brunette? Redhead? Dark skin, fair?"

She paused with nacho halfway to her mouth. "Intelligent, witty, and capable of a conversation are usually my starting points."

Right. Another Frankie. I could respect that. She crunched the chip and shot me a smirk.

"You wanna dance, Rach?" Coop asked and we both stared at him. "What?"

"You're not hurting yourself dancing on my watch," Rachel said firmly.

"Well, then you two go," he said pointedly. "Because sitting over here with us is not getting you laid."

She made a face. "Can't we just be out and have some fun without me having to find a hookup?"

I frowned. "I thought that was what you wanted to do tonight?"

Rather than answer, she ate another nacho and stared moodily out at the dance floor. Girls. I really didn't get them. Then again…

"Look, if you need me to go feed Walsh his dick, I can do that too."

The corner of her mouth tilted up. "Thank you, Jake. But I'm fine. I think I just want to kind of soak up the atmosphere and maybe dance a little. But we can go home when y'all are ready, I'm mostly tired." Then she slid off the chair. "Just going to hit the restroom boys, don't have too much fun without me."

She didn't wait for our response as she sauntered toward the hall leading to the restrooms. I tracked her movements automatically and if I hadn't, I'd have missed the blonde pixie bartender hurrying down the hall after her.

Fuck me. "Do you think…?"

"Yep," Coop said as he took another drink. "I do. Though, I'm not sure she was that interested."

"How interested did you need to be when a girl offered you a blowjob…"

"Dude." He frowned at me.

"You know what I mean, don't be a dick. She may not want to date her, but a hookup to take the edge off?"

His frown deepened.

"What?"

"I'm worried about her. She keeps putting herself in these bad situations. It's like she wants to fail."

"You know, you start psychoanalyzing her…"

"Yeah. Yeah." He waved me off, but we were both keeping an eye on that hall. Now that he mentioned it, he wasn't wrong. Rachel didn't seem like she wanted anything to succeed. At least not relationship-wise.

Man, I didn't want to have to do the feelings thing. But somehow, we might need to do it. "We'll get her drunk," I suggested. "Or stoned."

Coop paused. "That could work."

Great. We had a plan. Wingman meant more than just getting a person laid.

Well, sometimes.

But hey, at least we accomplished one thing tonight.

WTF Deconstructed Coffee

Frankie

"That is not a fucking thing," Rachel argued with me, and I snorted.

"I didn't make it up, it's why I sent you pictures of it. Ian and I even went inside." I shook my head as I walked over to the windows and stared outside. "Literally, tables and tables of people having their deconstructed coffee."

"Girl, you need to get the fuck out of California. That sounds like cult behavior."

I laughed. "A cult of deconstructed coffee?"

"I've heard of weirder. Manson was a thing, you know."

"He was a person and not a coffee."

"So? I've seen what you'll do for coffee. If deconstructed is all the trend, suddenly it'll be the only thing that gets you through a day and I'll have to stage an intervention and like deprogram the deconstruction. Do you know how messy that could get?" Rachel sounded equal parts scandalized and determined.

"You could always use it as the basis for a photo essay. You could call it the Deconstruction of Frankie—a tale told in pictures, beware some might fill you with horror."

She burst out laughing and I grinned.

"Oh my god," she said with a sigh. "That's really not a thing, right?"

"Totally a thing."

"Did you order any?"

"Hell no."

"Now you gotta go back," Rachel said. "Research."

"Pfft. I thought you were worried about a cult."

"True, but I'm curious."

"Well, check in New York and see if they have it there."

Dead silence greeted that comment.

"Rach?"

"I'm here, just trying to figure out what brain bleach I'd need to get rid of this concept if it actually has made its way to the city."

I snickered. "You should totally check. What cult is going to get you?"

"True, I'm suspicious of everyone."

This time what came out of me was a genuine cackle. Cause if that wasn't the definition of an understatement, I didn't know what was.

"You know what I want to know?" she asked.

"*Why* is it a thing?" Truthfully, I wanted to know too.

Chapter Twenty-Seven

BURNT

Frankie

Five days in Malibu turned into a week when we stayed over the weekend. When we got back to KC's mom's place, I sought her out that first morning and found her by the pool, half-asleep with an iced coffee. The housekeeper caught me on my way out the door and asked me if I wanted anything. Since I didn't quite feel comfortable raiding her kitchen, I asked for more coffee and maybe something light for breakfast. She promised to bring it out.

Ian had gone running. He had some of the tracks we'd already been working on loaded onto his phone and he wanted to listen to them. I offered to go with him, but he'd just given me a lingering kiss and told me he was fine to run by himself today. I could go with him the following day if I wanted. Sneaky man, he got me to agree before I remembered we had to be at the studio by seven. That meant we'd be going running *way* earlier.

Mean. So mean.

Still, the sound of his laughter when I pouted at him as he left had been a wonderful thing. After a week of wild emotions slingshotting the whole range of emotions, I couldn't complain. I mean I could, but I definitely wouldn't. Ian deserved all the good things, he'd put up with so much from me and made so much better. I also kept the put up comment to myself. My ass was still a bit tender from the play this week.

Worth it, but still sore.

KC rolled her head to the side as I walked over to join her. The huge sunglasses made it hard to see her eyes but the fact she reached for her iced coffee said she was awake. "I gotta admit," she said, by way of good morning. "It's weird having someone around who likes to get up early."

I laughed. "Honestly, if we hadn't just gotten back last night, I'd probably still be asleep."

"Sounds reasonable," she said and motioned to the lounge next to hers. I settled back on it and stared over the pool. It seemed hard to believe we were in a "neighborhood." The closest house was a half-mile away. There was a kind of warm peace just gazing at the pool and the landscaping. The whole house was a showstopper. I almost hated to sit on the furniture, but the girls didn't seem to have the same problem. "You doing better?"

I didn't answer right away, instead, I turned the idea over in my head. "I am," I said slowly. "I'm sorry we bailed on you."

"Don't worry about it," she murmured as Davina brought out a tray of coffee for me, along with fruit and croissants. My stomach let out a voracious hell yeah at the sight of it. "Seriously, don't. I should have thought about how overwhelming it can all be, but you guys seemed to be doing so well."

After setting the food down on the table between our loungers, she fixed KC with a look. "Your mama called. She said to tell you they've extended the trip because your papa is already back in town."

KC's whole expression fell.

"She said if you don't want to see him, you can fly out to meet them in Costa Rica. Then on down to Brazil for the rest of the summer."

My heart squeezed for her, KC's disappointment seemed to hover in the air like some cartoon cloud frozen in space, before she pasted on a smile. "I'm good, thank you. If she calls to see if I'm coming, could you let her know I have to be back at school in two weeks?"

"Of course. I'll take care of it." Disapproval echoed softly under those words. I took a sip of coffee, trying to not be in the way. I wasn't sure if the disapproval was for KC's response or her mother's. "If your papa calls?"

"I am *way* not here. You haven't seen or heard from me and I'm probably heading back to school if you were to hazard a guess." KC's fervent answer worried me, but not Davina, still I bit the inside of my lip to keep any comments to myself.

After she left, I glanced over at her. "I told myself I wouldn't ask, but are you all right? I've been preoccupied but you seem—different." I hated that word but it was the closest I could come to expressing what had struck me. Granted, KC and I didn't know each other that well. We'd communicated more via emails and texts than anything else. But she just seemed off.

"You lost your mom," KC said. "And signed your first recording contract. You have every right to be preoccupied, especially when I basically ambushed your time with Ian to drag you into my drama."

I twisted to sit up on the lounge and faced her. The coffee was damn near perfect, Davina had definitely figured out what I liked. "First, you ambushed us because you were being supportive as hell. I can't thank you or the other girls enough for how great you've been. As for the rest, I've been floundering, but I'm better now. Tell me what's wrong? I don't know if I can help, but I'd like to."

With a heavy sigh, KC sat forward and took a long drink from her iced coffee. "How much do you know about my family?"

"Probably not much more than you've told me. Which is nothing outside of Yvette and Aubrey." The girls were so tight, they were practically sisters, only without sharing blood. I grimaced. "And you know, the occasional TMZ article."

KC laughed, shoving her sunglasses up to perch on her fading blue hair. In the three, almost four weeks since we got to California, she hadn't touched up the color. My blue streak from the summer before was a distant memory. Maybe I should add it back again. Or make it purple—Jake would like that. Shuttling that thought to the side, I focused on her.

"Mom is an actress, Dad's a rock star."

That I knew.

"Mom used to be a singer, she auditioned to be one of his Sunshine Girls back in the day, that's how they hooked up." KC twirled her finger in the air. "They got hitched in Vegas, and before Elvis could finish pronouncing them man and wife, she was knocked up and he was banging another backup singer. I think they lasted fourteen months? A lifetime in Hollywood. I don't actually remember them ever being together, just the contract negotiations for when I got handed off between them."

That was—horrible.

"Now, before you feel too sorry for me," KC said without a hint of irony. "Realize they are both loaded and I had double everything. Double birthdays. Double holidays. Double bank accounts. The one area they couldn't seem to let go of was competing for who could give me more."

"Things aren't affection or love." I knew this. Maddy had "done" right by me. Okay, not always. She always made sure we had a roof over our heads and, most of the time, there had been food on the table. That didn't mean she'd been kind or loving or any of the things you wanted your mom to be.

"Eh, that didn't bother me as much when I was younger." Pretty sure that was a lie, but maybe the kind you got so used to telling yourself that it didn't feel like a lie when you said it.

I'd told myself any number over the years. Hurt like a bitch to rip those blinders off. Hurt even more each time she failed to live up to those expectations no matter how "realistic" I thought I was being.

"Doesn't really bother me now," KC said. "For the most part. Torched has been touring or in the recording studio since we were eleven?" She frowned. "Before that, it was boarding school and only home for summer breaks—not always here or there. Depended on whether Mom was making a movie or Dad was on tour. I spent a lot of summers bouncing between roadies and movie sets. One thing I got out of all of that was a solid grasp of the business."

And a lot of loneliness. No wonder the girls were so tight. "That sucks."

KC flashed me a half-smile and a shrug. "Most people would tell me they envied me for that glamorous lifestyle. Red carpets, movie premieres, sex, drugs, and rock and roll."

"I have my—issues with my mother, some that will never get resolved. But I always knew where home was. I can't imagine never knowing where you were going—"

"Or who you would find there? I think Mom is on her fourth husband?" She frowned. "Did she marry this guy? I don't know. He's like twenty-two and a stud. He got his start in skin flicks and moved his way up, though the skin flicks are supposed to be hush hush. Dude has—" she held her hands apart. "A dick."

I bit the inside of my lip.

"Course, he's also boning my mom, so that kind of reduces the attractive factor. They may not be married. I know she's been married four times, including to my dad. Twice she almost got married but the engagements went tits up. The last one, 'cause she was sleeping with her fiance's son."

I stared at her.

"No lie, TMZ didn't get that one but holy shit the scandal that would have made." KC laughed "Dad's not much better. He fucks 'em, knocks them up, marries, then divorces. I've got like four or five half-brothers and sisters. We're not close. We are, but we're not. We have a group chat." She dug out her phone and flipped a couple of screens before she held it up. I gaped at the chat name.

"KC!" I mean I tried not to sound appalled but holy crap. "That's terrible."

"Eh, I think it's funny. I didn't come up with it, that was Bronson. He's got six months on me—no wait, seven. His mom was pregnant when Dad hooked up with Mom, she didn't say anything until, you know, after he was born and she sued for child support."

Holy crap.

"Bronson's cool though. He has like zero interest in any of this life. He's gonna be a vet. You'd like him. Anyway…" She held up the phone and waved her family chat at me. "We could have been in a condom. We think of it as a motto and a way to remind ourselves things might have been worse—or better."

I rubbed a hand over my face trying not to laugh. "That shouldn't be funny."

"Come on, it's hilarious." She shrugged. "Anyway, it's not them I'm worried about. They're great. Most of them have really radically normal lives. Bronson's mom actually just got custody of our youngest sister— Penelope."

"The one you were worried about because of the cancer diagnosis."

"Yep, and because her mom is a fucking crack addict. She's more interested in her next hit than her daughter's treatment. I pay for it cause she can't afford it, but Bronson and I aren't old enough to be legal guardians. Jackie, however, can be, so she got emergency status as a foster parent. Bronson and I flexed some star power—mostly me but he's got a cheeky grin and the social worker likes him—and we got her taken away from her mom and put in Jackie's custody."

"What about your dad?"

"He didn't care, just wanted to know where he should keep sending the checks."

What. A. Dick.

"Besides, currently, *he* is the bigger problem."

"I'm almost not sure I want to ask how." And I wasn't, cause that sounded horrid.

KC shrugged. "He got married last year during Torched's final tour, you know for like the fifth or sixth time. I legitimately can't remember because he's had a couple of twenty-four-hour marriages."

"And?" Cause just based on this…

"His wife has kids and he loves these boys, apparently, he's been a real father to them over the years and they think he hung the fucking moon." Her whole expression puckered. "And all *three* of them are at my school. Assholes. All of them. I hate them."

Oh boy.

"Ouch."

"Yeah," she said. "It's worse because I didn't realize *who* they were and they thought I was just being a stuck-up cunt." KC rolled her eyes. "Anyway—fuck them all. Tell me about what's next. I know you guys need to go back for more recording and to get the album cover shot. What can I do to make that easier?"

Just like that, she twisted that spotlight back on me. "Yeah, I have to apologize to Sammie."

"Who's Sammie?"

"The makeup artist I freaked out on last week." I crossed my fingers. "Hopefully, she doesn't think I'm a nut. So much of what we've done so far hasn't really felt real. And I feel like none of it is how we imagined it."

"Well, two things," KC said, reaching for a croissant. The act reminded me I was hungry, so I took a long drink of the coffee before I reached for one of the croissants myself. "First, it can always get worse. In fact, every concession you make will encourage them to keep asking for them. So be sure you dig your heels in when it's important. They will try to throw their weight around, they're the label, blah, blah, blah. But independent musicians, is where it's at. You are your own brand ambassador, so you and Ian decide, *not* them."

"Okay," I elongated the two syllables. "And the second thing?"

"If you need us to throw our weight around, I'm more than happy to do it. In fact, Yvette, Aubrey and I were talking about our next album. We want you and Ian to record a song on it with us. You're a lot more valuable than Roll City Records, so they better treat you right. Because here's the thing, you've got star power. Both of you. You're gorgeous, you've got charisma and personality for days. The fact you're dating four hot guys will set the gossips on fire, but—" She raised her hands when I started to protest. "That's none of their business. The point is, don't let the music scene dictate your life. You dictate how much of it you let in and then you do this for you, not for them."

She drained her coffee then slid her sunglasses back on as she settled back against the seat.

"And never, ever, read the reviews of anything and stay off any hashtag trending that's related to you."

"Oh," I said with a shudder. "*That* one I already know."

"Good." She smiled. "I may not know everything, but this business I know."

"Actually," I said slowly. "I could use your help with something if you don't mind."

Excitement seemed to just bubble off of her as she sat up again. "Anything."

"You shouldn't promise 'anything' without hearing it first."

"Girl, have you met you? You wouldn't know asking for too much if it bit you in the ass. Tell me, what can I do?"

I sucked up my courage to ask. "It's about the music…"

"I'm all ears," KC said with a smile. "What dreams can we make come true?"

Chapter Twenty-Eight
ONE MOMENT IN TIME

Ian

The week following our sojourn in Malibu went far smoother. Frankie relaxed, not only into the music but also the cover shoot. I had to admit though, seeing her in ripped jeans all painted up was far sexier than I imagined, even after seeing the photos the first time. We did a lot of different angles and shots. Almost all of them ended up with her half-naked and that part irked me. She wasn't an exhibitionist for just anyone, but they went skimpier and skimpier.

Today, they had her in almost not there denim shorts and a bikini top that might as well not be there. In fact, from the sounds of what she and Sammie discussed as they came out of the back, the thing had been for her to be totally topless and that was *not* okay. There were easily a dozen or more people in this room, from the producer to the photographer to their assistants

305

and a few people I hadn't met or who hadn't been introduced.

"Boone," I said as I walked past him. "A word." I didn't slow down. One thing I'd learned in both sports and life, act like you were in charge and a lot of time people followed. I was also a solid believer in you got more with honey than you did vinegar—thanks for that Mom—but I was down with giving the guy a reason for stitches at the moment.

"What's up?" Boone asked as we moved out into the hallway away from the chaos of lighting and pictures. If today didn't net them what they were looking for—and at the moment I had zero fucking clue of the goal—they were talking about going out to do some live, candid shots. Maybe get some full on nudes.

"The album cover."

"Yeah," Boone said in a tone that conveyed he understood my frustration. He couldn't possibly, but I would rectify that. "It takes a while, art and marketing have to agree and there's a lot of cooks in the kitchen kid—"

"I'm not a kid," I said, keeping my tone light and even. "What I am, however, is not interested in watching all of you demote my *partner* to sex appeal."

"Okay," Boone said slowly. "I can understand that. But her body is going to sell more albums than your face. Arguably, you're a good looking guy and we're stripping you down shirtless for a lot of these shots for the same reason. Like it or hate it, sex sells."

"So do apples and naked babies in swimming pools." Did he really want to say those albums didn't sell a shit ton? "If you make it all about the cover, then you're not focusing on the music." My music didn't have to compete with Frankie's beauty. "We're not using her this way."

"I hear what you're saying, I do." Well, there was that. "The point is, we still have to look at who you are, what the public knows about you, how do we get their attention."

"And you think stripping her down and flaunting her body will get their attention and the music won't?" Because if that was the case, then we needed to rethink the recording deal. "Be honest, if you don't think the music is going to sell, then there's no point in putting anyone through this."

"Not what I'm saying." Boone held out both his hands like he wanted me to calm down. "The world doesn't know much about you at all. Who is Bound Hearts? Have you done an internet search on that? All you're going to find is they were a surprise at the final Torched concert. You might pop a YouTube video with the two of you on stage with the Torched girls. Most of which are from a hell of a long way away. What can they make out? Our girl has a banging bod."

"She's not *your* girl." He needed to figure that out right now.

"I meant metaphorically." Boone frowned. "I'm getting the impression you don't trust me."

"Well, I'll say your instincts are pretty on the money." Folding my arms, I kept a tight fist on my temper. "I get what you meant, but she's still not yours. Bound Hearts, we're a team. We're partners. We're a unit. She's not a sex object. She's a singer."

"Harsh life lesson, she's going to end up being both. Girls are going to want to be her. Guys are going to want to fuck her."

I would not punch him. It would be bad for business.

"The same can be said of you." He spread his hands wide and I'd give him points, he seemed to mean what he was saying. "You're a good looking guy. Girls are gonna want to fuck you and guys are going to want to be you. You'll both get some cross-gender appeal, it happens."

Frankie's comment about girls throwing their panties at me echoed in the back of my head.

"Sex sells, absolutely. But it's not just sex we're selling. It's fantasy. It's mood. It's a story that the listener gets to be a part of. Music is every bit as personal to the audience as it is to the performer. Will they fantasize about you? Sure. They might even get their rocks off imagining it's you or her. You're never going to police people's thoughts and you don't fucking want to. So what we do—is we package up the fantasy and we deliver it in a palatable form. One that helps us sell songs, helps you get to keep doing what you love, and gets your names out there."

I sighed.

Boone studied me for a moment. "I get it, you want to do right by her, and you don't want to capitalize on her sex appeal. Problem is, whether we do or not, the audience is going to sexualize her. So why not control what parts of the fantasy we can?"

That actually made a lot of sense. Even if I didn't care for it.

"Tell you what, let's talk to Frankie. If she's not comfortable with whatever direction we're going in, we'll switch gears. I think you two have amazing chemistry both in the studio and in person. Let's put the focus on that."

"How do you propose we do that?" Because, I thought we had already, so what had I missed?

"Can you take your eyes off her when she's in a room?"

"Nope." And I wasn't too proud to admit it.

"Then that's what we'll show. We'll play up that connection. That's where we keep our focus." He looked thoughtful and then a grin spread across his face. "That's exactly where we focus it. That's *exactly* where we focus it. Good talk, Ian. Good talk." Then he was heading back into the studio and I stared after him for a moment before I followed.

I hadn't expected the conversation to be challenging, yet, it felt like we'd lost the thread there and he'd gone charging off in a different direction. Frankie glanced over at me as I came in and there was a quizzical look in her eyes. Closing the distance between us, I was careful with how I cupped her carefully made up face and dropped a kiss on her upturned lips.

Sammie let out a little laugh. "I'll leave you to it."

"Sorry," I murmured to the makeup artist, but she'd already moved away. Truthfully, I wasn't that sorry. Not really. "Didn't mean to chase her off."

"It's okay, we were just discussing the different things she's heard when she's done people's hair and makeup. Did you know she's a wax specialist too?"

I leaned my head back and Frankie gave me a wicked teasing grin.

"And how uncomfortable are you right now?" Because if that meant what I thought it meant.

"Not bad at all, she's a damn magic worker and I was definitely due."

Didn't bother me in the slightest. I loved Frankie in every form, but if it made her happy. "Date night?" I kept the question light, but her smile grew. "Good. Any preferences?"

She shook her head slowly.

"Excellent, I have an idea." Then I gave her another kiss. We hadn't actually gotten our date. Though I was not complaining about the week in Malibu. KC had also calmed down a great deal since we'd been back. She would be heading back to school soon. Frankie and I told her we would move to a hotel, but she argued with us. If we had to sublet a place, we would, but I wasn't all that comfortable staying in someone else's house when they weren't there. Especially since we didn't know her mother at all.

That, however, was a problem for a different day.

Finally, the photographer called us over after a conference with Boone. The producer gave me a thumbs up as we moved to take our marks. "All right people," the photographer said. "Let's get to work, crank up the music."

"That," Frankie said as Paul let us out of the car at the nightclub, "was so much fun. Paul, you have pipes!"

Our driver grinned. "Thanks ma'am, I appreciate that."

"Oh, God, please don't ma'am me."

He laughed. Her smile was infectious. "Fine, I'll try to just call you Frankie."

She'd pestered him for the last two days with that and I held out my hand. He shook it. "She's right, Paul. You've got some range. Remind me to give your card to Boone."

His eyes widened a fraction. "I'd rather not. Personally, I keep my singing voice for church and the occasional car karaoke."

"Well, if you change your mind," Frankie said. "Definitely tell us. Also, thanks for finding this palace."

The Cup and Saucer—which boasted a sign of a flying saucer, and I wasn't even going to try and interpret that—was a karaoke club that Paul recommended to us. Fun place with a good vibe. Exactly what I wanted.

"Thank you. Do you know when you want me to pick you back up?"

I frowned then glanced at my watch. It was just after seven and we had an early call the next day. "Ten?" I glanced down at Frankie.

"Ten is fine," she told me. "We can go back earlier if you're worried about me running tomorrow." She stuck her tongue at me and I snorted. Two things relaxed her before a session—running and sex. I rather enjoyed both.

"Ten sounds good," Paul said. "I'll be a couple of blocks away. There's a diner where I can study." As it turned out, Paul was also in college. "So just send me a text when you're ready to go."

Inside, I gave the hostess our name and reservation and she took us to a huge table on the side. Way bigger than we needed, but the booth was deep and offered privacy, so I'd take it. As it was, Frankie scooted in and I followed her. A waitress popped over to get our drink orders along with food—they served pretty generic bar food, but I was fine with that and Frankie got a huge tray of appetizers.

Something else I was glad to see. Her appetite returning.

"You going to tell me what's been on your mind all day?" she asked once we were alone. There was a singer up on the stage absolutely slaughtering a Whitney Houston song. And I only wished that they would put the poor song out of its misery, because holy hell that was bad.

"Just had a talk with Boone earlier about how they were doing the album cover. They've been all over the place with the vibe." In all honesty, today had actually been the best shoot we'd done and they'd taken her out of the bikini and super short shorts and put her in a dark green razor back tank top and bikini bottoms—now, while I thought that was a *little* better, her reaction to the motorcycle boots that they added to her outfit had sold it to me.

Also, pools were our thing. The fact she helped them douse me in water, good times.

Chin propped in her hand, she studied me and I settled my hand on her leg. She'd changed into a flirty little shorts dress that looked fantastic on her. The ring on her left hand gleamed. The larimar had become something she tried to wear all the time, unless they asked her to take it off. Like the ring Jake gave her, Coop's ring stayed on her hand. We were going to have to find a way to blend four rings into one—kind of like how Jake did the class ring.

"I think they don't know what to do with us, we're too rock and roll for country and we're too country for rock and roll."

Chuckling, I said, "I don't know that I'd put it that way."

Her shrug and smile said it all. "I like how we sound. They'll figure it out and we've had fun with some of the experiments." We had. "But I don't want them to take away the poetry in your soul when you write your ballads. I love how you write them and I love how you sing them."

"You don't need to compliment me," I teased her. "I'm a sure thing."

That earned me a real laugh and then our food was there. "Smartass." She pinched me but she was smiling. She was eating a mozarella stick when she shifted her seat and pulled out her phone. It was a message from Jake.

So, if I beat up your lawyer, how bad of a conflict of interest will that be for you? Also, Arch said he'd cover my attorney fees if yours pressed charges.

Frankie raised her brows and looked at me. I shook my head. "No idea. Probably about Rachel."

"Hmm." She fired back a response and showed it to me before she hit send.

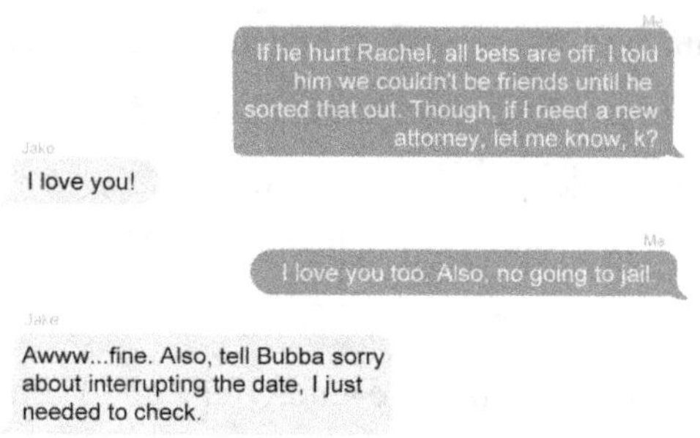

I snorted. "Five bucks says he already punched him."

"No takers," she countered. "Though I really do hope Dominic and Rachel can figure this out."

"You like him." It wasn't a question.

"I do, but I like her more. I also respect him and I like what I see in his eyes when he looks at her."

"Then I'll keep my fingers crossed for them." As soon as we were done eating—and after a few others gave it a solid go at the karaoke, most of them pretty damn good—Frankie made faces at me. "What?"

"Are we gonna go up?"

"Do you want to go up?" I teased. "I thought you were tired of being in the center of attention."

Eyes crossed, she stuck her tongue out at me and then gave me a kiss before she slid out of the booth. She headed over to sign us up. Ten minutes and one drink later, they called her name and not me.

"Hey," I protested but she just grinned.

"Trust me." Then she winked.

It wasn't all that long ago that she would rather have died on the spot than get up on a stage in front of a room full of strangers, *by herself* no less, and perform. The music started and it was my turn to gape. The Veronicas *Untouched* was not an easy song to sing, but she was right into it and her gaze fixed on me as she rolled between the notes. From the faster beat to the slower moments, she captivated me.

I'd bet if I looked around, I wouldn't be the only one staring, and then it hit me. Boone had been right, people were gonna look, they were gonna want—but we weren't about anyone else. We were about us.

And that was the key. The last song I'd been working on crystalized. When we got to the studio the next day, I knew what to tell Lauren we wanted to try. It would fit her voice and mine, more it would fit *us*.

Chapter Twenty-Nine

WE NEEDED A DISTRACTION

Archie

"We haven't missed it yet, right?" I asked as I took the stairs two at a time. Jake and I had been meeting with the contractors and safety inspectors at the new shop we were converting for ourselves. Grandpa came through in spades. I knew he would. Not only had he turned the land and buildings over, he'd made sure the local licenses were all up to date. The code inspector had given us a list of improvements and after the meeting today, we'd have a team onsite to begin the work the following week. It would take another month, possibly two, but we could switch most of our projects over and have all the room we needed to keep developing.

"Nope," Coop said from the living room where he was already set up with popcorn and drinks. "Pizza is on the way. One perk of them being three hours behind us is we can be a little late." He motioned to the screen. We were connected but the smaller screen where they would appear was blank. "They're usually running later than we are."

"That has got to be driving Frankie insane," Jake said as he followed me into the room but headed for the stairs up. "I'm gonna grab a five minute shower and change. Is Rach in or out?"

A door slammed downstairs and the alarm chirped as it was reset. "I got the ice cream," she called from downstairs. "Don't let them start before I get up there."

"You're fine," Coop yelled back down. "Grab sodas and bring them up with you."

"Yeah yeah," she said, though there was a smile under that grumble. With his question answered, Jake headed up the stairs.

A message hit my phone and I pulled it out to check it. Edward wanted to see if we were free for another game this weekend. So far, we'd gone almost every Saturday since our lunch. "You busy this weekend?" I asked Coop as I told Edward that would probably be fine, but I'd let him know if the plans changed.

"I'm working with the kids in the afternoon on Saturday, nothing on Sunday yet, but with classes kicking off next week, I figured I'd get ahead on my reading."

I nodded. "Pickup game with Edward, Saturday morning?"

"Count me in." He tossed back another bite of popcorn and went back to reading on his phone. I'd ask Jake when he came back down, but I had a feeling the answer would be yes. Rachel appeared at the top of the stairs, she had her camera bag over one shoulder and a pair of six packs in her hands.

"Have you guys considered getting a fridge for up here?"

"Yes," I told her as I stuffed my phone in my pocket and rose to take them from her. "But Jeremy vetoed the idea. Besides, he likes to keep everything stocked in one place so he can update the lists as needed."

Not to mention, the only reason we'd put one in here was pure laziness—or a gaming marathon. I filed that away for later.

She grunted then glanced at the screen. "They're late."

"Yep," Coop said. "Don't worry, we've got time. Jake's showering."

"Is that a hint?" Rachel snarked.

"Not touching that with Archie's ten-foot pole," Coop retorted and I laughed. "I learned a long time ago you don't tell a girl they smell or need a shower. Just bad etiquette, Rach. You should hang out with a better class of people."

Her grin was wicked. "I really should, but since I'm stuck with you guys, I'll have to make do."

"That was a low hanging fruit," I told her as I cracked open one of the cans and handed it over to Coop, before I snagged some of the popcorn from his bowl.

"Well, we all have our burdens to bear." She smirked and I shot her a middle finger. I rolled my eyes and returned the favor. "Well, if we have a minute, I'm taking this upstairs. Did you order the pizza?"

"Yep," Coop said, thumbing a page over on his phone. What the fuck was he reading so intently? "And I remembered to get you the vegetarian with extra onions and garlic."

"Oh, you do like me." She made a fist pump. "I'm gonna put my camera up and grab my laptop so I can work on stuff until we start." Then she was heading up the stairs. I stared after her, bemused.

"It's weird," I muttered once she was out of sight.

"That it's not weird she's here?" Coop asked and I glanced over to find him grinning at me.

"Yeah," I said, dropping to sit in one of the recliners and popping it up. Fuck, I was tired. Late nights going over plans, early morning workouts, and long days getting a machine shop setup that Jake and I could use before the academic year started. All of it keeping me busy and none of it letting me sleep. "When did that happen?"

"Probably somewhere between her becoming Frankie's best friend and us getting back here after vacation." He sat forward and set the popcorn bowl between us.

"What the hell are you reading on your phone that's so goddamn interesting?"

He chuckled. "None of your business. Why are you so grumpy?"

"I miss our girl. Why aren't you grumpier?"

Coop shrugged. "Cause I know she's chasing a dream and we're supporting her. It's not that I don't miss her. I do, but she's sounded good the last few times we talked to them and they're getting close."

"Yeah." Another reason to be grumpy. They had their first performance coming up, but it *and* Bubba's birthday fell during the first week of classes. Which was just shit. I wanted to blow the week off but the new requirements and the classes I'd signed up for made it a little harder to just say fuckoff to the west coast for a couple of days.

Adulting fucking sucked.

"Hey," Frankie's voice came from the screen and I sat up straight to lean forward.

"Hey, Babe," I grinned as I drank in the sight of her. She looked great. Her hair was wet and her face gleaming. The puffiness of her lips told me all I needed to know about *why* they were late. Goddamn, was it weird to envy Bubba and be grateful for him at the same time? "How you doing?"

"I'm good. Much more relaxed. Pretty sure Ian's going to spank me preemptively if I don't stop freaking out about singing in front of other people."

Right. *That* was why he was gonna do it. Coop snickered and Frankie's flushed cheeks pinkened. Bubba appeared behind her and he reached around to pass her a drink. "Hey guys."

"Hey."

"Yo," Jake said as he came down the stairs. "Where's our girl—there she is—looking nice and freshly fucked. Good job, Bubba."

Frankie burst out laughing and I chuckled even as Coop snorted.

"Way to be discreet, Jake."

"Why be discreet?" Jake fell onto the sofa next to Coop and then grimaced when the other guy winced. I could almost hear the mental swearing from here but they both restrained it, and I handed Jake a drink to distract him.

"Probably because I'm here," Rachel said as she descended the stairs. Jake had changed into shorts and a t-shirt. Rachel had switched hers out for leggings and oversized shirt. "Not that you have to, unless we're going to get into some kind of dick measuring contest in which case, count me out."

"Fuck that," I told her. "Your dick is bigger than all of us."

"Speak for yourself," Coop said and I narrowly caught the pillow before it hit me in the face.

"Oh, I miss you guys—hi Rach!" Frankie pulled our attention again.

"Hey bitch, looking good. California boy there being good to you?"

"Very. Are my boys being good to you?" Her eyes sparkled. Actually fucking sparkled. Okay, I could handle just about anything if she was going to smile like that.

"Absolutely terrible," Rachel deadpanned.

"Yep, cause if we were being sweet, she'd vomit or throw things at us," I deadpanned in return. Rachel grinned at me.

"See, he gets me."

Oh, I got her. She was a shit, but she was our shit, so yeah. She grabbed one of the drinks and folded herself onto the loveseat and pulled a blanket down over her legs. It wasn't that cold in here, but it might be.

"Is Jeremy there?" Frankie asked. "I wanted to thank him for the care package he overnighted."

I snorted. "No, he's out this evening. Don't ask doing what, he didn't deign to share his plans beyond the very crisp instruction that there was food in the fridge that could be reheated or we should order pizza."

The doorbell rang and Jake popped up. "That's the pizza."

"Oh, that sounds good." Frankie sighed.

"Ours is coming," Bubba told her.

"We should have ordered it before the shower. I'm starving." Her pretty little pout was all teasing, and it satisfied something deep inside of me. Granted, they were just a two-foot by two-foot square on the huge television screen, but it was almost like having her here.

"It'll be here soon, Angel," Bubba soothed her. The return of her appetite was a huge thing. Bubba had kept us up to date on that, after her meltdown during the photo shoot, she'd turned a corner. I could only wish it had happened sooner, for her sake. But I was glad it happened at all.

"We're doing movies," I said. "How do you not have Twizzlers somewhere?"

"Oh!" She bounced up. "Those were in the care package. Be right back." The angle of the camera on their screen gave me a good peek of bare ass when she stood up and I grinned, then I glanced at Rachel.

"You didn't see that."

"Dude," Rachel said in the driest tone. "I've seen the goods. I admire the goods. I'm not worried about the goods."

Coop's pillow landed and nailed Rachel right in the side of the head. She paused then picked up the pillow, expressionless.

Shit. Coop was about to die.

Then she winged that sucker right back at him and nailed him. Already expecting his next volley, I hit him with a pillow before he could wing one at me.

"What are they doing?" Frankie said, delight in her voice.

"Pretty much what it looks like. Coop started it."

"I did not," Coop called. "I'm innocent."

"And I'm the pope," Jake retorted as he made it to the top of the stairs. "Ceasefire. You fuck up the pizza, you starve."

Yep. I stopped. So did Rachel. Then Coop winged one, but Jake caught it one handed as he walked between Coop and Rachel.

"Nice," Rachel complimented him.

"You're welcome." He whacked Coop with the pillow before he sat down and then leaned to pass Rachel her pizza. "So where were we before the clown crew got stupid, Baby Girl?"

"Just me drooling over your pizza," she said, holding up her Twizzlers. "But Jeremy saves the day."

"He does that." I snagged one of the plates from Jake before putting three pieces of pizza on mine. He and Coop pretty much did the same. Rachel watched us with a bemused look. "What?"

"I'm wondering how many hoops you guys are gonna have to play with Frankie in California, if you keep eating like that."

Frankie's fresh round of laughter filled the air as I flipped Rachel off. "We get in enough, keep it up and I'll make you bring your melancholy ass with us."

"Pfft. Good luck with that." She leaned back in her seat. "I don't play basketball."

"Me neither," Frankie admitted. "But I'll give it a shot when I get back. I'm really suffering some FOMO right now."

"You're more than welcome," Jake said. "You can be on my team."

"Or mine," I said. "If we're doing two on two, though with both of you back, we can go three on three."

"If you boys turn me into some kind of sports fanatic, I'll never forgive you," Rachel said, but there was no real sting in her words "Did you guys ever decide what we were watching?"

Silence greeted that question.

"Right. Whose turn is it?" I took a bite of the pizza and glanced around the room. It had been a while since the five of us—now turned six—had sat down to watch a movie. One rule of thumb to keep arguments and debates to a minimum, and also to actually *get* to the movie, was letting everyone take turns.

"Shit," Jake said after a beat. "I don't remember. Who picked last time?"

"I did," Bubba said. "We watched Inception."

Right. Mindfuck of a movie. "Then it would be…"

"Let Rachel pick," Frankie suggested. "She hasn't gotten to choose one."

Munching on her pizza, Rachel glanced at us. "What are the rules to picking?"

How she managed to chew her food and talk without spitting any of it out was impressive. "No horror," I said in the same breath as Jake did.

"Frankie doesn't do horror," Coop said. "Nothing where the animals—"

"Oh, Tiddles, there's my boy," Frankie cooed as the black cat appeared on the back of the sofa and walked across it to where I was sitting. I moved my plate and the cat landed in my lap and immediately started to purr. "Oh, I miss my babies. How are Tory and Tabby?"

"Tory's asleep on the bed upstairs," Coop said. "Tabby's either up there or in Jeremy's room."

Frankie let out a little sigh.

"Hang in there, Babe," I said. "Couple more months and you'll be home, home." That was what I kept telling myself too.

"I know and I know this is all worth it," she admitted. "It's just hard some days."

"It's hard every day," Jake said. "But nothing worth having was ever easy, Baby Girl. You two have this and we're all really fucking proud."

"Yeah," Coop backed that up. "Now just don't suck, okay?"

I hit him from one side and Jake got him from the other, but it was Bubba who laughed and Frankie just shook her head. "Terrible. All of you, just terrible."

"Yet, you love us," I reminded her.

"I do," she said with another sigh, then a doorbell sounded and she bounced up. "Oooh, pizza."

"Hey," Jake and I said in the same breath, but Bubba caught her arm and pointed her back at the chair.

"I got it."

I blew out a breath and so did Jake. Frankie answering a door in nothing but a shirt? Not. Happening.

"Okay, Rach, hit us." We needed a distraction. "What are we watching?"

Chapter Thirty

ABOUT TO GET CRAZY

Frankie

I rolled over before the alarm and propped myself up on my elbow to watch Ian sleep. He had one arm tucked behind his head and the other resting on my thigh, it had just moved from one leg to the other when I turned to face him. His hair had gotten a little longer over the last few weeks. I didn't think he'd done more than get a trim since we'd been in California. A lock of blond fell in a curve over his forehead.

No one should look so perfect in sleep, or when they woke up. I always had scary hair and if I forgot to wash off my makeup, raccoon eyes. Hell, Ian even looked good in the cosmetics they'd used on him for the photo shoot and it didn't soften his features at all. If anything, it just enhanced them. Gave him a more chiseled set of features.

A sigh worked its way out of me and I ran my fingers over his cheek, just lightly tracing his fingers.

"I must be dreaming," Ian murmured, not opening his eyes. "My angel is never awake this early."

"Your angel is excited."

"Is she now?" He cracked his eyelids open and smiled at me. "Why are you so excited?"

"Well, one," I leaned down and brushed a kiss to one corner of his mouth, careful to not exhale. No one needed morning breath greetings. "It's the birthday of one of my favorite people."

"Hmm—I get that. And two?"

I kissed the other corner of his lips. "Tonight, Bound Hearts is taking the stage for the first time as us."

"Correction, second time." He ran his hand up and down my thigh lazily. "London counts, Angel."

"That was terrifying." I made a face.

"And you were brilliant."

"*We* were." Still, just the thought of that crowded arena and how many people had shown up to see Torched perform and then walking out there— oh, my stomach bottomed out.

"Breathe." The command might have been offered in a light voice, but it helped. Some.

"How are you so calm?" He had been from the moment we got here. He'd just *handled* it. Handled me. Handled everything they'd thrown at him. When he didn't like something or I hadn't, he'd handled that too.

"Simple answer?" Lifting his brows, he raised his hand to rub his knuckles gently against my jaw.

"Do I need coffee for the more complex one?"

He chuckled. "Probably, but the easiest answer is, you need me to be calm. You needed me to be steady."

I made a face. "That doesn't sound fair to you."

"Angel, being there for you is all I've ever wanted. Being there for you and getting to perform with you? That's just icing on the cake."

Propping my head against my hand, I studied him with a smile. "Sometimes I wonder how I got so lucky."

"I wonder the same thing every day. About me," he added the last bit with a teasing grin. "Not you."

"Nice save."

"I liked it." The doorbell rang and I frowned. We were staying at an apartment in a high rise in Los Angeles. It cost a ridiculous amount, but the commute from Malibu was ridiculous and this from a Texas girl, where everything was super far apart.

"Did you order us breakfast?" Ian asked as he threw the blankets back and climbed out. I watched him reach for his shorts and gave a little sigh. There was definitely something to be said for how regimented he was in his workouts. Normally, he rolled out of bed and right into pushups.

Crazy man.

Then again, he had a crazy kind of good looking to his body, right down to the way his muscles rippled when he moved.

"I can feel you staring at my ass."

"I like your ass."

He glanced over his shoulder after dragging his shorts up and grinned. "Stay right there."

"Yes, sir," I purred and then winked.

The doorbell rang again, and he growled. "This better be important."

I flopped back against the bed as he strode out. Staring at the ceiling, I half-listened as Ian opened the door. His voice drifted back toward me. "Thank you," he said. "Please, bring it in."

Bring it in?

A minute later the smell of coffee hit me followed by bacon and…

My stomach growled. Shoving the blanket back, I snagged his shirt from the end of the bed and pulled it on. Then padded to the doorway to peek out. There were two men setting up a rolling table. It had covered dishes on it and a pot of coffee. Ian held a clipboard and signed for it.

"Anything else?"

"No, sir. When you're done, just push the table out into the hall. We'll have someone pick it up later today."

Okay, if we were in a hotel that would be one thing… Ian's expression seemed equally bemused when he turned back toward the bedroom after locking up.

"Is it safe for me to come out?" I hoped so, cause I could swear I smelled french toast. Real french toast. The kind of french toast Jeremy made.

"Yeah, I think so Angel, no sense in letting the food get cold."

He plucked a card from a stand in the center, then opened it. I lifted one of the silver covers and moaned at the rich scents of cinnamon and nutmeg with powdered sugar goodness sprinkling the crispy to perfection french toast.

Someone loved us.

"Mr. Ian, I wanted to wish you the happiest of birthdays. As tonight is your debut performance with Miss Frankie, I thought the best way to start the day off was with a meal of your favorites. I took the liberty of contacting a good friend and chef that could prepare everything and make sure it arrived promptly. While we cannot be there with you this evening, know we are all thinking of you. I've also made arrangements for a birthday cake to be delivered tomorrow when you can both enjoy it. Kindly, Jeremy."

My heart melted as Ian read off the note. It was a really amazing and thoughtful gesture. "He sent us breakfast."

"Yes, he did," Ian said as he lifted his own silver lid to look at the steak and eggs waiting for him. My stomach wasn't the only one growling. The whole service even came with silverware and mugs, as well as orange juice. He'd thought of everything. "I'm just trying to figure out how the hell he knew we'd be awake." He flipped the note over while I filled his glass.

"He knows you like to wake up early. We told the guys I've been running with you to keep you company. And cause it's good for me." Breath control I'd found, got easier with all the running. Some of the notes we'd been singing meant I needed to be better at my breathing. That and it also helped take the edge off.

Once I'd poured the coffee, I leaned up to press a kiss to his jaw and Ian smiled. "What was that for?"

"Just you being you. You get as flummoxed as I do when someone goes out of their way for you." I didn't know how many people would recognize that, but I did.

He rubbed at the scruff on his chin and gave me a rueful smile. "I am, but I'm also not going to let that stop me from eating the food—or you."

Heat rushed up my face. "Sounds like you have a plan."

"Birthday boy…" he began and I laughed as I slid into the chair. The french toast wasn't going to eat itself. The whole time, my tummy curled in anticipation. We didn't have anywhere to be until later this afternoon. It was already shaping up to be a good day.

That night, we arrived at Club 404 ninety minutes ahead of our set. The band was already there and hanging out in the blue room in the back. Boone grinned when he saw us and to my delight, Sammie *and* Lauren were both there. "Hey guys, how are you feeling?"

"Like I'm about to piss my pants," I admitted. "I won't, but my butterflies have butterflies."

The guys from the band—Xavier, the drummer, K.O. bass player, and M.J. who handled keyboards and sang backup vocals for me while K.O. and Xavier did for Ian, all laughed.

"Come on," Sammie said, beckoning. "You too M.J., let's do a touch up and get some spritz to hold everything in place under the lights. I'll even teach you a few tricks."

I kissed Ian, then followed the girls to a little room that couldn't be more than a closet. Lauren tagged along and she practically buzzed with excitement. While my nerves were all over the place, I was also so excited I could burst. Ian had been riding a cloud all day and I loved seeing how happy he looked. I couldn't wait to get out there and sing with him.

"Hey Lauren," I said as Sammie ushered me into a chair, "could I get you to do me a favor tonight?" I hadn't expected her to be here. Honestly, I hadn't expected either of them, but I was so happy they were here.

"Sure, want me to go score you a drink from the bar?" The offer made me laugh.

"No, I don't want to puke." I'd drink later though, I didn't think I'd need the alcohol for a buzz.

"Well, we definitely don't want that."

M.J. laughed. "Stick with water. You'll be shocked by how dehydrated you get under the stage lights." Oh, that sent my butterflies into hurricane force twirls.

"I was gonna ask if you could video the set for us, or as much as you can."

We had seven songs in the first set and if it went well, another seven for the second. Over half the songs would be on the album, with five covers of other popular tunes, including a Torched song that KC insisted we do—it was the same one we sang with them in London.

"Oh, hell yes, I can," Lauren said, her eyes brightening. "Let me go see if Boone brought his digital camera with him. If not, I'll just do it with my phone."

"I love you!" I called after her and Sammie smiled at me.

"You're feeling better."

"I am," I said. "I feel good about tonight, even if I also feel a little crazed."

"It's going to be great," M.J. declared. "We're not going to let it be anything else."

While I didn't know our bandmates that well, the time we'd spent in the studio together had been fun, and they seemed pretty enthusiastic about everything. Mental fingers crossed, I sat still while Sammie did my cosmetics and got my hair all styled. In the end, our vibe and "style" had come down to the same thing —we were a couple of kids from a small town in Texas. We had a lot of traditional background beats, but we were making our own way.

Ballads, rock and roll, and a little pop thrown in for good measure. We wouldn't be pigeon-holed. Boone had been all in after we laid down the first three tracks. We'd done them his way, then melded in a secondary style, and our third attempt had been Ian making the sound our own again while still using some of their ideas.

The quiet pride in him when we listened to the final result had been unmistakable. It was us, maybe a little enhanced and a little fancier, but still us and I'd loved it. Thankfully, so had Boone and Lauren. After that, we'd gotten to work on the rest of the album. We had almost all of it set.

That meant we'd also be performing in clothes we were comfortable in. I had on ripped jeans and white sleeveless top that left my midriff bare. Ian wore a matching white shirt and jeans. He'd even rolled up the sleeves on the t-shirt to give himself a more muscle shirt look. The only concession I'd made to a "stage" presence was the heels I'd put on. They weren't five inch stilettos but a far more sensible three inch with a hint of a platform, so I didn't kill myself.

Baby steps.

Tonight was the first of what might be many nights for us to come. It wasn't all that long before I stood with Ian, hand linked with his. He had his guitar, I still couldn't quite play mine while we were deep in the middle of the sets, so I'd just be singing.

My heart raced and I swore I was already sweating. Ian lifted my hand and brushed a kiss to my knuckles. When I glanced at him, he smiled and more of my nerves melted away. "We did it," I whispered.

"Yes," he agreed softly. "We did."

"Club 404," the announcer's voice cracked over the speaker as the dance music faded. "We've got a special for you tonight. You might have seen them on YouTube performing with Torched in London, or caught a clip of their song on the concert tracks they released—but tonight you'll get them in person. We love launching bands here, so let's give it up for Bound Hearts."

Surreal didn't begin to describe the next few minutes as we headed out to the stage. The microphone was right there and the lights on the stage were intense, it threw the rest of the place into shadows. As my eyes adjusted though, I could make out the fact there were more full tables than empty and people were still coming in. One of the reasons Boone picked this club was they did a Quench Your Thirst Thursday, that meant half-priced drinks all night.

A well-lubricated crowd, already in a good mood, would be more receptive. Or so he said. A distant hum of conversation reached us in the bubble of light. The sound of dishes being moved. The hiss of a drink dispenser. And I swore my own heartbeat.

Turning my head, I looked to Ian and found his gaze on me. One. Two. Three. He tapped against his guitar, and then he hit the first two chords with the rest falling in with him on the third. Our song was the one we were opening with. It was so full of angst and hope and life, that I thought we should start with something more upbeat. Then again, birthday boy got what he wanted.

It was—magic. Every single note had me on edge and I forgot the people and the room. It was just us, singing like we had in his bedroom, or mine, or at the brownstone. It had always been us. When the last note faded, applause jarred me a little but Ian was already segueing into the next song and I followed his lead.

Just. Magic.

Chapter Thirty-One
QUISQUE HABET STRATIS

Coop

Pen between my teeth, I left the lecture hall with my backpack half-opened and my digital tablet in my hand. We had both standard textbooks and ebooks. I worked better studying off paper and writing out notes. But I took faster notes on the tablet, without having to try and read my own writing later. Frankie's penmanship was so much better, and was half the reason I borrowed her notes in high school. That said, I'd been managing. I moved into an empty alcove to set my bag down and repack it. I had roughly—I checked my watch—forty-five minutes between PSY 309, and Latin 201.

My advisor had said the course load I'd chosen was challenging. Yeah, the psych classes were interesting, and I was definitely invested. Latin, not so much, but I could *use* it going forward, so I'd stick with it. I'd debated going back to French, just to get Frankie to tutor me. The minute my dick got hard at the thought, I switched to Latin. There was no way I could survive her tutoring me and actually learn anything.

No, I'd just be trying to get in her pants. A lot.

That thought went straight to my cock and I grinned. Okay, a semi I could deal with and there was no sting. Hell yes. I snorted a laugh to myself as I checked the tablet to make sure the notes were saved, then tucked it into the bag. Removing the pen from my teeth, I slid it into the zippered pocket then dragged the backpack back on. I had time to go get coffee and send my girl a message to wake up to.

I took the stairs down the six flights rather than wait for the elevator— it was faster—and I'd just stepped into line when Dominic Walsh walked through the door. Not rolling my eyes, I focused on the barista ahead. Maybe he'd think I hadn't seen him.

Nope. Asshole walked right up to me.

"You got a minute?"

"Depends," I said, cutting him a look. "You about to be an asshole?"

The other man stared at me steadily, almost contemplatively. "I haven't decided."

Well, at least he was honest. "Buy me coffee and I'll give you five minutes."

The attorney nodded, then said nothing until we got the barista. "Coffee, black," he said. Then glanced at me.

"Like your soul?" I drawled then grinned at the girl behind the counter when she laughed. "Just a latte. Extra shot."

I'd need it for Latin.

After Dominic paid and our drinks were ready, he motioned to the tables outside. Considering how crowded it was getting in here, probably not a bad idea. I made a show of checking my watch once we were out there. I still had thirty minutes until class. "Your five minutes starts now." I set my bag down between me and the storefront as Dominic took the seat across from me.

"Rachel," Dominic began, his expression contemplative.

I resisted the urge to say, "no shit," barely. Instead, I pulled out my phone and opened up the message thread I had with Frankie and debated what I wanted to write her.

"You said you'd give me five minutes."

"I can multitask," I informed him. "And clock's ticking."

The impatient huff threatened to make me grin. For an attorney, he lacked the cool head of a negotiator where Rachel was concerned. I got that. She could drive a priest to drink and probably all the nuns too. It'd be a hell of a party.

"Rachel is no longer taking my calls, particularly now that she's moved in with you." His expression had gone to something bordering on neutral. But having seen this guy in action when he was defending Frankie's interests, there was a lot more in the way of emotion than he had been when it was business.

Good.

"While she has made herself clear, I also think it's bad form for her to just fill in for Frankie while she is in California."

Wait. What?

"Rachel can be tempestuous, and I understand she wants me to jump through hoops. Hoops, I will say, I'm finding increasingly challenging. An—"

I held up a hand. "If the words affair, sex, or some other direct or indirect intimation that we're cheating on Frankie comes out of your mouth, you're going to need a good dentist and surgery to fix your jaw."

Anger flash-fired through me. I would never and neither would they. Dominic's eyes narrowed. "You sound very certain."

"Asshole, I am certain. Rachel is family. We'd never treat her like that and we sure as shit wouldn't do that to Frankie." Something in the way the corners of his mouth moved tipped me. "But you knew that. You wanted confirmation. Why?"

"Nothing to concern yourself with," the attorney said as he leaned back in the chair.

"It must be, if you needed to ask me…or is she shutting you down so hard the only way to get information is a fishing expedition?"

Dominic shook his head slowly. For a microsecond, I felt for the guy. I really did. It sucked to be in love with, or desperate for, a person who didn't know you existed. Then I shook that off, because Rachel absolutely knew he existed, or she wouldn't be cutting him off. So far, she'd been rather tightlipped on the subject.

I had a few ideas though.

None I was inclined to share with this guy.

"That it?" I asked. "You still have sixty seconds to go."

"What would it take to get you to invite me to dinner at the brownstone?"

I didn't spit out my coffee. Barely. I also didn't laugh in his face. "First, I'd want to have dinner with you. I don't. Second, Jake and Archie would have to be all right with it, pretty safe bet the answer will be no. Because the most important person in that equation wouldn't want you there." Rising, I picked up my backpack and slung it over my shoulder. "Sorry, man. You're going to have to earn your way back into her good graces with an approach that doesn't go through us. Because it won't get through us."

Didn't think I could make it any clearer.

"With that, your five minutes are up." I drained my coffee. Instead of walking away, I stared at him a minute. The hot August air already had my shirt sticking a little. "Look…for what it's worth…" I debated my next words carefully. "If you really want Rachel to want you, then you need to respect her. Show her that respect. If that means backing off, then back off. If that means a new approach, it means a new approach. But this—going around her and trying to manipulate a way in the door, is just going to alienate her further. She's not a woman you'll ever control."

And on that note, I really needed to get her drunk and talking. I had a feeling she didn't let much out without a little assistance, and if we were gonna figure out what she wanted, then that might be the only way to do it.

I tossed my empty in the trash and started to turn away, but Dominic rose and put his hand out. I stared at the hand a moment then at him. "Thank you," he said.

"I didn't do anything," I said, honestly. "Keep that in mind with whatever you do next."

"Noted—one more question?"

"Time's up." But he just chuckled at the reminder.

"I just wanted to know if Frankie and Ian were getting along well in California. I've been playing telephone tag with her on some paperwork."

"She's great, they're both great. I'll let her know you asked about her."

"Thanks."

Not giving him a chance to ask any more questions, I headed back across the street and up the block. I wouldn't have much time to leave a message for Frankie and I absolutely wanted to, cause Latin would take the next three hours of my life.

Kill me.

Archie was just coming out of the doors with a river of other students. The first couple of weeks were always insane. Largely, because we had to navigate new routes to new classes and it was just crazy making.

"Hey," he said, glancing past me. "What did he want?"

I didn't have to look to know Walsh was still there. "What does he ever want?"

"Man has it bad," Archie mused with the faintest touch of sympathy. Very faint. Like, almost nonexistent.

"Apparently, though he needs to figure her out rather than just try to corner her."

"Hmm." Archie grunted then looked at me. "Text me what you want the flowers to say. It's your turn to write the message."

I grinned. "Will do." Since debuting on Bubba's birthday, they had begun appearing in clubs all over California, a couple in Arizona and one up in Washington state. The plan was for them to make their way east soon. We'd gotten to see a video of that debut performance and she'd blown me away with her confidence and her sound. Hell, they both had. While we'd been getting snippets and clips of their tracks, the video was the first time we'd gotten to really *hear* them and the new sound they'd put together.

"I've got lunch with Grandpa," Archie said, glancing at his phone then at the street. Probably waiting on a car. "Just fire it over when you're ready. Bubba said tonight they're at the Giggle Room."

"Giggle Room?" I shook my head. "That sounds more like a comedy club."

"Right? But he said they do both. They're actually the headliners tonight."

"Hell yes." Pride flooded my chest. "We need to get our asses out there and surprise them."

"Already working on it. We just need to get all our classes locked down and then go. There's my car…talk to you later." He lifted his chin and then was gone.

I glanced down at my phone. I had maybe five minutes to get to class, but I'd be late before I blew off sending her a wake up message.

I grinned before adding a couple of kissy faced emojis and hitting send. Morning text messages weren't the same as being there when she woke up, but it was as close as I could get. I climbed the stairs to the third floor, where the Latin lecture hall waited. My phone buzzed just as I slid into my seat and I pulled it out, along with my tablet and tabbed open the message only to close it immediately.

Yep. Time to switch seats. I grabbed my stuff and climbed up to the top row, where no one could sit behind me. It was kind of like the nosebleeds in academia, but worth it. Cause I opened the message to find the topless picture of Frankie blowing me a kiss with her hair all in disarray.

Beneath it, a single message popped up.

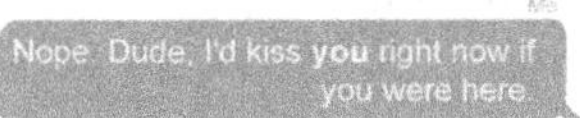

Not bursting out laughing took far more self-control than I knew I possessed.

Frankie sent back a series of laughing emojis and an *I love you.*
Definitely gonna be a good day.
Even if I might start associating naked Frankie with Latin.
It was still a romance language, right?

The picture, and everything associated with it, sustained me throughout the day. Bubba sent a couple of quick updates about their gigs and possible schedule changes. Also, that they were going to be back in New York in October, one way or the other. Frankie wouldn't miss our birthdays.

While that still seemed forever away, we could do this. The yelling was the first thing to hit me when I let myself in. My eyes hurt and so did my head. Latin for three more semesters might kill me. But it would be worth it, or so I kept repeating.

Jeremy stepped out of the kitchen and glanced down the hallway. "Good evening, Mr. Coop. I have your dinner set aside on a plate in the warming drawer."

"Thanks, Jere," I said. "I'm gonna go get changed and grab a shower, then I'll get it." I needed to wake up because I had a lot of studying to do. More shouting drifted down the stairs. "Do I want to know?"

"I believe Miss Rachel is handing Mr. Jake and Mr. Archie their asses in one of the video games. Apparently, they were misinformed about her skill level."

I didn't know what was funnier, Jeremy saying hand them their asses or Rachel actually nailing the guys.

"Would you like me to bring your dinner up in a few minutes, after you've had time to shower and change?"

"I can come get it. Also—weird question. You don't know anyone who speaks Latin, do you?"

He favored me with a droll stare. "Very few people actually speak Latin, Mr. Coop, it's a dead language. It is used in many contexts and provides the source material for many other languages, but no one actually speaks it as a native."

"Right. I knew that. I just need a Latin tutor. I don't want to fall behind."

Jeremy gave me a measuring look. "Bring your homework down after breakfast tomorrow and we'll go over it. You don't have classes until the afternoon tomorrow, correct?"

"Right—you speak Latin?" Why the hell was I surprised? This was Jeremy.

"As I said, no one speaks it like a native," Jeremy said. "I have, however, done my own studies. Tomorrow morning. After breakfast. Don't be late."

"Jeremy?"

"Yes, Mr. Coop?"

"Can I ask why you learned Latin?"

"Of course."

So, I did.

He gave me a small smile. "Hoc est secretum meum." With that, he returned to the kitchen and I chuckled. Jeremy had layers.

Blowing out a breath, I made it to the top of the stairs when Jake let out a groan of disbelief and Rachel chortled.

Flawless Victory.

Oh yeah. Jeremy wasn't the only one with layers.

Chapter Thirty-Two
FAR AND AWAY

Frankie

The internet connection in the hotel sucked. We could have stayed at a more expensive place, but this one was close to the venue and the other members of our band were here. Solidarity. That said, the internet *creeped* along. I'd actually switched to using the hot spot on my phone, but it wasn't much better.

Almost any other time, I'd have just waited until we were back at our place in Los Angeles. The fact I was thinking of it as our place was also weird. It wasn't home. August had segued into September when I wasn't looking, and we'd completely missed Labor Day. In a little over a week, it would be October and the number of clubs and appearances had gone up, not down.

Ian said he'd talk to Boone. We were supposed to get a break at the end of the recording before we started doing the club appearances, but they were trying to generate buzz for us with a couple of singles having dropped on Spotify. They wanted to try and put together a video so we could drop one on YouTube.

The last time I messaged KC about it, I'd asked her why I ever thought this was a good idea and she'd given me a pep talk. Well, more of a, this part sucks but it is worth it, talk and then she'd asked me how I knew I loved the guys.

There was a question I wasn't entirely certain how to answer, because it felt like I'd always loved them. Man, we were a mess.

And the little clock ticking down in the corner of the window didn't help my mood. I had to finish this test. It was more of a "did you actually do the reading" kind of thing and I had, but I was really tired. We'd been up late the night before, making the drive from the last town to this one and getting into the hotel.

"No more whining," I told myself as I rubbed my eyes. "You can do this." Ian had his own work to do, but he'd volunteered to stop at the coffee place a mile away, just to get me coffee *after* his run. 'Cause my boyfriend was a saint. All four of them were.

It took me about fifteen minutes total, when I stopped daydreaming and mentally complaining to focus on the questions. They were pretty detailed with the choices of answers being subtly different. Fortunately, I *had* done the reading. When I finished, I hit submit and got eighty-nine out of ninety correct.

I legit shouldn't give a damn about the one I missed, but I took the review option and skimmed down until I found it. Second question, when I'd been whining. Eh, figured. Ugh. I switched over to the discussion tab and found this week's reading assignments and the actual work assignments.

There were notes too, including one in my inbox about Grandpa Ted serving as my mentor. He'd been approved, I needed to check in with him weekly and email reports to both him and the teacher. Oh, I could totally do that.

While I was thinking of it, I got the email sent off to Grandpa Ted, we'd chatted a couple of times. Mostly surface stuff. He'd actually asked me a lot of questions about the music business, the contracts, the negotiations and said it was a good model for both product and service. That made a lot of sense. Now I had to wonder if part of his thinking was, that I use my current situation as research for this project.

We were producing a product—songs via different mediums. Contracts required us to participate, but also held the companies we were working with to some specifics as well. A constant stream of negotiation went on, and while we hadn't been altogether as happy with everything, we had gotten some concessions that the company hadn't wanted to give. When I told Grandpa Ted about that, he'd laughed.

"Young lady, let me tell you that's how you know you have a solid deal. Because if one party or the other walks away from the table happy, they've likely just screwed the other guy. If you'll pardon the expression. If they both walk away unhappy, they both had to make concessions, but it works out to be a more equitable deal."

Food for thought. I fired off another email to him and then reached for my phone so I could text Archie, when the door lock tumblers activated and then Ian slid inside. He was drenched. Oh, crap. I shot up from the desk and hurried into the bathroom to grab a towel. Laughing, *and dripping*, he set the drink carrier down as I held up the towel.

"I didn't even hear it start raining." I glanced at the window, guilt nibbling at me. Now that I was focusing on the present, the whooshing sound of rain was clearly audible.

"It wasn't until right before I got to the parking lot." He got this soaked, that fast. I passed him the towel and took the coffees. After setting those aside, I helped him strip out of the wet clothes and he dragged me in for a morning kiss. "At least I'm not sweaty," he teased as the dampness soaked through my tank top.

Laughter eddied through me, and I wrapped my arms around his neck then half-jumped. He dropped the towel and caught my thighs as I gripped his hips. "No, you smell like rain and coffee," I groaned a little with that before adding, "and Ian."

"Glad you added that last one there," he retorted, then scraped his teeth over my lower lip. When he lapped at it, I tilted my head to kiss him. Even after being rained on, his skin was hot beneath the dampness. One moment we were upright, then he twisted and we fell onto the bed with me on top.

He swallowed my laughter as he fisted my ponytail and then he yanked the scrunchy holding it off my face. The hair tumbled down in wild disarray. The combination of hairspray, sweat, and then sleeping on it had left it a bit of a nightmare. Not that Ian seemed even remotely deterred, as he fisted my hair. His kisses grew hungrier and more demanding.

I pulled back only long enough to let him get his hands under my shirt. As he pushed up, I peeled it off and then his lips were locked around a nipple. Holy fuck, everything inside of me clenched. Scraping my nails over his scalp, I let out a soft cry as he sucked the peak so taut it spiraled pleasure through me even as it stung. It was right at the edge of too much.

Heat from his palms scorched down my sides as he reached for the lace panties I had on. There was a rip and both of us froze for a moment. The blast furnace of lust that hit me when I realized he'd torn the seam on my panties took my breath away.

Ian pulled back for a split second, his deep blue eyes heavy-lidded and his sensuous mouth a slash of a smile as he ripped the seam on the other side. One had been an accident, the other? I swore, I was soaked before he got the panties all the way off.

"Sorry," he murmured before latching onto my other nipple.

"No," I groan-whispered and arched my back, aching for more contact. "You're not."

His answering hum thrummed through me, and then two of his fingers speared into me and he let out another sound. This time it was a torturous twist between pleasure and demand. Normally Ian took lead on everything, he loved the control and I loved surrendering it to him. But right now, astride him while he sucked, licked, and vibrated my nipple, I began to roll my hips. His fingers didn't quite have the reach, but he curved them every time I sank down on him.

"Not enough," I managed through pants and pulled back. The act earned me the sting of his teeth, but I reveled in the way his pupils dilated. Rising some, I reached between us to free his dick. It was hot and heavy in my hand. The silky skin beckoned to be stroked and I locked my gaze on his as I began to fist his dick. Up and down, gliding my thumb over the tip.

"You teasing me, Angel?" The husky note in his voice pulled a slow smile from me.

"And if I am?"

"You might be playing with fire."

"That's okay," I whispered as I dipped my head and added, "you can handle me," before I kissed him. He opened right up to me, with his hand in my hair he tilted my head further. The hungry thrust of his tongue left me aching and I shifted my grip. Angling myself forward, I teased us both with just rubbing his dick against my soaking core.

The raw sound he released unlocked something inside of me. A shudder raced over my skin and then he gripped my ass and thrust upward in the same motion. I groaned into his mouth as he filled me. It took us no time to find our rhythm as he thrust upward and I rolled my hips. With every twist, he struck deeper and I clamped down on him, but he pressed on, pulling out and then shoving back in until we were panting through our kisses.

I was so close, but Ian wouldn't let me speed us up. His hands were locked on my hips, controlling the rhythm. He struck one stinging slap to my ass and I swore my vision whited out. The startled scream I released deepened. The pleasure rippled over me in waves, he followed me shortly, thrusting up into my boneless body as I reveled in every delicious stroke.

Eventually, my racing heart calmed enough for the ragged sound of our breathing to fill the room. "Good," I managed between little gasps for air, "morning."

His chuckle reverberated against me. "Good morning."

It took a couple more minutes for me to get the wherewithal to slide off and move to sit on the bed. His discarded wet clothes were on the floor, along with the forgotten towel. I reached for the coffee cups, still decorated with water drops from the rain and after removing the drink stoppers, I passed one to Ian.

Sitting next to me, he pressed a kiss to my shoulder. Gradually, the air conditioning in the room reminded me of the fact we were both damp and now naked. I glanced down at the shredded lace on the floor and a giggle escaped.

Ian followed my gaze and his lips twitched. "I suppose I should take a picture of those and send them to the guys."

That sent a fresh wave of laughter through me. "Pretty sure they would consider that cruel and unusual."

"Nah," Ian said as he reached for his discarded shorts. After handing me his coffee to hold, he dug out his phone. "Besides, I've been really sympathetic to their plight of missing you. It's time to give them hell."

"Mean," I commented.

He winked at me. "Trust me, they'll appreciate it." Then he hesitated a beat before hitting send.

"Problem?"

"It occurs to me that you may go through a slew of shredded panties after this."

Snickering, I shrugged. "Just means Archie will buy me more." As much as I used to resist him showering me with stuff like this, it never stopped him and he enjoyed it. The simple fact was, I enjoyed it too.

"True. And you did promise to throw all your panties at me." The sly look on his face set me off laughing again. He hit send and I passed him back his coffee, then leaned against his arm as the responses started rolling in.

The emojis were funny, but Jake's cursing was far more clever and heated. Archie's succinct "dick" made me laugh even harder and Coop's only response was "Pictures or it didn't happen."

At that, Ian shot me a look in question. Mischief in his eyes and his smile warmed me from head to toe and chased away an element of chill. He missed the guys. So did I. Missed them like we would a limb.

"You can take one if you want to send it," I said. "Shall I lean back and pose?"

His smile grew. "I love you."

"I know," I said with all the gravitas of Han Solo. Ian's answering laugh cracked me up. He had me scoot up against the pillows and snapped a picture of me with the sheet strategically placed. Then he hit send. While his phone buzzed in his hand, he took a couple more, easing the sheet down.

It tickled me to see him having fun with this.

"Money shot?" He double checked and I took a long drink of coffee then stripped the sheet off and sprawled on the bed, legs curved so they could get a peek.

"I'm kind of still messy."

"Even better." Two more snaps, and then he sent a message before he started sending the shots. Shifting over, we sat side by side so I could watch the chat and laughter spiraled through me when the guys' responses grew more colorful.

"Fuck, I've missed this," he said, and I glanced at him.

"We'll see them soon," I told him, then kissed his shoulder. Tucking my head there, I waited for the money shot to be fired over and their responses set me off laughing all over again.

"Angel," Ian said before dropping a kiss on top of my head. "You may not be able to walk for a week after we get home."

"Worth it!"

And for just a few moments, I basked in the feeling of being there with them. The movie nights over video conference, the phone calls, the text messages—it was a Band-Aid on a bullet hole. At the same time, these were the kinds of memories I wanted to treasure, too. Because it wasn't just the sex I missed, it was their laughter, their teasing, the way they supported each other and me. How they picked on each other and even how they competed.

My laptop dinged and I groaned.

Homework. As much as I hated distance learning, I refused to fall behind. Forcing myself off the bed, I scooped up my discarded clothes and grabbed fresh panties before heading to the shower.

We would see them soon.

I couldn't wait.

You Are The Reason

Archie

Leaning back in the chair, I put my feet up on the desk. Fuck, I was tired. We'd been working longer hours to get everything the way we wanted it. Between the shop, school, and then running every damn day, I was almost tired enough to fall right into a dreamless sleep. Almost.

"Archie!" Delight curved through Frankie's voice when she answered the phone. "I thought I was going to be talking to Grandpa Ted."

"Technically, I usurped your appointment," I said. "I know I'm a poor substitute…"

"Oh, shut up," she said, half-laughing. "You are not a poor substitute for anything. I just didn't know you were going to be calling."

"Well, then my cunning plan worked. I surprised you."

"Yes, you did." She made a groaning sound and I raised my brows. "Sorry, these shoes were killing me—no, Ian, I'm going to talk to Archie for a few, you can shower first. I'll grab one in a minute. You want me to order us food?"

Bubba said something, but I couldn't quite work it out, it was too muffled.

"Big burger," Frankie said. "Huge. Everything on it. Um…fries? Soda?"

I chuckled. Bubba was ordering her food before he showered.

"Okay, sorry, Archie, just sorting that out. We just got in."

"You sound tired."

"I am, but—it's worth it. I think."

"You think?" I mean, I got it. The work on the shop was worth it, too. I thought.

"I mean—it's crazy making and there's so much going on and some days I think I've bitten off way more than I can chew." For a split second, the cheer evaporated from her voice. "And I *hate* online classes. Hate. Hate. Hate. Loathe entirely."

A soft chuckle escaped me. Even in a "temper," she managed to make me smile. "I'm sorry you hate them. If you want, we can work on investments, do some stock splits, buy out the school and ban them forever."

Dead silence.

"You're tempted, aren't you?"

She giggled. Honest to god giggled, and I grinned wider. "That's a terrible thing to do."

"Maybe, but if it makes you happy, I'm down."

"Also, can you even buy a public university?"

"Babe, it's me." Really, was she doubting me already?

"True," she agreed and I leaned my head back and closed my eyes. "You really have never met a challenge you haven't wanted to beat."

"That's the point of a challenge, it makes you step up. Or get out of the way." I rubbed my chin.

"Now you're the one who sounds tired."

"I'm not that—" A yawn interrupted my claim and she laughed at me. "Well, I was going to say I'm not that tired."

"It's after two there, Archie."

Was it? I squinted over at the clock. It was. "I knew that. Grandpa was gonna call you so you could discuss the East Asian markets and why watching them is a good thing. Because even at two in the morning on the East coast, the markets in Asia are open and trading."

"Do you really want to talk about stock markets?"

"Nope. I just want to talk to you." That was the truth.

"Tell you what," she said, her voice softening. "Get into bed and I'll tell you all about our night."

Sounded like a plan. "And the Asian markets?"

"They'll be there," she murmured. Good enough. I stripped down and climbed into the bed and burrowed against the pillow of hers I'd stolen. "You tucked in?"

Another yawn stretched my jaw, but I managed an elongated, "I am."

She started to tell me about their day and I tried to focus. I really did, but the soothing cadence of her voice and the fact she was whispering in my ear in the dark, and I was out. When I woke up the next morning, I was still cuddling the phone and there was a message from her that just said:

Frankie

I love you. Listen to your voicemail.

With a frown, I checked. There was a message from her. She'd recorded a long message too. But this one wasn't about her day, it was just about random things and thoughts. Just something to hear her voice.

See, another reason why I loved her.

She got me. She understood what I needed, even when I didn't fully get it myself.

Saving that message, I settled back against the pillows and played it, eyes closed and imagining she was right there.

Chapter Thirty-Three

VIVA LA VIDA

Jake

I took the corner at speed, legs pumping and heart hammering as I raced against the wind. Archie was a hairsbreadth behind me. We'd been pacing ourselves when we dragged Coop out of bed to go with us. He'd healed up enough that I no longer felt guilty about taking him along. Also, the workouts were good for all of us. In a little over thirty-six hours, we would get to see our girl, in person. We'd get to hold her, kiss her, hug her, and fuck her.

My dick twitched, but I ignored it and pushed my legs harder. I wanted to feel the burn everywhere. Especially after Bubba sent those fucking pictures of her. Goddamn, she'd looked great. It was weird to feel like I hadn't seen her that relaxed and happy in a long time. At the same time, all I'd wanted was to slide into that bed next to her and curl her into me.

The pillows had lost their scent, but that didn't stop any of us from wanting to keep them close. Or—and I wasn't too proud to admit this—I'd stolen back one of my shirts she wore often, just so I could have it. Yeah, next tour they did needed to be when we could fly out and join them. Even if it was every other weekend or something.

Archie gained on me, I caught sight of him from the corner of my eye and I pushed. I made it to the steps of the brownstone just seconds ahead of him. Breathing hard, I doubled over. We needed to do more of these rush sprints. It was something Bubba and I had done to keep fit for football. Fuck, I had a stitch in my side.

Leaning against the railing, Archie panted as hard as I did, but there was a manic smile on his face. "You trying to kill me?"

I laughed and paced in circles. My muscles needed the cool down and there was no sign of Coop. "Where is he?"

"He's coming," Archie said and pointed. I followed his gesture to where Coop *jogged* up the street toward us. He wasn't out of breath or huffing like we were.

"You get lost, slowpoke?"

He flipped me off as he reached us. "No, I just didn't sign up for a five-hundred-meter sprint."

I laughed. That was hardly a third of a mile. "It's good for you."

"Right, so is coffee and sleeping in. Tell me again why the fuck you made me do this?"

"Cause you needed a break," Archie said as he pushed away from the railing. "You've been stretching yourself thin between classes and work. This is good stress relief for what ails you."

His derisive snort made me laugh. "He's just worried about you getting older," I said as Coop headed up the stairs. "We're supposed to look after our elders."

"Fuck you," Coop and Archie snarked. Once inside, I took the stairs two at a time. The smell of breakfast chased me. Shower, change, then food.

Fifteen minutes later, I slid into a chair at the table. Jeremy was already carrying out plates piled high with food. Eggs, bacon, sausage, pancakes, and fried potatoes had my mouth watering. Rachel smirked at me where she sat with her cup of coffee, and what had probably been a bowl of yogurt with granola.

"Don't look at me like that," Rachel said. "Not all of us are Frankie. I'd kill for her metabolism."

I chuckled. "We all would." Frankie's ability to eat was just one of the many things I adored about her. Archie strolled around the corner and into the kitchen. Instead of straight up black coffee or juice, he went to the espresso maker.

"Morning, Jeremy," he said, and the older man gave him a nod and a smile.

"Mr. Archie. I've made the arrangements for the suite at the hotel in Maryland, along with the extra rooms and other special touches you requested."

"Thank you," Archie said. "You sure you don't want to come with? The cats would be fine for a night or two if we left them setup. Frankie and Bubba would love to see you."

Jeremy chuckled. "As much as I support their efforts and admire the music, I rather doubt the club scene is for me."

"C'mon, J," Rachel chipped in. "You don't have to be into the 'club scene,' because they aren't heavy metal at all. In fact, they've got quite a few ballads and I know you like those."

He gave her a distinguished, if firm, look of rebuke. "Miss Rachel, what have I said about teasing me?"

"That you're not used to it and would prefer if we kept our shenanigans to ourselves," Rachel parroted that back so precisely, I damn near choked on my bite of eggs, and had to wash it down. Behind Jeremy, Archie looked flat out entertained.

"She's right," Archie said. "And Frankie has *missed* you. Don't think I don't know about the care packages and special treats you've been arranging for them. Even if you only come in long enough to listen to a couple of songs, she'd love it."

"What are we talking about?" Coop asked as he wandered in, he sported a brand new Bound Hearts t-shirt.

"Dude," Archie said. "You're supposed to save those for when we see them."

He laughed. "Lighten up. I have a half-dozen. I'll be wearing them all week." When Jeremy handed him another fully laden plate, Coop grinned. "Jeremy, you're a god among men."

"Exactly," I threw in my two cents as Coop dropped into a chair. "That's another reason why Frankie would be over the moon to see you. Pretty sure Bubba misses you too. Or at least misses the food, cause he said half the stuff they've been eating on the road is crap."

"Oh, you're going with us?" Coop asked, brightening up. "That's a fabulous idea. If you don't want to drive down with all of us, you can fly down and we'll snag you at the airport."

Jeremy frowned, his expression considering.

"That's four to one, J," Rachel said. "I think you should just concede the battle right now."

"One only concedes when one has no options left," Jeremy corrected her. "I have many, including the ability to say no. I appreciate the invitation. I truly do." He turned away from all of us as Archie carried out a couple of lattes. He set one in front of Rachel and a second in front of Coop. Both of whom murmured their thanks.

"You want one?" He looked at me, but I shook my head.

"Thanks, maybe later. The regular stuff is hitting the spot."

"K." He returned to making his own drink and Rachel gave an exaggerated sigh.

I shot a questioning look her way and she tilted her head so that they couldn't see her face from the kitchen, then winked. I glanced at Coop and he shook his head once. Nope, he had no idea what the hell was up either.

"Man," Rachel said with another long, if too heavy sigh. "She's gonna feel bad, you know."

"Yeah?" Coop said and then gave me a little shrug like 'what?' Trust him to play along. "I think it'll be all right. I mean she gets to see us, you know."

"But like—Hank can't make it. I'm sure Grandpa Ted isn't going, and I don't think she's even told her grandparents where she'll be." Rachel lifted her latte and took a thoughtful sip.

Oh.

Got it.

"Well, she's been achieving for a long time without worrying about adult support or parental applauds." I chewed on a piece of bacon. "And she did send us the video. Pretty sure Jeremy watched that a couple of times."

"Five," Archie offered, as he headed out of the kitchen with his coffee and accepted the plate from Jeremy. "Isn't that right, Jere? You asked me to put it on the house cloud so you could watch it on the television."

"Indeed," Jeremy said, his tone all crisp, no nonsense.

"There, see, he's seen her perform. He doesn't *have* to see her in person. It's not his scene," Archie took a seat, his back to Jeremy.

"But the video was kind of small and from the back. She looked so nervous at the beginning," Rachel challenged. "Imagine how much happier she'll look when she glances out across the crowd and sees all of us."

"It is what it is. It's not fair of us to push Jeremy into doing something he doesn't want, just because—"

"That will be quite enough from all of you," Jeremy said as he came out to stand at the table. He looked around the table. "Emotional blackmail doesn't look good on anyone."

"But did it work?" Archie asked him. "Because we all know it's an effective technique."

The scolding look Jeremy gave Archie could have boiled water, but

Archie didn't flinch. In fact, his smirk just grew.

"C'mon, Jere. You want to go, you know you do. You just think your place is here keeping the home fires burning. And while you might work for us, you're also family."

"You're definitely family," Coop said firmly, and I pointed my fork at Jeremy.

"She loves you like family. I know for a fact that Bubba respects the hell out of you. It'd mean a lot to him, just like he's appreciated our support through this whole process." Bubba never asked for much, but then he did a lot more than most of us noticed. Just like Jeremy.

"Don't look at me," Rachel said when Jeremy fixed his gaze on her. "I think you're cool, J. I know you'd both enjoy it."

"You're not going to take no for an answer, are you?"

"Well, I would," Coop said in all seriousness. "But it's my birthday in a couple of days. We have rules in this family."

"Hell yes, we do," Archie said, grinning broadly and I laughed.

"That is indeed a fact."

Rachel snorted. "Right, the birthday boy gets what he wants."

"Suck it up, Manning," I told her. "It's the rule and if you didn't disappear on your birthday, Frankie would do the same thing to you."

She just flipped me off, but Jeremy huffed.

Wait for it.

"Fine," he finally committed, and Archie gave me a little fist pump. "I will, however, forgo the drive with all of you and I'll take the train rather than the shuttle. It will give me time to read. Now, eat your breakfasts. There's a great deal to be done before we all leave."

With that, he left us to our meal and Rachel clapped her hands. "That was fantastic. He so deserves the break."

"Yes," Archie said, agreeing. "He also needs to see that Frankie and Bubba are in one piece. Healthy and happy. Here's hoping she hasn't lost any weight." He raised his coffee cup and I grimaced.

"You don't think she has, right?" Cause, one, there would be hell to pay with Jeremy, and two, there would be hell to pay with me.

"Maybe," Archie said, sober and serious. "But I don't think it's bad. I was more worried about it when they first went, but she seems—*better*."

Coop didn't respond to that, just looked thoughtful, and Rachel let out a little sigh.

"Okay, no Debbie Downers at this table," she said firmly. "We're going to go, we're going to have a great time, you three will kiss her until she can't see straight, and I get to scream at her from the audience. We're going to have a fantastic fucking time and so is she."

"Sold," Coop said firmly. "Birthday boy gets…"

"Yeah yeah," Archie agreed with a laugh. "You get what you want."

"You guys better eat everything and stay in Jeremy's good graces." Rachel stood and carried her bowl and cup into the kitchen.

"What are you going to do?" I asked, more out of curiosity than anything else.

"I'm going to go see if their first video has gone live yet. Frankie said they recorded one a week ago between two of their shows, and at the shows."

Holy shit, I'd almost forgotten that. I started shoveling food as Rachel sailed out of the room, and I wasn't alone. Coop and Archie ate faster too.

The video probably wasn't—a whoop carried down the stairs and I was digging out my phone. Coop found it first and we all leaned over to watch on his little screen as the video came on.

There they were, our girl and our best friend rocking out and living their best life.

Chapter Thirty-Four
BALTIMORE

Frankie

It seemed so weird that our "official" tour kickoff was scheduled for Baltimore. What had the last six weeks been, if not the official tour? The "unofficial" tour according to Boone, who had met us when we flew in the night before. Our hotel was not that far from the venue, and it was a slight step up from the one we'd stayed in the day before, but not by much. At least Ian and I never had to worry about sharing our room with anyone else. The guys, K.O. and Xavier, split a room and M.J. got her own.

We had two queens in this room instead of a king, also fine, but we used one bed for luggage storage and the other to sleep in. When Boone showed up at our room not ten minutes after I woke up, I was irritated, but the man vibrated with excitement. Like, actually seemed to be shaking so much I worried he had the caffeine jitters or something.

The only thing saving his life was he brought coffee with him when he knocked on the door. Ian had made him wait while I pulled on clothes and then let him in. "You two might need to sit down for this," Boone said and I quirked a brow.

We were sitting down.

"Right," he said, pacing back and forth on the faded sienna and gold carpet. "So, when we first discussed the recording contract and the touring, I told you we would be starting small and then building steadily. We'd use momentum from earlier appearances, including reviews and some online comments to generate buzz."

I vaguely recalled the thing about reviews, but I hadn't actually seen any. Had people actually reviewed our performances? Did I want to know? Wasn't that what KC said? Never read the reviews? Or was that to avoid the online comments?

Shit. Neither? Both?

"You mentioned that it was also to get us comfortable performing in front of gradually increasing crowds," Ian said, before he took a sip of his coffee.

"Exactly, my boy, exactly. You cannot teach stage presence. You can teach the craft. You can teach the moves, but the presence? That you have or you don't."

Oh shit. My stomach bottomed out. Ian's hand came down on my bouncing knee and stilled it.

"You kids have it in spades. It was a little rough at first, I admit that, and we had some bumps along the way in recording and getting the album cover done—but we're ready. You're ready."

"Wait—it's done?" I knew we were close. He'd mentioned that a couple of stops ago in Bakersfield? Or was it Portland? It might even have been Riverside—no it was Renton, in Washington. I really had no idea what the other towns were named.

"It's done." He spread his hands, his excitement contagious. "We'll be dropping it online tomorrow, using tonight's show as the platform to launch it. That's why we're here and why we're using The Old Colonial Wharf as our launching point. The hippest new bands play there, it's part of the music scene here in Baltimore, and it's great for East Coast buzz. You've already made an impression on the West Coast. Then we'll be booking you guys right up until the New Year—"

"Uhh," I said with a quick look at Ian and he gave my knee a squeeze.

"Christmas," Ian told him. "We're going home for Christmas." Before Jake's birthday, because there literally hadn't been five minutes to get back to New York since we'd started on this wild ride.

"I think you guys are going to be missing out on some great opportunities," Boone said. "Especially the New Year's Eve jams."

"I don't care," I said slowly, and Ian glanced at me with an encouraging nod. "I mean, I care because I want everything to be successful. But we're not already booked for those dates and we're not already selling tickets. I don't want to add more stops to our plans. I want to just do everything we promised and then go home. I miss—my classes. I miss my friends. I miss the boys."

Boone frowned, then rubbed his chin. "What if you get the break then we still book the New Year's Eve somewhere—maybe even right there in New York? I mean, it's harder to break into clubs and venues there, cause they book months out, but not impossible. We make you look hard to get, irresistible and exclusive. Not a lie. You guys are gorgeous—might have to rely on that sex appeal." The last he said to Ian.

"Nice," Ian said in a dry tone. "We'll let you handle the marketing, you tell us what dates you might get, but we need at least two weeks at home."

At the very least.

Shoulders dropping a little, Boone nodded. "This might not be the best time to slow down. If you want to break out and really start making numbers, we need to widen your scope, add more appearances, more dates…"

"Boone," I said quietly. "Ian and I have talked about this. We love singing and working together."

"But we also love our family," Ian told him. "We're not going to sacrifice one for the other. If we have to make any sacrifice, then it's going to be the career for our people. That said, if it takes us a little longer or we remain small town appeal—I'm okay with that, too."

"So am I," I murmured and bumped Ian's shoulder. "Is that going to be a problem for you?"

I'd get it. The producer had been so enthusiastic and pushing us a lot. While I didn't always agree with him, I respected the fact he had listened and worked with us.

"Not going to lie, you guys could really go places if you were one hundred percent all in," he said slowly. "Not saying you still can't, but I also get that you have priorities and those priorities are important to you."

"They are," I confirmed. "I don't know that I'm totally cut out for the music business twenty-four seven. Not knowing where we are, always moving on to the next hotel room, the next club, and forgetting what the sun looks like cause we're up so late to get on to the next spot."

"We really appreciate all of this, Boone," Ian told him. "Seriously, and we're all in for the next few weeks."

"How about I get you guys a weekend off?" Boone offered. "You have been grinding pretty hard."

I would not say no. "Do you mind if we get the weekend right before Halloween?" That would let us go home for *Archie's* birthday at least.

"Done," Boone said. "All right, drink your coffee, get some food in you and do what you need to do to get ready. Tonight, you are going to make a splash."

As long as we didn't drown, I was all in.

The day blew past us. The guys had sent a couple of messages and I'd sent Coop a happy birthday text and tried to call him, but it went straight to voicemail. They probably had classes, but it also sucked, cause I didn't want to miss actually *talking* to him on his birthday. Especially since I wasn't there.

Ian tried to cheer me up and helped me make a video with me singing him happy birthday, like I was Marilyn Monroe—it took us five attempts, cause I kept breaking out laughing, because playing seductress was not my thing. Still, Ian packaged it all up, bloopers too, and we sent it.

"There," he murmured as we got ready to leave. The car was coming to take us to the huge club and nightspot we were performing at. It was Friday night, too. They could handle over a thousand people at The Old Colonial Wharf. I wished that Boone hadn't mentioned that little factoid. No way there would be that many people there tonight, right? "Don't think about it," Ian said. "Or I'll have to fuck you in the bathroom at the club, and while I'm up for it, I don't think you want everyone to hear you screaming in there."

About that…

Granted, the mere suggestion distracted me from the number of people to the idea of getting frisky in the bathroom. To be honest, the idea had *never* appealed to me. It was a public restroom after all. That said, I couldn't deny the fact that lazy tension began to coil in my stomach at the idea.

Ian chuckled as he opened the back door of the car for me. "Someone's thinking about it."

A laugh escaped me, and I jabbed him lightly with my elbow. "Well, of course I'm *thinking* about it."

He was still amused when we pulled up to the club. I'd never been to

Baltimore before and I didn't know how much of the place we'd even get to see, but we passed this massive aquarium and it looked so cool. Maybe if we had time…

The cars—because M.J. and the guys were in the one behind us—pulled in behind the club and we were let in the back doors. Our equipment was there, but Ian had his guitar. That traveled with us, not the band's stuff.

"Hi!" A bubbly blonde greeted us, her cherubic face alight with bright openness. "I'm so excited you guys are here! Come on and follow me. Our blue room is pretty comfortable, but I want to show you everything in case you have questions. We also have facilities back here for you, so you don't have to worry about going up front once we get packed. We *will* be packed. They've been promoting the show all week."

My stomach dropped but I didn't have time to worry about it as we followed our hostess.

"I'm Megan, by the way," she said with a laugh. "I should totally have introduced myself first, but I got so excited. I'll be your waitress tonight, too. Anything you need from the bar or the kitchens, I'll take care of it—except alcohol." She paused on that note and pushed open a door that was like one and half times normal size.

Their blue room was actually blue. Three sofas in various spots, a couple of chairs, a television, a monitor that looked out on the club. There was also a coffee maker and magazines. It was like a little lounge.

"You two," she indicated to me and Ian. "You're not old enough to buy alcohol, so I can't serve you. I can, however, serve your bandmates."

She gave us a very significant look. Got it. So M.J. and the guys could order for us, but Megan couldn't bring it to us.

"Your equipment," she continued, breezing on, "is already on the stage. Our doors open in an hour so you can go out and make sure everything is set up for you. Dalton is already here—he's our sound master—and he'll make sure you guys are good to go. Let's see—if you need changes for the equipment or placing, tell him. I'm going to ask for your dinner orders now so I can put them in as soon as the kitchen is officially open. We have two acts going on before you guys tonight. They won't be using your stuff. But they'll warm up the crowd for you and then we'll introduce you, as well as the fact that your debut album drops tomorrow."

She gave a little handclap at the last, her voice warbling up a couple of notes in excitement.

"I can't wait. I saw your video and it was amazing. I cannot wait to hear the rest of the album. Will you be doing all the songs from it tonight?"

I wasn't sure if she was ever gonna take a breath and it worried me, but she just charged right on and I couldn't keep myself from smiling. Her cheerful attitude was even better than a jolt of caffeine to brighten the mood.

"We're singing all of them in the sets tonight—there's two, right?" I checked with Ian and he nodded. "So, we'll do seven in the first and another four or five in the second, with some covers thrown in."

"That's so exciting!" Megan beamed at us. "All right. Let's hear those orders."

Honestly, the last thing I wanted was food, but I still put in an order anyway. My nerves had nerves. As soon as Megan was done, she showed us how to get out to the stage from the back. The interior of the club was so much bigger than I'd imagined.

So.

Much.

Bigger.

"Breathe," Ian said, grinning. "Once the lights are on, it's just us on the stage again, and we've done this a few dozen times now."

He was right. I knew he was right and still, the place was not only huge, it was tall with three floors over us all looking down. There were tables, and bars on every level and dance floors. While all the lights were on right now, they'd be turned down and traded out for strobes and colorful lights, to amp up the dance atmosphere.

Why did this feel like a thousand times more real than anything else we'd done? I couldn't answer that, but we ran through the soundcheck. It took a couple of attempts to get the equipment where they wanted it. M.J. was irritated by her keyboard's sound and we had to get Dalton to get her some new cables. That fixed it.

Then, we were back in the blue room and getting ready. The club opened and people were filling the place. I tried to keep my gaze off the monitor, but I only managed a couple of french fries to eat. Three times I checked my phone, finally I got a message from Coop, but it was just a voicemail. How had I missed a call?

"Hey Beautiful, I love the birthday song. Gonna save that and play it every year. Maybe when we're in the same place I can get a live performance, you know, in our birthday suits. Love you." The message made my heart soar and crash in the same moment.

I'd *missed* his call.

"Hey," Ian said. "It's okay."

I sniffled as he brushed away a tear with his thumb.

"I missed his call," I whispered.

"It'll be fine, Angel," Ian told me, his expression firm. "Trust me?"

"I do, I just wish…"

Was I going to miss his whole birthday? I hadn't miss one of his birthdays—like ever—in all the time I could remember birthdays.

"It's going to be fine," he whispered and pressed a kiss against my forehead. "I promise."

Still, I couldn't escape the melancholy as I finished getting ready. Even the jitters of performing couldn't quite escape it. Twice more I called Coop, but I went straight to his voicemail, so I sent him a quick video of me blowing him a kiss. Then promised I'd text him as soon as we were off stage.

When the announcement came, I was not ready. Holy Hell, I wasn't ready, but Ian held my hand as we walked out there, and the applause that hit was damn near deafening. I couldn't see past the lights, not yet. They were almost too dazzling.

A scream cut through the sound, then another yelling my name and I squinted a little as the guys started warming up. A shrill whistle, I knew damn well, cut through the music and I turned and focused.

There they were.

Archie.

Jake.

The birthday boy himself, Coop.

Rachel.

Holy shit, Jeremy was with them.

And sitting at their table was KC, Yvette, and Aubrey, all of them sporting Bound Hearts shirts.

I damn near burst into tears, and the lights strobed cutting off my view of them for a second, then I looked over and Ian grinned at me.

Dammit, he'd known they were coming.

I was going to kill them all.

Later. Later, I would kill them.

Assholes.

Wonderful, beautiful, adorable fucking assholes.

All of them.

Suddenly, I was smiling so hard my cheeks ached and when they began the countdown to our first song, I blew out a breath.

A one.

Two.

Three.

Four…

Chapter Thirty-Five

MAGIC NIGHT

Archie

My throat ached from yelling, cheering, and applauding. Jake put his fingers to his lips and let out a shrill whistle. One that could cut through a crowd and yank your attention to the field. Frankie's head snapped to the side. The dazzled shock on her face gave way to the most brilliant smile. My heart squeezed at the gleam of tears catching the lights and reflecting them.

"Yes, you glorious bitches! Yes!" Rachel's cry sent a wave of wild amusement through me. Goddamn, she was standing up on her chair swinging her arm. Yeah, no one would mistake her for anyone but a fan.

Fuck it, I climbed up on a chair too and cupped my hands to my lips. "You got this!!" I had no idea if she could hear me, and it didn't fucking matter. This moment was imprinted indelibly in my mind. The throngs around us were already going nuts and they hadn't even started playing.

Jeremy, bless him, continued applauding, but I hadn't missed the earplugs he'd stuck in his ears before even settling in at our table. He looked pleased. Pleased and proud. Damn right. That was *our* girl and our best friend up there. Bound Hearts was their band, but it was also all of us.

From the opening riff of their first song to their last, we were all shouting. I cracked up when I realized KC and the girls were singing along with them. They'd come "incognito" or as much as they could when KC's vibrant blue hair stood out. Then again—maybe it didn't. There was a lot of colorful hair in the room.

Jake had a hand over his heart when they hit one of the ballads, and it didn't matter how many times we'd listened to this music together, how many times I'd heard the practice tapes, the samples, or even the final results as they put the album together over the last year. Some of these songs just resonated within me.

Like the song she'd sung for my birthday, the first time I'd gotten a real taste of the power she had in that voice. A voice that Bubba had helped her find. Goddamn, would I be forever grateful for him finding a way to cut through the bullshit her mother had tried to bury that talent in. No sooner did Maddy pop into my head, than I shoved that bitch right the fuck back out.

Not welcome here.

When they drifted into their last song of this set, I swayed with everyone else. They'd started low-key, almost demanding everyone to listen to them, then ratcheted our pulses higher with so much energy you had to move and now, they soothed us back to our seats. It was time for a breather.

As the last chords faded away, the applause rose, and I hopped down from the chair. Someone else hopped up onto the stage to announce a break for the group and they would be back out shortly. Sweat gleamed on Frankie's and Bubba's brows, their smiles were wide as she grabbed him in a hug and whatever she whispered in his ear set him off laughing. Her mock angry expression told me it was probably scolding him about us, as they left the stage.

A blonde waitress approached our table. "You guys *are* the birthday party, right?"

Coop grinned. "That would be us."

"Come on back."

"Go," Rachel said, waving us off. "I'll see her after."

I thought for a second KC and the others might want to follow too, but they KC nodded her head to Rachel. "Same, go. We'll protect our table."

Considering just how crowded it was and how loud it had grown with the band off stage and house music on, they didn't have to tell us twice. Jake, Coop, and I followed the waitress to a side door, then bypassed a kitchen and down a hall to another room.

She barely got the door open when Frankie's squeal of delight—a genuine squeal, which I would totally tease her about later—preceded her slamming into me with a hug. Yeah, birthday boy was getting her tonight, but I wanted this first hug. Sue me.

I squeezed her as I lifted her right off her feet. "You guys killed it," I told her against her ear. "You keep taking my breath away." She pulled back and then kissed me fiercely, and as much as I wanted to hold onto her, I handed her over to Jake who crowded me for his own hug. Blowing out a breath, I grabbed Bubba's hand and gave it a good shake before I just gave him a damn hug too.

Jake

The first thing I did when I dragged her close was take a deep breath. Even with the kitchens, the bar, what had to be some kind of perfume and sweat, under it all was Frankie. Fuck, I'd missed this. It was like the last three plus months collapsed as I hugged her. She gripped me with a kind of fierceness that reminded me she'd missed me too. Even after watching her do the same thing to Archie, I laughed as she pulled back and then kissed me.

Yeah, this was better than watching it. I'd always been more into participation than spectator sports. The warmth of her lips and the hint of salt and sugar on her tongue just added to the wildness of her. I nuzzled the kiss, desperate to sink my hands into her hair and my body into hers. As it was, I had to remember we were still semi in public.

Coop gave me a nudge and I walked Frankie into the blue room, where our audience still included the waitress who led us back here, and the other musicians performing with them. Shit. Frankie finally reached past me and I twisted in time to see her grinning almost tearfully at Coop. "Happy birthday, you stinker! I thought I wasn't going to get to talk to you today and it was killing me."

"Aww, Beautiful, I'm sorry. We wanted to surprise you." The kiss he gave her was so sweet it took just a bit of effort to pass her over. He balanced her easily and their kiss gave way to words. I retreated a step to give them a bit of privacy. Birthday boy and all that. Fuck, my dick ached and I was already itching to pull her back to me.

Force of will had me turning to Bubba and I greeted him with a back slapping hug. "Fucking killing it," I told him bluntly. "You sound so goddamn good together, I almost don't resent you for getting her all to yourself for months."

Bubba chuckled. "Thanks man, right now, she's happier than she's been in weeks." He nodded to where Coop was laughing, as she continued to scold him. Yeah, we'd definitely wanted this to be a surprise, but I hadn't realized it might sting if she couldn't get him on the phone.

Note to self, this kind of "surprise" wasn't as much fun for her in the lead up to it as it was for us. The waitress was saying something about drinks and food, but I didn't much care about that right now.

"Thanks, Megan." Bubba nodded to her and gave her a smile. "Water is what we need and maybe a couple of ice-cold Cokes?"

"I'll grab those for you."

Coop had Frankie tucked under his arm when he joined us. He held out a hand to shake Bubba's, though he made no attempt to let Frankie go.

She grinned at all of us. "Please note that I am really mad at all of you." She wagged a finger at us. "Including you, sir, so don't look smug." The last she said to Bubba, and he just grinned at her.

"So noted. Though if this is how you get mad at us…"

"We really need to piss you off more often," Archie finished for him in a dry tone, though he seemed to be having as hard a time keeping a smile off his face as I was.

Frankie stuck her tongue out at him and then leaned into Coop, looping her arms around his waist. I took a good long look at her, and Bubba was right, she did look happy. Happier than she'd seemed even in the pictures and video chats. Then again, I was happier than I'd been since the last time we'd seen her in person.

Coop would call that a correlation. I just called it facts.

The waitress was back. "Food's coming in too. More snacks. You have about twenty minutes before you need to be ready to go back out. So hit the bathrooms if you need them." She hustled through like the most cheerful drill sergeant ever.

"Hydrate," Bubba said, and Frankie made a face but she was already twisting to go for a drink. "Also, you guys, this is M.J., K.O., and Xavier. We told you about them. Guys this is Archie, Jake, and Coop."

Yeah, pleasantries with the band. We all sort of nodded and waved but I followed Coop and Frankie over to the other sofa where he sat down and she perched in his lap as she knocked back about half the water. "You're gonna need to pee if you keep that up," Archie teased her, and she just flipped him off.

I laughed, a little giddy, like I'd actually had more to drink than just a soda. At her curious look, I caught her hand and kissed her middle finger. "Missed this."

She stared at me a beat and then we all started laughing. This was better. So much better. Twenty minutes was a drop in the bucket and flew by way too fast. "We'll see you after," I promised. "We've got a huge suite and the girls are out there. Probably be a bit of an impromptu party. But we're not going anywhere—except back out to watch you sing."

"See you in an hour?" Frankie said, damn near glowing, and if that didn't make me feel good—hell, if it didn't make the other guys feel good—I didn't know what would.

"You won't be able to miss us," Archie promised.

"Go on," Coop encouraged her. "Go make the rest of the place fall in love with you two. But you're leaving with us."

"Deal." She blew us kisses and then let Bubba guide her out. The waitress was back to take us out to our table. As reluctant as I'd been to let Frankie go, I was ten times more reluctant to miss even one moment of the show.

Coop

In the history of birthdays, this might be my favorite. Once we were back at the table, the girls had a dozen questions about how they were, but I let Archie and Jake field those. I didn't want to miss a single note of their performance. More than one song left me hard as a stone when they were up there singing it.

Memories from the studio back in Texas, to the studio at the brownstone, flowed through my mind. I didn't think I'd ever be able to listen to her sing without thinking of the way she came, strapped down to the piano bench, while her music serenaded us. Those were good memories. The fact she flushed during one key song told me that memory was very much alive and well in her.

If Bubba had wanted to find a way to cure her of her stage fright, he'd long since found it. The songs were magnetic. Maybe it was the live performance, maybe it was the fact that the whole club was jazzed up by them, but it was electric and then…

"Hey, we wanted to thank y'all for coming out here tonight," Frankie said into the microphone. "Seriously, so many of you out there having a good time makes us feel great about this. If you don't mind, I need a little favor—"

Then the lights swiveled to hit us and I blinked a little at the dazzling array and then Frankie began to sing Happy Birthday to me in that sultry, sultry tone and yeah. I was a goner. Somewhere behind me, Jake muttered, "Lucky prick."

"Don't hate," I said over my shoulder, not taking my gaze off our girl. Best birthday ever. Definitely in the top five. The roaring applause for my birthday had me standing up and taking a wave before I blew her a kiss and she mimed catching it.

God, I loved her.

They went on for three or four encores. The crowd was electric with affection for them and when they finally broke into a Torched song and Frankie cast a look at our table, I could almost see the invitation.

The girls hesitated, and then KC glanced at her besties and they bounced up to go and join them.

If the crowd was already on fire, they lost their fucking minds when Torched joined in. They went over an hour longer, and the girls stayed up there with them for three more songs. Rachel wore the same pride on her face I was pretty sure we were all feeling.

Not that I was remotely sorry when they finally finished for the night. Jeremy was already up. "Cars are coming," he said. "I'll escort the ladies, you boys will take care of Miss Frankie."

"Yes, sir," Archie said. "Jake? Head back and…"

"Already on it." Jake nodded to us, before he headed toward the back. He would get KC and the girls out from the back to meet us at the cars. I was going to head out front with Rachel and Jeremy. Archie would get Frankie.

Ten minutes later, we were piled into the back seat with Frankie and Bubba and I had a lapful of giddy Frankie, kissing me like she needed me for oxygen. No complaints here.

I could almost feel Archie and Jake's envy. Wait, there was no *almost* about it. But neither one was going to push in the door, even though I'd never close it to them. Maybe I'd give us a couple of hours first, then just tell them to get the fuck in there. My birthday or not, she deserved time with all of us and they were going to be on the road again in under twenty-four hours.

Back at the hotel, not only did we have a huge suite, we also had the whole floor. Archie had taken precautions if the Torched girls came out of retirement for the evening. I also didn't miss a couple of familiar Pax security guys. Frankie made a face, but she didn't complain. Not tonight. No one was taking any chances. The last time we relaxed, shit had gone sideways.

I'd rather overthink it. It was still another hour after we were at the hotel before I managed to steal her away to a private room and lock the door. The guys all had keys if they needed in. Frankie grinned at me. "I should still be mad at you," she told me.

"Absolutely," I agreed. "I was a bad boy. I let you think you wouldn't get to talk to me, terrible man-child that I am."

Her laughter was a balm for my soul.

"But while we're on the subject," I said, unbuckling my jeans before I stripped off our custom made shirt. She had lost her shoes somewhere and she watched me with burning eyes as I toed off my shoes before yanking down my jeans. Thank fuck I could wear the damn things again. Matching me clothing item for clothing item, she stood there in just a pair of panties and no bra—cause apparently that top didn't require one, and I kind of just stopped to drink in the sight of her.

"While we're on the subject?" she prompted.

"Yes," I said slowly. "Right. On the subject of being angry and me being a bad boy. I have a secret."

Frankie raised her eyebrows as I closed the distance between us, I couldn't stand not having my hands on her. I traced my fingers down over her skin, circling her puckered nipples then down to the gorgeous little gem at her navel. I hadn't missed the fact she was wearing my ring and the class ring.

Running her tongue over her lips to wet them, Frankie said, "What kind of secret?"

"The kind that's a surprise for you and I think it will get me out of the dog house."

"We don't have a dog house."

"Yeah well, going into the cat house would get me in even more trouble." I locked my gaze on her and made a face.

She burst out laughing. "Agreed, so dog house."

"Exactly." Setting my hands on her hips, I murmured, "Truth or dare?"

"Truth."

"Did you really want me to get pierced?"

"I love the idea," she whispered. "Not gonna lie, and I love playing with not so little Coop and his delightful piercing."

My cock twitched. Yes, those calls had been a lot of fucking fun, even when I didn't dare try to tease myself into coming.

"Good to know."

"Truth or dare, Coop?"

"Truth, Beautiful."

"What's your secret?"

I loved that she got me on every level.

Every. Single. One.

I took a step back and peeled my boxers down. "Surprise."

The look of pure shocked delight knocked her earlier surprise flat. That right there, that pleasure in her eyes was worth every single uncomfortable second.

"Truth or dare?" I whispered.

"Dare." Zero hesitation.

"Come get your surprise."

Chapter Thirty-Six

SURPRISE

Frankie

I was riding on an adrenaline high. I had to be. But when Coop slid his boxers down, I froze. His cock, his beautiful, thick, heavily veined, and ridged cock had a beautiful piercing curved through the tip. Dropping to my knees, I stared at it and then up at him. The smile on his face was equal parts trepidation and pride.

"Coop."

"You said you wanted one, Beautiful," he murmured, not moving as I started to lift a hand to touch him.

"I said I'd love to try one—and you made me the not-so-little-Coop."

"And you loved it," he reminded me.

"But this had to hurt." I mean, it was one thing to want one, and another for him to suffer.

"Worth it," he whispered. "If for no other reason than the wonder in your eyes just now."

I licked my lips, still hesitant, even if I could feel the heat from his cock and it didn't look angry or inflamed. Okay well, it looked eager as hell and I really had *missed* his dick. I'd missed all of their dicks. A little laugh bubbled up out of me.

"Truth or dare," he whispered.

Licking my lips again, I said, "You just went."

"And you're not moving, so come on, Beautiful. It's my birthday…"

I shot him a look and he grinned. The shit was truly enjoying himself. Then again… "It is your birthday, my birthday boy with his beautiful cock all eager for me and so beautifully crowned." I ran my fingers along the underside, the silky skin scorching to my fingertips.

He let out a long sigh at the barely-there caress. I couldn't get over the fact he'd done it. He really had. "This is why you looked sick a few weeks ago, but insisted you were fine and then *promised* me you weren't sick."

"I wasn't sick," he told me, running his fingers over my hair. "And yeah, it wasn't the most fun thing I've ever done—she's kneeling right in front of me by the way, if you were wondering—but it also wasn't as bad as I thought it would be. Rachel also provided moral support."

I grinned. "You told Rachel." That—that made me inexorably happy. "You guys really are becoming friends."

"She's not so bad once you get past all the prickly parts, and I'm currently her favorite because—look what I did for you!"

Another laugh burst out of me and I leaned in to rub my cheek against his dick ever so slowly, not looking away from him for an instant. "Promise me if this hurts—at all—you'll tell me?"

"Beautiful, the only thing I feel is you. The only thing I want to feel is you. Touch me before I die, yeah?"

"Then dare, Coop."

I ran my cheek up the other side of his dick, just whispering my lips against his tip and his mouth opened as his pupils dilated but no sound came out. Twice more I stroked him, then I wrapped my hand around his base to lift him up so I could run my tongue up the underside, following the thick vein that throbbed against my tongue.

A pearlescent bead of pre-cum glistened on the tip and I wrapped my mouth around him. Being ever so careful with my teeth—I didn't want to inadvertently tug. No pain for him. I still couldn't believe he'd really done this. We'd teased and joked and talked, but he'd done this...

With a harsh exhale, Coop stroked his thumb against my cheek. "No tears, Beautiful. I mean it. This is for you. Haven't you figured it out yet? There's nothing I wouldn't do for you."

"I love you," I said around his dick and his soft expression filled with mirth.

"Say it again."

I chuckled and he sucked in a breath. The vibrations seemed more intense. "I love you," I said around my mouthful and then locked my lips around his pierced tip and hummed.

"Fuck me," he groaned as he slid his hand up into my hair. With pleasure, I told him in my head and hopefully he read it in my eyes, cause I widened my mouth and he pressed deep to my throat and then back.

The second thrust was shallow, but the third actually took him into my throat as I swallowed around him, and I swore he froze there for a moment. I had my hands on his thighs and I could feel the piercing just tickling my throat.

"Holy. Shit...Frankie...I want to fuck you everywhere, but I don't think I'm gonna last long. I haven't even managed to jack off since I did this."

My eyes widened.

He grinned down at me. "My hand is a poor fucking substitute for you. You have no idea."

Tears leaked from the corners of my eyes and he swore, this time pulling back so I could breathe and swallow. A thin line of spit trailed from my lips to his dick. Impatience and need seemed to fill the air around him as he lifted me up. I barely had time to swipe at my mouth before his lips crashed down on mine.

Yes, I'd had Ian for months and thank fucking god for him. He'd driven me out of my mind more than once. But I ached for Coop. I ached to feel him, to touch him. And wrapping my arms around him, I sighed in relief at the contact of his skin on mine. Hunger punctuated his kiss as he stroked his tongue against mine. He went to one knee on the bed and we went down sideways. Not once did he let up on the kiss, other than for a brief gasp of air, before he swooped in again.

His hands were everywhere, stroking me, teasing my nipples and then he was smoothing them over my lace panties. It was on the tip of my tongue to tell him to wait, but he sucked my tongue hard as a sound of ripping punctuated our panting gasps and then another wave of laughter rippled up through me.

Goddammit Ian, a distant part of my brain noted. But the rest of me just went soft and slick and wetter. They described the shredding of panties in a lot of those books I read.

It had nothing on the real thing. The scraps of fabric vanished and then he had his dick in his hand and my thigh lifted over his hip so he could stroke against me. The metal was warm, not at all cold. It was warm like him. Every time he teased me with the tip, he would run it up to my clit and my legs started to shake as I strained to follow him.

His groan echoed mine and when I closed my hand on his, I opened my eyes to find him watching me. Finally, he lifted his head. "I've missed kissing you."

"I've missed everything with you."

Together, we lined him up. "Slow," he whispered, his voice firm despite the ragged note on that syllable. It was always a lot to take Coop, his thrusts were slow, shallow, just pressing into me. The piercing served as an electric sensation against my inner walls as he deepened his thrusts. I stretched for him, I always did. There was something so fucking awesome about how much work it took.

I was hardly a virgin, and my body knew his so goddamn well, but that piercing. The moment he pushed deep, I tilted my head back to let out the cry. Oh man, it was…another thrust, this one firmer and my whole body bucked as I gripped onto him.

"Holy fuck," Coop muttered and then he pressed kisses to the column of my throat. "Does that feel good to you? It feels fucking incredible to me, you're spasming around me like you don't want to let me go."

I didn't. I tried to answer him and he began to piston his hips. Rational thought fled and I was sensation incarnate. He struck that one spot that had me seeing stars and when his mouth found mine, I was crying from the orgasm storming through my system. He levered me over onto my back as I shook and trembled and then rose up on his knees.

"Hang on, Beautiful," he said, his voice thready and taut. "We're doing that again." I didn't have the words for the ferocity of his thrusts and I barely had the focus to arch my hips up to meet him as he tested his piercing.

Goddamn. I needed to send every single author—oh fuck, I was already coming, and I swore my body went from soft and slick to taunt and tense, but oh so wet and when he gave a shout, I surged up to kiss him. The heat of his release just lit me up and added another layer to the sensitivity he'd ignited in me.

When he pushed me back into the pillows, I clung to him and his mouth found mine. The kiss went from hungry and fierce to lazy and loving only to go back to fierce.

"Happy birthday," I whispered against his lips.

He gave me another lingering kiss before he raised his head. Smoothing my hair back from my face, he stared down at me. "You're not going to get much sleep tonight."

"Probably not," I said, laughing. "I don't care. I don't want to miss a minute with you."

"Me neither." He sucked at my lower lip. And I read the question in his eyes. Slowly, I nodded. His grin grew as he stretched over to the side of the bed, never leaving me. The movement only served to shift him inside of me and we both let out trembling laughs.

His hands were shaking as he held up the phone and it took both of us to steady it.

"Jake first," he said. "Unless you want Archie…" Then he paused. "Or both—yeah, both. We'll get Bubba in here. Lucky bastard deserves a reward for how well he's looked after you, and I want to see them both fill this beautiful pussy of yours."

My eyes must have rounded and Coop chuckled softly. "Didn't think I knew about that? Yeah, I caught some of it. I love watching you fall apart. Not sure I can get my dick in with one of theirs, but I'll gladly try if it won't hurt you."

"Coop…" A strangled laugh escaped me, and he grinned, this time all smug and proud.

"I know, my cock is the best. I fill you up and then some. But you can take me, Beautiful." He shifted his weight and I swore as that softening cock began to stiffen again. "And look at that, not-so-little-Coop is fucking ecstatic to be back where we belong."

He finished sending whatever and then tossed the phone over his shoulder somewhere. He'd just rolled over so I was astride him when the door opened.

"Brother," Jake said from behind me. "I love you."

"Yeah, yeah," Coop said grinning. "Tell our girl."

"Fuck yes, hey Baby Girl." He was on the bed behind me and tilting my head back to him and then he kissed me as he massaged my breasts. Oh, this was where I belonged. With all of my guys. Movement caught my eye and Archie was there, Ian right behind him. The door closed and it was just the five of us.

I swore I caught on fire.

We found new ways to come, with me sandwiched between Coop's pierced dick and Jake's long beauty. Another where Archie and Ian filled my pussy and Coop fucked my mouth. Again when it was Jake in my pussy and Ian in my ass. At some point, I passed out and I woke up to Archie stroking me through the laziest and longest orgasm in a long time.

Coop held me against him as the guys' took me one at a time, soaking up my nearness and honestly, if I never left, this would be paradise.

At least until hunger struck sometime near dawn. That sent Ian and Jake stumbling out in search of food and coffee, while I showered with Coop and Archie. The hotel bathroom was nice but it was too crowded there and we ended up just leaning on each other while we washed.

Curled back up in a different bed—no I didn't envy anyone who had to deal with the one we'd been in all night—we just talked and talked until the guys got back with food and coffee, then we talked some more.

"I learned something tonight," Coop said, holding up his coffee. "Brothers are worth their weight in gold and our girl is a gift. But chafing on my dick is a bitch."

I don't know who started laughing first, but we all dissolved into the giggles. Still, I refused to sleep. Not one minute would I miss with them.

Not one.

Chapter Thirty-Seven

THIS IS OUR LIFE NOW

Frankie

It was another week between Coop's birthday and our "break." Well, almost ten days and I was feeling every single one of them. We had appearances every single night following our Baltimore "launch" and the last show we did was in Orlando before Boone put us on a plane for New York. It was so weird to be back in Florida and at the same time, I couldn't wait to get home.

Our album had live released online over the last week, and our YouTube video had been getting traction. We'd even been introduced to our new social media manager, Andrea. She was a damn gift. I loved her. She didn't need us to do anything. Instead, she just created the content, ran it past us and then went with it. She was so freaking creative, she almost had me liking TikTok.

Almost.

I had no idea how she just dove in and did it all, but she was the best. The only time she'd really needed me to do anything big was the day she had me pull up a lot of old costume pics, then she made a Halloween TikTok, or TreatTok as she called it. It was freaking adorable. But like Boone, she told us not to worry about anything for the next week we were home and I was *ready* for it.

Between the gigs and the homework, I wasn't sleeping more than four or five hours at a time. We had to do sound checks at every new place. Some were big, like the place in Baltimore, and others smaller. Either way, we'd blown up online, thanks to the impromptu Torched appearance. KC had been so tickled, she tagged us on all *her* social media too.

That was when I learned to *stay* away from the comments. The sheer number of people who were judgy as fuck, like we weren't real people, would probably bug me more, but I'd survived Sharon and her bitchy reign of terror. These people didn't know me, they just wanted to feel important.

Especially the chick who kept posting these lists about how we'd copied everything from Torched and that we were blowing up when Torched did it first. KC's text had been a reminder to just ignore it. There were always trolls and they always got their panties in a twist about something. At the same time, some of those comments were just fucking mean.

Rachel sent me a scolding text like she had some super secret psychic power that said she knew I was reading the comments.

> Ignore them. They don't know you. They think they do. They think they know everything. Hey look, you sing songs. So does KC. Clearly, you're copying her. But you just get more dick.

The message damn near made me die laughing.

> Rachel
> Now picture the troll's face if she realized just how much dick you were getting for real, you know?

> Me
> I love you.

> Rachel
> That's cause I'm the best. Now ignore them and come home.

She was right, I deleted the apps wholesale off my phone. For the next week, at least, Bound Hearts was going on the shelf and we were just gonna be Frankie and Ian again. After Halloween, we were flying to *Texas* of all places—define some irony—to do some appearances in the Lone Star State.

Ian's parents were ecstatic. So were Jake's sisters and Trina. I'd have to make sure, when we were close to them, we sent them tickets to get in. We were still doing the smaller venues and I was fine with that. No way did I want to do something like the American Airlines Arena. Just the thought made me want to vomit.

The guys were waiting for us at baggage claim. It was colder in New York. A lot colder than it had been in Florida and I hadn't even thought about that when I dressed to get home. Jake wrapped me up in his coat and I curled up between him and Archie on the drive. The brownstone looked like heaven when we got there.

Seriously—I hadn't realized just how much I'd been missing home until I fell on my bed. The cats came from all quarters, yowling at me in scolding frantic tones for having abandoned them. I spent most of my first afternoon after I showered and changed into pajamas just hanging out on my bed and talking to the boys as they drifted in and out.

Dinner that night, we caught up with Jeremy. He seemed so pleased to have us home. Almost as much as the guys, and it wasn't until I was about to fall asleep pressed between Archie and Coop that it hit me why—he loved looking after us. All of us.

With Ian and I on the road, he didn't have us where he could see us. In his soul, Jeremy was a caretaker and I made a mental note of that. Jeremy needed someone else to look after at some point. On Archie's birthday, we headed off to meet Grandpa Ted and Edward for dinner.

The funny thing was, Archie apologized about that. If he'd realized I'd make it home for his birthday, he would have just booked us a suite somewhere and kept me in bed for the night. While he was only partially teasing, I shook my head.

"No, don't mind seeing them at all. I should probably check in with Ted while I'm here and it feels so strange to be here. It shouldn't, but it does."

Holding my hand, he grinned at me. "That's because you and Bubba are becoming boneified stars. Our quaint little life may not be enough for you anymore."

Teasing or not, I twisted to face him in the back seat and thumped him.

"Ow," he said, laughing. "See, already putting me back in my place."

"Knock it off, Standish. I'd give up everything for our so-called quaint little life. Nothing about you is little."

"Thank you," he said, smug as fuck. "I knew that, but I always appreciate confirmation."

I groaned. He was so bad sometimes.

"Besides," he told me. "I get the culture shock. It's not that this isn't home, but you were in a rhythm. Then we took our trip and before we were even home a few hours, you and Bubba were off. You haven't really been back here in New York since the end of May."

That was true.

While I'd spoken to Grandpa Ted, I really hadn't seen or spoken to Edward or anyone else here who wasn't in my immediate family. I needed to call Hank, but we only had a few days in the city and as much as I would love to go see my dad, I didn't want to miss a minute with the guys. Hank and I had been in regular contact on the road and I'd been sending pictures and fun facts to the kids.

They liked that.

"Where'd you go?"

"I was thinking about Hank, that I should probably call and let him know I'm close."

"But you're worried he'll feel bad if you don't want to go up there for a visit." Archie knew me well. "Babe, call him. Hank adores you and he'll get that this is a brief stop at home. He's not going to hit you with a guilt trip."

True. "It's so weird, did you know he and Edward have been talking and having lunch?"

"I heard," Archie said and he made bug eyes. "Talk about weird."

I laughed. "I guess it's better than if they didn't get along at all?"

"Maybe," Archie agreed. "Then again, maybe an alliance between them would be even more formidable." He pulled a face that cracked me up. Dinner, as it turned out, wasn't at a restaurant. No public places we couldn't secure for a while.

I appreciated that. Just like I appreciated the fact that the minute we'd started blowing up online, security had taken a more prominent tone in our lives. Our band mates were entertained, but as M.J. put it—as long as our security was hawt, she had no complaints. The fact one of our main security was also female, had also not been lost on me.

When we were in public venues, she was the one who went to the bathroom with me. Weird, but effective and maybe, just maybe, I'd stop having little paranoid daydreams of what could go wrong in them.

So, dinner was at Edward's apartment on the west side. Fortunately, Muriel wasn't in attendance "Yeah, they aren't back together, thank fuck," Archie told me as we stepped into the elevator. "She's actually dating some dentist and they're currently on a cruise to Alaska, I think. I didn't really ask."

I clasped his hand. "But you and Edward are doing better?"

"Shockingly, yes." The sheer amount of surprise in his voice never seemed to change no matter how often we talked about it. "He's almost—human. And no, it doesn't change the past and I'm not sure I fully trust it and at the same time—"

"He's trying to be a dad."

"Better," he told me. "He's trying to be a friend."

The elevator dinged open right to his penthouse apartment. That was so weird. I didn't ever want to live somewhere that an elevator could open up in my living room. Granted, Archie had a keycard and a code, still.

"Good evening, kids," Edward said. "Happy birthday, Archie."

"Thank you, Edward."

He held up a bottle of wine. "Dad and I were just discussing what would go best with the lasagna and tiramisu we made. I prefer red, but I wasn't sure about you kids. Frankie, do you like reds?"

"I haven't had that one," I told him as Archie helped me out of my jacket. I wasn't sure what part had floored me more. The fact that Edward was dressed in jeans and a button-down shirt with the sleeves rolled up and *no* shoes or…

"Did you say you *made* the lasagna and the tiramisu?" Archie asked, his expression frozen in disbelief.

"Not going to guarantee it's any good," Edward said. "But yeah, Dad and I made it. I forgot we used to do that when I was a kid. One night a week, Mom would go out with her lady friends to play cards and gossip."

"Your mother didn't gossip," Grandpa Ted announced, as he left the kitchen carrying a huge glass baking dish with bubbling lasagna in it. It smelled correct. The rich scent had my stomach growling. "She played cards with the ladies and they discussed ladies' business."

He set the dish down on the table that had been set for four of us.

"Dad, isn't that gossiping?" Edward asked in a dry voice.

"No," Ted told him firmly. "Gossiping is when you don't know what the hell you're on about. Your mother always knew." With that, he turned on his heel and went back into the kitchen. "Open the wine to let it breathe. We can always get out a second bottle if the kids don't like it."

I put a hand over my mouth to try and not laugh, but Edward's rolled eyes was so Archie it made my heart hurt. Archie, for the most part looked like someone hit him in the back of the head with a board.

"Let's do cocktails, regardless," Edward suggested. "Archie, do you mind starting on those, you'll know more what Frankie would like."

When Archie didn't respond, I elbowed him and he shook his head.

His wide-eyed gaze was adorable. "Sure, what do you want, Babe?"

"Whatever you're having will be fine," I told him and he nodded. He took my jacket over and hung it on the rack then glanced around.

"No servers tonight?"

"No, I gave Cassian the night off. I wanted this to be family. Cassian's still a little too stiff for my taste. Might have to send him over to Jeremy for some lessons, unless you're willing to part with—"

"No," I said in the same breath that Archie did and Edward grinned at us.

"I didn't think so."

"Eddie," Grandpa called. "Something's wrong with your chiller."

With another roll of his eyes, he waved us into the living room before he vanished into the kitchen. "Should we worry?" I asked Archie as I followed him over to the wet bar. He studied what they had and then opened the cabinet beneath. Pulling out the rum, he fixed a rum and coke for both of us, and then handed me a glass before he poured two glasses of single malt whiskey.

"That they've been taken over by pod people?" He tossed back the shot for himself and put the glass aside before adding a single finger to a fresh glass. Then he retrieved his rum and coke and lifted it to me. "I already am. My safe word is Peaches. If I say it, we make a run for it."

Clinking our glasses together, I laughed. But oddly, he wasn't wrong. When Edward and Ted finally joined us, Ted's hair was in a bit of disarray, his face flushed and a bit sweaty and they were both just—not put together.

"We're out of practice," he said by way of apology. "We should probably change."

"You don't have to," Archie said as he took a seat next to me. Both his father and grandfather had taken the single straight-backed chairs across from us. "Seriously, we dressed up because dinner usually meant dressed."

"Fair," Edward said. "I thought about having it catered, then Dad reminded me we used to cook and well, I wanted to do something different for your birthday this year."

"You showed up, that's different." The hard words landed between them like a grenade and I settled a hand on his thigh. When he covered my hand with his, he sighed. "I'm sorry, that was uncalled for."

Grandpa Ted said nothing, but Edward looked at us for a long time. That sadness in him was still there, but so was something else—acceptance.

"No, it wasn't. I deserve that. I've missed more than my fair share. I can tell you, I'm working on it, or I can show you."

"How about both?" Grandpa Ted suggested. "Maybe next time, you and Archie can make dinner."

Panic flooded me, but Archie squeezed my hand. "I don't think that's a good idea, Grandpa. Not because I wouldn't be willing, but simply—most of the food I make turns out to be inedible. Maybe we can bribe Frankie into coming over and I'll be the entertainment, while you two cook."

I laughed.

"What do you mean, you can't cook?" Ted and Edward both stared at him and I wasn't sure who looked more concerned, Ted, who'd voiced the question or Edward.

"I can rebuild an engine and I've actually designed a functional robot. So, food ingredients are not my thing." His ears turned a shade of crimson as he took a sip of his drink.

"Dad," Edward said slowly. "Am I mistaken or did my perfect son just admit he isn't perfect?"

"Nope, you are not mistaken, boyo. Sprout absolutely admitted that there is still something he can learn from us old folks. You clear a night for us," Grandpa Ted said. "Frankie's got to finish her tour. That reminds me young lady, we should talk business tonight, but after supper. While you're gone, Eddie and I will get Archie all sorted out."

Oh boy. "Just promise me you'll have a fire extinguisher handy."

Edward laughed and Archie frowned at me. "Damn, even my girl is out to get me."

"No, I'm out to make sure you don't blow up another oven. I like you just the way you are."

He grinned, wrapping a hand around my nape and kissing me lightly. "Right back atcha."

Dinner turned out to be amazing. Maybe there was hope for Archie in the cooking department. Maybe. We finished all of the wine and moved on to coffees before conversation turned to business and my classes. Ted had a lot of pointers and comments, while Archie and Edward threw in theirs too. It was a wonderful evening. Even better than I could have imagined.

The best part of it all was the quiet pleasure Archie took in the whole thing. He may not want to admit it, but Edward kept proving he did choose his son and Archie deserved that, and so much more.

Chapter Thirty-Eight
ALREADY THERE

Ian

"I'm telling you right now," Andrea said as she sat across from us in the restaurant. "Don't read the comments. I'll do that and I'll put together a sanitized version for you to read."

"Sanitized means censored, right?" Frankie asked before she took a sip of her coffee. We were in Houston today. It was our last show in Texas. We'd be going up to Chicago next, then St. Louis, and a couple of other stops before we broke for Christmas. Boone was so damn pleased with the tour and the sales, that he said we could afford to take a breather.

After the holidays, he wanted to discuss our second album. I just left that in the back of my head for the time being.

"Yes and no," Andrea told us. She adjusted her glasses. "Look, guys, I'm not going to lie and tell you everyone and their Aunt Mary loves you.

But you are developing a vocal fanbase. The online world just makes it a lot easier for haters and jerks to be haters and jerks. They don't even have to dislike you, to dislike you looking like you're doing better than them, and you don't need that kind of negativity in your heads."

"That seems fair," I said after a moment. I'd taken a look after Frankie had mentioned in passing that she had been checking out the comments. I was with Andrea on this one. Frankie didn't need that in her head, and I didn't want it in mine. "But if they are genuine criticisms, I think they should stand. Sometimes, critics will tell you what the people who love you won't."

"And opinions are like assholes," Andrea retorted. "Everyone has one. That said—" She held up a hand. "If it seems genuine as an art critique and not a mean-spirited bitchfest, I'll leave it alone."

"Thank you." I couldn't really ask for more.

"I can't believe we have a social media footprint," Frankie said, making a face. "Or that you have to spend this much time managing it."

"It's the cost of doing business in the modern age. But I'll pull the statistics you ask for your assignment. Actually, let me make a note of that right now." She typed into her phone. "I'm going back to Los Angeles tomorrow. I have enough material from the road that I can take care of everything from there. So, at least you're off the hook for now."

Her teasing grin pulled a reluctant smile from Frankie. She liked Andrea. So did I. While she'd been a bit shy in the beginning, once she was in her element, she'd just taken over. The control she'd exerted, along with her confidence, had actually made - what could have been a painful experience, with an uncomfortable learning curve -relatively painless.

"Also, I'll be sending you guys some questions now and again. Probably no more than five or ten at a time. All you have to do is answer them in little 30 second clips and fire them back to me and I'll take care of it from there."

Frankie gave an exaggerated sigh, but her smile was genuine. "We can do that. No offense, Andrea, I'm really ready to go back home after this."

"Girl, me too." Andrea flashed a grin at her. "I love the energy of being on the road, but it does take its toll. Boone mentioned you guys wanted to keep me on as social media manager even after the tour. Are you sure?"

"Yes," I said. "Frankie suggested it and I agree with her. Neither of us are really going to have time to take it over. You've spent the last four weeks with us and gotten to know us. Whether we tour like this again is debatable, but we don't want to lose momentum now that we have it going."

"Sounds fantastic. I appreciate it."

"If you're game, we can also put you under private contract," Frankie said. "My attorney can draw it up. I already talked to him about it. I know you work with the record label, but you don't work for them."

"Nope, I'm a contractor. I like working for myself, though if they need me to go places, it's also nice that they pay for it. So, I'm definitely game. I have a contract that I can send over to your attorney too and we can work it all out."

Sounded good to me. We spent another ten minutes chatting before parting ways with Andrea. We had to head back to the hotel and get packed so we were ready to get on a late flight after the show.

A really late flight.

"Have you thought about it?" Frankie asked once we were in the room.

"About another tour?" I asked. We didn't really have that much to pack. We'd been sending our clothes out to be washed anytime we were in a place longer than two nights, so it had time to get back to us, and we'd gotten into the habit of packing clean clothes in one case and dirty ones in the other. We'd also condensed our personal items down. Mostly school work, guitars, and laptops to go with our chargers and phones.

When we'd gone home in October, we'd left a lot there. Pretty sure it was wishful thinking on our parts. Then, I didn't blame her. I'd *liked* being home too. Even with Rachel there as an added dimension. She fit.

"Yeah," Frankie said as she sat down on the bed and pulled out her guitar. She puttered with it, getting it tuned.

"Some," I admitted. "This has been a hell of an experience. One I'm very glad we did."

"Agreed," she said, glancing over at me.

"But…you hate doing the distance learning."

She made a face. "I really do."

"And college is important, particularly because this isn't your career choice."

"It's not, not my career choice," she said, and I grinned at her.

"Angel, you wanted to do this with me. If it was just you, this wouldn't have been your first choice."

"I could say the same about you," she countered. "Your music has always been important to you and I love being a part of it, Ian. I really do."

"I know that." I moved over to sit next to her. "But being on the road for months at a time? This wasn't even a lot of stops compared to some tours. KC mentioned they did their first worldwide when they were thirteen."

She pulled a face. "I don't know if I could go on something like that without the guys. I mean—obviously we could, but I miss them every day."

"Same." I exhaled. "Look, I think we stick with our plan. We did the album, we did the tour, and now we're going home and back to school. You don't have to keep sneaking peeks at the school schedule. I know you want to get back into classes with the guys."

When she strummed a few notes and looked thoughtful, I waited her out. "What if…what if we work on a second album while we do the social media thing with Andrea and work on school. Then do a mini tour next summer after June, but we go back in the fall so we can finish our degrees."

"Works for me." It really did. "I love just working with you."

"Yeah?" She teased, fingers brushing the strings. She'd been getting more confident with her guitar, but she still wasn't willing to take it up on the stage with her. "I couldn't tell."

"Don't make me spank you. You weren't that thrilled with performing in Lubbock."

"That's because you did it a half hour before we had to go on stage and ripped my panties off."

Grinning, I shrugged. "Someone promised she'd throw her panties at me."

"Oh my god," Frankie said with a groan and laughed. When I would have stood up, she said, "Actually, can you wait a minute? I want to play something for you."

I raised my brows and settled back in.

"I've been working on something on and off the last few months. Something to try and figure things out, but also a place to put all my emotions."

I got that.

"Okay."

Licking her lips, she made one more minor adjustment on the guitar and then began to strum it. The chord started deep and slow, then began to pick up the pace. Frankie's voice didn't falter once as she started to sing about a small town with a lot of friends and strangers. A place where she was home and nowhere. Because home was never there for her. Then she shifted gears to how a home wasn't a place, it was people.

It was her people. Our people. We made home. Home could be on the road. It could on a boat or an island escape. Home was where we were. I found it hard not to mist up at the forlorn note when she talked about someone trying to take away that home, take away her people. The person was the one who should have been her home to begin with. The last few notes faded away and then she picked up the chorus again about finding her home and her people. That was where she would stay. No more dark clouds, no more people trying to take them away.

When she finished and lifted her head, I wasn't remotely surprised by the fact she wavered in my vision or that there were tears spilling out of her eyes. She'd written a song about her mother. She'd found a way to get it out.

"That was truly beautiful," I told her. "I'm so goddamn proud of you,

Angel, you have no idea."

She smiled. "I asked KC for help—I know I could have asked you."

"Shh." I pressed a finger to her lips. "You did what you needed to do and I absolutely love the song."

"Yeah?"

"Oh yeah," I whispered before I pressed a kiss to her forehead. "Teach me?"

We spent the rest of our day practicing the song, until I had it down. It was beautiful. I loved every gorgeous note of it. While she didn't tell the guys about it, said she wanted to share it when she was home, I worked on getting her to perform it.

One of the things she'd been doing on this tour had been purging her past. Purging the darkness and the scars that Maddy had left on her. Scars her grandparents' actions or lack of had added to her heart. More, the fact she was healing from them.

We were in Minneapolis, our final show of a three-night stay. We were four days away from Christmas and Jake's birthday was right around the corner, when she said, "Maybe tonight."

Just like we had for every other last night, we'd packed before we came to the venue. A car would be taking us straight to the airport and fingers crossed the weather would hold and we'd get to be home in just a few more hours. This wasn't the first time she'd said maybe tonight, but it was the first time she'd said it while we were at the actual venue. We were between sets. One more set stood between us and home.

"Whenever you're ready," I told her and I meant it. She never had to perform it in public, but I thought in some ways, it might help. But I would not force her. This song was hers. When it was time, she carried her guitar out with her to the stage, but set it just off to the side. I'd mentioned to the guys that we might be doing an unplugged at the very end.

We played through the rest of our list and a couple of bonus songs, including some Christmas tunes, and then Frankie glanced at me as we finished the last one. Leaning forward, I said into the microphone, "Thank you Minneapolis for having us tonight. Seriously, for Bound Hearts—for me, for Frankie, M.J., and the guys, it's a dream come true. Tonight's our last show. So we thought we'd close out on something special, something personal and something no one has heard."

Frankie moved away from the microphone and retrieved her guitar, then she came back. Someone brought her a stool and she settled on it with the guitar. The applause died down and the lights went low.

Lifting her head, Frankie stared out at the crowd. "Earlier this year, my mother died. We weren't close by the end, there was too much between us for that. Still, the loss left me a little—disconnected. This tour, this music—these people, and my family—they brought me back. Ian and I have worked on songs before, but he's the musical genius, don't let him tell you otherwise."

I chuckled and the crowd laughed.

"When I wrote this, I never thought I'd perform it. I may never perform it again. But thank you for being here with us. Thank you for having us. This song is for you and your people and it's for mine. For my family and my home."

Then she started to play and the others stayed quiet. For this, it would just be the two of us, and I joined in to play the backup to her main line and when she began to sing, the crowd went quiet. More than one phone was up and pointed at her, but she wasn't paying attention to them. She was lost in her song.

On the chorus, she glanced at me and I began to sing. Frankie was my home. So were the guys.

I felt this song all the way in my soul.

When we finished, there was a profound moment of deep silence and then applause battered at us. She'd done it, with tears streaming down her face, but she'd done it. As soon as we were offstage, I texted the guys to be on a lookout for the upload. They blew up our phones before we were at the airport.

Somewhere mid-flight, she fell asleep with her head tucked against my shoulder. At the airport, the guys were waiting for us and the drive through the snowy streets back to the brownstone was festive, even if Frankie curled up next to Jake and went right back to sleep. She deserved the rest. Hell, I needed some.

Maybe we'd never tour again and I was okay with that. Really, I was. Rules and Roses was our first album and I was fucking proud of it. If it was our only album, then goddamn, go us. Back at the brownstone, the house draped in Christmas, Jeremy waited with mugs of hot cocoa and welcome home.

Yeah, we were already there.

Chapter Thirty-Nine
CUPS OF KINDNESS

Frankie

Home was a whirlwind of shopping, Jake's birthday—and seeing him play hockey for the first time. Yes, Ian and Coop kept me warm while Jake got his crash on the ice. He looked so damn happy and his amateur league was perfect for him. The boys had been up to all sorts of things, including signing up for flying lessons.

The day after Christmas, I took the train up to see Hank and the kids. I couldn't stay but one overnight, mostly because I'd *really* missed the guys and we had a surprise for Jeremy. The guys picked me up at the station when I got back and then we drove out to Jersey, where we met with the family who had puppies. They were the most adorable chunky little babies, in all black. They were lab mixes the lady told me, they weren't totally sure, still they were perfect.

When I'd told the boys Jeremy needed more to look after than just us, they'd all gotten that panicked look in their eyes. The cats might disown me, but a puppy would be perfect. From the first brush of her puppy breath to my cheek, I was in love. It was hard not to take them all, but I settled for a chunk and we took her back to the city with us.

Jeremy's reaction was priceless. It started out as faint disbelief and disapproval, followed by pensiveness. Finally, he asked me for her name.

"I don't have one yet," I told him. "I just—couldn't say no to her, you know. And I know that there's gonna be a lot on my plate this spring. I probably should have thought about that beforehand."

Coop gave me an impressed thumbs up from behind Jeremy. Rachel wasn't due back from her family's for another couple of days, but I bet she'd be impressed too.

"Nonsense," Jeremy said. "Of course, I'll take care of her." Without hesitation, he took her from my arms and examined her. "She'll need proper training and gear. I can get everything ordered promptly. She should probably be crate trained and I'll keep her downstairs, at least until we have the potty training sorted out."

He hummed.

"Puppy proofing is a must."

"Archie and Jake went to get stuff for that," I volunteered, and Coop hid his smile behind his coffee. "But Jeremy, I really can't ask you to do all of that."

The look he gave me could have peeled paint. I'd never once, in all the years I'd known Jeremy, earned one of his reproving looks. "You, Miss Frankie, possess a beautiful heart, but you are a terrible liar. You want me to have company while you kids run all over the world. Your cats are quite lovely, but they are very independent and little Miss Abigail here will need proper attention."

I bit my lip. "Don't be mad."

"I'm not mad," he said, caressing the puppy under her chin, she was half-asleep next to Jeremy. "Not in the slightest. I'm also *not* giving her back to you."

I didn't laugh. It about killed me, but I didn't. "I wouldn't dream of asking you."

"Good. Very well, no time like the present to begin some leash training and rewards, if you'll excuse me."

As soon as Jeremy and Miss Abigail were out of sight, I made a little fist pump at Coop and he did a distance high five. "You called it," he said softly and I grinned wider. "Jere's right though, you're a terrible liar."

Yeah well, I wasn't going to let that bother me. The next few days passed in relative peace, or as much peace as one can manage with an energetic puppy. Jake sacrificed a pair of shoes. I lost one of my socks. Ian managed to save his guitar case, but Jeremy lost more than one tie before we managed to keep the puppy away from the things she wasn't supposed to have.

The house became a minefield of puppy toys and Tiddles was so disgusted with all of us, he refused to descend to the first floor. Tory stalked the puppy and Tabitha stared at the puppy from one of the cat trees, but like Tiddles, she didn't deign to get down and play with her.

The cats would come around.

Or they'd shit in my shoes, according to Jake. We'd figure it out. Jeremy though—Jeremy was happier than I'd seen him in a long time and he was totally in his element. We went out on New Year's Eve, braving part of the cold to go to a party on campus. We stumbled home around five in the morning as Jeremy was taking Miss Abigail out for her morning constitutional.

He just gave us an amused look and reminded us to hydrate and if we could be so kind as to confine our vomiting to the bathrooms, he would appreciate it. I wasn't hungover, but I was exhausted. I managed a shower and had just settled into bed when Archie came into the room. He was still dressed, before I could tease him though, he turned haggard eyes on me.

No.

No. No. No.

No more losses.

"Dad called…Grandpa Ted passed away last night. He went to bed and didn't wake up."

My heart broke for him and I was across the room and wrapped around him a second. Coop climbed out of bed and went for the guys. Soon we were all there, just holding Archie. Grief was a strange thing. It came in waves. Growing up was like that too.

It was a new year, but we were starting it without Ted and that—that hurt. Grandpa Ted meant the world to Archie. I adored him. The guys loved him. After a while, I coaxed Archie into a shower and got him to clean up. Then we went to Edward's. All of us, even Jeremy came along, and he took charge once we were there.

Edward, like Archie, seemed just as lost. But we'd get them through it. Just like they all got me through Maddy.

Grief came in waves, but home? Home was us.

Frankie and the Boys will return in

Legacy and Lovers!

To keep up with Heather and all her series as well as enjoy bonus scenes and other content join her reader's group on Facebook:

https://www.facebook.com/groups/HeathersPack/

Afterword

Deep breaths.

Maybe get a drink and a tissue.

Yes, I know. I wasn't ready for that moment either. Yet, I always knew it was coming. Losing a grandparent is never easy, whether they go gently or not.

When my grandmother died, it was very much like losing a parent. She was the one who raised me, who taught me, who gave me so much and helped me become who I was.

Nothing prepares you to say goodbye, even if you know it's coming. I had gotten engaged just a few short weeks before she passed. I remember one of the last conversations we had was that she was happy that I would be okay. She didn't have to worry about me anymore.

In a lot of ways, this was reflected in Grandpa Ted's death. That moment of knowing Archie would be okay. He had his family, his people, Frankie, Jeremy, and now—now he has Edward back.

Eddie is going to be okay, too. I know this isn't the greatest moment of comfort, but I feel the pain. I do. I'm also ready for what comes next.

Because as I said all the way back in the forward, life goes on…

Thanks for being the best.

xoxo

Heather

Legacy and Lovers

When did *we* become the adults? When did *we* become the ones who had to make the hard calls? One by one, we've all left our teenage years behind. College brought new challenges even as Bound Hearts brings us more.

Whether we're making music, love, war, games, or trouble, we've found a good balance. That's my story and I'm sticking to it.

Together, we know we can do anything.

We've learned that even being apart doesn't mean we aren't together.

Life has a habit of throwing curve balls. School, careers, new hobbies, friends in need, and family demands are hitting us from every angle. We're going to need each other more than ever.

Archie, Coop, Ian, Jake, and I are a team. We're constantly figuring it out and sometimes, we fight. We also make up.

And we'll have each other's backs, today, tomorrow, and into the future.

**Please note this is a reverse harem and the author suggests you always read the forward in her books. Contains some bullying elements, mature situations, violence, and is recommended for 17+. This is the eleventh in a series and the story will continue through future books.*

Pre-Order Now

About Heather Long

USA Today bestselling author, Heather Long, likes long walks in the park, science fiction, superheroes, Marines, and men who aren't douche bags. Her books are filled with heroes and heroines tangled in romance as hot as Texas summertime. From paranormal historical westerns to contemporary military romance, Heather might switch genres, but one thing is true in all of her stories—her characters drive the books. When she's not wrangling her menagerie of animals, she devotes her time to family and friends she considers family. She believes if you like your heroes so real you could lick the grit off their chest, and your heroines so likable, you're sure you've been friends with women just like them, you'll enjoy her worlds as much as she does.

Follow Heather & Sign up for her newsletter:
www.heatherlong.net
TikTok

Also by Heather Long

82nd Street Vandals

Savage Vandal

Vicious Rebel

Ruthless Traitor

Dirty Devil

Always a Marine Series

Once Her Man, Always Her Man

Retreat Hell! She Just Got Here

Tell It to the Marine

Proud to Serve Her

Her Marine

No Regrets, No Surrender

The Marine Cowboy

The Two and the Proud

A Marine and a Gentleman

Combat Barbie

Whiskey Tango Foxtrot

What Part of Marine Don't You Understand?

A Marine Affair

Marine Ever After

Marine in the Wind

Marine with Benefits

A Marine of Plenty

A Candle for a Marine

Marine under the Mistletoe

Have Yourself a Marine Christmas

Lest Old Marines Be Forgot
Her Marine Bodyguard
Smoke & Marines

<u>Bravo Team Wolf</u>

When Danger Bites
Bitten Under Fire

<u>Cardinal Sins</u>

Kill Song
First Chorus

<u>Chance Monroe</u>

Earth Witches Aren't Easy
Plan Witch from Out of Town
Bad Witch Rising

<u>Her Elite Assets</u>

Featuring:
Pure Copper
Target: Tungsten
Asset: Arsenic

Fevered Hearts

Marshal of Hel Dorado
Brave are the Lonely
Micah & Mrs. Miller
A Fistful of Dreams
Raising Kane
Wanted: Fevered or Alive

Wild and Fevered
The Quick & The Fevered
A Man Called Wyatt

<u>Going Royal</u>
Some Like It Royal
Some Like It Scandalous
Some Like It Deadly
Some Like it Secret
Some Like it Easy
Her Marine Prince
Blocked

<u>Heart of the Nebula</u>
Queenmaker
Deal Breaker
Throne Taker

<u>Lone Star Leathernecks</u>
Semper Fi Cowboy
As You Were, Cowboy

<u>Magic & Mayhem</u>
The Witch Singer
Bridget's Witch's Diary
The Witched Away Bride

<u>Mongrels</u>
Mongrels, Mischief & Mayhem

<u>Shackled Souls</u>

Succubus Chained

Succubus Unchained

Succubus Blessed

Shackled Souls (Omnibus)

<u>Space Cowboy</u>

Space Cowboy Survival Guide

<u>Untouchable</u>

Rules and Roses

Changes and Chocolates

Keys and Kisses

Whispers and Wishes

Hangovers and Holidays

Brazen and Breathless

Trials and Tiaras

Graduation and Gifts

Defiance and Dedication

Songs and Sweethearts

<u>Wolves of Willow Bend</u>

Wolf at Law

Wolf Bite

Caged Wolf

Wolf Claim

Wolf Next Door

Rogue Wolf

Bayou Wolf

Untamed Wolf

Wolf with Benefits

River Wolf

Single Wicked Wolf

Desert Wolf

Snow Wolf

Wolf on Board

Holly Jolly Wolf

Shadow Wolf

His Moonstruck Wolf

Thunder Wolf

Ghost Wolf

Outlaw Wolves

Wolf Unleashed